MEN AGAINST WOMEN

MEN
AGAINST
WOMEN

A NOVEL

LAURA HART McKINNY

STONES THROW MEDIA

Stones Throw Media
703 Coliseum Plaza Court
Winston-Salem, NC 27106

First Edition

Cover design by Kevin Morgan Watson

Cover art Copyright © 2015 by Hayden Tedder

This book is a complete work of fiction. Any resemblances to actual events or
persons, living or dead, are meant to be resemblances and not actual
representations of events or persons, living or dead.

Printed on acid-free paper
ISBN 978-0-9962351-0-5

In loving memory of our mother,
Marjorie June, who hung the moon

It is what it is, but it becomes what you make it.
—Pat Summit

Night Girls

Asbury Park, N.J., 1961

Morgan started making secret audiotapes the month after her mother died. "I can feel Samantha when she cries at night," was her first recorded utterance. Morgan was her best friend Samantha's self-appointed protector. Chronicling her concerns about Samantha kept Morgan from slipping back into her own personal grief pit. Late at night, Morgan whispered the day's highlights into a silver microphone leading to a reel-to-reel tape recorder under her bed. *"When Samantha sat next to me on the school bus this morning, her eyelids were puffy like two tiny Twinkies, so I told her not to worry — I'd take care of everything."* But Morgan couldn't take care of everything: she was only thirteen.

The tapes were secret, or at least Morgan didn't let anyone else hear them. The recorder had been a condolence gift several months before from her great-aunt Tilly. For weeks after Morgan's mother died, she had been mute to everyone — her dad, teacher, schoolmates, even Samantha. Then one day great-aunt Tilly brought her a gray square box. Morgan figured it was a record player until she lifted the lid and a dozen round, shiny recording tapes fell out, along with a note in blue fountain pen: *You can't lose a love that's endless.*

Morgan eyed the tape recorder, a useless hunk of metal offering no hugs or hope. She buried it in her closet and stared for hours at the blurry clouds on the sky blue bedroom ceiling her mother had wallpapered.

But sulking just made her dwell on the pain. She had to fill her head with something else, anything, even the sound of her own voice. So, three days later she hauled the tape recorder out and dictated spelling words, leaving a few seconds of silence between each one, so when she played them back in the dark, she could give herself Thursday night practice tests. After a couple of months she had enough words on tape to host an unattended spelling bee at midnight in which she and an imaginary player whispered letters under the bedcovers, fighting it out to the last word: obscene. Morgan forgot the silent "e."

She branched out to dictating class notes, mostly science, her favorite subject. Her voice on tip toe, enunciated Einstein's Theory of Relativity: *"…the speed of light is absolute: the one absolute…"* she'd editorialize, *"good."* With so much breaking off and falling away in her life, she found some solace in the assurance that the universe was fixed — that everything was essentially connected.

As she became more intimate with taping, she strayed from spelling lists and class notes, whispering her own confidences. Then after one harrowing Christmas Eve at Samantha's house, her hushed narrative suggested that maybe everything wasn't all that connected.

On this particular night before Christmas, over a year since her mother's death, Morgan planted her bare feet on the cold, hard wood, tiptoed towards the window, crammed her long braids underneath her baseball cap, pulled on her overalls and boots, and stood motionless, listening to the burst of canned laughter from *Burns and Allen,* her dad's favorite television show. Staring at the illuminated life-size nativity scene across the street reminded her that theirs was the only house on the cul-de-sac without outdoor lights. She couldn't even get her dad to replace the bubble lights for the sorry Christmas tree he'd picked up at Woolworth's at half price: a four-foot aluminum pole with a couple dozen ill-fitted holes for nearly the same number of tweaked silver branches. When she asked if they could go cut down a real tree in a nearby forest, her dad told her not to worry because the following year they were going to be Jewish. No Santa, no tree, no lights.

Samantha's grandmother was Jewish, too crippled to manage trees or lights, but she did order presents for Samantha from the Sears catalogue. Since Morgan had read the *Diary of Anne Frank*, she'd gotten her hands on a book about Jewish customs and holidays, so she knew something about Hanukkah. She'd never been won over by baby Jesus anyway, and now without her mother's Christmas enthusiasm, she figured if they became Jewish, eight days of presents was a pretty good deal. She suspected though that her dad was about as well versed with the miracle of oil lasting for eight days as he was with shopping for a trainer bra.

Again the chortles followed by George Burns' familiar closing, "Say goodnight, Gracie." And her dad laughed. He never laughed unless it was a comedy show. Apparently, he didn't find anything in life remotely funny. Then Gracie Allen's sweet retort, "Goodnight, Gracie. And Merry Christmas, everybody."

"Good night." And clap, she thought. Everybody clap. Go now.

At the sound of applause, she opened the bedroom window, flicking the snow off the ledge. She lifted one leg through the window. Once she was outside on the frozen ground and her shoes stopped sliding on ice, she glanced up and stared at the massive oak tree in her yard, mesmerized by sparkling stars mingling in the bare branches, but it was too cold to dilly dally. Samantha's house was four long blocks away.

The side of the paved road was crusted, frozen in ruts and ridges from an unusually warm New Jersey mid-day rain, turning the streets into a muddy, now icy, slush. She wondered what her Dad would say if he knew she'd slipped out the bedroom window again. Hard to say. He wasn't one for saying much.

By the time she reached the end of the first block, the balls of her feet, exposed to the hard ice through the holes in her boot soles, were numb. Her mother would've made her wear extra wool socks. Her mother, small and delicate with a clear and musical voice, had made Morgan's life sing. And this night, culminating in Christmas Eve Midnight Mass, had been her mother's annual hallmark, lovingly reflected in her daughter's new dress clothes. Morgan always swallowed her embarrassment, and, with a starched smile, wore her new black patent leather shoes, perfectly pressed red wool dress, unblemished thin white gloves and gray coat with the gold anchor buttons. They had to walk several blocks to the town's only Catholic church. Her mother didn't drive and her father worked late shift at a distant plastics factory, so by the time they arrived, there was standing room only, usually near but not close enough to her Aunt Tilly.

Aunt Tilly had been an outspoken social feminist, still proudly wearing in one lapel her 25-year law enforcement pin, as one of Portland's first female detectives. This wisp of a spinster, poised in her dark blue velvet Christmas dress with her pin centered on a white satin collar, had been a staunch advocate for Portland's "fallen women."

After Mass, Aunt Tilly and Morgan's mother made a big deal about setting out the milk and cookies for Santa. Morgan always presented her mother with a tiny clear frosted-glass bottle of her favorite perfume, Shalimar, gold lettering on a red label, for which her mother thanked her profusely and, in grand fashion, lifted the pointed stopper and tapped a dab behind each ear lobe. And, in the morning, while Morgan's dad slept in, it was her mother who sat with Morgan and watched her open the traditional stocking half-filled with salt-water taffy, oranges, fudge, two pencils with erasers, and a new steno pad. Her mother always gave her new sneakers and a handmade school outfit, usually a bulky wool skirt and knit vest. She also gave her daughter a board game — Monopoly one year, Risk the next, then Clue — and the next book in L. Frank Baum's *Oz* series.

The day was so totally free of responsibility and worry that after opening the presents, eating breakfast and popping the stuffed turkey in the oven, Morgan's mother would stack the dishes in the sink and leave the kitchen. She would start reading the new *Oz* book aloud. Several chapters later, they might go sledding, build a snowman, or play card games. After the turkey dinner, they stacked even more dishes in the sink, played more board games and read another few chapters until they couldn't keep their eyes open.

Morgan's dad joined them for hotcakes, and then he would draw the curtains in the den and sit in front of the television all day. He didn't believe in Christmas. Thought people spent too much time and money for one meaningless day. Said it depressed him because it was fake: the whole Jesus story and Santa stuff was just crap. Morgan's mother would explain away his attitude, "He doesn't like surprises or presents." Morgan wondered how a woman who loved to *give* could marry someone who didn't like to receive. Maybe she didn't know he was such a Scrooge when she married him.

Earlier the year before, around Valentine's Day, her father had caught a bad flu and was sick in bed for several weeks. Morgan was delighted. She didn't feel a shred of guilt about how happy his confinement made her. Her delight, in fact, increased the longer he was ill. And, simply overjoyed not to have to negotiate around his extreme moods, she secretly hoped he would die. It would have been a perfect arrangement, him supine, drugged, asleep, indefinitely, except her mother stayed up with him day and night, practically hand-feeding him, until she contracted walking pneumonia.

He finally recuperated; then, when Morgan's mother was so terribly ill she couldn't get out of bed to go to the bathroom, he reluctantly went to the market.

That year of her mother's illness had been rough. She had some good days, and then some mornings she was so dizzy she couldn't even sit up in bed. On those days, Aunt Tilly came by with a huge pot of potato soup. The soup didn't put the color back in Morgan's mother's cheeks, but the 1960 Presidential election did, briefly. Several weeks before Kennedy's election, on a particularly healthy evening, Morgan's mother had hung JFK's picture in the dining room near but not presumptuously close to an 8X10 of Jesus Christ surrounded in a ring of light.

Midway through dinner, her father glanced up to ask Morgan for the mashed potatoes and noticed the Kennedy glossy. He demanded an explanation. When none followed, he banged the table, instructing Morgan's mother to get "that rich upstart" off his wall. Unlike some of the West Virginia coal miners Kennedy had won over in the primary, Morgan's father mistrusted anyone with a broad-A accent or a southern drawl, and he pledged to his buddies if Kennedy would've come to his plastics assembly plant, he would've refused his hand — Catholic or not.

Morgan's father leaned forward, face beet red, charging her mother to remove the photo from the wall or he'd take it off. She had just finished slicing a piece of Irish soda bread and handed it to Morgan, who could never forget the calm expression in her mother's sapphire eyes as she looked across the table at her husband. "I like looking in the eyes of the man of I'm voting for," she said, then proceeded to butter a slab of bread.

Something bestial snapped in her father: he lurched forward and in one sudden move was to the other side of the table, screaming, "You won't live to vote." And before Morgan realized what happened he'd slapped her mother so hard she shot from the chair.

Morgan rushed to her mother's side, placing her rawboned body between the heap of woman on the floor and her father's half-crazed stare.

He swiped his daughter to the ground like a weed and was about to hit her mother again when Morgan bit him on the calf. Just thinking about it, she could feel her teeth crunching his muscle.

Now, Morgan almost bumped into the familiar tree trunk leaning onto the sidewalk before she realized she had reached Samantha's house. Her friend's giggle floated down from the second story open window. Golden and sparkling, her laugh was like the tinkling of bells. Samantha could sit for hours drawing trees. Morgan only wanted to climb them.

Morgan waved and started to climb the leafless willow tree towards Samantha's china-doll face and long, curly billowing blond hair. Her smile helped Morgan forget this lonely holiday without Santa. Her father's indifference to Christmas was robbing her of the last breath of childhood, and late night escapes to Samantha's were her way of stealing it back.

Samantha set her potholder loom, a red-pronged metal square the size of a hot plate, on the ledge and leaned out the window to give Morgan a hand.

Her half heart-shaped gold mitzvah flashed, reflecting the bright headlights that turned into the driveway and shone hard on Samantha's solemn expression. Morgan regretted she'd left the other half of the mitzvah on her bathroom sink. Necklaces bothered her, but she tried to remember to wear it around Samantha. The mitzvahs reminded Samantha they were locked in a permanent friendship bond; they reminded Morgan of tragic deaths — Samantha's mother, her own mother.

"It's your dad." Morgan indicated the car lights with her head as she wobbled onto a branch.

Samantha's eyes darted to the closed bedroom door. "But he's not s'posed to be back until tomorrow morning."

"So what? I'll be gone before he gets up." Morgan held out her hand. "Samantha, c'mon before he gets inside. My fingers are freezing."

Samantha reached out, clasped her friend's hand, and helped her inside.

Morgan peeled her overalls off her nightgown, stuffed them under the bunk bed, and then started to climb onto the top bunk

"Morgan," whispered Samantha, "the window."

Morgan made a face and rolled her eyes at Samantha, who was already curled up in a ball under the covers, then she climbed back down and crossed to the window. Accustomed to the temperamental warped wood, she whacked it, wincing. "Is your grandma asleep?"

"Yes."

Snuggled again in bed with her back to the wall, Morgan silently identified the sounds downstairs: a key jiggling in the lock, the front door opening and shutting, thud of a suitcase, heels scuffing across linoleum to the refrigerator. The freezer. Probably looking for ice cream. Forget it. Samantha never had ice cream. A whoosh of air from an open beer bottle. Shoes clunking up the stairs. What an elephant, Morgan thought, sure he would wake up Samantha's grandmother, sleeping in the bedroom at the end of the hall.

Samantha's door creaked open. Morgan, hidden on the top bunk behind a couple of pillows and a big teddy bear, lifted one eyelid just enough to verify Mr. Deaver's bowtie in the hall light.

He stopped nibbling a chicken leg, "Sweet dreams, Samantha hon." He stared at the bottom bunk waiting for a response. When there was none, he leaned in, calling softly, "Samantha? Are you asleep?"

Take a guess, thought Morgan. Mr. Deaver tiptoed into Samantha's room, carefully shutting the door behind him. Beer and grease stink preceded him as he crossed to the bed, whispering, "Daddy's home, sweetie. You asleep?"

"Yes."

"I missed you, sweetie. You want my drumstick? C'mon, share it with Daddy."

"I'm not hungry," came Samantha's soft, small voice.

"You sure? I bet you didn't eat with Grandma, did you? Here, have a bite…"

She said she's not hungry, you moron, Morgan wanted to tell him, but she listened instead to Samantha counting almost inaudibly, "…hun-dred roses…nine-ty eight ro-ses…nine-ty six ro-ses," and Morgan realized she was counting the red buds they'd painted on the bottom bunk over Samantha's head, "ninety-one ro-ses."

Mr. Deaver chewed until she reached the seventies, then he told her to stop counting. The sound of a zipper sliding was followed by Samantha's muffled protests. "C'mon, relax. What do I have to do tonight? Tickle you? Does Daddy have to tickle his little girl, huh?"

Samantha was giggling. No, coughing…hacking that subsided to tiny coughs.

"That's better," he said, inhaling deeply, then exhaling. "Better. Now squeeze as hard as you can, and…that's it…yes…oh, sweetie…that's the ticket…yes…you got it…that's the…tic — " he sucked air and his words trailed off unintelligibly into a deep guttural groan. What was he doing?

Morgan's eyes widened saucer-like, as the bed shivered, a violent quake, then stopped abruptly, leaving only the sounds of Samantha's faint sobs between the Bowtie's heavy breathing. "Samantha, Daddy's girl. Samantha. Hush now."

A chill swept through Morgan, warning something was incredibly wrong, but utterly baffled, she lay so rigid that she could feel the end of her braid dangling into the bottom bunk. Don't let him know. Don't move. Don't breathe.

But she could feel him sit up and had no time to brace herself for him to see her long braid, clasp it and tug it so hard that her head jerked back, wedged between the wall and the bed frame.

He cleared his throat. "I wonder what your daddy'd say about you being out on a school night, little girl?" He jerked her braid again, then let it go.

She wrenched her neck and stared at the sliver of light under the door. Holding her breath, she waited for him to stand, to confront her face-to-face, to pull her from the top bunk and bodily fling her into the hall. But he didn't move. And in that moment of stillness, where she could sense him thinking and all she could hear was Samantha's soft sniffle, Morgan felt herself sit up. She shifted the teddy bear to the side, so, when Mr. Deaver finally stood to face her, nothing came between her and his stony stare.

"I said, what would your daddy say about you being out on a school night?"

"Beats me," she said, without taking her eyes off him, "why don't you ask him?" And she knew that even her dad, especially her dad, who didn't like Christmas, Jesus, Santa or Kennedy because they were fake, would hate this guy.

He held her stare without blinking, then crossed to the door. Turning the knob, he paused, "I'd be real careful what I go telling to your daddy or anybody else." He flicked on the light switch and left Samantha and Morgan squinting from the naked, overhead bulb. And Morgan, afraid to even tell her Aunt Tilly, was real careful from that moment to only tell the private stuff to her microphone:

Safe, I'll keep you safe, Samantha. I promise…promise… promise.

1

FIRING RANGE

Los Angeles, 1984

Morgan was careful not to tell anyone, especially her daughter, that she loved to fire a gun. She leaned against her Jeep, waiting for Sam to get off the school bus stopped at the corner, planning to ask her if she wanted to ride along to the police academy firing range. For her 13th birthday, Sam had asked Morgan to take her to the desert and teach her to shoot. "Maybe when you're sixteen," Morgan told her, remembering the first time she'd fired at a target: the rush of adrenaline had swelled, then settled into a still calmness and assurance unlike any other feeling. She wasn't sure if she were calm because she was confident she could fire accurately, or she fired accurately because she was calm. *"It's this stone-still body shiver,"* she'd taped into her recorder. *"A sustained high note, better than sex. Well, a helluva lot better than what I was getting from the butcher's son."*

A gun was power. She could feel it when she pulled her gun in the field. She liked her daughter to go with her to the police academy so she could observe women performing in a typical men's world. But, watching Sam, a gangly pre-teen with her father's shocking red hair worked into a loose braid, hurrying towards her, chattering with her neighborhood buddy, Morgan was certain she didn't want to pass on this love for shooting a weapon.

"Mom," Sam responded to Morgan's invitation to the firing range, "I would but it's Friday and I promised Nat I'd go to the swim meet with him." She eyed her friend Nat, who shrugged at Morgan as if he were powerless to change her mind. "Besides," added Sam, indicating Gramma Sofie's shadowed face poking out from their drawn living room curtain, "I don't think we should both go there together for a couple of days. She's afraid I'm going to follow in your footsteps. I thought she was going to bite my head off," she told Nat, "when I asked her last night if we were going to have a party to celebrate my mom's three years on L.A.P.D."

"We should," Gramma Sofie had nodded, poking at the last slimy herring on her dinner plate.

Morgan took a bite of brisket, waiting for Gramma Sofie to finish her thought, a thought that would certainly reflect how much she hated that Morgan was a police officer, how much she hated that Morgan never listened to her begging from the grave of her dead son Jacob, Morgan's husband, Sam's father, a war hero, no less, who died for his country — from his very grave Gramma Sofie could hear him crying out that Morgan should stop with this policing, stop policing and go to work for the butcher.

"We should," Gramma Sofie continued, still nodding, "make some kind of celebration." She cocked her head, conceding, "Every day you make it home is a special occasion, so three years as a policeman should be a milestone?"

Now, Morgan jockeyed her Jeep through downtown Los Angeles traffic, slowing as she crested Academy Drive. Just as well that she never told Gramma Sofie that she'd requested a transfer to a more dangerous inner city division. It hadn't come through.

She missed her opportunity for a spot on the street, so she circled the jammed parking lot a couple of times, then waited for a tan Ford pick-up to inch out of a narrow spot. Just as she was making her move to turn in, a candy-apple red Camaro, whipped towards her, coming from the opposite direction, and turned into the space. She pressed on the horn, rolled down the window, and yelled over Springsteen's "Born in the U.S.A." blaring on her radio: "Hey, what's your problem?"

A bald African-American, shoulders like a quarterback, bolted from the driver's seat, pushed the door closed with his racquet. Running his thumb and forefinger over his mustached lip, he faced her annoyed look. "Wait a minute," he indicated his shiny vehicle, "I'll be back in a few...I'm saving this spot for you." She wanted to show him what he could do with his toothy grin, but wouldn't give a jerk like him the satisfaction to turn his back on her erect middle finger.

Waiting for two captain's wives to decide who would drive a nearby blue Impala, she turned up the music and tapped the steering wheel. Springsteen thundered. Although Morgan was partial to his adolescent tributes like "Thunder Road" and "Born to Run," she could have listened to this loner in battered boots and faded jeans sing about anything. His words went right to her heart. The folks in his songs longing for a better life were like so many of the people she came across every day on patrol.

Sometimes when she was in a bind, she'd even think: What would Bruce do? She trusted him. Maybe it was because both of their fathers had worked in the same plastics factory, or that at concerts he shared anecdotes of his wretched relationship with his father. When she'd heard Springsteen say that as a teenager he'd felt more comfortable in the local phone booth than his own house, she knew their fathers were cut from the same blue-collar cloth.

Finally parked, she scaled the stone steps from the parking lot to the first terrace and headed towards the firing range, located on the upper tier of the twenty-one acre complex, beyond the main entrance and the courtyard. Her stomach was a little queasy. Hunger or nerves. She wasn't sure. What had she eaten for breakfast? Nothing. She had time to grab something at the Academy gift shop before she scaled the mountainside steps. Qualifying at the firing range was the only time Morgan had a reason to hike up to the area. She generally confined herself to the lower workout track unless she was meeting a friend for lunch or picking up something at the gift shop for her daughter.

Since Morgan rejected Sam's request for birthday shooting lessons, she'd been asking for M-16 military/tactical body armor. She practically slept with a framed photo of her dad, short and well-built, in full face paint and protective camouflage gear, posing on a training reconnaissance before he'd been shipped off to Vietnam. Morgan reassured herself she still had over a month to find Sam an outfit that didn't offer such complete ballistic coverage, one that made less of a fashion statement for a rising seventh grader.

The sole customer, Morgan walked the gift shop aisles jammed with everything from padded training suits to monogrammed L.A.P.D. pencils. She passed the ballistic carry bags and flotation gear, moving towards the corner of the store where Sam had helped Señora Blanco, the former gift shop manager, arrange the caps on a spinning rack. They were gone. They'd been replaced by a tactical body armor display, a completely concealable police/military enhanced shield for maximum coverage.

She sighed, noting how the police-look increasingly resembled that of armed federales. She scanned past the small arms loading pouches. No baseball caps. Maybe Sam would settle for a pouch. There were pouches for door wedges, nightsticks, handcuffs, shotshell ammunition, radios, side-arm magazines, gas masks, holsters, and grenades, not to mention the various size utility pouches.

"Can I help you to find something, Officer?" a soft-spoken woman addressed her.

Morgan turned around, "Baseball caps…Señora Blanco," she smiled, "que surprisa," as she crossed to the cash register, embracing the gaunt white-haired woman. They fell into the lap of Spanish chatter: Señora Blanco relating her long, lonely recuperation after the electrical fire a year before that had sent her tenement house up in flames and killed her husband. She'd left almost overnight to stay with his distant relatives in Nogales.

Now Señora Blanco smiled, admitting she couldn't stay away forever: the relatives were too distant and Nogales was too dirty and she missed her friends in her Los Angeles barrio and her son, José, who had a desk job in a big police office. "Besides, I like too much working here. So, José asked that they give back my old job." But she didn't want to talk about José. She wanted to know about

Sam. Was she still playing baseball? Did she still hang around with the boy, what's his name, down the street…Cole…no, Nat…named after Nat King Cole. That's right.

Ten minutes later, when Morgan exited the gift shop with a new L.A.P.D. baseball cap, she could hardly wait to tell Sam that Señora Blanco was back.

Morgan passed the academy's cafe, noting the fluttering turquoise and orange banner that publicized the upcoming Olympics. She crossed the worn path through a rock garden around water cascading into several pools. At the top of the rock stairs, Morgan spotted Big Mac, the corpulent range supervisor sitting on a chair near the gate, filling out a report and humming a melody Morgan couldn't quite identify. But he didn't look up even though Morgan knew he saw her. He never let anyone cut him off in the middle of a tune, famous as he was for what he called the timeless values of Celtic music.

When he finished, Morgan said, "Hi, Mac. What was that?"

He frowned, "And you, a lassie. I'm ashamed of ya, Morgan Fraser. That was 'Tonight My Sleep Will Be Restless,' and for not knowing it, yours will be, too."

They bantered briefly. He teased her about never needing a gun in her bucolic north San Fernando Valley police division, commonly referred to as Sleepy Hollow, so it was too bad she had to bother to qualify. She badgered him about the trashy condition of his area, pointing to a couple of paper cups resting on the ledge of an otherwise spotless range. Then she requested the last firing stall at the end of a row of twelve, and told Big Mac that before she did the emergency reload test, she wanted him to work her right side with a few silhouettes. Left-handed, she had good reflexes for movements coming from the left, but she sensed her reflexes were slower on the right, not by much — a millisecond.

"That's using your head," he tapped his forefinger on his temple, "'cause as a lefty, you're at a disadvantage. You know, people move to their dominant side first, the right."

"So?"

"While everybody else is moving to the right, there you'll be looking to your dominant side, the left, away from the action."

She gazed at his ruddy face a moment, her eyes twinkling. "What if the suspect's facing me?"

He studied her, then a grin split his face, "So, you'd be wanting to work on hammering all those suspects coming at you from the right."

"You can't be too sure."

Morgan took her equipment to the last stall. She felt at home here because the bull's eye target at the end of the cement corridor reminded her of the strike zone at the end of the back yard pitching run she'd made for Sam. A week ago she'd tried to remember how she mentally approached firing a gun so she could give her daughter pointers to help her pitching. Focus on the strike zone, she'd said, ignore the heckling. But Morgan could never quite put into words the mental process that muffled all her brain chatter. Just before she shot, sounds disengaged, voices, although identifiable, were like disembodied spirits as though part of her were listening through plexiglass; then a pinhead of light shimmered across the dark meadow of her mind, and in that utter mystic silence, she shot for the light. Experience told Morgan that Sam would have to find her own internal centering. It wasn't a gift given from parent to child; like so much of growing up, it must be self-taught.

Morgan blew a lock of loose hair from in front of her eyes, started to withdraw her gun from the holster, then stopped and deftly rewove her hair into a thick braid that dangled down the center of her back. She was careful about keeping her hair out of her face when in uniform. After all, men didn't mess with their hair.

She withdrew her gun, shut her left eye and stared down the cement corridor at the human silhouette moving erratically along the wire.

The silhouette stopped for an instant, and she aimed at the stationary target, concentrating: Steady. Steady. Make it easy on yourself. Exhale. Aim.

The gun felt glued to her hand.

She fired six rounds and stepped back. All hits.

Big Mac stood at a discreet distance, pointing out her impressive marksmanship to a couple of male officers on their way to the racquetball courts. Morgan knew one of them, Gladstone, and recognized the other as the driver of the red Camaro.

Catching Morgan's glance, Gladstone, Mr. Bad News, an aging steroidal bull with a bleach-blond crew cut, sauntered over and leaned against the railing. "Hey Morgan," he called, "what's the bad news?" He dragged his racquet across the chain links to get her attention. "Not too shabby for a white Barbie," he said with a wry smirk, less for Morgan's benefit than for his black racquetball opponent, who was busy lifting a glob of brown chewing tobacco from a green and white Redman pouch.

She glanced back, expressionless. *Funny, Gladstone, real funny. You're a fuck for brains,* she wanted to tell him, but she'd survived on the force by not always speaking her mind. Instead, she messed with Gladstone's small one, "Did you know, Gladstone, that if Barbie were life-sized she'd be seven feet, two inches? And her measurements would be 39…23…33. What a pair you'd make, huh? Midget Mind and Towering Tits."

Gladstone smirked at his racquetball partner, who gave Morgan a quick visual critique. She noticed perspiration glistening on his bald head. His mustache rode a crooked grin, as he apparently identified her as that woman he was saving a parking spot for.

Morgan turned away and waited for Mac to hook a fresh cardboard target on the wire. If she didn't respond to Gladstone, he'd probably leave. No such luck. She could hear him tapping his racquet on the fence behind her back. He had an audience to impress. He was going to stand there for her entire emergency reload test. She really wished Sam had joined her. Gladstone hated kids and he wouldn't have stopped to annoy her.

Morgan forced herself to concentrate — the rings closest to the heart counted most.

When Big Mac called out the course of fire, she would have three seconds to shoot three rounds. She nodded 'ready' to Mac and he called out, "Fire."

She fired the first round, hit the release with her left thumb and, reaching for her full clip with her right hand, noticed with dismay that the magazine hadn't dropped. Gladstone muttered something as she manually yanked the magazine clip out with her right hand, then clicked the full one in and got off her second, then third round successfully.

Mac yelled out her score, "258." She passed, but she knew she would have scored over 280 without the clip jam.

Of course Gladstone had something to say about that. "You better practice your ass off. At the 77th you might actually have to kill someone to stay alive."

Morgan lowered her gun.

Gladstone continued, "Williams is down at the gym. Wants to see you ASAP. And you better check the transfer board, hotshot: your days in Sleepy Hollow are numbered."

Morgan checked Gladstone's glib expression, "The 77th, huh?" she said, stalling for time.

"You heard it here first and we kick some bitchin' butt in the 77th. One day there is like a month anywhere else. Tell her, Teddy Bear."

Teddy Bear nodded, sucking air through his teeth.

Gladstone nudged him. "Now, tell her who your partner is."

Teddy Bear spit a stream of brown liquid into the nearby grass. "Ben Fender. See you in roll call." He smiled broadly, then followed Gladstone's racquet's indication to head to the courts.

Morgan knew the 77th had become a Fender stronghold, far enough away from the suburbs that an arrogant cop like Fender could find a home among the good old boys who looked like Robocops with dark glasses and no feelings.

She'd put in for a transfer several months before, but hadn't heard anything. She had intended to reapply because the job at Sleepy Hollow was boring: most of the calls were sleepers — loud radio or louder spouses. It was hotter than hell. Smoggy. Traffic was a bitch. She admitted to herself though, it wasn't the heat, smog or traffic that spurred her to request the 77th. It was Fender. *"He has done everything he could to keep me from graduating from the police academy. Every other woman but one, Lola Day, has dropped from this class, and she has sued his ass. But I'd walk on hot coals before I'd give him the satisfaction of a sexual harassment suit. The brass at Parker Center have to do something to keep women from crashing and burning. Rumor is they're going to revamp the program — send Fender, Gladstone and his bunch back on the street. Lovely."*

Morgan had made a point to be at her academy graduation, also the day Fender cleaned out his office. It was family day, the time when cadets were encouraged to bring family and friends, so Sam was with her. She knew Sam liked to hang out with Señora Blanco in the gift shop, or, safe on police grounds, do her imaginary sleuthing — hiding behind classroom bungalows, concealing herself in shrubbery, standing on the toilet seat in the bathroom stalls and eavesdropping on conversations. That day Sam had promised to meet Morgan on the front stone steps with the long metal railing.

Even as Morgan made her way down the academy corridor, she chided herself for wanting to see him so badly. *"If he hadn't fought with Jacob, he wouldn't be clogging up my head like chronic hay fever. It's as if he has the combination to Jacob's security deposit box filled with his last wishes, words, and worries. But his lips are sealed. So, it's a royal pain in the ass, but I have to stay in his face, stare him down — remind him he has information that belongs to me."*

Fender's door was ajar and Morgan could hear him rustling paper inside. There'd been rumors that Fender wasn't attending graduation ceremonies, and she didn't intend to miss the last opportunity to talk with him.

The papers stopped rustling; Fender opened his door and, seeing Morgan, stood there a moment. His head was shaved clean, giving him a monklike appearance. On one hip he balanced a box filled with papers, files, fishing and gun magazines. A large framed document was under his other arm and he clasped a multi-colored pheasant stuffed in mid-flight.

"No autographs today," he said and moved by her, the box riding high on his hip.

"No sir, I didn't expect so." Morgan hurried to catch up with him, as he walked briskly down the nearby steps to the trash dump-site in the parking lot.

"Well, maybe for you. Have a pen?" He kept walking.

"No. No pen. I just wanted to say thanks." Her words, to her ear, were strained, artificial, although since she had survived his indifferent, often humiliating instruction, she could act objectively, make decisions — unemotional decisions. If forced to she could sum up what he'd taught her, like his detached maxims: don't get love on the street; one night's victim can be the next night's suspect; respect the honor code between partners: if you make a mistake, don't bring your partner down. Clearly, he took his last maxim the most seriously. Don't bring your partner down.

Jacob had been his partner in battle, but Fender declined to talk about him. What was Fender hiding? Who was he protecting? That connection between them forced her to ask about Jacob's death. Cheated by the government's *killed in action* boilerplate, she wanted a play-by-play description of what happened, and only one man alive could tell her.

She watched him drop his box of papers and old magazines in the garbage bin, turn and face her, his expression impassive.

She held out her hand. "Good luck, sir." He kept his hand still by his side.

"You're making the mistake of a lifetime, Fraser." He glanced at Sam sliding down the metal railing to the stone stairs, and then leveled a look at Morgan. "She's the spitting image of her father."

Morgan wavered, caught off guard by his personal comment. Then he took the framed white document from under his arm and held it out for her to see. She read the bold black lettering: The United States of America has awarded THE BRONZE STAR MEDAL for heroism in ground combat against a hostile force in The Republic of Vietnam. It was the award he won trying to save her husband in battle — the bronze star and flowing red and blue ribbon were close enough to touch.

She wanted to wring that damn combination out of him like a sponge, but she drew in a shallow breath and stated simply, "You have no idea how I'd appreciate anything you could tell me about what happened with Jacob that last day."

She felt her face flush, groveling.

Fender readjusted the frame under his arm, away from view. His eyes narrowed and Morgan sensed he was holding something back from her, some terrible detail about the way Jacob died.

He made a move to leave, then stopped and looked at her. A flicker in his eyes flashed a sober recollection, then he sighed, disappointed and tired. It was obvious, his last day at the academy wasn't tugging on any heartstrings. He shook his head as if talking about Jacob was completely out of the question, but he would do the next best thing. "I'd do anything to keep you off the street," he said, sadly.

"I'm sorry you feel that way, sir." She forced herself to maintain eye contact, then glanced at the plaque tucked under his arm.

His gaze dropped to his war award. "Keeping you off the street," he shrugged, "I owe him that."

"And what about me?" The words slipped out, candid and sincere.

Fender responded as if he hadn't heard her. As she watched him head toward the station-wagon that turned into the parking lot, she wanted to run after him, shake him, plead with him to tell her the details of the ambush that took Jacob's life.

Then for the first time, she considered that maybe he'd promised Jacob to protect her, given a pledge to his comrade as she'd pledged once to protect her childhood friend.

Fender nodded to his wife, Phyllis, gripping the steering wheel and slowing to a stop; several kids called "Daddy" to him from the backseat. Heavily perspiring and unsmiling, Phyllis scooted to the passenger seat, and Fender slid behind the wheel without a backward glance, as if he were escaping — from the academy headaches, from Morgan and the memory of Jacob's death.

His station wagon turned out of the asphalt parking lot and Morgan was left alone, thinking of Jacob. She still missed him, how he'd swept through and changed her life. Jacob's last letter referred to Fender as if he were a friend. Hard to imagine. But there was a lot she didn't know, and just then she'd caught something in Fender's glance that said he knew much more. She told herself that sometime, somewhere she would find out.

"Morgan Fraser," Mac's resonant voice yanked her back to the firing range, "are you wanting me to call you room service?"

Morgan made her way down the corridor to the entrance of the firing range.

"Thanks," she told Big Mac as she handed him the metal box containing the semi-automatic.

"Better to have that magazine stick here in the firing range than on the street," trying to make her feel better about her unusually low score. But his words could've just as easily slid out of Gramma Sofie's red-painted lips, reminding her for the umpteenth time she was pressing her luck. That if she made it to her third year anniversary she should celebrate being alive. Morgan managed a smile, told Big Mac she'd come back the following month to take the test over to improve her ranking.

"That's the way," he said. "If it doesn't kill us, failure can be a great teacher."

As she crossed from the firing range to the gym, Morgan thought, I can't afford to fail. With each step though, she felt herself moving out of her patrol car comfort zone, lounging on a couch, to an inner-city footbeat, walking on ice.

By the time she reached the gym, she was prepared for the outside chance that Gladstone might not be kidding. Shifting her weight to her left foot, she leaned against the wall, and let herself stare at her name on the transfer board: FRASER, MORGAN: 77th NIGHTWATCH. Cheese and rice! What'll I tell Gramma Sofie: she'll want to know where I'm being transferred. I'll say closer to home. Downtown. Not mention the exact location: South Central L.A.

Morgan glanced around the gym foyer at the poster-size portraits of police chiefs and city leaders, all men. It reminded her of the marble memorial in the entrance of Parker Center, the downtown police headquarters. The plaque had been dedicated in 1971, two years before the first woman police officer entered the Academy. It read: *In Memory of the men of Los Angeles Police Department who have given their lives in the line of duty.* "There's no need to change it yet," she'd told her daughter, "but one of these days they'll have to break down and add *women.*"

The academy gym was a dumping ground for every imaginable policing activity. Brochures described it as an all-purpose gym room, serving as both a space for staging an event on the proscenium, conferring certificates on graduates, or holding a banquet for city notables. But Morgan's auditorium experience mostly included suffering the body-slams of wrestlers on remarkably thin mats.

Morgan recognized a male voice yell, "Okay, let's whip out the mats," and she crossed to the double doors that led into the cramped gymnasium, where her friend, Tony Williams, a burly physical training officer and serologist who specialized in identification of body fluids in major crimes, stood with his arms crossed alongside a dozen women pre-recruits with their last names painted on the fronts and backs of their sweats. They were unrolling a massive yellow plastic floor mat.

Tony shook his head, "Just slap it down, girls, you're not making a bed."

He glanced up and, seeing Morgan through the glass, told his girls to take a break and burst through the gym door. He rushed Morgan to a bench outside. "Glad you caught me. It's my last week here. I'm going back to serology."

"Blood, saliva and semen?" she smiled.

"Yep. Bring on those body fluids."

"But you're doing such a great job with the pre-cadets."

"Thanks. And don't get me wrong. I've enjoyed working with the ladies, but I miss the intellectual charge I get in a lab coat. I kinda like sitting over a microscope in a dimly lit room, stuffing my face with junk food." He peeled the wrapper off a Hershey bar, handing her several squares. "Stick with chocolate and don't sweat it," he assured her, "it's a tough division, but you'll kick it. In the early 70s, I worked in Harlem with the captain in the 77th, Lewis Drummond. Good guy. Controversial as hell though. Thinks we shouldn't be taking a life unless it's absolutely necessary."

"Imagine that," she grinned. "How'd he get that assignment?"

Williams shrugged and handed her another chocolate square, popping the last one in his mouth. "You know who's there?"

He read her nod, continuing, "And you can imagine how well Fender gets along with the woman lieutenant there. Herdahl. She's a real ballbreaker, but I also got the word she's not long for her job there. Busy working her way up the chain of command. She's chomping at the bit to slip into Chief Gates' hot seat."

She indicated his pre-recruits congregating on the sidewalk. "Your break's over."

"Right. Remember, stick with chocolate. And don't be a stranger in serology."

She watched him join his class, jockeying them into position. She marveled at his personal fusion of patience and inspiration.

Clearly, he believed in his women, yet getting them ready for real academy training had frustrated the hell out of him.

Morgan ran the hilly obstacle course before heading home. Puffing as she pressed forward, as usual, her stride fell in step with the familiar cadence from her cadet training: "Man's fight…one right…one way…I say…"

"Cadet Fraser!" She could hear Fender's bark, "move it, move it!" She could almost feel him breathing down her neck, as he burst out, insulting and taunting, "Zero lag time, Fraser. Be a fucking man."

Her pace slackened as she approached the hill, the wall. Be a fucking man. She had to laugh at the thought of how Fender's voice used to egg her on. How men were born fighters, women weren't. And Marines, of course, were born, not created. She wanted to take a break before she reached the crest, but just thinking about Fender's unrelenting attack drove her to exert more than even she thought she had to give.

"C'mon, Cadet Fraser," she imagined Fender's bellow, "stay with me, you splittail. If a suspect had a gun in his pocket and you didn't see the gun, but somebody told you: 'hey, he's got a gun in his pocket…'"

Wincing, hissing air through clenched teeth, she made a final effort to reach the top, "Fraser, you with me. This suspect's hand is on the trigger, draw your weapon and point at him. Cock the revolver and wait for his hand to move. When you see a weapon, shoot him…"

She gasped a dull chuckle, "Duh." Arriving at the summit, she paused an instant, ran in place, absorbing the familiar Los Angeles skyscrapers, Elysian Park, Dodger Stadium, then she pointed her index finger and shot at a nearby tree trunk.

"Fraser!" She smiled to herself, simulating Fender's histrionics, "Do that and you will lose.…Why? You wanna know why? Lag time, Cadet Fraser: your finger has still got to wait for your eye to see the gun…"

She crossed the road and turned into a dirt path, which led through some woods and opened onto an obstacle course "…to send a message to your nerves to pull that trigger…" She ran past a row of metal pull-up bars. "…but the suspect's finger is already pressed, waiting. He knows he's going to shoot you…Fraser…are you with me, or what? He's going to shoot you."

She leapt over a fallen tree branch, slowed, balanced herself with outstretched arms, then shimmied her shoulders, hips and head as if moving to her own music flowing through her, revitalizing her from her inside.

Turning towards a ten-foot-high wall, marred from signs of defeat, she swerved drunkenly towards it, then ran directly ahead, starting to pick up speed. "…and Fraser, when he moves to shoot you, he will fire at the same time as you…" She approached the wall, her heart thrashing wildly. "…and beat you, every time…" She appeared to be too close to the wall to scale it. "…every fucking time, Cadet Fraser."

Then suddenly, she leapt up, planted her left foot in the wall center, grabbed the top with her hands, smoothly flipped her right leg and body over and dropped to the other side, hunched over, gasping. "Now," Fender's words burst in her head, "that's something for you *splittails* to think about because you do not have zero lag time and in three years at least one of you'll be fucking dead."

Morgan looked up, took a deep breath, and shook her head. "Not me."

Driving home, she considered that since she'd been transferred to a much more dangerous division she would have to have a serious talk with her daughter. She and Sam had discussed facing danger, that sometimes in order to do the right thing, in order to win a fight, you had to dare to face rejection, hostility, danger. They'd had that talk after Sam caught a junkie's daughter writing *your mom's a pig* on her gym locker. Sam pinned her against the lockers, held her by the hair. "That's right," she said, "my mom helps people and arrests people for a living. I'm okay with that. Now let's write what your mom does for a living on your locker." The girl socked Sam in the stomach and Sam punched her back harder, then let her go. But Sam kept the graffiti on her locker the rest of the year, pointing to it occasionally, grinning at the junkie's daughter, almost challenging her, or anyone else, to make a disparaging remark about her mother.

Morgan reconsidered. Maybe a talk about the difference between Sleepy Hollow and the 77th wasn't the answer. She didn't want to alarm Sam, and she certainly didn't want to give Gramma Sofie more verbal firepower.

Morgan recalled the people she'd loved and lost — her mother, her childhood best friend Samantha, her husband Jacob, and Aunt Tilly. She tried, in vain, to remember anything they'd said or done to prepare her for the possibility that they could suddenly be gone — forever. But what could they have said to prepare her to face such a shock?

2

Six Inches of Steel

Pigeons had made a nest under the neon "O" in Tia's Tacos. B. Jay Moon, a ten-year veteran of the 77th Division, tanned and rugged, stopped carving a wooden chess piece long enough to stare up at the birds. He and his partner, Earley, were at a table outside the taco house across the street from a boarded up fried chicken drive-through and a crack house. Moon set down the blade and the piece — an unfinished knight — and picked up a half-eaten burrito. Eyeing the birds, he licked some refried beans spilling down the side of the messy flour tortilla off his gooey fingers, then wiped them on his jeans. "Smart, those pigeons, damn smart," he said to Tyrone Earley, also dressed undercover in jeans and a chambray work shirt. Earley, thick and sturdy, palmed his kinky-cropped mane and sipped coffee, maintaining a steady gaze at Bo's Chicken drive-thru across the deserted South Central Los Angeles street.

"See," Moon jerked his head in the direction of the sign, "the 'O' up there's the only letter that lights up at night. Keeps those little buggers warm as toast."

Earley's dark eyes, alert for the next move across the street, were drawn instead to the light in the window of the rundown crack house next to Bo's Chicken. Just then, a lean young male opened the crack house front door, closed it behind him and descended the front stoop. "Not much action over there tonight," Earley said, as the guy crossed the driveway toward a parked '64 Falcon that looked like it'd been put together with baling wire. He opened the trunk, placed a brown shopping bag on top of a mound of clothes, slammed the trunk and walked back indoors.

"I don't know." Moon stuffed the rest of the burrito in his mouth. "Kinda dicey."

"Could just be clothes for the Salvation Army."

"Or snake oil."

Earley shrugged.

Moon had a feeling they should shake the boy down. They made it a practice to shake down just about every person caught going in and coming out of drug houses. They tagged two, sometimes three dealers or users a week from various suspected narcotics dealing pads, usually got drugs or hypes, carted the suspect to jail and called it a night. But this Bo's Chicken dude, probably a minor, hadn't done anything except saunter out his front door and drop a brown bag in his trunk. It was the way he sauntered that bugged Moon, too leisurely for after midnight. Moon knew he'd need more than a suspect's breezy gait to convince Earley to go knock on the door.

Moon pointed at Earley with his burrito, "That's the problem with you, Earley. You don't think the worst of people. See, if you think the worst, you'll never be disappointed."

Earley shook his head in disbelief, then looked away for a moment, down the street, and Moon swiped his last few tortilla chips. Earley glanced back and, missing his chips, said, "Moon, you raised in a fucking zoo, or what?"

"Jungle," Moon said, grinning, sleepy and playful. His body language, nonchalant with a killer's confidence, said: *don't mess with the king.* He tapped a beat with his open palms to the syncopated rhythms coming from the tape on the cook's trashed ghettoblaster. Tia, the owner-chef, a white-haired Sonoran woman, listened to the same static-filled tape every night. Same guys, sounding like a bunch of Boy Scouts around a crackling campfire, singing in Spanish to a strumming guitar. Same speech by the leader, then the chorus of voices followed by wild clapping and cheers. Moon had gotten so sick of hearing the defective recording that he gave Tia *South of the Border*, a Herb Alpert and Tijuana Brass cassette, but she never played it.

Not much action at Tia's tonight either. Where was the colorfully half-dressed Bob Marley stand-in from central casting, who usually filtered over from the adjacent shabby apartments with the torn window shades? Just as well he hadn't made his midnight appearance. Earley would go off on Marley's meaningful message about global suffering and the survival of African Americans. And where were the two light-skinned hookers in mini-skirts and maxi red henna curls, who batted dark eyelashes at Earley and exposed big teeth behind their slick ruby lips? If they only knew they were exhausting their facial muscles on a devoted family man.

Moon and Earley had been partners for over a year. Moon's last partner, Stan the Man, had taken a shot in the chest from a jumpy addict during a domestic violence call and retired early on disability. The first night Moon worked with Earley they'd also been sitting at Tia's Tacos as flames suddenly lit up the sky a couple of miles east. Earley had leapt up, exclaiming, "The clinic." In six months, this one women's health center had already suffered a fire, an eviction, several blockades, death threats to doctors and staff, an assault and battery, and a boric acid attack.

Driving to the fire, Moon complained that if the damn clinic stopped doing abortions they wouldn't put everybody in such danger. But Earley's wife, Amberlene, had written a book on the social necessity of women's health care, so Earley trashed Moon's ignorance, giving him a crash course in all the other free community services, including but not limited to abortion, the clinic provided. Now every time they received a radio call while they were at Tia's Tacos, Moon would jump up and cry out, "Oh my God! The clinic!"

So when the dispatcher's monotone issued from Moon's inside jacket pocket, "Code 6 at 2025 Lincoln," and Moon sprung up, in mock alarm, "The clinic! Oh my God Earley, it's the clinic!" Earley simply ignored him; Moon shrugged and sat back down. "Possible GTA suspect," continued the dispatcher. "Car 5 responding."

Moon slipped the faceless miniature knight in his breast pocket and started to get up again, but Earley motioned for him to forget it. "Sarge has it. C'mon man, I'm beat."

"No back up requested," the dispatcher concluded the radio transmission.

And it was quiet again except for the Boy Scout camp leader shouting from Tia's ghettoblaster, all worked up about something. The only word Moon could make out was *libre.* Free. Free, of course. They were Mexican: they expected things in the U.S. to be free. Pleased that he'd translated what the Boy Scouts were singing, he gave Earley a look, then sat down and handed him back a few of his tortilla chips.

"Thanks," Earley said. "You'll never be famous: you've got scruples."

"Don't want to be famous. I want to be infamous, so people just leave me alone."

"Just like the Lawman," Earley nodded. "He said it like it was."

"What Lawman?"

"Burt Lancaster: the Lawman."

Moon shook his head, withdrew his knight from his pocket and rubbed the figure's undefined face between his thumb and forefinger.

"C'mon, the Lawman is you, man. Every kid saw that movie," Earley said. "This big white guy comes into town because a bunch of do-gooders hung the wrong man. And he's going to arrest all of them, but they're all prominent citizens, so he goes to the sheriff and says: 'I want these six mothers in jail.'"

"Don't tell me," Moon said, holding up his palm, "Sheriff goes: 'Well, they're all prominent citizens, I can't do that.'"

Earley grinned at the retelling. "I knew you saw it."

"I didn't."

Earley didn't care; he was on a roll. "So, everybody in town knows the Lawman's there, right. He's in the saloon eating breakfast; a bunch of townies get their backbone up and they go in. He just looks at them and says: 'Who's got the words?'" Early added, "I love this part."

"I can tell," snickered Moon and poured them each another cup of coffee.

Earley bristled, cocked his head and butchered a Burt Lancaster impersonation. "'I know what you're gonna say; you don't want me in your town. You don't need me to be here and take care of your law. Well, why don't you all get out of here and leave me alone before somebody dies. Like you, storekeeper.'" Earley poked Moon in the ribs. "'You'll be the first to go…'"

Not far away, in a parking lot adjacent to a cluster of old brick office buildings, Officer Rhonda Slattery, petite and trembling, ran her fair-skinned palm under the dark-skinned perp's pant cuff. Slouched, he had his arms crossed casually behind his head. She could smell his sweat, a faint whiff of dusty socks and sugary peaches. She couldn't help but notice how his ivory lamé T-shirt clung to his chest. Her partner, Sergeant Matt Ross, had spied him on a storefront stoop, exchanging a pouch with a pubescent girl; the teenager had slipped away, but Ross nabbed the suspect. He'd been hanging around the neighborhood all week, moved in from Crenshaw, and the word on the street said he was using pre-teen girls to traffic drugs north on the Greyhound bus.

Rhonda Slattery continued the hand search up his leg and felt the suspect shift his weight. He darted a glimpse at her partner. She could tell Ross had already checked out the suspect's potential and figured she could handle it alone, so he took a guard position, standing to the side of the building.

The suspect squirmed again, but Slattery was afraid to look into his face. She was afraid to look into any black man's eyes except for Ross or Earley, knowing she'd see the look judging her as that stupid white girl, a tag she'd been working hard to avoid. She was a sheltered white woman, nearly a tennis champion, and working eight hours a night in a black universe was, for her, like stepping into a dark fantasy where people played by different rules, or no rules.

He shifted again and exhaled deeply. "Why don't the brother homie do me?" He nodded towards Sergeant Ross. "You in training tonight?"

"Stand still," Slattery said, as she patted the inside of the suspect's other calf with the palm of her hand, moving up the inside of his thigh.

Certain the sergeant was out of earshot, he whispered, "Hey baby, you like that?"

She ignored him.

But his low, husky voice lured her to explore. "C'mon, little higher, baby, and you got six inches of steel."

Her eyes avoided the prominent bulge in his groin, and she briskly terminated the search and stood, the top of her head level with his armpit. She took a step backward to offset his towering stature and nodded to Sgt. Ross, who gestured with his hand to let him go.

"All right," she said, averting her eyes, "you're outta here."

The suspect slapped his arms to his sides and fastened his stare on her, until she was forced to look up at him. "I said you can go."

He shrugged his shoulders, grinning, head tilted to one side. "You know you want it. Change your mind, just ask around for Boots." He pointed a thumb back to his chest. "I won't say nothin' to nobody." He brushed his palm down his thigh, winked at her, then turned and strutted down the alley.

Back at Tia's Tacos, Earley gulped more coffee, resuming his tale. "Then the Lawman gets on his horse and rides out, like he's got no feelings whatsoever."

"Good move, you can't get all wrapped up in this horseshit," Moon said, raising his eyebrows with a sigh.

"That's what I tell Amberlene when she tries to get me to talk about my job. Leave all the work bullshit in my locker. Don't want to take it home and stink up my house. Why I wouldn't let the crap that goes down at the 77th close enough to fertilize my marigolds." Earley remembered something and, privately cursing himself, hissed air through his teeth.

"What?" Moon looked up from his carving.

Earley brushed the thought away, "It's okay," he said. "I just forgot to spread fertilizer on them this morning. A gardener's work is never done," he declared flashing a grin, swilling down his coffee and glancing toward the nearby stainless pot. "I have to stay awake through Lily's first tap dance recital this morning. She's a tree." He started to pour Moon some more coffee.

Moon covered the cup with his palm. "Nope. Going home and sleep."

"I'm jealous. What I would give for a Saturday morning without my kids." A sudden thought erased the smile on Earley's face. He glanced at Moon and shrugged a wordless apology.

Moon smiled mechanically. "S'okay, just don't be jealous of me, partner."

Earley nodded, then flashed a concerned look at Moon who'd been a mosaic of stress since his divorce three years ago. His wife had asked for a divorce on the grounds of irreconcilable differences. Moon had admitted to Earley that everything irreconcilable between them had started with the death of their son.

Tia poked her head out the window, "Hola, taco de pescado."

"Another fish taco," Earley marveled. "What she won't do for you."

Moon plunked his knight down and got up. "Yeah, so long as I keep Immigration off her back."

Moon watched her count with her fingers, then pull a stubby, chewed pencil from behind her ear and jot down numbers on a paper bag. Tia had been making Moon fish tacos almost every night for two years. Her son had brought her across the border from Kino Bay in northern Mexico, where she had a shack on the beach and made fish tacos for locals and tourists.

"Why don't you tell her son how to get her a green card."

Moon made an anguished expression. "And give up my free fish tacos?"

"I've never seen anything like it." Earley shook his head. "You have a hollow stomach?"

"Heart," Moon thumped his chest with his fist, "hollow heart." Moon lifted the yellow paper off his taco, peeked inside and nodded approvingly, handing a bill to Tia, which she declined and he kept. He scooped up his taco, took a huge bite and walked back to the table. He eyed a dude in a shiny white T-shirt, ambling across the street, and Moon recognized him as a new player on the 77th front line; he'd seen him before, but couldn't quite place him.

Earley had been watching him too. "I'm gonna get you a glittery suit like that for your birthday." Earley indicated the sparkling T-shirt dude, who looked as though he was heading for the crackhouse, "'Bout time the Captain gives us the high sign to bust the cow shit outta that place, don't you think?" But the dude didn't go inside. He looped back.

"Shit, Glitterboy's going for the car," Earley said.

"That's right." Moon nodded, encouraging him. "Go for your goodies in the trunk." The mere thought of what might be in the paper bag — a 100-kilo cocaine bust — shot icy adrenaline through Moon's veins. He waited for Glitterboy to do something that would confirm his suspicions. Nothing to pick him up on yet. Moon watched him open the driver's door and slip in. Maybe it was his car after all. Dude might've parked it there in the afternoon. Hardly. He was starting to think like Earley. Any dude driving a car from that crackhouse had to be a drug dealer.

Glitterboy closed the car door, hesitated before he turned the ignition, then backed slowly out onto the street.

He was probably a pimp, too. And all pimps should be shot, just like all drug dealers should. As far as Moon was concerned, they were dragging down the whole human race. Moon worked himself into a hot sweat while he carved his knight's metal breastplate, feeling the Falcon turn onto Century and drive cautiously past — Glitterboy not so much as casting his eyes in the direction of Tia's Tacos. Like a lion in pursuit of prey, Moon continued sculpting and, with half an eye, observed the car move at a snail's pace down the street.

The Boy Scout song leader was yelling "*libre*" again when the Falcon stopped at a yellow light with plenty of time still to make a left turn westbound onto Century Blvd.

"Dyn-o-mite," Moon said, "you're busted, you son-of-a-bitch." His eyes fixed on the bucket of bolts stopped too short of the pedestrian crosswalk. "My great grandmother had enough on that light to make it."

"What are we going to stop him on, excessive caution?"

"Right rear brake light's out."

Looked fine to Earley, but he gulped his last swig of coffee and sighed. "Why does this always happen at the end of our shift?"

Moon was half way to their beat up late-model Ford. "C'mon, we'll close out with an easy bust. This dude's loaded."

"If you do the report," Earley said.

"You got it. Let's go kick some ass."

"Adíos," Tia called from the window, as the Boy Scouts launched into *"Cancíon de Adíos."*

Earley swung onto Century, tailing the Falcon, as Moon situated the red light on the dash and flipped on the siren.

Glitterboy pulled over right away, and Earley parked ten feet behind and a couple of feet to the left of the car in order to keep an eye on the driver.

Moon sniffed. "He smells like shit, look out."

"That's your fish breath blowing back in your face, man."

Moon half-smiled, cracking the door on the passenger side. He leapt out before their Ford stopped, and started to walk up to the right rear of the suspect's vehicle.

Earley jammed the car in park, opened his door and moved towards the Falcon.

It wasn't until he was standing next to the patrol car's headlight that he apparently noticed the driver's door was ajar, barely, held shut by the suspect. Earley yelled out, "Put your hands on the windshield inside the car." Just as he turned his head to signal Moon, the suspect threw open the door, dropped his head between his shoulders and rolled to the pavement exposing a 30-caliber pistol in his right hand. He fired twice.

The first shot hit Earley right over the heart and, like a fist to the chest, Moon could see it shoved him backward a couple of feet.

The second shot hit him below the belt, through the pelvis. Doubled over, Earley shot at the suspect three times. All misses.

Slumped, Earley melted into the pavement, cussing, "Fuck. Shit. Piss."

As the suspect stood, trying to maneuver back to the Falcon, Moon fired six rounds, hitting him all six times, on the right shoulder, abdomen, and thigh.

Earley crawled towards the Ford, pulled his torso up onto the driver's seat. He could feel himself starting to lose consciousness, so he grabbed the radio and yelled into it. "Officer needs help! Century and Saint Andrews."

Moon heard Earley yelling, "Officer down." Then nothing. And Moon was out of bullets.

Struggling to still stand, the suspect aimed to shoot, staggering forwards. Moon ducked, threw down his .38 special and fumbled for his back-up gun with his left hand just as Earley, half-dangling outside the car from the front seat, seized the gearshift and yanked the still running Ford into drive. The car lunged forward.

Glitterboy turned and shot out the front windshield. Glass splattered on Earley as the front bumper slammed into the Falcon, giving Moon a shield against the suspect's fire.

Earley got back on the radio mike, a different man. Now he knew what was happening to him, and he murmured, quietly sober, "Please help us. Jesus, God. Help us." His voice failed, as he dropped the mike and passed out.

Moon shot Glitterboy once, twice, three times with his back-up gun. He stumbled, but fought dropping to the ground. Moon vaulted the car bumpers and pumped three more shots into his bloody T-shirt until he slumped and tumbled sidewise like a human bowling pin. Moon felt a pulse and handcuffed him.

Moon rushed to Earley, who was barely conscious, sucking in quavering breaths. Moon stared an instant at his friend's denim shirt that glistened from the street light bouncing off the glass slivers that covered his chest.

Easing into the driver's seat, Moon felt as if electric shocks were being pumped into his brain. He gently lifted Earley's head onto his lap, and picked the glass shavings from his partner's face. Moon heard the approaching sound of the Boy Scouts harmonizing what sounded like the Spanish version of Beethoven's *Ode to Joy*, and looked through the glassless dash at Tia hobbling madly down the sidewalk past boarded storefronts long vacated. She must have seen the shooting from the taco stand. Now, stumbling off the curb, she hurried towards the patrol car.

Whispering through sobs, she opened the passenger door, kneeled and clasped Earley's hand in her nicked, creviced palms. She held her dented portable cassette player near Earley's ear and adjusted the volume on high, as if she really wanted him to hear the Boy Scouts' scratchy song because it was the only solace she could give to release him from his agony. She prayed in a language Moon came to hold in higher esteem, prayed with them until the red, flashing squad car lights scared her. "Vaya con Angel," she kissed her fingertips and blew Earley a kiss, repeating, "Vaya con Angel," then she slipped into the shadows, away from the conspicuous pulsing lights.

Minutes after the shooting, when the three support units finally rolled in, Moon was yelling, "Goddamnit, where the fuck's the RA!"

Officer Sara Ann Engels stepped out of the passenger door of one of the police cars. *Engels, dynamite*, thought Moon. *Just make my fucking day.*

She crossed to the Ford and swallowed a gasp when she saw Earley, covered in blood and glass, slumped on Moon's lap — Moon trying to staunch the bleeding in Earley's chest with his own shirt. "Don't you have a first aid kit?"

Moon looked at her blankly.

Earley lifted his hand and offered a limp wave.

"Hi," she said, clearing her throat.

He motioned with barely moving fingers for her to lean closer. She bent over and he spoke in a whisper, "I need a gigantic band-aid." He inhaled sharply, then added, "Two."

Engels gritted her teeth, too choked up to speak. She touched his hand, indicating for him to take it easy.

"I know he looks like shit," Moon told her, picking the shards of glass off his partner's forehead, "but Rescue's on the way, the RA's on the fast track, and he's gonna be okay."

She managed a nod, took a deep breath and then turned sharply as if she had to escape the reality of her favorite cop, a close friend, so badly shot up. She made her way towards the suspect.

Behind her another assist unit pulled up, and Officer Ben Fender exploded from the passenger seat and hammered his feet towards Moon's car. The driver, Teddy Bear, hung back in the driver's seat to dash off a call, dipped his head in swift prayer, then jammed in a wad of chewing tobacco.

Moon fired Fender a look of desperation, "Where's the fucking RA?"

"Teddy's getting a fix on 'em."

Fender eyed Earley unblinkingly, grit his jaw, then shook his head. "Fuck." He exhaled deeply. At a loss for words, he stalled,

"Look at you. You make me wolf down my Big Mac for this: a fucking scratch." He pointed to Moon's blood-drenched shirt wadded on one of the wounded cavities in Earley's chest and pelvis, then pounded his own chest with his fist. "Heartburn to die for."

Earley's wince would have accompanied an apologetic shrug if he could've moved his upper body.

Sergeant Ross hustled, trailed by Officer Rhonda Slattery. Ross' anxious eyes asked how bad it was. He and Fender exchanged a wooden look that erased any shred of hope. Ross blinked hard several times before he bent over to look in the car. "That's butt ugly," Ross said, grimacing at Earley's open chest. He leaned closer, touching Earley's thigh, "Got any chips and salsa in there, brother?" He indicated the take-out bag from Tia's Tacos, then waited on Earley's weak nod. "Well, you don't have to offer me any."

"That's cool, 'cause I wasn't," Earley started to tremble. "I'm just fucking with you. Help yourself, Sarge."

Teddy Bear got out of his patrol car and sprinted up. "RA's on the way." He spit tobacco juice on the curb.

Moon and Ross exchanged an uncertain glance that Moon clarified. "Where they coming from is the question?"

Teddy Bear took one look at Earley and hit the door jam with his fist. "Tyrone," he said, shaking his head at him, "goddamnit, now you really done it to yourself." Teddy pitched a lob of his chewing tobacco on the ground, then indicated he wanted to relieve Moon. Carefully, Moon eased out from under Earley, as Ross and Slattery looked on in stunned despair. Fender backed away from Moon's car and trudged a dozen yards on the dirt sidewalk to check out the suspect.

Officer Engels, entranced, was standing over the suspect, staring. She grimaced at the twelve rounds spread from his neck to his groin. She leaned over, stretching her hand towards his neck to check for a pulse.

"Don't touch him!" bellowed a voice from behind.

She straightened up. "Fender, no, you can't just let him — "

"Stand back." She hesitated, but he glared at her. "You. Back."

She stepped aside, her face sagging.

Moon had moved next to Fender. "Earley didn't get a shot. I hit him twelve times."

Engels interrupted. "You had to shoot him this much?"

Moon and Fender ignored her.

Fender just shook his head. "For Chrissakes, you have to be fucking Daniel Boone today to bring a dude down with the shit ammunition we've — "

"You hit him twelve times," said Engels in disbelief. "You didn't have to — "

"Will you shut the fuck up!" Fender shoved her aside with his shoulder.

She jabbed him with her elbow and he raised his baton, flashing her a hard look, as if it would give him infinite pleasure to stick his baton in her. She held her ground, glaring at him.

"For Chrissakes you two," Moon snapped.

Engels backed off a moment. "Well, at least cover him up."

"I'm gonna let him lie here and fucking bleed to death," Fender snarled at her. "Get it, bitch?"

The suspect cried out in agony, his lips spilling blood.

Engels regarded him in silence, keeping it together until the suspect's bullet holes started bubbling blood like a spring, then she dropped to the ground and gagged uncontrollably.

Without even looking down, Fender said to Moon, loud enough for Engels to hear, "She's number one on the Sergeant's list. Score 95. I don't fucking believe it: she could be our next boss."

"Yep, I can see it right now," Moon agreed.

Fender inhaled deeply then exhaled in a disgusted burst, "Yep. Captain's going to give her a fast-track into a detective position because she's done such a bang up job on sexual abuse against women."

Moon glanced down at the vomit-splattered pavement and cringed.

Fender crossed his arms and gave her a long, hard stare, then he said in a lowered, ominous voice, "Say somebody shot you up like that," he tilted his head towards Boots, "which parts of your body would you want donated?"

"Moon!" Ross yelled, pointing to Earley and shaking his head.

Engels darted a glance to Moon. "You're a witness to his threat."

But Moon was scanning the empty boulevard. "Fuck the RA," Moon said, "I'll take him."

Teddy Bear moved out of the front seat of the Ford, Moon slid in, scooted Earley over onto his lap and slammed the door. The siren split the air as he screeched westbound.

Slattery looked up at Teddy Bear who was still staring at Moon's departing Ford. "He can't die, man," Teddy Bear shook his head, eyeing Engels and Fender. "You know yourself, Earley's kept those two from killing each other more than once."

Slattery nodded, adding her barely audible assurance that Earley would be okay.

Sergeant Ross patted Teddy Bear on the back. "Shit is gonna fly. Be up to you then to unplug the fan." Slattery noticed Ross level a look she didn't understand, but figured it must be some brother thing, some sort of black man's interplay. Both men moved towards the suspect.

Slattery followed. The suspect was oozing blood, but his eyes were open, watching. She leaned in closer to get a better look at his face, then dropped back as though hit by a sudden gust of wind. She looked around for his gun. There had to be a gun. Did he have it when she searched him? No, he couldn't have. Her eyes passed her partner's. She felt Ross' eyes regarding her quietly, in disbelief, recognizing Boots as the suspect she'd searched at their last call in the alley.

She wanted to back away, leave the crime scene entirely, but Boots gazed up at her, silently replaying his earlier taunts in her head: "C'mon, little higher, baby, and you got six inches of steel." The gun could've been in the car, she told herself again, but she doubted Boots had the gun under the driver's seat. And he confirmed her fears with a knowing wink, then he whispered the word, "steel." And she knew: she'd been caught off guard by the bulge in his groin…she'd missed the gun at his waist. She should have searched farther. It was too soon after Slattery's probation as a rookie officer for her to miss a gun. Too soon.

She glimpsed around to see if anyone else read his intimate flicker; no one did. She tried to flag Engels, who was too upset with Fender to catch Slattery's gesture.

When she glanced back at Boots he was just staring at her silently repeating the very words she couldn't stand to hear: stupid white girl.

Moon swerved out of a side street onto Florence, empty but for a *Los Angeles Times* delivery truck. He glanced down at Earley, who was staring wide-eyed up at him.

"Not a great tactical shooting, I know, partner. But it took a lot of balls, whuddusay?" Earley smiled, fading.

"Don't you die on me, you son-of-a-bitch! It'll look bad in my package. And my personnel file looks like shit — it's already the size of *War and Peace.*"

"Don't worry. Aren't we supposed to get old, wilt and go in the ground?"

"Right." Moon slammed on the brakes and skidded around a produce truck through a red light.

"Well, that's my plan. Live to fight another day…"

"That's better, keep talking."

Rhonda Slattery watched her partner's back, standing nearby, staring intently at Boots, still breathing. Earley's wounds were more serious than everyone was letting on: he was struggling to live with every breath, and the connection between Boots and Earley was inextricable, as if they were now on a singular life line, inhaling and exhaling with increasing difficulty, together. Ross kept his back to her because he couldn't look her in the face right now, and Slattery wondered if he would still want her as a partner, or if Earley's loss would be so painful he would have to request another partner. Ross was fair, firm, sincere; her oversight was tragic: his disappointment in her must be utter and complete. Guilt seeped out from every fearful pore.

She shuddered not at Ross' silent, professional grief, but at what Fender would do when he knew the significant role she'd played in this fatal scene. Ross would have to identify Boots as the suspect she'd searched in the alley. Fender would put two and two together.

Even if Boots hadn't been concealing a gun, Fender would insist he was and Slattery missed it. On the edge of tears, Slattery stopped thinking about her fear of Fender for a moment, realizing that as bad as she felt, Ross felt worse: he wouldn't have missed it.

Sergeant Ross turned abruptly and walked to their car, without looking back. He returned to the station alone, leaving her at the site by herself with Fender, now the senior officer in command.

Slattery was the first to spot the rescue ambulance unit finally pull up and race towards Boots, but they wouldn't be saving any lives here. Fender, standing guard over him, checked to see if any of his wounds were gurgling, which would mean air was going in, blood was circulating — and he was still alive.

Two paramedics pushed through, blocked by Fender's impenetrable stance. "You're a pound light and a day late."

They missed the point and maneuvered to go around him, but he shifted his weight. "Officer Earley's half way to the hospital by now."

The male paramedic pointed to Boots. "He's alive."

"And I'll let you know when you can have him."

Engels burst out, "Now, Fender! They can have him now." She appealed to the other paramedic, who cocked his head, "Don't know if we can save him."

"Not a chance." Fender ignored both paramedics, but glared hard from Engels down to his soiled shoes and back to Engels.

Engels darted a look entreating Slattery to say something. Slattery, silent and still, directed her gaze at Boots.

After a long, soundless minute, Boots' shoulders trembled and he sighed a tremulous breath that he shivered to catch and didn't. Slattery stiffened as Fender brushed by her, ignoring her entirely. Then staring at Boots' still body as the paramedics hoisted him onto a stretcher, she sighed softly, felt her heart stop racing, and turned away from her suspect, careful to conceal her relief from Engels.

Moon sped down the highway, one eye on the road, one on Earley. Something must have ruptured inside Earley. A gaseous smell filled the car and now the seat of his pants was entirely soaked in the blood flowing from the holes in Earley's chest. He thought of stopping to apply pressure to reduce the bleeding, but he was less than a minute away from the hospital and every second counted. "C'mon, keep talking. Talk to me, partner."

"Just get me plugged up quick," Earley said, wheezing badly.

"You got it."

"Gotta dancing tree to — " His words cut off as though he suddenly turned down the volume.

Moon touched his shoulder, "I hear you, buddy." He kept his eyes on the road, not daring to look down at Earley.

"Ever want to learn to tap?" Earley said slowly.

"What?" Moon turned onto the final stretch of road and pressed the accelerator to the floor.

"Tap dance."

Moon glanced down at his bloodless face. "Hell no. Did you?"

He smiled, then fixed a long, glassy look on his partner.

Moon headed for the green light in front of the hospital emergency entrance, wondering why he waited for the RA as long as he did. Why hadn't he driven Earley to the ER immediately?

Earley's stone stare was now riveted on Moon's face. Moon reached to check his partner's pulse, and his eyes narrowed as if he were looking into a bright light. As the light melted into dark, he could see the shadowy image of a tree and his own young son running towards him grinning, arms outstretched.

By the time the memory faded, the Ford had slowed somehow, stopped at the red light across from the emergency room sign. Moon stared transfixed through the shattered windshield. The light turned green. But the Ford sat alone in the empty intersection, lights flashing, siren screaming.

3

Dancing in the Dark

The alarm went off with an intolerable bleat. Morgan willed herself to come out from under the covers and flicked off the alarm. She squinted at the digital numbers:1:55. That would be a.m., she noted, recalling that she'd forgotten to reset it.

Awake in the dark, she stared bleary-eyed at the photo next to the clock. Her arms were wrapped around the waist of a man who was holding a baby on his lap, sitting on a carousel horse; she was ten years younger, ten pounds heavier, ten times happier: she was in love with her man, with her toddler, with her life.

She'd dated in the past few years, but like her Aunt Tilly, she'd never found somebody she could love and respect — sleep with, maybe, but she wasn't very good at sex without a personal connection. She figured when Springsteen decided to let a woman as close to him as he did his audience, she'd think about it again. Right now, she was about to hang it all out there, do what she believed she could do best, protect people, in the bloodiest precinct in the L.A.P.D., and she didn't want any man to get in her way.

She closed her eyes, yawned and dropped her head, hiding for a moment in her long, messy hair, then bolted out of bed. Shivering in a skimpy nightshirt, she slid into a pair of jeans and a blue oxford shirt dumped the night before on the wood floor. A few brush strokes before turning on the nightstand light, then she leaned over and gathered her hair into a high ponytail on the top of her head. Divided the hair into three equal strands, braiding them to the end, wrapping the braid in a knot and securing it with a couple of black pins. Then she slipped into the moccasins Jacob had bought her on their honeymoon.

Just before she went out the door, she remembered to sprinkle fish food in a tank too small for the ten-inch goldfish.

The hall nightlight was out. She watched her step so she didn't trip over one of the invariably bunched-up throw rugs. A stumble trap for Gramma Sofie, her permanent charge, whose idea of contentment was to get through another day without slipping and breaking an arm or leg. Morgan flicked on a bathroom light that lit up the hall, casting a shadow on Sofie's colored photo of the Western Wall in Jerusalem next to a black-and-white print of Golda Meir.

A loud clank redirected her to the next room, where a baseball bat had rolled on the hardwood floor next to Sam's bed. The headboard was in the shape of a baseball glove, and from the twisted blanket, it looked as though the buried little leaguer had been wrestling with the covers. Morgan picked up the bat, resituated it in the nook of Sam's outstretched arm, next to a worn glove. A bold scrawl across the inside glove pocket advertised a Police Academy slogan: ONE RIGHT, ONE WAY. Morgan leaned over to kiss Sam's forehead.

She tiptoed through the living room, stopping briefly to ease a blanket over Gramma Sofie who, reclining in an E-Z Boy lounge chair, snorted gulps of broken wind until Morgan eased the front doorknob, which triggered a sense alarm that jarred her from a sound sleep, "Where are you off to in the middle of the night?"

"Drive. I'm going to check out my new precinct. See if I can find out my days off. Meet my new partner, maybe."

"Nightwatch is no job for a woman with a child."

"Sofie."

She sat up with a grunt, resettling her broad bottom in the cushion. "That's all I'm saying."

"You'd probably sleep better in your own bed."

"Oh God, that I should sleep." She flung back the afghan. "Don't worry about me." Morgan wasn't sure what to say. *Okay, I won't worry about you.* There had to be some sort of response appropriate for a self-absorbed mother-in-law, and maybe Jacob could have found it for his mother, but Morgan couldn't. Not at 2:00 a.m. Not since Gramma Sofie had moved in last year with her and Sam.

"I'll be back in a couple of hours," said Morgan, too harshly, she considered, especially since she was going to have to depend on Gramma Sofie to take care of Sam at night. "I'll stop at Mort's on the way back and pick up some bagels."

"Egg. That last onion one gave me heartburn."

"Right," Morgan said, adding, "why don't you listen to some music? Relax."

Morgan checked and secured the locked door behind her, then, as if she'd been shot with adrenaline, bounded off the porch, sprinted across the front lawn and half leapt into her topless Jeep parked at the curb.

Although Morgan's East Los Angeles neighborhood certainly wasn't crime-free, it wasn't the hub of hot car parts that some snooty, uninformed West Los Angeles residents assumed either. Morgan's block residents had adopted their own non-electronic neighborhood watch: their captain Sidney, the block's only Mr. Mom, a writer for the *LA Weekly*, monitored the street every Friday night and signed adult residents up for a 10 p.m.-6 a.m. night shift every couple of months. Morgan flicked on her lights, rolled down her windows, and crawled along the narrow, residential street, until she reached the end of the block, where she waved to Sidney, crew-cut with thick horn-rimmed glasses and a white T-shirt, sitting in a lawn chair, sipping coffee from his *Sesame Street* thermos between typing strokes on the block's only Kaypro laptop.

He nodded, toasting her with his Big Bird thermos cap, then pointed down to the box next to him with several lab-mix puppies clamoring to get out. She grinned, giving him thumbs up. Nat,

Sam's best friend, wanted to give her one of the puppies for her thirteenth birthday. He'd picked out a female that he wanted to mate with his dog, Jax.

Morgan had little success convincing Gramma Sofie to think about getting a puppy—a loving family addition. "What's to think about?" Sofie had said. "Loving? Licking maybe. What's more, they grow big and smell bad." "Sam would keep her clean," Morgan assured her, adding, "and a dog barking at strangers is good protection." Gramma Sofie shrugged, "I have a policeman daughter-in-law who wants to get a dog for my protection. And one dog usually has more dogs. So much protection I don't need." To sell this idea, Morgan would have to omit mentioning the mating plan.

She turned onto the boulevard, then popped her *Born in the USA* tape into the cassette player and stepped on the gas "…you can't start a fire…" smiling at the wind "…without a spark…" blasting those last few die-hard freckles on her face.

Towel drying his hair, Moon noticed Iggy—stocky and sexy maybe to the women, but the men's piñata—slumped in his briefs on the edge of the bench in front of his locker. Eventually, Iggy would have to get dressed, but right now, he was in a kind of daze, his elbows planted on his bare knees, head resting in cupped palms, removed from the men's clubhouse conversations, probably thinking of Earley—how just before they'd gone out tonight, the three of them talked about getting together on Sunday for a pot luck. Iggy offered to make his famous ceviché. The thought of lime-marinated raw fish turned Moon's stomach; he liked his seafood cooked, preferably canned, but Earley feasted on the crude stuff. Moon stared at the crooked wall mirror and became aware of a couple of cracks in the center resembling a tired capital "T." "T" for Tyrone, he thought, and supposed Iggy noticed too. Moon wiped the sweat from his brow.

Dripping wet, Ben Fender stepped out of the shower and into the locker room, ranting about Earley's shooting. "Just poke my eyes out, just poke my fucking eyes out." All the men except Iggy stopped dressing and looked up at Fender, watching him push his index fingers into his closed eyeballs.

Moon could tell Iggy was not ready to lock horns with Fender. He kept staring at the droopy "T." When someone you care about dies, thought Moon, when a human life ends, how ridiculous the people around you look, how shallow their concerns, how annoying their mannerisms. Iggy had recently confided to Moon that he hated Fender's voice, a hammer hovering in the air overhead, crashing to the ground. He hated the way Fender could get so worked up he seemed to have mastered talking while breathing in.

Still yelling, Fender flicked water on Iggy in passing. Iggy's dark eyes shifted towards Fender. Too late to trip him, thought Moon, as he rested an untied hiking boot on the wooden bench that ran the length of the dozen lockers, wondering how long it would take this group to unravel without Earley, a straight-shooter who'd never been in awe of Fender's power. Earley had always laughed at Fender or disregarded him, but Iggy took everything Fender said to heart. Iggy wasn't in the mood for listening to Fender's self-indulgent view. "Is it just me," Iggy said to Moon, "or you notice anything that happens lately is against Fender. Like he's the center of the fucking universe."

Moon let Fender's hot air blow around him like the Santa Ana winds; Fender's temper was provoked by too much wind, rain, sun. Who knew? Moon had learned to work around the man's moods. He had a way of diverting Fender's attention. "Just think, Fender," Moon had recently helped him get a grip on an emotional outburst, " in ancient Egypt, a guy like you, a leader type, would've probably been a priest and had to pluck every hair from your body." The very idea put the brakes on Fender's flare-up. "That's disgusting. Every hair?"

Moon nodded, "Eyebrows and eyelashes." Deflecting Fender's outbursts, Moon, the encyclopedia of weird information, emerged as Fender's right hand man — the critical link to Nightwatch's delicate balance.

But now, the night of Earley's death, Moon didn't interject any quips or attempt to diffuse his buddy's tirade. He watched Fender storm around the locker room insisting the men, one by one, poke out his eyes in mock contrition as if eliminating his sight would erase the memory of Earley, bleeding and shimmering in glass shards; Engels, fussing and throwing up on his shoes; and Boots, spurting and gasping oxygen. But why, Moon wondered, was the focus on Fender? How had Fender so completely dominated the room that the guys weren't asking Moon the particulars of the stop, the suspect, the shooting, and Earley? He assumed they wanted to talk about Earley, but they were so upset about the shooting and his death they couldn't talk about him directly. So, instead of directing their hungry questions to Moon, they allowed Fender, a locker room Elmer Gantry with orchestrated wild eyes and gestures, to direct their frustration and anger.

Fender punched his locker with his flat palm. "Ten years ago this was the best division in the fucking city," he said, as the locker, too old to be slammed evenly shut, bounced back in his face. "The world's passing me by and I'm sitting here with niggers and females on a police force that used to be great." Now he was talking to his dependable sidekick, testy Norm Gladstone. Gladstone, grim and gun-metal tough, sat nearby on a bench slicing calluses off his big toe with an exacto knife. If Gladstone wasn't cleaving dead skin in the privacy of the men's locker room, he was snipping the whites of his nails, or digging a bit of grime from between the corner of his thumbnail and flesh. What about Gladstone? Would he question Fender's influence? Gladstone had been a college jock, a catcher, too light for pro ball, though he'd spent the last twenty years filling out. He struck Moon as an unlikely dissenter.

Fender puffed up his chest, imitating Engels' stab at justice, "'No, that's not right, Officer Fender, don't let that cop killer die.'" Moon had to admit Fender nailed Engels big-sister act.

Bow Wow Tufford, fat and balding, nineteen years in the same division but nobody's fool, stuffed the remains of a coffeecake in his mouth. "No sir," he said, his voice hoarse from chain-smoking, "wouldn't wanna let a scumbag-mother-fucker-shit-for-brains-dope-dealer die." Bow Wow shook his head in awe and dumped a clod of baking soda in a glass of water. "Makes me want to puke." How about Bow Wow? Moon wondered if he'd speak out against

Fender, and instantly dismissed the thought. Bow Wow was delighted to live in Fender's commanding shadow.

Gladstone swiped off a little too much skin and winced. "A motherfucker with a car full of shit who's just gunned down a police officer. What happened to our compassion?" Gladstone's sarcasm echoed Fender's. "He's a human *being.*"

Bow Wow finished off his baking soda brew. "Nope. NHI. We had ourselves another No Human Involved tonight, ladies."

Fender nodded his agreement, apparently comfortable with these men who didn't question that certain situations called for old-fashioned police methods. But what about Iggy? Moon wondered how Earley's death would tilt the locker room minority faction. Fender was always demanding proofs of loyalty from the men, especially when it came to harassing women officers. Ignore them, he would instruct his men, pretend like they're not in the room, in your car. And if you absolutely have to communicate with one of 'em, don't look 'em in the eyes.

If Moon drew a line on the cement floor, Gladstone and Bow Wow — steadfast and unconditionally loyal — would be on Fender's side; Earley and Iggy on the other. Earley and Iggy disagreed with Fender, but Iggy had learned to keep his mouth shut, treating Fender like a hateful wealthy relative he couldn't afford to piss off. Now, with Earley gone, Moon supposed Iggy could already sense the certain power shift to Fender's side. And Moon, preferring to at least imagine he chose sides, was uneasy shifting automatically onto Fender's team. Leaders like Fender needed to be questioned, tested by men they respected such as Earley, whose own aggressive presence kept Fender in line, kept him from getting himself in too much trouble. Fender would miss Earley, but wasn't smart enough to understand why.

"There's only one right in the war we got on these streets," Fender said. "If you have to *think* about it," Fender paused, pumping his fist like a boxer at Teddy Bear who was slapping aftershave on his bald scalp, "...you're dead." Fender drove home his point with a final punch in the air. And Moon had to wonder about Theodore D. Bear. On the surface, he seemed overjoyed with the freedom his job gave him for a discreet, little known personal life. Did he really set up his two-man pup tent and camp at the beach every weekend? Alone? With a woman? Another man? Or had he been moonlighting, saving up his pennies to move into another line of work? Hard to say. And if you asked him directly, he'd brush you off with some aside. "What are you writing, my biography? *Unauthorized*?"

Teddy Bear was their funny-man, and he'd been under comic cover for so long, Moon wondered if, alone, he ever stripped his camouflage to expose his serious concerns. Teddy Bear slipped his aftershave in his shirt pocket then hung his head over the dented metal trashcan, preparing to spit his flavorless wad. The clod hit with a thud. Teddy Bear liked riding with Fender because he could chew and spit his Redman tobacco as he pleased; all the other guys gave him a rash of shit every time they caught a little brown drool in the corner of his mouth.

Gladstone grinned, pointing his penknife at Iggy's knife-scarred cheek. "Splittails like Engels can think about whatever they want for as long as they want: they got Iggy to watch out for 'em. Ain't that so, Ignacio?"

Iggy, his handsome face made more mysterious by the deep slash, looked up from polishing his shoes, then shook his head at Gladstone's insinuation. "I watch out for me and my partner, ain't that so, Bow Wow?"

Bow Wow punctuated his weak nod with a belch.

Iggy tossed his polishing rag at Bow Wow. "Don't let me down, partner."

Teddy Bear, having substituted bubble gum for chewing tobacco, snapped his gum. "You got eyes in the back of your head then." He prepared to blow a bubble. "'Cause lately, the ones on your face have been wearing a hole in A-li-see-ya's ass."

Iggy offered him a cool look. "Alicia," he corrected.

Teddy Bear, always stretching for a laugh to break the tension, cracked his gum in front of Iggy's nose. "Look at those red-weary, yellow eye bulbs. Pitiful. Don't tell me, *Alicia's* keeping you up all night."

All eyes were on Iggy, who didn't react. Moon supposed he should say something, because now is when Earley would've come to his rescue, saying Alicia was a good cop and Iggy's eyes were jaundiced because he'd picked up hepatitis from the contaminated water in that hellhole of a shower. And that hepatitis A, a highly contagious liver disease, came complete with nasty symptoms — diarrhea, stomach agony, puking — which could turn you into human compost. And what, Moon thought, could you say to that? Earley's metaphors either drew a parallel to film or the miracle of rebirth and refuse. God how Moon would miss him.

"Hey Bear," Moon interceded on Iggy's behalf. "I don't hear you telling us who you keep up at night."

"Shuddup," said Teddy Bear.

Moon had hit a nerve, but it was pointless to speculate what was going to happen in this infected cavern, decided Moon, frowning at himself in the mirror. Just stay cool and don't get involved. Get out to the site and help with the report. He had to move, take his mind off the acid seeping up his esophagus, acid that tasted of a half-digested burrito. He waved goodbye. "I'm outta here."

Fender nodded and winced, yelling what had been Earley's nightly departing refrain, "Christ, what the fuck's that smell?"

But Moon was out the door, swallowing the bitter lump that had moved to his throat that reminded him he was connected, even in his absence, with the men he'd left behind: they all knew that the odor was the rotten fish wafting in from the dumpster outside the window. Old Man Worsley down the street used the police refuse heap for trash too malodorous or bulky for his own small aluminum can. And Fender's echo of Earley's signature question was the closest the 77th men would ever come to a group hug.

Morgan slowed her Jeep to cruise by the 77th. She went around the block, settling for a parking spot on the street, then turned off the ignition and inhaled deeply. This was nuts, driving here at after two in the morning; she could hear Gramma Sofie reproaching her later, but now she was pumped up to check out her new division.

Morgan closed the ragtop, locked her Jeep, then faced the grim 77th Station. She licked her fingertips and smoothed the straggly hairs off her forehead. She should have taken the time to re-plait her hair, but she had already spent a couple of hours braiding hair that evening. Her daughter's pre-teen friends on their block often stopped by Friday nights for lessons on French braids, ribbon braids or her famous fishtail flipover. Sam was always annoyed that her friends were more interested in Morgan as a hair stylist than they were in her life as a police officer. Only Nat liked to hang out with her and listen to Morgan's work stories.

Morgan stopped to notice the bullet holes in the side of the building, then came through the front door of the 77th and introduced herself to Sergeant Matt Ross, who was writing a report at the front desk. Ross seemed to be preoccupied, but making every effort to be as civil as he could be. "Yep," he nodded, "those bullet holes are from '65 Watts riot."

"Impressive," she said. "A historical building."

"No bullet holes in your Sleepy Hollow building?"

"Nope, no bullet holes."

Ross dipped his head, that figures, then noted, "In Devonshire, I bet you don't even see heaps of abandoned cars, graffittied-walls, broken street lights, and barred shop windows."

"That's because the community keeps it out," Morgan said.

"Right," he said, unconvinced. So she told him about the street she lived on in East L.A. How they'd cleaned up the eyesores — trash, car parts, graffiti — and worked out a mandatory community watch patrol where every resident signed up for an eight hour monthly shift or arranged for someone else to cover for them.

Sergeant Ross stopped filling out his report and listened to her.

But she could feel the nervous energy in her voice making her sound like a high-strung PTA parent.

"Folks have a tendency to think big problems need big solutions," said Sergeant Ross, "and the truth is they didn't get to be big problems overnight."

He reminded her of her buddy Tony Williams. Turned out Ross and Tony went to the same church. Ross knew Tony had worked with Captain Drummond in Harlem, so that opened up a new line of communication. He talked more freely, gave her a sense of the pecking order at the station. He was the sergeant, her immediate line superior, of course. Then there was Lieutenant Linda Herdahl, very accessible and who would probably be encouraging her to take a promotional exam as soon as possible. Next there was Captain Drummond.

Sergeant Ross told her about widow Rodriguez who baked them white bread with heaps of butter and white sugar every Friday, and Shawn, the single mom who sent her kid from the 75th Street school across the playground daily to buy candy from the police vending machines, and of course, there was that mother who stopped in once a week to find out if there were any new afterschool programs to keep her pre-teen out of gangs.

Then Ross turned serious. "We had an officer gunned down tonight, and we're in for some powerful aftershocks."

"Who?"

"Earley. Tyrone Earley."

"Killed? Oh god, I'm sorry." She could feel the blood rush to her head. What an idiot. Me babbling on about graffiti and garbage. She wanted to erase her visit, dash out and return on Monday, but she kept her feet planted and held her breath, then inhaled deeply and mentioned that on the way over to the station she'd passed what looked like a crime scene unit at Century and Saint Andrew, and Ross confirmed they were the same.

Officers in the 77th were frequently involved in shootings, wounded on the job, but the last time she remembered hearing of an officer killed on the job was the one found dead in the spring of 1974, not so long after her husband Jacob left for Vietnam. She asked Sergeant Ross if he remembered the officer's name.

"Michael Edwards," Ross said without hesitation, then pointed to one of five pictures on an adjacent wall. She walked over and studied the brass cards under the photos. Michael Edwards, Ross added, had been shot through the head, probably with his own gun. His hands had been manacled behind him with his own handcuffs. She shuddered at the image that reinforced the dictum for any officer: never let the suspect get your gun.

She resisted the urge to turn away and moved onto the image of Charles White, July, 1962, killed in a car chase; Richard Hallenbeck, December 1960, surprised by a robber, and Roland

Kent, May, 1948, the year and month she was born, who'd been shot five times answering a "routine disturbance" at a bar.

She spotted the square where Earley's photo would hang next to the others on the wall, and she pictured what she'd known all along: it could happen to her. She forced her likeness from the wall, glancing away from the slain officers' photos. "What a loss," she said softly, avoiding the sergeant's eyes.

"A big loss," Ross said. "For the men and the women. He had a way of keeping the kernels around here from bursting into popcorn." Ross got up. "Alicia Herrera is supposed to show you around on your duty day. Lemme see if I can get her to give you a little advanced tour." He disappeared around the corner.

Morgan was probably rushing it. She could've waited until Monday, her official duty day, when an officer would introduce her and explain the procedures particular to that precinct, but curiosity had compelled her to just show up. She'd been on the track team in high school, and it was the same instinct that used to move her to drive to away meets the day before the event. She would walk the course, getting psychologically keyed up. Out of a certain respect, she would never run on an "away" track until the day of the meet.

Ross returned with Officer Alicia "La Chola" Herrera, in a short, sleeveless purple dress, half zipped up the back, trudging a few steps behind, none too happy about her charge to "show the new transfer around" at after two in the morning. "If your new partner's gonna be who I'm thinking: Moon," Alicia informed her, "he's a super cabrón."

"Thanks for the heads up."

Alicia made it clear to Morgan that she had a late date. "So, I'm just gonna take you into our lockers, and I'll show you around the station on Monday."

"Sounds good." Morgan had thought there might not be any women at all on Nightwatch. She was surprised there were four.

Alicia escorted her into the women's locker room where Morgan winced at the rotten odor and was informed it was a combination of Old Man Worsley's trash mixed with mildew from permanently decaying baseboards in the dressing room. The gray walls, repainted so many times they looked like tin sheets, testified that this room had been subdivided and slapped together from the men's basement shower area.

Relative newcomers like Alicia, who'd been recruited in '81, complained about the facilities, but the women who remembered when they had to dress in a glorified outhouse, standing on crates to elevate themselves above the dirt and vermin, didn't complain about the mildew, the crooked mirror or the permanent "tripper" crack on the cement floor, compliments of the '72 earthquake.

Steam from the adjacent showers poured from an open breezeway into the dressing area towards Alicia and Morgan. "Alma Blocker," said Alicia, pointing to a black woman, whose locker happened to be next to the foggy cave.

"It's like dressing in a rotting tropical rain forest," said Alma. She was somewhere in her forties, over six foot and meaty. Morgan guessed she was rarely pressed for her police I.D., let alone her age. Alma glanced past Morgan, offering no indication she wanted to be introduced.

Stepping from the misty shower area, Sara Ann Engels, identified by Alicia, almost tripped over a pair of tennis shoes on the floor. Engels turned to a soaking wet woman trailing at her heels. "Will you stop worrying?" Engels said.

"Rhonda Slattery," said Alicia, pointing to the dripping woman with the creased brow.

Engels reached for a couple of towels from the bin, "You searched him, right?"

Slattery nodded, thinking hard. Soaked and dripping, Slattery's dark, curly hair gave her a bedraggled standard-poodle look.

Shivering, Slattery stood above Alicia as Engels handed her a towel, "Well, he probably had the gun under the front seat in the car. What you should worry about is Fender, who let him bleed to death in front of the paramedics."

Slattery and Engels were in the midst of an intense conversation Morgan couldn't focus on because she was sitting next to Alicia on the bench trying to pay attention to her guide's whispered background tidbits. Alicia indicated she usually listened to Alma Blocker because she had her head on straight. "She busted a chair on a cop during the 1965 Watts riots and was a teenage heroine in the hood," Alicia filled her in. "After ten years in the Air National Guard, Blocker began her policing career in the early 70s. She dove right in and fought for gender and ethnic rights, victims' rights, children's rights." Now, she threatened to retire every year, but Alicia didn't figure that would happen anytime soon. Blocker still had two teenagers and one son in college, and, as a single mother, couldn't afford to stop working. "She's been busting her butt studying though: Herdahl's encouraging her to get off the streets and take the detective's exam."

Slattery wrapped the towel around her slight frame. "He killed Earley, Sara." Slattery was still shivering — from chills or nerves, Morgan couldn't tell, but she didn't need Alicia to inform her they were talking about the officer shooting.

Engels glared at her. "For Chrissakes, this isn't about Earley."

"The hell it isn't," Blocker said from across the room, pouring a ton of baby powder down her top, slapping a handful under her armpits. "Asshole shot him down without even thinking about it. Now why do you think he'd do something he knew he couldn't get away with? Drugs. Protecting his goddamn drugs in the trunk." Blocker obviously had no problem speaking in front of Morgan, a stranger.

"Díos mio," Alicia nudged Morgan. "What did I tell you?" She shook her head, indicating Slattery and Engels, "Those two are enough to make you want to put a gun in your mouth. Thanks to God for Blocker."

"I don't care if that suspect shot down the President," Engels said, then apparently noticing Morgan for the first time, lowered her voice, driving the conversation back to her adversary, "Fender shouldn't be able to invent laws according to his whim just because this is supposed to be the worst precinct in the city."

Morgan could hear lockers slamming. Muffled male voices reverberated through the paper thin walls behind Engels' locker. "Hey guys," Alicia said, trying to interrupt Blocker's account of the only time she'd ridden in a patrol car with Ben Fender.

Hearing Blocker talking about her own former training officer at the Police Academy, Morgan had a sense she was glimpsing the preliminary steps of a wild tango between the men and women of the 77th.

Alicia said with a reproving tone, suggesting she'd announced this before and no one was listening, "If you guys'll shut up, I'm trying to introduce the new transfer."

Morgan touched Alicia on the elbow, indicating her appreciation, but it could wait.

Engels, pale, thin and tall as a flagpole, headed toward Morgan with an outstretched hand. "Welcome," Engels said to Morgan, gripping her hand with the force of a handshake that wanted to be remembered. "I'm Engels. Nice to have you on board."

Morgan nodded thanks, but before she could ask Engels' first name, Engels was back across the floor next to Blocker, tearing into Fender. "He thinks he's God, so he can save whoever the hell he wants."

Alicia bristled. "Kill a cop, I say you die too. If you're so upset, Engels, write him up for Godsake. I'm trying to intro — "

"So upset?" Engels stared at her in amazement. "So upset! Alicia, it's too bad you can't grow a dick and join Men Against Women."

Morgan had heard rumors about guys dubbing themselves Policemen Against Policewomen, MAW for short, with the mission of annoying and harassing women officers, but she'd figured it harmless gossip.

Alicia took up Blocker's support of Earley. "Engels, you got it all wrong, you know. Earley was one of us. And some things the criminal justice system takes care of — some things we take care of ourselves."

Engels pointed a stiff palm at Alicia. "Not on my police force," she said, with a firm tone that suggested she'd already passed the detective exam and was revising police procedure.

Blocker turned and got right in Engels' face. "Girl, you waste a ton of energy with all that dick-ass drama about how we been victimized, rapized, fuckized. Sometimes you got to take the emotional component into consideration and not just fly off the handle everytime somebody does something you don't agree with. I have a few years on you fighting for rights, and I'm not a fan of Fender, but — "

Engels cut her off, "Yeah well, you're as wrong as Fender was if you think — "

Blocker planted her index finger on Engels' shoulder. "Don't be walking around talking shit. Earley was my friend. My kids babysat his kids. And if I had been there, I wouldn't have waited for that asshole to bleed to death, I'd have put a bullet right through his motherfucking heart." Blocker slung her bag over her shoulder and stormed out, leaving in her wake several moments of stunned silence, as if everyone was privately remembering why Blocker and Earley had a bond that lasts a lifetime.

Alicia glanced at Morgan. "Earley and Blocker worked together for six years," she said. "One night, they pulled over this teenager from Fullerton — "

"Vernon," Engels adding, "the coldest night in '78."

Alicia rolled her eyes. "*Vernon.* So they pull him over — "

"No taillights." Engels couldn't help herself. Getting the details right were essential to the report.

Alicia ignored her. "And this kid's got an infant in the back of his truck. Said he'd given the father a ride from the homeless shelter to cash a money order. The father gives him a handful of quarters, tells him the baby had a crackhead mother who'd died in the shelter and he couldn't take care of an infant any more. Tells the kid, 'If you can find somebody to buy the baby, Lily, that's what the mother named her, you keep the money.'"

"He went in the liquor store around eleven o'clock," said Engels, "never came back out."

Blocker had told them that Earley held Baby Lily all the way back to the station. With twin toddlers, Earley was the only one who knew what to do with an infant at 2:00 a.m. He refused to take her back to the shelter, so his sergeant gave him permission to take her home for the night until they could contact Children's Services in the morning. Earley took her home, fully knowing Amberlene would never want to let her go.

Silence gripped them all, as if they were each visualizing Amberlene waking up in a few hours without Earley.

Alicia splashed on some cologne, broke the hush. "It's only a little time before Fender and his buddies are history. 'Sometimes,'

Iggy says," she said, smiling tentatively at Morgan, "'it takes death to give birth to new life.'"

Alicia's expression hardened at Engels' scathing look. "Another cryptic Iggy observation."

"You got a problem with Iggy?" Alicia crossed the cement floor to Engels, "or is it just Fender? Or maybe it's a gender thing, and you got a problem with all men."

Engels stared her down till Alicia finally pivoted and headed towards the door. Slattery glanced nervously from Engels to Alicia, who stopped at the door, shrugged and said, "Go ahead, you can write him up."

"That's precisely what I'm going to do," Engels said.

"Just know," Alicia added, fluttered her index finger at Engels, "I wrote Fender up ten times my first year. Nobody up there listens." She pointed at the ceiling, then slammed the door behind her.

Morgan hurried to catch up with Alicia, calling to her down the hall, "Alicia, thanks."

"*Por nada,*" Alicia waved, declining to even look back.

"Alicia," Sergeant Ross called from his entrance post.

She clicked her tongue and huffed, "Don't start with me." She swung out the door as Morgan reached the front desk. Sergeant Ross looked up and half shook his head. "What'd I tell you? Not a great night."

Morgan nodded.

"Bet it's a far cry from Sleepy Hollow in there." Ross pointed his thumb towards the women's locker room.

Within seconds of one another, Fender and Engels exited their respective locker rooms.

Fender headed toward the desk and Morgan's stomach dipped as though something inside capsized. She moved to the edge of the counter and lingered over a metal chair, contemplating what to do next.

Engels stopped at Sergeant Ross's desk. "Sergeant, can you leave a copy of that report for me?"

"I'll put it in your box."

Engels glanced at Morgan, then shoved through the front door as Fender moved to the sergeant's desk and positioned himself slightly to the side of Morgan, so wrapped up in his mission that he didn't see her. "She turn in a report?" Fender asked, nodding after Engels.

"Nope. No report."

"Make sure you get in *your* report then about how she threw up on my shoes," Fender enunciated at Ross' paper work, "on my shoes, and, along with all the other women we got here, she's useless…about as useless as — "

"Tits on a bull," Morgan finished his sentence. He turned to face her.

"I thought you were out in Sleepy Hollow," Fender said.

"I was."

Fender turned away. "Moon go out to the site?" he asked Ross, who shrugged. "All right." Fender walked out, saying, "Night," to no one in particular.

She turned to Sergeant Ross, who'd been closely observing both of them. "You guys related?" he asked.

"Fender was my training officer at the Academy."

"Fender? No kidding."

"Yep. Ol' hit first, think later. He taught me to poke 'em in the eyes, hit 'em in the throat, kick 'em in the face." She shook her head, confounded by her private wonder of Fender in the face of his consistent abuse of her and other women. "'To survive,' he'd tell us, 'you need to know before something's going to happen. Anybody can learn how to take a report, he used to say — just fill in the boxes,'" Morgan said, eyeing Ross' report and smiling. "So, there's really not much chance I can meet my new partner and check my days off."

"Afraid not. You'll probably have Saturday and Sunday off. But Lieutenant Herdahl's the only one who'd know that for sure, and she and the captain are with the O.I.S. unit waiting for the other officer involved in the shooting to do a walk-through."

Morgan thanked him, "See you Monday."

Ross gave a polite dip of his head and watched her leave.

Morgan parked her Jeep near Century and Saint Andrew. She had no good reason to show up at the site of Earley's shooting, and even as she leaned against her car hood, watching the buzz of activity, she thought she was probably pushing her luck.

She surveyed the scene, noting that the performance of a dozen homicide officers measuring distances, dusting for prints and shooting photos, looked more like preparing for a wedding than examining a crime.

She didn't recognize any of the homicide investigators from the Officer-Involved Shooting Section, but she figured they were the two men talking to the brass. Sergeant Ross had mentioned there were no witnesses, so homicide didn't have to worry about keeping them separate until they'd been questioned. Didn't look as if they had to bother with collecting and transporting trace evidence in those pain-in-the-neck plastic bags either. So there were too many people here with too little to do. She didn't like a mob of criminalists and investigators at a crime scene. Something was invariably moved, touched, removed from the scene and, even though every Police Academy student knows nothing is too insignificant to be overlooked, something always was.

In the midst of all the movement and business, Morgan noticed a man in blue jeans and a jacket standing utterly still, his arms cradled on his chest, waiting. She stared at him for a long time. He looked isolated, and occasionally nodded in response to a question or pointed to a specific area on the ground. She finally figured he must be the other officer involved in the shooting. He took a deep breath, and with no apparent provocation, turned and glanced in her direction. They exchanged a look, broken by the sound of footsteps on gravel. Morgan glanced away to face Ben Fender.

"What are you doing out here?" he snapped at her as if she were his cadet back at the Academy.

"Sergeant Ross told me what happened," she said. "I'm sorry. Did he have a family?"

"I hope you're not thinking of transferring here."

She made no move to confirm or deny it. "We don't play games here, Morgan. No simulated suspects or perimeter searches like at the Academy. You don't have what it takes." He motioned to the homicide crew nearby. "See, nobody in this city cares that a police officer just got killed. And I don't care if some citizen out there, who wants to test a policeman, dies. Spit on his body, and let's go eat a spaghetti dinner. It's nothing. It's devoid of feeling, like war."

Morgan shook her head. *It's feelings in chaos,* she thought.

She turned back to the crime scene, the aftermath of death. The flicker of lights, cameras and actors burst into a flash of inquiry, then puff, as swiftly as they came, they would go, and the blaze of questions would die, leaving only copious notes, crime-scene photographs, sketches made of the shooting.

The medical examiner wasn't even here. There was no body to examine, no wounds to check, no position of the victim to photograph. Looked like the still photographer was ready to pack it up, but the videotaping specialist was still there following the officer who had been staring at Morgan. A couple of print people were also prowling around, fully knowing they weren't given all the information about the crime. *Funny,* she thought, *in military combat you didn't have crime scene documentation.* She figured you just called it a skirmish or a slaughter, depending on the bloodshed, and let it go at that. But it was hard not to want to know certain details. She had to wonder.

Fender cleared his throat, forcing Morgan to look back at him.

"You know," she blurted, "I've been thinking a lot about you and Jacob being ambushed. About him almost making it, then taking those bullets just for the hell of it."

Fender looked at her, revealing nothing, but she sensed his weight shift to an aggressive stance. "This is not a pissing contest you're gonna win, Morgan." They stared at each other, soberly. Then he turned and strode back to the scene of the shooting.

Surrounded by dark shadows, strangers, secrets, she felt utterly alone. If only she could turn to Jacob...he helped even the inexplicable make sense. Sometimes even in death Jacob was so close; she could smell the Castille soap oil on his skin.

Moon noticed Fender walking away from the woman with the Jeep. He watched her draw in a deep breath, fix a long gaze on Fender, then stand totally still for a couple of seconds. Something going on there, he thought. Fender's new concubine. Hope to hell Phyllis doesn't find out.

He didn't judge Fender's extramarital activities, but he didn't much respect him for it either. Marriage meant monogamy, Moon thought, or why bother getting married? He had illusions of slapping some sense into Fender about how lucky he was to have a loyal wife and mother to his five kids. A senseless objective, he decided, and chose not to think about it.

"Moon," called Lieutenant Linda Herdahl, his thick-bodied superior, waddling towards him. "Captain wants you to tell Amberlene." Harsh streetlight shadowed the dark circles under her eyes. He looked away from her without a word, but Amberlene echoed in his head, like a voice reverberating under water.

Moon crossed to his Range Rover. As he pulled out from the curb onto Century Boulevard, he glanced in his sideview mirror just in time to catch the woman in the Jeep turn onto Century and pull up close enough for him to make out the famous raspy male voice wailing from her stereo speakers, "…can't start a fire sitting 'round crying over a broken heart…"

Moon decelerated slightly to get a better look at the woman's face behind the windswept hair, but the Jeep veered into the left turn lane. "This gun's for hire even if we're just dancing in the dark…" Moon watched her hang a U-turn and head in the opposite direction.

4

JACOB

Jacob, who would've been 35 now, had been shorter than Morgan, not by much, just enough for passersby to notice and nudge one another; he had not been short on sensitivity though. She'd met him in an oral communication skills class at East Los Angeles Community College. The instructor paired them up to develop speeches together and help each other iron out the wrinkles before they presented their speeches to the group. When Jacob asked her why she was taking the class, she told him that studies show when a person speaks in an average tone, they use 150 words a minute, when they're nervous about 175; radio announcers, about 200 a minute. She used about 250, had a hard time looking people in the eye, did a fair amount of head-tipping and smiled too much.

"Your smile," he said, "lights up your whole face. It's a keeper." He winked at her and she liked him more than she wanted to, but she didn't fall in love with him until his final speech.

As her workshop partner, he helped her learn to plant herself, stand straight and look people right in the eyes. He made her practice holding eye contact, then he made her look away; he told her people who have more power establish eye contact first and look away first because they have control of the situation. He worked with her on

slowing down her speech, not using bonbon phrases — in my
opinion, I feel, I think, I believe, this may not be important — to
diminish her impact. He seemed more like the instructor than a fellow
student. "Why did you take this class?" she asked.

"To meet you."

During weeks of coffee breaks going over each other's outlines,
finding the perfect opening, convincing middle and solid closing
remarks, they found out about each other. He learned her mother
had died when she was young; she learned his mother Sofie lived
with his father Thomas, thanklessly fighting the urban beach
development that was escalating property values and breaking up
their Yiddish community.

When Morgan would go back to her small apartment after night
class, she would tape her thoughts about him, some of their
conversations. He'd grown up the only child of Sofie and Thomas,
which offered insights into communication between the sexes that
he'd woven into his sociological understanding. Jacob and Morgan
talked a good deal about the ways men and women communicate.
He pointed out that women sometimes ramble. *"I've never given
it much thought,* she said into the mike, recording her thoughts,
*but he has a point. He says when you ask a woman if she got a pair
of new shoes, she'll start telling you about that place with the 50%
reduction around the corner from McDonald's…ask a guy if he
got a new pair of shoes, he'll say, yes."*

Jacob convinced her that more important than eye contact,
head-tipping, and bonbon words, was understanding how men
and women communicated and applying that to your job, your
personal life. Take a ride with me, he would say. You have a man
and woman going down the street. The woman asks him if he
wants to stop and get a bite to eat. "No," he says, and when they
get home, she's upset. Two women are in a car. One woman asks
if her friend wants to stop for a bite to eat. "I'm not sure," says
the friend, "Would you like to get something?" "I don't know."
They may take a while to come to a decision, or they may get
home before they've reached one.

Now you take two guys in a car; one asks, "You want to get a
bite to eat?" The other one says no, and nobody's upset.

"Men and women are different, just different," he keeps telling me, and he encourages me never to apologize for who I am — for what I want to do in life…Jacob calls me several times a day. I like that he lets me know where he is, what he's doing, but, until I met his mother Sofie, I wondered how he evolved this intense kind of communication. He invited me for dinner at his parents' apartment. We barely walked through the front door before his mother said, "Jacob, you sick?" "No, Ma. I'm fine." "You didn't call me yesterday." "Sorry Ma, I got busy and I didn't have anything to say." "So, that I shouldn't worry, call and tell me?" "Okay Ma." I would tell her to get off my back, but they've worked out kinder communication: she knows he doesn't want to call her if he has nothing to say; he understands she needs to hear him say it.

Jacob's final speech left everyone dumb. He stood easily away from a podium, quietly competent, his thick, red hair falling over his forehead. He talked about sexual violence against women and how the fear of that violence restricted everyone. And he spoke in images to burn into his classmates' consciousness the reality that victims adapt to humiliating, embarrassing, life threatening situations. They even adapt to death:

"This biology teacher comes into class," Jacob says, "with a burner, two pails and two frogs. He puts one frog in a pail of cool water and turns on the burner. The water heats up and the frog adjusts. Water heats up and heats up and before a horrified audience, the frog dies with not even a last protest. He heats up the second pail, throws the live frog in and it leaps out unhurt. And Jacob looks at me for a moment and says, 'So, when in doubt, leap,' then he sits down…This is the guy."

Morgan and Jacob moved in together the following week. They were married during winter break, spent their honeymoon alternately cuddling in front of a fire at a friend's home on Long Island and skating, gliding in a sea of red-nosed skaters under the Christmas tree in Rockefeller Center.

Samantha was born the following October. And because Jacob had a student deferment, they enjoyed eight months juggling school and family life. Then when his father died during finals week, he'd arranged to take a couple of exams early, turn in a Philosophy paper late. His physics professor, however, wouldn't let him take the final early or late, so he left without taking it at all and failed the class.

The next fall semester he lost his student deferment and was drafted almost instantly. Two months in boot camp, one month infantry training, one month in machine gun school, two weeks in recon school, and twenty days leave.

Then he was gone.

He'd been in the last Marine Corps offensive, about ready to rotate, when he and his Lieutenant Ben Fender were ambushed on scouting duty. An American flag folded in the shape of a triangle was tucked away in Morgan's nightstand drawer with one particular letter she'd received and was saving to give to their daughter someday:

Dear Mo: It may sadden you to know that the love of your life is no longer a cherry private. In your last letter you asked me to tell you what was in my heart and not to quote from manuals. Before I go on, I want to note that I'm still in a mild state of shock; but I need to record my feelings before this wears off and my senses dull.

Right now I'm sitting in a bunker with my buddy, Ben Fender, at our Fire Support Base writing this by candlelight, although it's about 8 a.m. here. Ben started a letter to his wife, Phyllis. But he wadded it up and is putting the finishing touches on a fifth of rot gut whiskey. Pretty early to party, I know. But even Ben, who usually takes killing the enemy like exterminating so many cockroaches, is pretty whacked out this morning.

It started yesterday at dusk. I was writing a poem. All of a sudden, all fucking hell broke loose: rockets, mortars, R.P.G. (Rocket Propelled Grenades). A 122 took out the 'hooch' next to mine. That was followed by a ground probe of 'hard core' V.C. and North Vietnamese troops — 100-150 men. As the first rounds hit, Fender and I grabbed a thump gun (40-mm grenade launcher) and made it to the bunker. The enemy started coming and coming, Mo, unbelievable. Shouting pigeon obscenities, 'mother fucka, you die, GI's eat shit.' To which we replied, along with return fire, 'dinky dinky doo,' (meaning fuck your mother by your brother or cut your own throat). I hit a V.C. complete with satchel charge right off center with an HE (high explosive) round and blew him into about four or five big pieces.

Mo, I lost all sense of reason, I almost enjoyed killing, no I did enjoy it; such is the blood lust in the human animal. I remember the look on the face of a dying V.C., I think it was a girl. It was a look of utter disbelief.

Then as suddenly as it began, it was over. They retreated and melted into darkness. My hands were caked with blood and there was blood on my face and encrusted in my mustache and my mouth. I tried not to be sick, I really tried but I couldn't help it. I puked and puked my guts all over the field and I wasn't the only one. Gore, body parts and sweat covered me from head to foot. I wanted to burn my clothes, but I have no others.

Later, we were ordered to follow the blood trails. I found the V.C. I thought was a girl. I was right, but it's so hard to tell over here. I thought of our Samantha, and how I'm glad we live in a country where she doesn't have to kill. I can retain my common sense, if not good mental health, as long as I know I'm protecting you both, that neither of you will have to know what I have known, never have to do what I have done.

Forever yours, Jacob

5

BAD FOR MARIGOLDS

Moon watched the sun rise on Earley's award-winning marigolds that lined the front walk. Now, he checked the clock on the dash again: 7:55. He would wait until eight o'clock. Five minutes offered a world of possibility. There was nothing he could do about the shootout that had taken Earley's life, but he had everything to do with what was about to happen. In five minutes Amberlene would know.

Inside the house, Moon imagined that Amberlene already suspected something because Earley wasn't home yet. And he hadn't phoned. Occasionally, after a grueling arrest and time-consuming paperwork, he had an 8:30 a.m. court date that he'd forgotten to mention to her, and, rather than go home, he would just crash in the backseat of his car for a couple of hours. Maybe he'd had a court date and forgotten about the recital. But it was Saturday. She would probably wait to call the station until after the kids left for the recital. After all, she'd received no calls from the hospital. Emergency admitting had been instructed not to phone her. He was dead on arrival.

Lily was upstairs standing in front of the full-length mirror, sneaking one last look: green leotard and tights, green shoes and hair ribbon. Everything was perfect. Except when forcing a quick smile, she exposed that missing front tooth.

"Lily. C'mon, we're waiting on you," her mother's voice called from downstairs.

She grabbed her bright pink backpack and hustled towards the door, stopping just long enough to check off a square next to "brush teeth" on a plastic wall chart titled GOOD FOR ME.

A car horn sounded as she raced down the stairs to meet her twin seven-year-old brothers, Terrence and Anthony, leaning against the front door.

Lily's mother slipped the backpack over her shoulders, "Just take your costume now in case Daddy and I get there a little late." She handed her a child-size cardboard tree, indicating the grip in the back. "See, Daddy made this handle so it's easier for you to carry."

Lily looked up, concerned. "Late?"

"Don't worry," her mother assured, "we won't miss you. And we'll have a picnic afterward." She handed Terrence a couple of brown lunch bags.

He jammed them in his backpack. "Daddy probably arrested a bad guy and is making a report."

Anthony added, "Hope he shot him."

"Okay, that's enough, Anthony." She opened the door and, reaching for the screen, saw Moon sitting across the street in his Range Rover. She slammed the door.

Anthony, Terrence and Lily looked up at her. "Whatssamatter?"

"Nothing." She turned robot-like, guiding them with her stiff palms. "Mr. Walter's parked on the side. Let's go." She pointed to the kitchen and shuffled them down the hall.

Moon got out, closed his car door and stood watching the children file from the side of the house and clamber into an awaiting station wagon. Lily dropped the cardboard tree, then scooped it up, dragged it along the sidewalk and crammed it in the back with her, managing to smile back at her mother who stood waving from the kitchen window.

Moon lingered near his car for a long moment after the wagon had turned the corner and disappeared from sight. Yesterday, Earley's life was so normal, everything going along, more or less, just right. Then Amberlene woke up this morning unaware that someone, who didn't know her enough to care, had painted a red cross on her front door and changed her life forever. His mind drifted to victims lost in crashes, catastrophes and freak accidents, to their loved ones left behind who never got to say "I love you" one last time. He remembered his happiest times, his most fulfilling moments, were anticipating Lance's face at the living room window. Lance would open the front door and rush into his arms, screaming, "Daddy, Daddy." No other moment made him feel as important, as irreplaceable.

Moon finally forced himself to cross Earley's street. He turned up the manicured footpath and stopped, recalling how he'd stood in his own front yard, holding his breath, hoping his toddler wouldn't trip and fall on the cracked sidewalk before he reached his outstretched arms. He wished, as he had too often, that he'd never decided to fill the cracks with fresh cement.

Moon knocked softly on the front door.

No answer. He knocked again.

Still no answer, but he knew Amberlene was there just on the other side of the door, hunched, hugging herself, drawing trembling breaths.

"'Lene. It's me. Open up."

The deadbolt turned, locking the door.

"C'mon Amberlene. You've got to let me in."

He heard her body slide down the door and slump near the baseboards. He sat on the stoop and listened to her soft sobs through the wood.

"I'm not going to leave until you let me in."

He waited. Nothing.

Holding the screen door open with his foot, he crossed his arms and resituated himself against the doorjamb, careful not to lean too heavily against the screen. He took a deep breath, collected his thoughts and leaned his ear closer to the crack in the door, whispering, "'Lene, talk to me." His throat choked up, and he murmured, "You don't have to let me in. I'll just sit here with you and take care of the kids when they get home."

He cursed himself again for not shooting the suspect before he'd blasted Earley. Moon was good at preventing gunfire, good at protecting his partner, good at responding to crisis. Everyone, all the guys anyway, told him he was a helluva proactive cop. They didn't realize that after everything had collapsed, so had Moon. He didn't know which fragments to piece together first. A muscle in his abdomen cramped, and would have bowled him over, were he not sitting down. He hunched his head over his curled knees, took a few shallow breaths, then managed to inhale deeply, and whiffed manure. Glancing slowly around the yard, his gaze finally rested on a sack a few feet away. His eyes and nose filled with the pungent stink. Blinking back tears, he stared first at the full bag of fertilizer leaning on the porch railing, then lifted his eyes to the perfectly smooth front walk lined on either side by Earley's prize marigolds.

6

MAW

Tempers had been stretched at the end of Sunday's Nightwatch in the men's locker room. Alone, Moon stepped out the back door of the 77th, his peripheral vision alert in the dark to his left and right. He headed for his Range Rover parked next to Iggy's Camero. All the other guys had already dressed and left, were probably buying beer to bring to their "venting" place in a vacant park. Moon expected Iggy would hang around the precinct for a few more minutes, jaw with Ross, who never met with the guys at their after hours MAW sessions, but not because the guys wouldn't welcome his company.

Ross, like Earley, refused to join the PoliceMen Against PoliceWomen until the *little girls* were invited too. "And you have to admit," Earley would've taunted them all, "women would spice up those midnight meetings."

But the locker room had been dead to Earley's voice tonight. Their collective thoughts, however, had been with him. While the guys were stripping and putting on their street clothes, Sergeant Ross was making his way around them, collecting money for Earley's children.

Somebody should, thought Moon, glad it wasn't him. Asking for money was bad enough, but he could barely think about Earley for more than a few seconds without feeling razors spinning in his gut. It would paralyze him to ask for donations to buy kid-sized stuffed animals or some other inane gift for young lives forever changed by an indifferent spray of bullets.

Ben Fender was still harping on Slattery's blunder; he wasn't going to get it out of his system any time soon. He'd gone over and over how he'd found out she'd actually searched Boots before Moon and Earley had tagged him and she'd missed the gun.

Iggy offered another possibility. "Look, the gun could've been in the car. Why does everyone assume she missed the gun?"

"Of course she missed it." Fender dismissed any other possibility. "She's a fucking cunt," Fender grit his teeth and made a fist, "I thought 77th Nightwatch was the policemen's watch, where men stay to do real police work: kicking fucking ass. What's happening to us?"

Bow Wow shook his head, what can you do? Then he ripped open a cellophane bag of Oreo cookies, opening one to lick the vanilla center. He passed the bag to Fender who shoved Bow Wow's hand away. "So," he continued to Moon, "Slattery walked by tonight just as I'm reading in Sarge's report," he flicked a glance to Sergeant Ross, who was too busy calculating donations to notice, "that she searched the fucker right before he picked up his goodies in the car and you guys tagged him."

Moon held up his palm. "I don't want to hear about it."

Teddy Bear strutted in from the shower, lifted a handful of cookies off the bench next to Bow Wow, and nudged Moon in passing. "Whip up another one of your reports on her?"

"Done." Moon managed a hollow laugh. Known for his detailed, accurate reports and large, childlike cursive writing, Moon had written enough reports on Slattery to wallpaper the Captain's office.

Gladstone yelled across the room, without glancing up from his fingernail file. "Hey Fender, why didn't Sarge make an employee report out on Sara Ann Engels for throwing up all over your shoes?"

Moon grinned. "They already looked like shit, right Sarge?"

A few chuckles, then silence that begged a response from Sergeant Ross. Moon couldn't help but like Ross, even though his balanced, discreet sense of professionalism annoyed the hell out of him at times. Ross was a line supervisor, not a patrol officer, but at least he'd been on the streets for years and was a veteran, unlike Lieutenant Herdahl, their supervisor and general butt of female ridicule, who'd never spent a day on patrol.

Ross said simply, "I suppose nobody here's ever thrown up." Bow Wow opened his mouth to comment, but Ross cut him off. "Save the details. So she threw up," indicating Fender's bare feet, "sorry it was all over your shoes."

"Screw the shoes," Fender said. "Sara-Ann-the-fucking-Nightingale was trying to save the son-of-a-bitch who blew Earley away. Don't turn tail on me, Ross."

Ross shot him a studied look. "She's a good little girl. Drop it," he said, securing the lid on the donation can.

"Lit-tle girl," Fender enunciated in absolute disbelief, shooting a glance at Moon.

Fender tossed up his arms. "You don't get it. None of you get it. This is just the beginning. Missing guns."

Iggy adjusted the collar on his starched shirt. "C'mon Fender, you're a broken — " Iggy reached for the wrong word, " — television. You know, guys fuck up too."

Sergeant Ross put his hand over his mouth in mock horror, nodded to Moon and left.

Fender slammed his locker, ready to square off, and yelled across the room. "Ignacio, you tell me when's the last time you worked with a guy that fucked up on instant response to violent behavior."

"Last year." Iggy didn't miss a beat. "Nickerson Gardens stake out. Bob Winston shot himself in the foot."

"Bob Winston," Fender said, hardly containing himself, "was Mr. Magoo. These cunts make him look like Marshall Dillon. And he's history because nobody covered for him. Last I heard, he's selling life insurance in Bakersfield. I rest my case."

Moon shuddered at the mere thought of selling insurance. "He rests his case, guys. Stay the hell out of Nickerson Gardens with a female."

"Look, shit happens," Bow Wow garbled, finishing off the last of his Oreo cookies. "What about the broad in Metro, Lola Day, who shot a guy carrying a comb?"

"Right." Moon nodded. "Guy pulled a comb from his pocket and she shot him in the leg. Fucking A. Nothing happened to her. Justified shooting."

Fender let out a disgusted breath. "I was her T.O. Cunt. Damn, if I did that I'd be on fucking Terminal Island."

Moon poked Fender and shot a mischievous eye at Iggy splashing on cologne in front of the mirror. "Remember," he whispered. "MAW tonight."

Bolstered by the thought, Fender sauntered over to Gladstone, tying his shoes. Fender leaned down, face-to-face, and mouthed: "MAW." Gladstone grinned.

While Fender silently signaled Bow Wow and Teddy Bear, Moon approached Iggy, slapped him on the back and said loud enough for everyone to hear: "Hey Macho Man, MAW's meeting tonight. You going over to the park and have a beer?"

Iggy hesitated, his eyes flickering indecision, then he nodded reluctantly. "Sure."

Sometimes Moon wondered where Iggy got his good nature.

Now, Moon pulled out of the 77th police parking lot. He supposed Iggy would stop at a pay phone to leave a message for Alicia. He'd much rather spend his off hours with her, but the MAW guys, if nothing else, were his co-workers. And unlike Earley, who could afford to joke about MAW because he was a respected leader, Iggy was not a leader and details about his personal life with Alicia sparked their cliquish contempt. However cliquish and covert MAW had become, Moon considered that it had started out innocently enough. A bunch of malcontents, with no safe place to express their hostility about the wave of women officers, had started meeting after Nightwatch on Sundays. At 2:00 a.m. all the drinking holes were closed except the gay bars and men's clubs.

So, they'd met at Breaker's Lounge until the night Fender got so upset during the retelling of yet another humiliation at Slattery's hands that he got a little carried away with one of the strippers who'd been bumping and grinding in front of him. "There I was in the middle of Century right in this trucker clown's face, nailing him for running a red light," Fender said. "And he was all over my ass, so Little-Miss-Slattery-Temple butts in about not wanting to have to stop any horseplay between us and mess up her fucking manicure. Horseplay? That clown, the guy I'm about to ticket, checked out her manicure and then broke up, in disbelief, 'Horseplay?' he says, laughing at me." Eye level with the gyrating crotch, Fender slipped a folded bill under her g-string, and kept his forefinger hooked on the inside while she torqued her body, giving him the hot stare. He smirked, announcing in a fierce tone, "Horseplay. I'll show you some horseplay. I've got the pole baby, you've got the hole." She glanced over him uncertainly and began edging away, but he had his finger hooked into the elastic. When she caught the nasty gleam in his eye, she stepped back, and the flimsy shield ripped, exposing her shaved labios and spilling a dozen folded bills onto the table.

The manager of the lounge must have suspected they were off-duty cops because he sidled up to Moon and asked them to leave pronto, letting him know if his buddy wanted something beyond looking, he could take his business outside.

After the Breaker's incident, Iggy reminded the MAW guys they were meeting because they were frustrated about working with women, so why should they beat themselves up worse by meeting near women. Why not just let off steam in private? This made no sense to Moon. What better place for them to meet to discuss their anxiety about women than in a strip club? Moon agreed though with Iggy that the MAW guys could only push Fender so far, then when he got lit, they had to back up and let him explode. Better to have him explode in the privacy of a vacant, moonlit baseball field, a mountain firing range, or a wide-open stretch of beach.

Moon stopped at a 7-11 for a six-pack.

He parked next to Iggy's Camaro and a couple of other familiar cars under streetlights in a vacant Little League parking lot. He grabbed his six-pack from the passenger seat, slammed his car door and sauntered towards Fender, Iggy, Bow Wow, Gladstone, and Teddy Bear standing across the dark outfield.

By the time Moon caught up to the MAW guys, Teddy Bear had popped the top off another beer can, challenging a dare. "Iggy, anytime you wanna see me throw up, just tell me."

"I don't want to see you throw up."

Teddy Bear looked at Gladstone, who wore the hint of a smile behind his mustache as though he was up to something. But nobody could ever catch him doing anything.

Fender queried Moon, "What happened with that report on Slattery?"

"Waste of time." Moon shot him a beaten look, then described how he'd stood in front of Drummond, watching him read his report about Slattery, then finally looked up.

"Moon," Drummond had indicated the file in front of him, "what's with *this* report on Slattery?"

"She's incompetent." Moon stared down at him.

"You know," Drummond said, eyeing Moon, "women are here to stay, so you better learn to like it." He turned to the coffeemaker on the end table next to him. He poured the last of the pot of coffee into a black mug with a gold L.A.P.D. insignia on it.

Moon shook his head in mild amazement. "You change my whole department. I have absolutely nothing to say about it. And you expect me to like it?"

"Look, I know it's difficult adjusting to new gender dynamics and it's going to take time for some of you guys — "

"Difficult," interjected Moon, "doesn't cover it, Captain. Suicidal is more like it."

Drummond held Moon's fixed glare, maintaining calm under pressure. "With a little effort on your part, Moon — all right, a lot of effort — the adjustment is doable. My experience with women here has been really good so far. There's an obvious need for more women in — "

"Slattery's oversight of the weapon that gunned down Earley is not an exception to the rule: she is the rule. That's what happens every fucking day. Every day one of us is in jeopardy. You have to admit," he continued, "if she had searched him even haphazardly around say his waist, the gun would have been obvious. She was afraid. And frankly — "

"Moon, my hands are tied. I have no witnesses. Nobody saw her overlook the gun. What do you think I can do with this?" He shoved the report to the front of his desk.

"What you can do with it, Captain, is put it in her file, then when she has a big file you can kick her off the force."

"This isn't about Slattery, Moon. Let's face it. You think I don't know that you're out to get women, that you've got an illegal organization going here that's against having women on the force. All women. You better watch your step. You're the one with the mother of a file."

Moon chugged a beer and shrugged at Fender, "So, the dickhead basically turned the tables and threatened me."

Fender pressed him, "Write another fucking report on her. Flood the entire fucking chain of command. Leak something to the press. You've got to. Who else can do it? You're the only one left at the scene who can write the report." Fender raised his palms skyward. "And you *know* she missed that dude's piece. She was scared shitless to search that big nigger."

Bow Wow nodded. "Yeah, she's probably missed shit before. She's got no clue."

"That's what I told Captain Dithers." Moon took a big gulp. "But I left out the part that she needs to work in a soup kitchen. Last week, you're not gonna believe this, she buys five boxes of girl scout cookies, eats a few and passes the rest out on the street."

"Like I said," Bow Wow hustled to keep up. "She's got no clue. You don't give girl scout cookies to crackheads. Were they mostly savannahs or those chocolate mints?"

Teddy Bear grinned and tossed Bow Wow a beer. He caught it on his big belly. Bow Wow worked the Nightwatch because there was no brass, and it was where the veteran rebels hung out. An agitator in his own day, he still gave the probationers a hard time, especially the women. He routinely asked all new women officers their cup size.

The men spread out on the bleachers. Teddy pulled a beer tab, protesting to a doubtful Iggy. "I'm telling you I can throw up anytime."

"No way."

"You don't believe me. C'mon, put some money on it." Teddy Bear was not one to let an issue fizzle out. He grew up in Detroit, so he learned the ropes in a school with inner city blacks. If a dude looked at him oddly for being honey-colored, almost white, he jumped on the guy — probably figured he might as well start the fight and get it over with. Survival in the streets bred his own personal sense of ethics. Moon had heard that last week Teddy Bear stopped a green-haired skateboarder and, convinced the rider had stolen the board but unable to arrest him for it, put the skateboard underneath the front car tire, got back in the passenger seat and said to Fender, "Okay, let's go."

Teddy Bear pushed for a bettor. "C'mon, just put your money where your mouth is. We got a pool here? Get on board. Train's pulling away."

He coaxed a dollar from each of them. Fender reluctantly contributed. "Between Engels and my three-month-old, I've been barfed on enough this week."

"I'll double your money if I can't do it." He pointed at Iggy. "And you get to say: do it." He chugged down his beer, shot his empty can in the trash and gave them a giant smile.

"Do it," Iggy said.

"Watch this," Teddy Bear held up his index finger.

"Just fucking do it," said Fender, pressing to move on. "Don't talk us through it."

Teddy picked up a paper cup, sucked in a gulp of air, threw up the beer, then, without taking a breath, drank it all again.

"Bitching," Moon nodded, impressed, and they all broke into laughter.

Gladstone poked Fender. "That's worth a buck."

"I want to call a *tri*-bunal for Iggy," Fender said.

All conversations stopped.

Automatically, four of the guys got in a circle around Iggy, who belched, then shook his head, as if he was expecting as much. "All right, what are my charges now?"

"Shuddup," Fender ordered.

"Shuddup?" Iggy straightened. "You shuddup."

Fender ignored him, impassively going through the motions. "Do you have a defense rep? Will anybody here," Fender yelled as though he were addressing an outfield of lawyers, "act as Mr. Ignacio Rivas's defense attorney?"

Moon could tell Fender was really into his Grand Dragon role tonight. He glanced at Teddy Bear who was studying the thin air as though waiting for a legal advisor to step from the shadowy outfield. But nobody appeared, so Teddy sighed. "Oh, okay."

"Good," Fender said, "and Bow Wow, you're the prosecutor."

"Again," Bow Wow groaned, ripping off a fart that amused Gladstone and Teddy Bear, but which Fender ignored.

"Moon," Fender called out in his most austere military fashion, "Sergeant at Arms, stand by the defendant." Moon took a step next to Iggy. "Now your charges are as follows, Ignacio Rivas," Fender said, then took an exaggerated deep breath. "You were seen *having coffee* with one of the enemy."

Moon, Gladstone, Bow Wow chorused a gasp, followed by Teddy Bear bemoaning, "I'm always the last to know."

Fender frowned at him, snapping, "You're the one who reported it to the MAW infraction committee, so shuddup."

Teddy Bear frowned, "You just watch your mother: I'm not your nigger."

Fender disregarded Teddy Bear and leveled a sausage finger at Iggy. "You were seen kissing," he winced, "one of the enemy, off duty, and conversing with a smile on your face, cavorting with rather than demeaning the enemy. Now, how do you plead on these charges?"

"Innocent," Iggy said, then added lightly, "you guys are too much. C'mon. I played racquetball up at the Academy with Alicia. No big — "

"Okay," Fender cut him off, "trial will begin. Jury take your places. Prosecution?"

Bow Wow lumbered forth and finished the last of his beer before he bellowed full of fire and brimstone, "I aim to prove beyond a shadow of a doubt that this man here is a lowly Missouri scum — "

"Mexican," Moon said. "He was born in Mexico City."

Bow Wow dismissed the correction. "Missouri scum who should not be allowed in our venerable Policemen Against Policewomen brotherhood because he violated all of our principles by talking to a female officer, touching a female officer, and…" he glanced at the notepad and pounded his heart, "oh God, kissing one female officer on duty in uniform and embarrassing us all."

Teddy Bear stepped forward, warning, "My defendant will not be…"

"Railroaded," Moon coached.

"Railroaded in this manner. He has his rights and — "

"Fine, fine," Fender cut him off like a conductor with a downbeat of his hand. "Now, does anyone have any real evidence to produce?"

Moon sensed Iggy was getting restless. Ready to call it a night. Probably regretting the date he'd called off with Alicia to put up with this circus act.

"Yes, Grand Dragon, sir," Gladstone said. "May I present mine?"

Fender offered a regal arm sweep. "Certainly." He stepped back, downstage, as if the protagonist in an outdoor play, offering Gladstone the prime performance position.

"On May twenty-fifth," Gladstone referred to his pocket-sized notebook, "I observed the officer in question not only kiss one Alicia, the Chola, on the ass — "

Iggy took a step forward. "Fuck you!" Moon blocked him.

Gladstone raised his voice, "But he turned around, shrugged and said: 'It's just a piece of ass — '"

Iggy lunged towards him. "That's a fucking l — "

Moon held him back. Iggy had had enough roasting, but Moon could tell Fender was going to turn up the fire, maybe too much, and he didn't like it when Fender went over the line, forgot they were simply letting off steam and moved the show from slapstick to scary.

"Sergeant at Arms." Fender nodded to Moon. "Silence the defendant."

"Grand Dragon, sir," Moon said, "the defendant and the Sergeant at Arms are ready to call it a night. See you mañana."

"Mañana? Where you women going?" Fender demanded, wagging his pointed index finger, "Deal with me, the both of you, or you won't fucking deal at all."

"Let's just get this over with for tonight," Moon said, urging Iggy to play along. "He's way ripped," Moon indicated Fender, who turned his head towards Gladstone, Bow Wow and Teddy Bear. "All right Jury, how do you find the defendant?"

"Guilty," the threesome said, not in unison.

"Okay, as the Grand Dragon, I need a moment to think before I pronounce sentence on you." Fender scrutinized Iggy's hard expression. "Sergeant of Arms, take him into the outfield while I confer with the members."

Moon nudged Iggy to move forward, escorting him about twenty feet away. "You shouldn't have made that stupid ass comment about Slattery finding the gun under the seat."

"You know," Iggy inhaled deeply, looking out over the infield, then exhaling, "I put up with a lot of crap from you guys 'cause you're my buddies, but I just don't happen to think when women put on that uniform they turn to shit."

"C'mon Iggy, I know Fender's slapping it on hard tonight, but that's because you're fucking one of 'em, for Chrissakes."

"That's my business. Fender's just jealous." Iggy said.

"Whatever you say."

Iggy nodded, sure of it. "Why wouldn't he be jealous? What kind of a life does he have?" He gestured to Fender leading the distant caucus. "He has a bad temper, too many kids and a battered wife."

Moon checked his look. "You talking about Phyllis?"

"Yeah, I'm talking about the way he treats his wife."

"That's between him and Phyllis."

Fender had never admitted to hitting Phyllis, but he talked big about always getting what he wanted, "In my house," he'd brag, "it's my way, or the highway," so the accusation didn't surprise Moon.

Iggy toed the dirt. "Bueno, I don't see it like that. My dad beat my mom, beat all my brothers and sisters."

Mood nodded, thinking. He couldn't predict what Iggy would do when they rejoined the group. Openly publicizing this domestic abuse indictment, however, could escalate Fender's verbal sparring to a physical battle that would play out beyond the park. Domestic abuse at the hands of some police officers wasn't exactly staggering news to Internal Affairs, but tossing around personal accusations was never good for locker room morale. Moon had to refocus the controversy to Slattery…to Iggy's relationship with Alicia. He had to center issues that related to policemen against policewoman because that was their reason for gathering.

"Look," Moon said, "If you were my partner instead of Earley, we wouldn't be having this conversation. You know that gun wasn't under any damn seat."

"You don't know that. And you don't really know these women. You've never even talked to Alicia, so you've got no idea what she had to live through in Segundo Flats to — "

"Iggy, Iggy…" Moon motioned for him to relax. "Look, if she were down on the ground all the time getting dirty and kicking and stomping ass, she still wouldn't belong here."

"What makes you sure?" Iggy tried to reason with him, "You might not have anything to do with policewomen, but you have a helluva lot to do with women everywhere else when you're out of uniform. Why, you drive into the valley to go to a woman *dentist* for chrissakes."

"That's right." Moon sighed, privately relieved they were back on track. "I used to live there, and she's a good dentist. My civilian life and my professional life are two different things. My life doesn't depend on the ladies I see when I'm not working. My life depends upon how good the people are I'm working with, and you know and I know, they are not good enough."

Moon and Iggy walked back to the others in silence. The MAW members turned their backs, chanting, "Shame. Shame. Shame."

"Okay," Fender informed Iggy, "your punishment is we're not going to talk to you for a week. Maybe longer — I'll decide when we let you back in."

Iggy jeered. "What a good break for me."

Fender glared at him. "This is no fucking joke. And we're gonna help you see how it is when all you have to talk to is female officers. Then you can baby-sit them, change their diapers, be their little buddy."

Moon leaned in towards Iggy, quietly suggesting, "And the regular size diapers are not gonna fit the Lieutenant's," he spread his open palms wide, wider to indicate her butt, "you'll have to use Depends."

Iggy ignored him and glared at Fender. "You're a real fuck." Then he turned, waving his hand. "You're all fucks." He looked for another second into Fender's eyes, cold and unblinking. Then

Iggy turned on home plate and hiked across the infield. Moon could tell he was relieved to get away, get over to see Alicia.

This time, Fender had gone too far; Iggy wouldn't let himself be humiliated again. Iggy's squared shoulders and firm step crossing the infield suggested a new attitude: he didn't care how long the MAW guys gave him the cold shoulder. He didn't care if they started ignoring his calls for back up like they did with some of the women. He didn't care if Fender put razor slashes in his car tires like he'd done to the woman rookie who'd quit a couple of months before. Iggy wouldn't get down on his knees to perform for the Grand Dragon's satirical amusement. It wasn't the least bit amusing anymore.

7

Roll Call

Moon had been at Earley's memorial Monday morning, standing near his partner's canopied cemetery plot, indistinguishable from hundreds of silent uniformed police officers. The somber unity of the officers for one of their own killed in the line of duty did not escape him, men and women at attention, a blur of blue.

He spent the afternoon on a picnic with Amberlene, Lily and the twins. But he hadn't eaten anything. Didn't much feel like swallowing peanut butter and jelly sandwiches; and his head felt full of rocks, sliding against each other. He should have called in sick, taken a mental health night off, but it never occurred to him not to work under emotional distress.

When Moon showed up that Monday night he stopped to read the assignment posted outside Captain Drummond's office. "Figures," Moon muttered, glancing incisively at the Captain's closed door. "Punish me with a transfer. Dynamite."

Ben Fender strutted by, saw Moon's chagrined expression, checked out the board and shook his head. "Don't tell me, he dumped a transfer on you."

"Yep," Moon sighed. "From the West Valley."

"Well, if he's keeping you on Nightwatch, but dumping some valley clown on you, it's probably my month to change Slattery's diapers. You know — " Fender stopped abruptly as though he remembered something disturbing. He leaned in and squinted at the board. "You're shittin' me. Morgan Fraser." He sighed and shook his head.

"That bad, huh?" Moon checked the name again. "You know him?"

"I was *her* T.O. at the Academy."

"A girl?" Moon said. "Another one? What a slap in the face."

Fender glared at the assignment board as if he were trying to figure out how to rip it off the wall. "I mean," he said, thinking aloud, "what's the point? What are we doing here?" He looked to Moon for an answer. "I thought we were doing a helluva job." He banged his head twice so hard against the assignment board that Moon had to grip his shoulder.

"Take it easy."

"Take it easy? I got reserves who tell me they can do my job as well as I can, and dumb niggers who tell me that, and people who can barely speak English who tell me that, and 20-year-old females who are 5'1", 90 pounds who tell me that…"

"You got a lot of people talking to you, man."

Fender eyed him. "Don't mess with me."

"I hear you," Moon said. "If someone can do the job with an IQ of say 80, and is tiny, illiterate and ugly, where does that leave us? I hear you, man."

"It's all bullshit, man." Fender faced the Captain's closed door. "The thing that you don't realize, Captain, is anytime you have to justify an action in a police department, it means you're grasping for straws so civilians won't shoot you down with all the knee-jerk reasons why you shouldn't have done it in the first place."

Fender shot another look to Drummond's office door, "It's as clear as the pimples on his ass. If this department were all six feet, 180 pounds or more, all aggressive, all marital-arts trained — "

"Blond-hair and blue-eyes," Moon interjected.

"…and sniper qualified," Fender said, nodding, "what would the city have to justify? They'd keep it quiet because the jobs are being done, and done quietly and intelligently, and they don't have a lot of problems."

Fender inhaled then exhaled in a slump. "No, they don't care about us like they used to, Moon…so the hell with 'em. I'll just sit in my car and answer my calls. Me, rush to a call? No way. No more. It just pisses me off we've come to this. You know, if I didn't have six mouths to feed, I'd go to the press and tell them most good policemen would like to take certain people in the alley and blow their brains out."

Captain Drummond opened his door and stepped into the hall, following Lieutenant Herdahl, and caught Fender's last few words; and *blow their brains out* echoed in her icy stare. Her eyes, dark bullets set in a doughy, pale face, watched Fender and Moon planted together, arms crossed, in front of the assignment board.

Moon emitted a low warning growl to Fender, then, pretending not to notice Drummond's raised eyebrows or Herdahl's harsh glare, declared with a broad smile, "Heigh ho, heigh ho, it's off to work we go…" Nodding to Fender, he strolled past Drummond, and lurched off following the lieutenant down the hall.

Fender imitated her waddle. "There she is," he indicated in a loud whisper, but not audible enough to force her to turn around, "our Baby Dumpling."

"Room enough to seat four comfortably," Moon said.

They burst into laughter and turned into their locker room.

Unlike most of the women who earned nicknames by what wrong action they did or didn't do, Lieutenant Herdahl earned her nickname by appearance alone: 5'5", 35 years old, slumped shoulders, braces on her teeth and a pouch Moon often swore was big enough to hide two cats. At least once a week Fender flared up before she walked into roll call, reminding everyone that their "little" lieutenant had never worked in the field. That she sued the police department in order to get promoted to the job. She did have to go back to the Academy for a two week "brush up," but she'd never worked in a police car. She'd never even been in uniform until she became lieutenant and was assigned to the 77th.

Moon didn't think much about her; thankfully, he considered, she wasn't working on the street. He only spoke with her when he absolutely had to. She apparently mistook his silence as a form of acceptance, and tried to generate some sort of office rapport with him, that is, until, some months before, she bumped into him at Lucky's meat counter.

She had wedged her shopping cart between a couple of others, reached over to pull a service ticket and slipped, pushing her cart into Moon's. Made up at the division as a woman of profoundly indeterminate age, in the store she was stripped of all pancake base, which left her sallow-skinned, hollow-eyed. He avoided her and looked instead directly inside her basket brimming over with steaks, eggs, bread, family-sized frozen waffles, quart soda pop bottles, and a couple of half gallons of vanilla ice cream, plus a half dozen assorted bite-size chocolate bars, several boxes of super plus absorbent tampons and a couple of packages of maxi pads wedged next to a family size bale of toilet paper. He was just going to ignore her, until he sensed that was exactly what she wanted: no acknowledgement or recognition, however brief, on either of their parts that would engrave the chance meeting on his memory.

But he couldn't resist. Shaking his head as a preface to a thought that caused her eyes to swell into an unspoken, *oh shit, he does recognize me,* he lightly, playfully, tapped her basket with his, which was filled with a dozen king-sized cans of oil-packed tuna, two gallons of milk, a few loaves of white bread, and several six packs of beer. "Ah," he sighed, indicating her basket contents, "the lonely idle."

Morgan watched Alicia make a Herculean espresso in her personal pot, conveniently set up in the women's locker room on a wobbly card table. Alicia reminded her that a little espresso before a long shift sent a swift shot of caffeine to the brain to fine tune those connections between body and mind. Morgan's queasy stomach needed a little fine-tuning. She gagged down a couple of her mother-in-law's matzo balls in chicken broth just to keep her from adding to her complaint rolodex: *didn't eat dinner on first night of new job.*

Morgan downed the espresso. She imagined the hot liquid rocketing to her stomach and detonating the great glob of matzo dough. Now, half an hour before roll call, she was surprised none of the other women were there, but the cramped changing atmosphere didn't exactly invite socializing. She hung her mitzvah in her locker.

She could already hear the male overtones laughing from the other side of the lockers. What were they talking about? Was Fender telling them about her? She'd already checked the board to make certain she wasn't partnered with him. What an assignment from hell that would be. It struck her that she had had it pretty good at Sleepy Hollow, got along with the men and women for the most part. Now, she'd really stuck her neck out, and was going to have to learn to work with a whole new set of problems and people.

Alicia nudged her, handing her another demi-tasse espresso.

"Thanks. I'll be flying. You do this every night?"

"That's right." Alicia smiled. "Bienvenidos," gesturing an open palm towards the confined locker corridor. "Mi casa es su casa."

Alicia seemed much friendlier than the previous Friday night. Espresso in hand, she gave Morgan a tour of the highlights of the 77th, starting in the basement property room that looked more like a concrete arsenal. Yellow-tagged weapons that had been confiscated since the first of the year were piled on metal shelves. Morgan spotted everything from a pearl-handled pistol to a row of shotguns buried under a layer of AR-15s and AK-47s. Alicia indicated the kit room where Morgan would have to pick up the equipment for Nightwatch.

On the way to the roll call room, Alicia stopped by the booking room wall and pointed to her personal favorite: a slip of paper from a fortune cookie was taped to the wall in the frisking room at about the eye level of a man who would be bent over waiting for the inspecting officer's fingers to pop into a pair of thin black rubber gloves to complete the unpleasant search. The fortune read: "This is your lucky day."

For the rest of the unremarkable walking tour, Alicia ticked off the Nightwatch's unmarried women on her fingers. Herself. Engels and Slattery. Blocker who'd as soon slug the father of her children as hug him.

"Like I told you the other night: we pay attention to Blocker. We don't always agree with her, but she's our man." Alicia did a fair imitation of Blocker, complete with open palms on her hips, "I tell you girls somethin' you don't forget about Nickerson Gardens," she tells us all the time, "if you a homie and you mess with an officer and win — you get away — why you be one bad dude. Everyone a them little black asses wants to get hisself a cop. And the only reason they let a nigger like me work in niggertown is I asked for it."

Blocker had evidently convinced the police board she wasn't going to show the homies any mercy: she'd come from nothing and made it out of there, so could they. She had big plans. Plans she got out into the community and talked about, "We can do something for real about cleaning up those mules and needle freaks on the street," Alicia mimicked Blocker's commanding voice.

Blocker didn't simply mouth off about what needed to be done. She did it. For the last year she and Tyrone Earley had been mentoring kids in the 77th, taking them on field trips, driving them to the central jail, the Sybil Brand Institute for Women, or the Hall of Justice Jail where some of the boys and girls would wave to their friends, but most of them learned they didn't want to go there.

Four unmarried women worked Nightwatch. "Actually five," recounted Alicia, "if you include the Lieutenant. The late work shift shoots down dating, then the equal opportunity development department, E.O.D.D., keeps me so busy recruiting women officers, I have no time to do my laundry, forget about nurturing a relationship."

It was generally suspected that the E.O.D.D., along with Internal Affairs, spied on every officer's personal life. Why would they spy? "Who knows why they do anything?" Alicia said. The department pressured her, their only Latin representative, as a panelist for their Saturday morning propaganda seminars to entice women to sign up for a seemingly endless process of written and oral tests, medical and psychological exams, and background investigations before taking on six months of grueling Police Academy training. "It's unreal, you know, but I got to do it, if I don't want to be the token *chica* forever."

The roll call room looked more like a prison classroom for high security inmates. Bars on the windows, no sharp objects, a blackboard drawing of Barbie bursting out of a bikini. Alicia erased the cartoon, muttering something in Spanish. She explained to

Morgan that the humans usually sat in the front, the animals and cut-ups goofed off in the back next to the "No Smoking Sec. 41.40-inch sign LAMC, Los Angeles Municipal Code, tacked behind a wall-mounted baseball trophy with a ripped-off bat.

Lieutenant Herdahl turned into the squad room. Without so much as glancing at Gladstone, Teddy Bear, Bow Wow and Iggy sitting in aluminum chairs around a cafeteria table and the handful of women sitting separated, but nearby, Herdahl marched purposefully to stand behind the podium in front of the room, slipping a video tape into a VCR and flicking on an overhead video screen.

It was the weekly video word from Parker Center. The assistant chief hailed L.A.P.D. for the new crime stats: Homicides were down 8%, he informed them.

Alicia nudged Morgan, indicating Moon as he made his way with Fender to the trashed baseball trophy in the back of the room. As Moon started to take what Alicia whispered was his customary roll call seat next to Iggy, Fender gave him a hard look, which he ignored. "Fender's getting the guys to ignore Iggy because he's seeing me. Is this grade school, or what?" Alicia faced the front.

Moon checked out the back of the women, identifying them easily by familiar coiffures: Blocker's puffy Afro; Alicia's geometric razor cut; Slattery's Shirley Temple crop; Engels' khaki thatch; and a long single braid resting on the back of what must be Morgan Fraser, that transfer from Sleepy Hollow.

Out of the corner of her eye, Morgan noticed Teddy Bear, smacking bubble gum, point to her and wink at Moon. It took a second for her to place Teddy Bear, but then she remembered he'd been Gladstone's chewing tobacco sidekick at the Academy.

She prepared herself for Teddy Bear to be another Gladstone, only black. Teddy Bear, Fender and Gladstone probably formed a trio here similar to the dynamic duo Fender and Gladstone immortalized at the Academy — mates tormenting new women transfers to the 77th.

Morgan avoided looking in Fender's direction. Why does he want me to fail so badly? Don't think about that, she warned herself. She squirmed in the hard metal chair and forced herself to concentrate on the videotape, not to think about Fender, about the Academy.

"So," the assistant chief wrapped it up, "I want to pat you on the back."

"Don't touch me, you faggot," Fender said.

His acrimonious voice grated on Morgan more than she wanted to admit. Get used to it, she told herself. You're going to have to put up with this jackass every night.

Gladstone backed Fender up. "Yeah, words are cheap, just slap me a raise."

An abrupt glitch in the tape suggested the assistant chief's hearty closing had been edited to give time for the police chief to express his sympathy for the fatal Friday night shooting of Officer Tyrone Earley. "We have a war going on here," he said, reminding them that it could have been any one of them. He droned on another couple of minutes about not wanting adrenaline to interfere with their judgment. "Don't lose control. Take that extra minute and assess the situation."

"Minute?" Moon said, questioning if their chief of police had ever even been in a gun battle. "Take that extra minute so you can watch everyone around you shot, stabbed, torn apart. Take that extra minute. Helluva piece of advice."

Not an entirely ignorant observation, Morgan thought.

Lieutenant Herdahl finally turned off the video and started roll call: "Today is May 28; your court date for tickets is June 15." She reviewed the partners posted on the board outside the captain's door. "Slattery, you'll be riding with Fender." Slattery sat motionless as Fender moved his hand towards his crotch. Herdahl didn't look up from her papers. "Not a fucking word, Fender?"

"No, Lieutenant," Fender said, offhandedly. "My balls just itch; that's why I'm scratching 'em."

Moon snorted into his palm.

"And a transfer," Herdahl continued. "Morgan Fraser will be working with you, Moon."

Morgan turned around and smiled, noticing that Moon was lighting up a cigarette right in front of the No Smoking sign. She recognized him as the silent man in blue jeans at the site of Earley's shooting.

Moon looked right through her to Herdahl.

"Seems somebody's dumping stolen cars in the end alley at 23rd again," read Herdahl. "So, you might make some checks in that area. Problem, Moon?"

"No, Lieutenant," he grunted. "Everything is dyn-o-mite."

His immediate snub summed him up to Morgan and she squared her shoulders as if to face this new challenge.

After roll call, Morgan crossed to Moon, but before she could utter a greeting, he told her: "Get the gear. I'll meet you outside."

She checked out the radios, shotguns and ticket books from the kit room and, with some difficulty, carried them to the parking lot. She set the heavier equipment down by Moon, who was talking with Fender. Moon spoke without looking at her. "My car's the one down on the end." He pointed, indicating the row of patrol cars.

Morgan took a deep breath, eyeing Fender a moment. She'd been considering how to handle their working relationship, and she'd decided that his arrogance probably commanded the same intimidation here as at the Academy. No indication, thus far, he'd had a personality make-over. But she wasn't afraid of him. What embarrassment could he deliver in the field he hadn't already delivered at the Academy? And the Academy was school, not a life or death situation, she reminded herself.

But what if Fender pulled the same manipulative tactics in the field? No, too dangerous. Besides, nothing in Jacob's letters suggested Fender was a heartless, incorrigible brute of a sergeant in *Full Metal Jacket* — physically and psychologically beating up his guys to prepare them for surviving guerilla warfare. She decided to treat him cordially, almost pleasantly, and never to reveal her real feelings towards him.

So, she shifted the gear in her arms, and as she started to move away, turned and nodded to Fender. "Nice to see you again, sir." Her glance swept past Moon. She could feel his lingering look, as though he knew he'd seen her before, but he couldn't place her.

8

Eight Hours with Moon

A few moments later, Moon strode up to the police car and stood next to Morgan as she tried to get the nut off the shotgun. Finally, he took it from her and stated flatly, "I'll do that. It's real easy, dear."

"Thanks," Morgan handed it to him, and, maintaining a casual air, opened the passenger door.

Moon turned out of the police parking lot and drove for several minutes in dead silence.

Then he declared, "We don't call each other by names out here."

"Okay, sounds good."

"If somebody gets your gun, you just remember to dive because I'm going to shoot."

"Okay."

"Do you wear a vest?"

"Yes."

"Why?"

She frowned at him, waiting for an explanation. He offered none, so she said, "My deodorant soap doesn't deflect bullets."

"Vest won't either. Do you carry a back-up gun?"

"Yes."

"Did you remember to bring it?"

She threw him a blank look.

"Always carry a back-up. Always."

Who was this guy? Spouting off routine reminders as if she were fresh out of the Academy.

He continued to drill her. "What do we each do at a traffic stop?"

Push-ups, she almost responded, but was interrupted by a 415 Juvenile group call broadcast from the car radio. "Shots fired in the alley at Hoover between 109th and 110th, Handle Code 2."

Morgan sat up anxiously and announced, "All right, let's go kick some ass."

Moon sighed and shook his head. "Unlock the shotgun, dear."

"The shotgun?"

"Right. Get it out." She got it out. "Good," Moon said. "You got it out. That's real good. You're real talented. Now, put it over on the side, so when you get out, you can kick the door open."

Nervous, but intent, she listened to him. "Now, when you get out, throw the door open. But, put your foot on it, so it doesn't come back and knock you over."

She tossed Moon a look. He was too preoccupied checking out the area to notice. He turned into a graffiti-covered alley. "Here we are in lovely Nickerson Gardens," he said, mocking a cluster of tenement buildings surrounded by sterile dirt plots and connected by cracked cement walkways.

Rolling at a snail's pace, he flicked off the lights, and enunciated as if he were talking to a first grader: "Okay, we're not going to drive right down there."

Just play along here with him, she thought. He's struttin' his stuff. "Right," she whispered, imitating his tone. "And if we really want to catch somebody, we shouldn't drive the big, big police car down the middle of a dark, dark alley where the bad guys can hear us half a mile away."

He looked at her, stopped the car and parked. "So, we're gonna walk down the alley. You on one side, me on the other. And don't shoot me or your foot, okay?"

"Okay. Let's go," she responded evenly. She threw the door open and stood waiting outside the car.

"You're gonna do some police work, dear." He forced a taunting grin. "Something you probably haven't seen the likes of in Sleepy Hollow."

She talked to herself: Stay calm. Pay attention to everything. Everything is important. Don't try to impress him.

They walked down on to a carport where five black "gang-bangers" in gang-affiliated golf hats were standing around. With his weapon out, Moon motioned for her to stay back a few steps. Then he called out: "Okay, everybody get your hands above your head now!" No one moved. "Now," he yelled. "Motherfuckers, put your hands up!"

Morgan noticed how his change of voice made the gangbangers obey. One particularly indignant black gang member, trying to dazzle his brothers, exclaimed, "Why you hassling us?"

"Shut your mouth, and put your fucking arms up!"

"Fuck off, pig!"

Seeming to come from nowhere, Moon's hand whipped out of the thin air and slapped the suspect on the side of the head. The gangbanger went down. Moon grabbed him by the hair, put the gun to his head, and said, "Now, let's do it right, dude…you know the routine. Let's do it by the numbers. I want everybody to stand there with your hands behind your head. I want you to spread your legs, and when I grab you by the hands, I want you to step one pace backwards, and I'm going to search you."

Automatically, Morgan, as the guard officer, moved to the unsearched prisoner's side, so if any of them went for their guns she could cover Moon.

An angry man stormed into the alley. "What's going on out here? This is the fifth night this week you been out here. What's it, dope? The liquor store get held up? What's it this time? I gotta be at work in four hours. This is my sleeping time and I'm getting damn tired of this."

Moon continued the search. "I don't blame you."

A woman in curlers, a bathrobe and stocking feet opened her alley gate. "I don't understand what's happening here," she said in a hoarse whisper.

"We had reports of shots fired here, ma'am," Morgan said.

"What shots? I didn't hear no shots," the woman said, her silver curler rods twinkling in the moonlight. "It's like everybody's guilty because they're black. This happens all the time. What are we all, garbage? Criminals? These boys are out here talking and you just embarrass the hell out of 'em."

Another woman spoke from the shadows. "That's right. The harder we try to help these boys, the more you harass them. I work with you people. The last time, you fellas came in and tore up my house, harassed my boy for months." She waited for a response.

Finally, Morgan said, "Ma'am, you know we're here so everyone can get a safe night's sleep. If you had called in a complaint, heard gunshots, you'd want us to come take care of it. We're not the enemy here, ma'am."

The woman's eyes flashed, then her curlers did an abrupt about face. She slammed her gate and went back inside. The other neighbors who'd gathered in the alley vanished into the darkness, muttering about helicopters, lights, sirens and gunshots.

Morgan switched back to where the majority of suspects had been searched. Unmoved by the residents' protests, she had her eyes on the last suspect.

Finding nothing, Moon said, "Okay, everybody put your hands down and bust out ID."

"Just mellow out," grinned the jester of the group. "Smile, brother."

"I got nothing to smile about."

Morgan could tell while this might not be a game for the Jester, neither was it entirely serious. "Oh my man," he said, "you got something to smile about: you one good-looking dude."

"Too bad I can't say the same for you," said Moon. "Now bust out your ID."

"Oh," the jester offered a dry chuckle, "oh you could say it, my man, if you told as big a white lie I just told."

A snicker rippled through the group.

"Lemme see your fucking ID," said Moon.

"We don't got to show you shit, my man," the leader cocked his head.

"I'm not your fuckin' man." Moon got in his face like a drill sergeant. "I'm not your cuz, I'm not your blood. I'm sir to you, dude, and if you don't like that, try to kick my ass. You can't kick my ass, I'll kick yours — get the picture?"

Eyeing Moon's gun, the Jester said, "He gets the picture; let's check out that picture," he nodded towards Morgan. "Who's your girlfriend?"

Moon jabbed him in the gut. "She's a police officer. And don't you ever forget it. Now shut the fuck up and break out some ID."

Moon checked their ID, then told them to disperse.

When Moon and Morgan got back to the car, she ventured that he wouldn't have jabbed the jester in the stomach if the neighbors had hung around. He made a vague silencing gesture, and she remarked that with his abusive attitude, it was no wonder police were treated like the enemy.

He assured her she didn't know jackshit about the lowlifes in these neighborhoods. "But," he smiled broadly, "now it's your turn. Let's see what you can bring to the party, Barbie."

He backed out of the alley, then drove in front of a low-income housing project, past a liquor store and the local gangbangers, hookers and homeless hanging out. He pulled to the curb near a carport where two black males were standing, talking. "Let's see if you can pat down those out-of-towners. Let's see how they react to you. You're going to check out those two ex-cons. I want you to tell them to put their hands behind their heads and turn around, that you want to talk to them."

"Why?"

"They don't belong in this neighborhood."

"Says who?"

"I'm telling you."

"Seems like an awfully hostile way to 'meet and greet.'"

"Then," he continued, ignoring her reaction, "assuming they turn around, you search them."

"Do I have probable cause?"

"You don't need probable cause. You want to know who they are. You know the area; you've never seen 'em before, so you want to talk to them. Introduce yourself to the folks on your beat, you know."

"Yeah, like a policing welcome wagon," Morgan nodded, got out of the car and stiffly approached the two men, who were neatly dressed with shaved heads.

Her limbs began to tingle and go numb. She yelled silently to her legs: *No. No, you don't.* Then, aware that Moon had gotten out of the driver's seat, his hard gaze driving her from behind, she managed to plant herself in front of the two behemoth black men.

"Evening," Morgan nodded and waited for an answer. There was none — only their black eyes rimmed in flawless white, riveted on her face. "You guys are new in the neighborhood, so you might not know about our random "on the street" weapon checks. Put your hands above your head and turn around," she said, offering more of a request than a command.

Mechanically, they did exactly what she said, almost as if they were staring right through her, watching Moon, who was standing next to the car with his hand on his gun.

Morgan searched each man thoroughly. "Thank you, gentlemen. Sorry for the inconvenience. But I bet you'll feel safer on these streets."

Quietly confident, Morgan returned to Moon, standing next to the car, and said, "Those are your ex-cons, huh?"

"Right," Moon nodded. "You were talking to two black Muslims that I've known for a long time, and both have been in prison for murder, and both would have snuffed your life in a second if I hadn't been here. Muslims don't have a shit of respect for cops if they don't feel like it. They can kill you if they want, whenever they want. That's why you females will never make it out here: you don't know who you're talking to and you never will."

She flashed a smile, then commented brightly, "Aren't you just a wonder. A *wonder* man."

He held her animated look briefly, smirked, "You have less sense than a fucking blind person," then walked away.

"Where you going?"

He indicated the sidewalk. "Footbeat."

"Oh." She caught up to him, "Actually, that's a misconception about blind people, like when we say, somebody eats like a bird. Birds really eat five times their body weight daily, just like blind people have really strong senses — "

"Who asked you?"

"Well, I appreciate the little helpful hints you're giving me about the street, so I just thought I'd correct — "

"Look, if you're going to work with me, just go along with what I say, and shut the fuck up. You cover my ass, I'll cover yours."

She pushed for a clarification. "Could you give me an example of when you might expect me to cover your ass."

He glanced at her askance. "Little things mostly."

"Like what?"

"Like jabbing that nigger in the ribs back there. That's not going in the report."

"I didn't think so. Do you routinely change the facts in a report?"

He shrugged, making it difficult for her to figure out if he had secrets and engaged in cover-ups or if he was just exaggerating, trying to impress her. Then he gave an example of how he'd changed the facts just the other night to make an arrest. He said he'd found a hype who was clearly under the influence, but he, Moon, could not find a fresh needle mark, so he squeezed one of the hype's old marks to make it look fresh.

"When it comes down to it," he assured her, "I'm not going to jail for you, but I'll take six months suspension, not because I like you, not because I think you belong here, but because you've got the uniform on and…I have to protect that."

"Thanks."

"Don't fucking thank me like I'm doing you a favor or something. You are fucking worthless. You can't do anything right."

"I can hold my own."

"Well, that'll get you killed deader than hell," he said, snapping his fingers. "That fast. You know how long you'd be in the hospital if I did nothing but hit you in the face? You'd be out of work for a month. I'd break every tooth out of your mouth."

"Probably."

"No probably about it."

They approached the liquor store. Several tough locals were hanging around outside. While Moon was talking, he fixed his gaze on a shirtless dude in a telephone booth.

"I mean, why don't you want to be a social worker."

"My great aunt inspired me to be a cop."

"Your great aunt, now isn't that special."

She nodded at him, then offered an encouraging smile to an unshaven man who looked like he'd been pumping iron for ten years and was carrying a battered trumpet case.

"Why are you smiling?"

"Why not?"

"Don't smile at these people..."

"Why not?"

He was silent a moment, and she realized that smiling annoyed him, so she made a mental note to do it often. She would study his gestures, mannerisms, and inflections and note those used by others that annoyed him.

"Well, my great aunt didn't inspire me," he broke the silence. "I always wanted to be a cop."

Oh, he's expressing a feeling here. Be sincere. Don't just blow him off. "I'm guessing they signed you out of the Marines?"

"I didn't even know what the pay was. I didn't care. Now you got all these splittails—hairdressers, bank tellers, preschool teachers—leaving jobs so they can triple their salary and they don't have the instincts."

Morgan considered for a moment, then asked as though she really wanted to know, "Then you really just disagree with women officers on the street?"

"It's ridiculous."

"Why?"

"Why? I've seen 'em! I've seen 'em lock themselves in police cars, cry over dead bodies, or puke like Engels did after the shoot out the other night. I've heard 'em call back-ups that I could handle with my hands tied. Just me standing here can make a guy do something that a splittail would have to point a gun to get him to do."

Uneasy, the dude hung up the phone, glanced at Moon, then walked too casually to his car, got in and drove away.

"See what I mean? You could never have made that pusher get off the phone and leave."

"Like I said, you're a *wonder* man."

It was after midnight. Moon turned off of Century, past Tia's Tacos. He made a move to turn in, then thought better of it and drove past. Morgan rode along, observing the neighborhood and enduring his silent treatment.

They stopped at a red light.

A beefed-up Chevy with several black guys, laughing and rapping, pulled up next to Morgan's window. She looked over at one stone face in the back seat who just glowered at her.

Moon pulled away. "So when was the last fist fight you were in?"

She considered briefly. "You give me the opportun — "

"No, no, I said when was the last fist — "

"In high school."

"With a man?"

"Yes." She looked at him directly. "With a man."

"Did you win?"

She thought a moment. "I'd call it an even draw."

"Did he try to hit you?"

"Yes."

"How big was he?"

"Oh, much bigger," she toyed with him. "About your size. Tons of muscles."

"So," he paused speculatively. "Other than that, you've never had an aggressive encounter with a man in your whole life?"

She took a few breaths, making an effort to remain calm. "If I'd have been put in the situation I would have, but I haven't — "

"That's not the point," he badgered her. "Tell me what you're going to do with some big nigger who's been in prison seven years digging ditches?"

She swallowed hard and tightened her lips. "I'd do the best I could."

"No, you'd do anything he fucking wants you to do."

She dug her thumbnail into her index finger, staring ahead.

Moon pulled into a 7-11, past a half dozen gangbangers, males and females probably all under eighteen, laughing and cutting up by the pay telephone. He swung around the back and parked in a handicapped spot near the bathrooms.

"Don't we have to enforce a curfew or anything after midnight?" she nodded towards the underage group.

He shook his head hopelessly.

They both got out. Morgan walked around to the front of the car and stood by the steps as Moon passed by on the sidewalk. "Moon," she said, looking directly into his eyes, "I'm sorry you lost your partner, and I just want you to know I won't let you down."

He regarded her for a moment, nodded, communicating nothing, then moved around her to the men's room. "Pick me up a can of tuna while you're inside, will you?"

"Packed in water?"

"Oil. I like it the old-fashioned way."

"How did I know that?"

Inside the convenience store, Morgan waited behind a bearded black man in a pressed khaki uniform. He smiled and handed Morgan a large cup. "Thanks." She nodded, and held it up to the ice dispenser. Crushed cubes spilled out. She filled it half way with lemon-lime soda, adding some Dr. Pepper and a splash of orange drink. She took a few sips as she walked the aisles searching for tuna. Just as she stooped down to reach for a can, a spurt of bullets shattered the glass behind her. Half bent over, she peered out the window to see the man in khakis drop on the hood of a Southern California Gas Company car.

The drive-by van sped down the street. Morgan dashed from the convenience store across the parking lot to the victim. The three dudes in the van — Driver, Lookout and Shotgun — were probably getting even more pumped up as she ripped open the man's khaki shirt and examined his massive chest wound. She imagined they were congratulating each other: "Fuckin' A, man!" "Yeah, I popped 'im good."

And when she peered between the legs of several onlookers and saw the van make a sudden, sweeping U-turn, she was right. They'd talked themselves into a second drive-by. No cover close enough. "Drop!" she yelled out. "They're coming back."

But two panicked teenagers stood and dashed for the 7-11 door.

They couldn't make it, but she banked on the brief second that Shotgun would be distracted by the running kids, sight them, and wait to shoot; she had just long enough for her to get her bearings in the group and brace her right shooting arm on her left forearm.

She propped her arm. Focused and intent, Morgan fired.

The right rear tire exploded hard enough to topple Shotgun against Driver who lost control just as Moon rounded the back corner of the 7-11 in time to witness the van skid into a parked car.

Morgan ran towards the crash and positioned herself several paces from the back of the van on Driver's side.

"Freeze!" Her arms outstretched, gun aimed at Driver's side mirror. "Everybody just freeze!"

Moon hustled to the back of the van and covered the passenger side.

"Driver," her voice rang each enunciated word. "Put both hands on the steering wheel at ten and two o'clock."

"Fuck you," muttered Driver, and started to lift his left hand casually from the steering wheel.

Morgan shot Driver's side mirror. It shattered, as did his confidence. "Another bad move and it's your head. Now, keep your left hand on the wheel; reach over with your right hand and open the door; kick the door open with your left foot. Then slip out with your hands above your head, and get on the ground spread eagle."

Driver followed her matter-of-fact directions exactly.

"Passenger," she continued, "open the door with your right hand…"

She checked Moon, who nodded an affirmative.

Minutes later, Morgan cuffed Lookout and thought she saw a hint of remorse, or possibly embarrassment, as he glanced at the surrounding bedlam in his neighborhood: scurrying paramedics, gawking neighbors, crying teenagers. He turned and spit at her feet, avoiding eye contact. Then, he slid into the back of the police car with his buddies, and Morgan slammed the back-door. She checked his stony expression, now filled with anything but regret.

A paramedic with a graying ponytail finished positioning the victim's stretcher in the back of the ambulance, pulled the doors towards him, and offered Morgan a thumbs up through the rear glass window. She watched the vehicle tear out of the parking lot, siren blaring. There'd been no time for a medical report, but the victim was still conscious, so maybe 'thumbs up' meant they had a good chance of getting him there alive. She'd call the hospital back at the station.

She opened her passenger side door, glanced across the top of the patrol car and caught Moon staring at her with silent approval.

"So?" he asked, as though he were waiting for the answer to a question she hadn't heard.

"What? You want me to drive?"

"Yeah right." He slapped the car top with his palm. "This is my car. You don't ever drive my car." He eyed her expectantly.

"What? What'da ya want?"

"My tuna fish?"

"Your tuna fish?" She got in, muttering, "My ass," but smiled a small victory.

After a cup of hot chamomile tea and honey with a dash of tequila, Morgan finally sunk into her bed and burrowed under her covers around four in the morning. The tense details of her first night in the 77th rushed through her mind, the serene finale settling in the women's locker room shower. She could still hear their laughter flowing through the dim light diffused in steam that enveloped and softened their naked bodies into shapes of cream and white and brown, embracing them in an ephemeral, foggy womb. She had locked that fleeting vision in her mind, then turned her face into the stream of water, just as Engels warned that she'd probably catch some flak from Captain Drummond for shooting out the sideview mirror. The "regs," Engels reminded her, strictly state: shoot to maim or kill.

"Fuck the regs," Blocker said, "She got four animals off the street."

"First night," Alicia yelled, pumped up. "I'd love to know what those Men Against Women muppets have to say about that." Shaking a can of soda, she moved across the slippery shower floor towards Morgan. "They got that stupid group, but we're gonna start our own, and we don't need to be against no fucking men because we are Las Mujeres."

Alicia popped the lid and soda sprayed on the wet bodies. "Viva las mujeres!" She thrust her fist in the air. "Viva las mujeres!"

"Thatta way! Girl, you tell it like it is." Blocker slapped Alicia on the bare butt, "Viva las mu-whatever!"

"Mu-jeres," Engels corrected her. "Viva las mujeres." She nodded approvingly at Alicia. "I like that."

"That's good." Alicia said, eyeing her closely, "just don't touch my butt."

"Mu-je-res!" yelled Slattery, getting into it.

Swept up in the camaraderie of the moment, they started yelling "mujeres" in unison, which evolved into a loud chorus of "bitches," that reverberated in the men's locker room and inflamed a resounding series of barks.

"That's Bow Wow." Alicia informed Morgan.

Morgan imagined Fender standing next to Bow Wow, dripping wet, egging him on. "You tell 'em, Bow Wow. Pack o' bitches."

"So she didn't fuck up too bad." Fender would confirm with Moon.

"She can point a gun." Moon would probably give her that.

And Fender would take credit for it. "Yeah, I can teach anybody to fire a weapon. Even a splittail."

"She's pissed off inside." Moon might have picked up on that as well. "You teach her that?"

"Not exactly."

9

ALMOST PARADISE

Morgan cracked her last salted peanut as the umpire called the second strike in the bottom of the ninth inning. She glanced at the scoreboard beyond centerfield: Home 1, Away 0. Bases loaded. The Pirates hadn't scored any runs on her daughter, but Sam had walked the three base-runners. A run now would tie the game, and the coach would pull her from the mound. Sam would be devastated. The one time the coach had pulled her, early in the season, she'd acted like there'd been a death in the family. She refused to eat and sat on her bed all day punching her baseball glove. Her friend Nat had finally broken her mourning spell with a chocolate milkshake from the nearby Foster Freeze.

"Strike two," the umpire called. Amidst the subsequent hooting and cheering, Sam stepped off the mound and watched the batter back away from the plate to scrutinize the bat.

Sam frowned at Nat, the catcher, when he tossed the ball back to her. "C'mon, Sam!" he yelled, "let's put 'em away." His voice rang out above all the others.

Sam caught the ball, took it out of her glove, and glanced down at the message scrawled on the inside pocket: ONE RIGHT, ONE WAY. She stepped back on the mound.

Morgan held her breath, watching Sam shake off Nat's sign.

Intent, Sam nodded yes and concentrated on the batter, giving him a cold, hard look, then she wound up and fired a bullet right down the middle. The batter swung and missed. Nat bagged the ball in his glove and flipped off his mask. Sam's team howled from the dugout, jumping on each other and tossing their hats in the air.

But it was Nat who ran out to congratulate her, screaming, "I knew you could do it!" He jerked her hat off and tugged on her rope braid. Her intense expression broke into a modest smile. He dumped water on her head as if it were champagne, and she socked him in the arm. She wiped her face with her sleeve and looked into the stands at Morgan, who was madly grinning and waving. Morgan wiped her tongue over the edge of her lip to stop tears from running into her mouth. How proud Jacob would have been to see his little girl pitch a no-hitter.

After celebrating the win at a local pizza parlor, Morgan had taken Sam and Nat up to the Police Academy. Then they'd returned home early in the afternoon because Sam wanted to work on their treehouse. After catching a game, then running at the Academy, Nat had no interest in building anything outside. He had cupped his head between open palms rigorously shaking his glistening Afro, but Sam wouldn't take his emphatic "no" for an answer.

Several hours, and three pitchers of lemonade later, Morgan was still outside the garage work area sawing one-foot wood hunks. She called out to the treehouse builders, "Hey you guys, have to wrap it up before Gramma Sofie gets home from bridge."

Gramma Sofie would view the treehouse as another lapse in judgment. She questioned any sudden decision or change of plans. The slightest modification in dinner would send her sulking. Morgan and Sam might decide they'd like to order pizza or Chinese food on a Sunday night, and Gramma Sofie would be upset because she'd already defrosted her cheesy meatloaf for three. And no they couldn't have the meatloaf Monday night: she'd already made a chicken pot pie. If they ordered a pizza, Gramma Sofie would complain that it was greasier than the last one; if they ordered moo shu chicken, the pancakes were drier than before. Gramma Sofie's glass was perpetually half empty, and Morgan wondered if her mother-in-law's glass, even in the best of times, perhaps when she'd moved with Thomas to the beach community after World War II, had ever been half full.

Sam and Nat either didn't hear Morgan calling to them or they ignored her. Either way, she didn't get a response, so she looked up to see Sam balancing on a tree branch, calling to Nat, and pointing the handle of her hammer at a piece of wood on the ground.

Nat picked up the block of wood, a foot long, one inch thick, stretched and handed it to her. She nailed it about eight inches above another block, making footholds in the trunk of her backyard tree.

Nat referred to his pencil-sketched treehouse plan on a piece of white construction paper. "You know," he drew a third guardrail between an upper handrail and a lower ledge. "We're gonna need a middle rail so nobody falls through."

"One's good enough."

Nat studied a diagram in a construction booklet, then glanced up at the proposed treehouse platform. "Yeah, for a fort on the ground."

"We'll never finish, you keep adding stuff."

"That's fine." He held up his hand in a gesture of surrender. "I'm just not getting up there with you unless it's safe."

Sam rolled her eyes and sighed, as if fully knowing they'd do it his way; they each understood the skills they brought to this business friendship: he made the architectural plans for her overall treehouse vision, then he supervised or did the grunt work while she did the serious hammering.

"I better get your mom to cut some more," he said, pointing to the dwindling wood blocks.

She nodded agreement, "And tell her we need a ladder."

Nat plodded over to Morgan leaning over a sawhorse. "We need about a half dozen more." He stacked wood blocks neatly in the crook of his left arm.

Observing Nat, Morgan leaned back against a late model Cadillac badly in need of a paint job it would never get. It had belonged to Thomas, Jacob's father; Gramma Sofie couldn't drive, but she wouldn't part with it. So, Morgan backed it out of the driveway once a week, sometimes she'd even maneuver the mini-tank down the narrow car-lined street and around the block.

Morgan watched Nat balance precariously stacked wood blocks on his slick ebony forearm. "Need any help?" she asked, handing him a wet towel for his dirt-and-sweat-streaked cheeks.

"Nope." He wiped his face, encouraged, "we just gotta carry up the 2x6 boards for the floor."

"Right. I'm glad you guys have it all worked out."

"After she wedges the boards in, all we need is another railing and a ladder to haul up our stuff and go to sleep." He glanced at her, waiting for a response. "You're supposed to ask, what stuff?"

"Oh, well I don't think you or Sam should let anything up there that you don't like a lot."

He poured her a glass of lemonade from a grimy plastic pitcher.

"Thanks." Morgan watched him surge back across the yard. Smiling to herself, she considered if Sam ever ran for political office, Nat would be her campaign manager. Gramma Sofie would be at the door selling raffle tickets for her apple strudel to Sam's grassroots coalition, and Morgan would be the unremarkable assistant passing out *Vote for Sam* buttons.

The image quieted that strange sense of alarm running through Morgan's mind in a futile search for a safe exit. The sense that crept in during her greatest times of joy and reminded her to relish that moment because it was as ephemeral as a cut gardenia.

Prior to starting her new assignment in the 77th, Morgan had spent her week off work with Sam and Nat. They were the oddest of companions: her daughter, so intense and outspoken; Nat, so earnest and polite. Sam, with no siblings and only a mother and a gramma to call her own; Nat, the youngest of six brothers and sisters, with an extended family of aunts and uncles that spread from North Carolina to New York City to East Los Angeles. Nat's father, an expert plasterer, had traced their lineage back to a great-great-great grandfather who'd been the first freedman on his plantation to buy land from his master. Nat's living room was a display case for family photographs, a scrapbook of his descendants portraying a living, rich community posing in private homes, gospel concerts, picnics, religious celebrations. A photo of Nat's grandfather, an ironworker on the Empire State Building, was predominantly displayed at the entryway. Both hallway walls were lined with formal and individual portraits highlighting the various stages of his ancestors' lives: infancy, childhood, parenthood and old age.

Over his father's piano hung William Claxton's black-and-white photo of Charlie Parker, a blurry silhouette in front of an open venetian blind, blowing on his horn. In the kitchen, Nat's mother had a framed poster with individual pictures of outstanding black Americans in civil leadership, education and science. Every school child learned about Rosa Parks, Martin Luther King, Jr. and Harriet Tubman, but Nat and Sam had eaten biscuits and gravy and greens under that poster so often they knew Shirley Chisholm was the first black woman elected to Congress and Benjamin Banneker was the mechanical genius who helped design Washington, D.C.

There was nothing about being black Nat wasn't proud of, and although it surprised Sam's baseball coach to learn Leroy "Satchel" Page was her pitching idol, it didn't surprise Morgan. There was nothing about having a black best friend that Sam wasn't proud of. Besides, Satchel was the greatest pitcher in the history of the game, Sam was quick to point out, even though he was not allowed to play in the major leagues so there were no statistics to prove it. Satchel, as Sam often mentioned in numerous school reports she'd given on him, was inducted into the Baseball Hall of Fame the year she was born.

Morgan ventured a sip of Nat's doctored lemonade — sugar water with the slightest scent of lemon — and gulped it down, fearing he might see her spit it out. She sat on an ice chest and observed their construction accomplishment.

Since they were toddlers, Morgan had been a silent partner in the children's imaginary and real adventures. Sometimes not so silent; occasionally she gave them direction, set limits, but they seemed to know she didn't hang around them because they needed her: she needed them. She gravitated to the middle of their constant chatter or solemn silence because it forced her to live in the existing moment.

It was Jacob's legacy to her, a gift or burden, depending on her mood. He talked about the simple exchanges of his day as if they took on a magical quality deserving of awe. His inspired attitude often exhausted her, but his fresh outlook still clung to her heart and compelled her to seek out people who lived in the present. Children, naturally grounded in the moment, kept her from slipping into the past, as she did with other adults whose memories tainted their emotional reaction to even the simplest event. It was only Sam and Nat who, still stepping into the twilight zone of fantasy, genuinely accepted her sometimes forced enthusiasm without judgment.

Perhaps they accepted her because it's hard for a child to find any adult who makes time for child's play. And since they did not belong to any clique, they hadn't become jaded or strongly influenced by any particular group to act in an acceptable way. True to their simple convictions, they just acted. Even in school they weren't identified with any club they hadn't organized themselves. They didn't always agree, but they supported each other, so they didn't depend on the strength of organizations.

Sam and Nat would never know, Morgan considered, what they had together, how beautifully they danced, until it was far too late, until they had tried dancing with others who might know some catchy steps, even an entire routine, but couldn't move well with the music turned off. In their perpetual state of exploration, powered by pure passion that knew no motive, she felt the seeds of what she relished about loving Jacob.

Sam and Nat's friendship reminded Morgan of the friendship she had shared with Jacob. They could talk about everything and nothing at all in the same breath. And now, Sam and Nat liked to talk to Morgan. They liked to ask her questions, especially about police work — about her new job in the 77th.

Before her transfer, she'd always given them the highlights in Sleepy Hollow: the six-year-old accused of stealing a 99-cent toy from a drug store; the mother who filed a missing-person report on her 12-year-old daughter who had disappeared with a boyfriend, and showed up several hours later with a big stuffed gorilla from a local fair; the man who reported he had been robbed, then broke down and admitted he made up the story because he spent his mother's bus money on a long shot, "Latin Lover" in the ninth at Hollywood Park; the confused 80-year-old woman wandering on a residential street under a Big Bird umbrella.

She'd wanted to give them a taste of life in the 77th after midnight. But she realized just how much she was editing from her night job, how much she couldn't tell them, how much she didn't want them to know: the pregnant woman who, scalded over half her body from someone tossing out a soup pot of boiling water, crawled into the station for help; or the teenage boy, shot, in shock, hunched and shivering on the front station steps.

Since she couldn't fill in the dots of her work life, she painted broad strokes, mostly about Moon. They'd given him the code name Mooseface. She did the Mooseface walk and Mooseface talk, sashaying hands on hips, leaning over nose-to-nose, "Lemme tell you something you'll never forget: Criminals pick on good people; cops pick on assholes." Or, mocking his confusion, she would hit her temple with the palm of her hand and rattle her head, saying, "I don't know. I'm restless. There's this restlessness in me. No matter where I am, I'm not going to be there long..."

She would improvise her Moon act until Sam and Nat bowled over laughing.

Inadvertently, she turned them on to the allure of secret investigation.

She'd been noticing a heightened interest in people watching. They hung around the front bushes with binoculars watching the bus passengers get on and off at the stop at the corner. They would scribble down details about clothes, hair, shoes, distinct mannerisms, disabilities, equipment or animals.

They would orchestrate a pretend traffic accident and fill out a collision report detailing weather, lighting, roadway surface and conditions, pedestrian's actions, and special information about hazardous materials, fires or defective tires.

When she would take them to the market, they would jot down details on pads they kept in their back jean pockets. While Morgan walked down the aisles filling the shopping cart with groceries for the week, they would position themselves at discreet locations in the store. When they found a good suspect, they would locate Morgan maybe — somewhere in produce picking through green beans. Siding up to her, Sam would whisper, "We got a 4204A, drinking alcohol in public, out by the newspaper stand," or Nat would swing past her at the meat counter and quietly confirm another 4115, dog in prohibited area.

Just the day before they'd surprised her at work. Morgan had called late in the morning to say she had to be in court all day and wouldn't have time to come home before she had to go to work. She would grab a bite at Tia's Tacos. In one of their bursts of inspiration, Sam and Nat decided to surprise Morgan and intercept her at the 77th station.

Later, Morgan pieced together a version of their escapade. They'd invited each other over, called their respective homes and claimed to be at each other's house for dinner, then they pooled their change and hopped on the local RTD.

When they stepped off, they were in the throes of disagreement. "I'm telling you, Sam," Nat held her by the arm, "I seen 'em lift this guy with just his five fingers. Five fingers, I'm telling ya."

"In your dreams," she rolled her eyes. "You can't — "

A boy whisked a satchel from the back of a woman's baby stroller and darted across the street.

Sam yelled, "484!" and chased after him, screaming repeatedly, "484! 484! 484!"

She sprinted across the 77th Police Station parking lot past Moon who had just pulled up in his car. Moon hauled his dry cleaning out of the backseat and slammed the driver's door, looking up to witness Sam overtake the boy thief, knock him to the ground, sit on him and pound on him.

"Holy shit!" Moon tossed his pressed shirts on the hood and bolted across the asphalt towards the fight, just as Morgan pulled into the opposite end of the parking lot, and recognized Nat running past.

Moon wedged his knee in Sam's back, leaned over and clasped her wrists, pulling her off the thief. Sam wrestled, yelling, "Nat!" as the thief scrambled to his feet. "Don't let him get away, Nat!" She watched Nat almost overtake him, until the swift robber scrambled over a block wall that Nat had to stop and think about. He banged his fist on it, and Sam just shook her head sadly.

Her wrists firmly wrenched behind her back by a strange man, Sam spied her mother running towards her and, indicating the block wall, gasped, "Ripped off…lady with stroller…"

Morgan smiled at Sam, then said simply to Moon, "You can let go of her: she's not going anywhere. She's mine."

Moon shot Morgan a querulous look, to which she nodded reassuringly, and he released Sam's wrists. "Sam, this is Officer Moon." Morgan indicated with a nod, then resting her hand on Sam's shoulder, she informed Moon, "This is my daughter, Samantha, and her friend, Nat."

Coolly respectful, Sam dipped her head. "Hello," she said, adding halfheartedly under her breath, "Me and Nat was hoping to get a load of that 'Mooseface' guy you been telling us about."

Moon and Morgan exchanged an awkward look, and Sam, suddenly sensing Officer Moon and Mooseface might be one in the same, looked to Nat, whose alarmingly bugged-out eyes confirmed it. With considerable poise, Sam turned and held out her hand to Moon, "Nice to meet you…" she darted a glance at Morgan, and then added, almost as a code word to a private club, "Mooseface."

As follow-up training to prepare them for their next encounter with a thief on the loose, Morgan had taken Sam and Nat to the Academy that afternoon. They followed Morgan up the Police Academy Hill to the obstacle course.

Nat muttered to Sam, "How come she still comes here if nobody's making her?"

"C'mon," Sam said, as if he was really too far gone to straighten out. "Let's see if you can climb this ten-foot wall as good as you could build it."

After several failed attempts to secure footing over the thrashed hunk of wood, Nat slumped against a tree trunk to rest. "It's okay," Sam assured him, "it took me a few tries to make it over." She stood next to him, hands on her hips, admiring the battered wood wall covered with shredded pieces of canvas padding that dangled from the top, testament to its years of use.

One of the Academy rookies recognized Morgan and called out, "Officer Fraser, ma'am, do you have a minute to show us how to…" she motioned to the wall.

Sam jabbed Nat in the ribs. "Watch."

Morgan scaled the wall nimbly.

With renewed energy, Sam turned to Nat, who was gawking at the wall as if it were Mt. Everest. "All right, Nat, which is your strong foot?"

"I don't know. I think I'm *ambeedendress*," he responded, staring wide-eyed at the jagged circular scar chipped from the wall's midsection.

"Well," she said, shrugging, "just start running all out and throw your strong foot on the wall. Put your hands on top and you'll blast right over. Go!"

Nat started, then stopped, thinking.

"What? What are you doing?"

Staring at the wall, trying to figure out what to do, he finally looked at her and shrugged, "I don't know."

"Then just don't think about it."

He hesitated.

"Go!" She hollered, and he jerked to a start. She yelled at his back, "C'mon Nat, there's a dude on the other side, with a gun, and he's got your partner — "

Nat hit just a fraction of an inch below the top of the wall, flew backwards like a spring and landed in the sawdust.

Sam raced up to him, "Way to go! Do you know how close you came? You were so close. This close." She indicated almost touching her thumb and index finger. "Try it again."

Knocked a little senseless, Nat shook his head, "No."

"Nat!" She plastered her face up against his, insisting, "You have to do your absolute max every time."

"Says who?"

"My dad," she poked his chest with her index finger, "that's who."

"Great," Nat mumbled, "he's dead." Then, sensitive to the hurt snap in Sam's eyes, he made a vague apologetic gesture, relenting. "Okay. Okay."

In spite of numerous attempts, Nat never made it over the wall that afternoon, so it was no wonder, thought Morgan, that his energy and enthusiasm for finishing the treehouse sagged with the setting sun. Later, by early evening, when Gramma Sofie's ride, a '65 Chevrolet, turned into the driveway and scraped along a hedge, finally coming to a clumsy stop, Nat was lying on the ground, his head on a wood block. Gramma Sofie, in her summer hat covering a white babushka, stepped out of the backseat and sweetly bade a Yiddish good-bye to several of her Jewish Center bridge chums. Turning around, she first saw Nat sprawled on the ground, then spied Sam balancing on a ladder, hammering the tree. "Samantha Lynn Fraser," she hollered, holding forth her assumed authority in any given situation, "get down from there before you kill yourself!"

Sam just hammered harder.

The kitchen was hot and stuffy that evening. Morgan filled bell peppers with hamburger meat while Sam, restlessly shuffling from one foot to the next, helped Gramma Sofie make a pie crust. Sam glanced wistfully at her nearly finished treehouse from the kitchen window. She jabbed the pie crust with her index finger.

"Don't touch it," warned Gramma Sofie, "you'll make it tough."

Sam grit her teeth and went back to chopping apples.

"Well, Nightwatch has worked pretty smoothly this week," Morgan said, entirely ignoring Gramma Sofie's heavy sigh, "but I miss not eating dinner together. So, Sam, now that baseball practice is over, can you be in by four o'clock so we can all eat an early dinner together?"

"Four!" Sam choked on an apple.

"Is there more butter in the box in the garage?" Gramma Sofie asked.

"Yes," Morgan nodded, but made no move to get it. She waited for Gramma Sofie to exit before she informed Sam that on work nights she had to stay inside after supper. Morgan didn't want Sam disappearing outside or at Nat's house until way after dark so that Gramma Sofie had to stand at the front door repeatedly calling her name.

Sam protested. "Mother," she put down the knife and scowled at Gramma Sofie walking to the garage. "I'm not a baby, and I don't see why she has to watch after me."

Morgan hugged her, fully aware that Sam's construction interests did not jibe with Gramma Sofie's expectations of her granddaughter as a placid, if not mild-mannered hygienic child — a little charmer for whom she could make frilly doll clothes and to whom she could serve lukewarm tea in tiny, delicate china cups. Gramma Sofie would never understand that cleanliness and china are anathema to explorers.

Sam filed her complaint. "Gramma Sofie won't even let Nat in the house when you're not here."

"I'll talk with her about that."

"Me and Nat don't have anything to do inside."

"Nat and I. Do homework."

"Homework!" Sam blurted. "Summer school homework's nothing." She flipped open her math book on the counter and defiantly pointed to her written homework. "There, figuring interest and bank borrowing, done."

"Where's your work?"

"Right there." She waved at a column of numbers.

"Those are answers. How did you get them?"

"With the calculator. My teacher says I can use a calculator."

"Wrong-o."

Sam made a wry expression. "Oh great. Wait'll Nat hears." She picked up the phone receiver, then, remembering, set it back in its cradle and sighed, "I can't speak to him before sunrise."

Morgan gave an affirming nod, encouraging without patronizing the early morning stage play to which Sam and Nat had earnestly committed themselves. For the last three Sundays they had met at the crack of dawn in the scrap metal dump behind the house.

From the second story bathroom window, Morgan witnessed their act. They didn't speak at first. They acknowledged one another with a stiff handshake. Then standing back to back, they gripped their saber-length curtain rods and carefully paced ten steps forward. One of them said, "Go." Then Sam leapt in a fitful start towards Nat, running towards him in a rush, madly waving her weapon. He usually stepped to the side when she flew by, as if he didn't have the heart to stab her senseless while she was out of her mind.

Watching them, it was apparent they were playing together, but not the same game. Nat understood the use of foil, epee and saber. He even mastered a couple of sophisticated moves to the torso with the foil after Morgan had shown him. Solemn and calculating, he had a sense of honor at stake. It was easy to imagine him calmly stating in the midst of a duel between himself and another gentleman: "Halt, blood has been drawn, honor has been satisfied."

Sam, on the other hand, brandished her weapon like a tomahawk.

10

NICKERSON GARDENS

Alma Blocker grew up in Nickerson Gardens and told Morgan that she could distinguish between the night sounds of a car backfiring, a Smith & Wesson, a woman's voice shrieking, a Glock, a door slamming, an M-16. Unlike the rest of the 77th Division, Nickerson Gardens was an entity unto itself. After the military stopped using it, the cement block, prison-like units became a federal housing project, a sprawling public apartment complex in the middle of a residential area. Then, after the Korean War in the fifties, it fell into disrepair, and the area soon became a Los Angeles Housing nightmare, the largest and most troubled public housing project, riddled with assaults and vandalism.

During her two weeks of Nightwatch in Nickerson Gardens, Moon had run Morgan into the ground on a footbeat through a dark maze of sidewalks, tenements and alleys. He ordered her to confront raucous drunks and dope dealers hanging around liquor stores and move them off the street, while he loomed over bookmakers resting on telephone booths, waiting to take bets. She summed up her first two weeks with Moon on her tapes: *He ribs me every chance he gets, complains about dickless cops,*

insists on driving. His parting words last night were, Sleep tight,
Barbie doll.

She knew, but for the time being forgot, that Moon was the
type of experienced officer who entertained himself by looking for
conflicts that put new partners, especially women, into situations
where they had to confront people who they wouldn't normally
even greet on the street. She wasn't at all happy about his
personalized hazing ritual, but she figured if she just overlooked
his wisecracks and pranks, eventually he would lighten up and they
could discuss old-style policing that she noticed had failed to stop
drug dealing in residential neighborhoods.

She had been talking about community policing with Blocker.
They had already agreed that unless police dedicated long hours to
surveillance they couldn't catch dealers in the act to make legitimate
arrests that would stand up in court. So what they needed was more
emphasis on helping local residents to organize and take action
around their schools, on their streets, in their housing projects.

When she mentioned to Moon the idea of infusing traditional
strong-arm policing with a community partnership using problem-
solving, other agencies and interpersonal skills to show folks how
to become more powerful about their own environment, he
laughed, assuring her that these people didn't give a fuck about
their environment.

"You are so wrong," she said.

"Let me get this straight," Moon said, kicking a beer can into
the gutter. "You're trying to tell me that people in this community
could be taught to pick up their own damn shit, so that their streets
are not attractive to drug dealers."

"They need to be given the support to clean up the area, board
up vacant houses, clean up graffiti, repaint buildings, haul away
abandoned cars."

"Oh yeah," he grinned, gesturing to the area with an open palm,
"I can see these lowlifes cleaning up their shit."

"I've checked into this, and they're already doing it in St. Louis,"
she said, "Cochran Gardens project. How are they doing it, you ask?"

"Don't put words in my mouth."

"By putting people who live there in charge."

They walked across a side street towards a liquor store. Moon was silent. Trying to put the situation in perspective, Morgan made the mistake of telling him what he was thinking, "You see, you have a tendency to think that big problems need big solutions."

"Did I say that?"

"No, but you act like these people are so lazy and incapable they couldn't possibly make a difference in their community."

"And you make it sound like a U-haul truck and a couple of dozen buckets of Mr. Clean will turn this into *Leave it to Beaver* land — "

"Wrong again. What makes you think for one minute anyone but you wants to live next to the Cleavers?"

"What I'm telling you is this place doesn't need paint and soapsuds, it needs a night gas blanket," Moon said, pausing for a moment to let it sink it. "We need to block off Watts to Inglewood and just send a lethal fog over the area."

"Knock it off."

"See, if I time it just right, the good people would be asleep in bed. They would never know what hit 'em; and the assholes, like always, would be out on the streets, lying down though, real still. Easy to scoop into a garbage truck."

"If people knew they were paying their tax money to have somebody like you protect them, they'd — "

"Love me. Because I tell it like it is. I don't fuck around with these little community touchy-feely policing ideas."

"You're crazy. You haven't listened to a thing I've said."

"Jesus H. Christ. Yes, I'm crazy, Morgan. What would happen if you took somebody from 1890 and put him in 1980? That's me. Like it or no, I'm stuck in the wrong fucking century. A hundred years ago, they'd've thought nothing of gassing horse thieves."

She stood silent a moment, staring into the liquor store.

"All right," he said, "maybe the gas idea is lower than whale dung today. I'm a little eccentric. Ideals that nobody understands."

"Don't flatter yourself. Those *ideals* go back way before the SS. And they're not complex. Neither are you."

"Ha," he nudged her playfully, "now, you're playing my song. Bet you don't even know how they chose the SS. Five generations of racial purity to be an officer. Three generations of racial purity to be enlisted. SS troops trained for two years. Officers graduated from Heidelburg, most were Prussian, most had Von preceding their name."

She made an effort to look at him directly, her eyes unblinking. It was impossible for her to even talk about that kind of social injustice that punched the spirit out of a life. Hostile, upset, trapped together for eight hours, they were forced to interact with one another, and therefore themselves.

He shrugged, "Okay, okay. Wanna talk about the American POWs in El Salvador?" Her head turned away slowly without a word. "No. All right. Let's try your community partnership approach." Moon stretched out his arms, palms open, making a sweeping pretense to compassion. "Helping folks recognize and clean up the little problems — trash in the gutter, graffiti on the walls, gambling on the streets." He nodded towards the liquor store alley where a half dozen guys were huddled around in a circle. "Craps," Moon said to her under his breath. "That's gambling." He shook his head and sighed. "You better go over there and tell them they can't play craps on the street or we'll have to take 'em in."

"I don't think so."

"It's the law," he assured her, shrugging. "Not on the street. Gotta draw the line somewhere. I'll back you up."

"Yeah, like with the Muslims."

He shrugged, tough luck, "You didn't see that one coming, first night and all." He jabbed her with his elbow in the upper arm. "C'mon, let's help the community help themselves."

Morgan took a swift, sobering breath and started towards the group, which, by the time she had made her way around a couple of broken crates, an abandoned, rusty jalopy and a metal can burning trash, had stopped playing. Her voice hung over the whites of their eyes like the first chord of a death march in the sluggish air. "Gotta take your game off the street, fellas," she said. They made no move to leave, so she stretched her hand out towards a dude palming the dice. He gave no indication of giving them to her, so she said simply, "Hand them over."

A couple of guys shook their heads in disbelief, then glanced to Moon, standing several yards away, smiling to himself. The two guys grinned in Morgan's face and the rest of the group chortled wisecracks, cursing the interruption.

Morgan, dead serious, was steadfast, and, refusing to enlist Moon's support, didn't turn to see his openly amused expression.

She opened a set of handcuffs and looked towards the dice thrower. "It's interesting to see you find handcuffs so funny." She watched him toss the dice in the air a couple of times with his left hand. A lefty. She always noticed lefties.

The dice thrower looked from Morgan to Moon to his buddies, then back to Morgan. He sniffed several times, wiped his nose on his sleeve, then stood obligingly, ignoring the snickers to his right and left. He handed Morgan the dice. "You know," he leaned toward her, indicating the handcuffs, and said, almost kindly, "We all can't fit in there." He eyed her steadily, waiting.

"My partner has a pair as well." She looked squarely into his sunken, bloodshot eyes.

He nodded repeatedly. She shifted her weight so she could feel her feet firmly planted on the asphalt, then added sensibly, "Look, it's simple, don't gamble in public or…" She paused, half assuming that the authority her uniform represented would give weight to the unfinished ultimatum.

Again, no response. A solitary despairing cry wrested her heart. They had no intention of moving. Nothing short of dynamite could make them. Or worse, a chill ran down her back: Moon. She would have to call him for assistance to move or cuff these harmless guys playing craps. Both Morgan and the dice thrower knew, standing toe to toe, by herself, she didn't have a chance in hell to get even one of them in the police car, let alone all of them to the police station.

"You got a good head," the dice thrower lowered his voice, darting a glance to Moon. "And I gonna make these dudes move outta here tonight, but we be back tomorrow night like always. This our spot, been our spot for years. Next time your partner there set you up like this, you tell 'em to go fuck hisself."

She flushed slightly as she grasped the truth of the hoax. She felt Moon laughing behind her back, but she kept her cool. She held the dice thrower's red-weary eyes and smiled discreetly. "I s'pose you pitch pennies, too."

No, he shook his head. "Dominoes. Fact, they call me Domino."

"Domino," she repeated. "Officer Fraser." She shook his left hand with hers. "Pleased to meet you. I don't have a problem with you gentlemen playing craps back here," she said, deciding she had to pick her battles and this wasn't one of them. "Seems you've claimed it as your space, so do you have any objection to working together to move that rust heap out of here and trash those crates?"

A few shrugs of minimal approval to Domino. "Sure thing. Shadow," he indicated the muscular, poker face next to him, "he's our Mr. Clean. He'll take care of if." Several low chuckles moved through the still immobile group. "Night, Officer Fraser," Domino turned and indicated for his buddies to rise and disperse.

Morgan watched them begrudgingly get up and saunter out of the alleyway. Then she turned, glided back to Moon, and uttered in passing, "Go fuck yourself."

Grinning, he tilted his head to one side. "Wrong way," he called out.

But she didn't respond. She was already heading towards Nickerson Gardens projects and acted as though she didn't hear him. He turned, crossing the street, and caught up to her. They walked through tenement life punctuated by sounds of dissonant rap, rock, jazz crisscrossing and muting a baby's cry, a television game show, a mother calling her son from his gang loitering on the dirt lawn. Morgan watched the boy amble inside, dodging toddler toys and a half-filled plastic pool. She stood over several neat rows of redwood-framed vegetable plots: some droopy tomatoes and limp greens. "Looks like somebody's trying to do something positive."

Moon waved away any sense of hope. "Kids'll just dig up the plants and have tomato fights."

They walked for a long time and didn't speak. Wary, Morgan was intrigued by the hostile, cold, passive looks from gang types, from residents rocking on their porches, taking out trash, unpinning work shirts and underpants from the clothes line.

"That's a blowjob hole," Moon informed her, breaking the silence, indicating an overgrown bush in front of a torn screened porch that camouflaged the action but not the sound of panting from the other side. Morgan moved to detour.

Moon touched her elbow. "Keep straight," he said quietly, then added, tauntingly, "unless you're ready to head back."

They passed the amorous gasps, then some distance away, at a fork in the sidewalk, stopped. "See, was it that bad?" he asked.

"No," she assured him coolly, "I just feel like we're walking through their living room, bedroom, bath."

"You are. It's your beat. You have to know it. And they have to know you're not afraid in here, and that you know the traps."

"You mean the clotheslines that choke you in a foot pursuit, the potholes that trip you up, the dogs that rip you apart?"

"That, and, of course, the local…flora and fauna."

He plucked a gardenia from behind him and presented it to her.

They walked in silence again for a few blocks, then Moon just couldn't help himself. "You know, Morgan," he chuckled, "you're pretty sharp for a girl. But there's really not one fucking thing you can beat me at. Doesn't that bother you? I can outwrestle you, outrun you and outswim you. There's not one thing you can do better, except make babies, and even then I have to assist. I can cook, iron, vacuum, sew — "

"Fence," she blurted, fiercely confident. "You can't out-fence me."

"So what?"

"So what?" She could tell from his jeering expression that he knew absolutely nothing about fencing and that training gap punctured his physical prowess.

She forced the issue. "So, it's something I can do better than you."

His brisk voice boomed, "En guard," and he feigned a jabbing move with his swordless hand. "You're dead."

She stopped walking. His pitiable fencing knowledge was not even worth addressing. "Look, just let up." He paused, staring at her as she laid it on the line. "I get the picture, okay? You may think I can't teach you a damn thing, but I'm learning a helluva lot about what not to do from working with you in spite of your racist, fascist, sexist bullshit. And you're stuck with me, so you can just knock off the verbal abuse because it doesn't become you, number one, and number two, that kinda crap is not going to make me run crying uncle to Captain Drummond."

"Dithers," he corrected, then eyed her with an attitude of perplexity. "We call him Dithers, and Lieutenant Herdahl is Our Baby Dumpling."

Stonefaced, she regarded him. "Very clever. We, I suppose refers to your little MAW group I've been hearing about." He shrugged, not quite hiding his dismay that he'd let a MAW confidence slip out to a policewoman. "And what do you call yourselves?" she looked at him, waiting for an answer that didn't come, so she suggested Alicia's reference, "The muppets?" With that she turned and continued walking alone, but her words left a trail of light behind.

Moon stood a while longer watching her back, possibly intrigued. She wondered. No, not possible. Then he called after her. "Okay, you're on. Fencing. Tomorrow. Twenty-one hundred hours. The Academy gym."

She kept walking. "Don't wimp out," she said, not daring to turn around for him to notice her irrepressible smile.

The next morning Morgan was staring at the coffee pot, waiting for the first sign of amber liquid to drip, marveling at the bonds of friendship that had roped her up at that hour. She'd had the weekend off, until Alicia convinced her to spend Saturday morning as a panelist for the Equal Opportunities Development Department, Alicia's EODD seminar to recruit women officers. When Alicia first approached her, Morgan just said no: it's Saturday; I want to sleep in — spend the morning cuddling with Sam in bed watching *Defenders of the Universe*. Absolutely not.

Alicia didn't take no for an answer. She'd planted herself between Morgan and their lockers and began her tirade on the importance of women cop role models to encourage more women to become police officers, "especially us working in the 77th, our butts on the line all the time. We're all going to be there to speak with a unified voice: It's a crime more women aren't cops," Alicia stared at Morgan, waiting for a reaction, then shrugged, admitting, "That's actually the EODD's slogan."

"I've seen the posters," said Morgan, unimpressed. She reached over Alicia's head, pulling a pair of jeans out of her locker. She started to explain why she hadn't jumped on the administrative bandwagon to recruit more women, then paused, wondering why she should bother to get into it with Alicia. Finally, she ventured, "Look, the truth is originally I didn't think I wanted to be a cop until my aunt nudged me, and I got involved in the coroner's office because I was intrigued with inexplicable death. After a while I got hooked trying to help people put the pieces of a victim's life together just so I could figure out the cause of death. I mean, at the very least family members should know why a loved one died, so they can put the mystery to bed. Move on, maybe."

Morgan reached for her socks. Alicia moved to the side, not taking her eyes off her, indicating for her to continue.

"So, after a taste of working day-to-day with people on the street, I knew my heart belonged to a foot beat. And I didn't need to go to any EODD meeting to get recruited. Did you?"

Alicia shook her head no.

"See? Did you need a bunch of women cops on a panel getting paid a few bucks to spend an entire morning trying to persuade you to tackle the Police Academy? No, right? I only completed the Academy because I had to, so I could do police work, street police work."

Morgan closed her locker, summing up, "I'm not panel material."

"How do you know? I hear you, but how do you know 'til you give it a shot?"

"What's the point? Frankly, I don't want to put my life in the hands of someone who's been enticed to do this job for money, prestige, power. Somebody who thinks it's cool to be a cop. I didn't feel very cool my first night patting down a couple of big Muslims. I felt like," she paused, "a girl."

Morgan shrugged and sighed. "I've got to do better than that," she said, describing a personal goal more to herself than Alicia. "I mean, I have to be able to physically carry out the authority of this uniform, or I'm getting equal pay," she paused, disturbed by the realization, "for less work."

Alicia thought a second, then touched her on the shoulder, "You know what I think?" she asked earnestly, and, without waiting for a response, told her, "We've got to build ourselves an outstanding group of women cops, so you've got to come to the panel on Saturday and tell them what you just told me." She eyed Morgan directly, stressing, "*Exactly* what you just said."

Amused at the prospect, Morgan smiled. "At least I wouldn't have to worry about getting invited back."

Alicia nodded, conceding the possibility. "But *I'm* asking you now because we have an opportunity here, chica, for one time in our life to build something special: Women cops *especiales.*" Alicia clenched her fist, getting worked up, "*fuertes.*" She stuck out her chest. "*Orgullosas, sensitivas.*"

Now, Morgan poured herself a cup of coffee, wondering about Alicia's presentation. The phone rang. It would wake Gramma Sofie.

Morgan jerked up, spilling her coffee as she spurted into the living room, and considered that worse than starting the morning with an EODD panel discussion would be a play-by-play of Sofie's morning pains. Every sunrise, she says, she wakes up in pain. Her hands shook so bad some mornings she couldn't put in her eye drops for glaucoma. So she would call Morgan into the bathroom for help. Trying to cheer her up, Morgan would get her to talk about the Jewish Center's agenda or her continually bickering friends, Hershel and Rebekah.

Maybe Sofie was sleeping on her side with her good hearing ear on the pillow, thought Morgan as she picked the receiver up on the fourth ring. "I'm up already. Getting dressed."

"Goooood." A man's voice, not Alicia's.

Morgan froze, listening, "Sharpening your sword?"

Why is he calling me at home? "It's sharp enough," she said, bracing for a curve ball.

"How you doing?"

She sat down. "Fine," she managed, as she mopped the coffee from her lap. "Just fine. How have you been since last night?"

"Got a new pair of tights. Forest green, and this matching blouse thing that kind of ties at the neck with a piece of shoe leather."

She paused a moment, imagining him in the Robin Hood get-up. "You gonna wear the blouse in or out?"

"Out."

How long is he going to keep up this dumb repartee? "You'll look pregnant," she said simply, and stymied his comeback.

"All right. Are we still fencing tonight at the gym?"

"Unless you called to cancel."

"Just a time change. Twenty-three hundred hours." Moon said.

"That's almost midnight."

"Very good. Too late for you?"

"No."

"Come alone. And don't wimp out." He hung up.

She stared at the receiver for a long moment. Wimp. Where did that word come from? One of his favorite stupid expressions: "what a wimp" or "pretty wimpy." Vaguely, she heard her daughter picking up speed on the wooden hall floor, and, Morgan hurried into the hall with a reproving look just as Sam was about to slide on a long throw rug.

Sam glanced up at her mother and grinned sheepishly, "Okay, let's compromise: one slide a day?"

"Not one. None."

"None is too few. C'mon, Mom, let's talk about it."

"Go talk to your pillow."

Sam frowned. "My what?"

"Clearly, the discussion we had about this just last night ran out of your ear onto your pillow."

"That's not funny, mom," she said, padding after her into the kitchen.

Morgan poured herself another cup of coffee, and set the pot back down on Sofie's needlepoint hotplate that read: *Cast Me Not Out in My Old Age But Let Me Live Each Day as a New Life.* She smiled to herself, knowing her daughter was regrouping for another attack. She had instilled in Sam a belief in her own personal power as well as the confidence to fight for what she believed in. And since most battles in preparation for life are practiced endlessly on the homefront, Morgan, ironically, wound up as Sam's main punching bag.

Morgan wiped the spilled coffee off the floor and poured herself another cup.

"You have to admit, Ma, it's a perfect sliding place."

"What if somebody happens to be coming around the hall corner at the same time you're sliding into home? You might knock them into the great dugout in the sky."

Sam smiled. "Somebody? The only somebodys are you and Gramma Sofie and," she added and discounted him in the same breath, "Nat. And besides, you can hear the sound of my feet, or I could yell 'home' like they yell 'fore' in golf." Sam followed her mother annoyingly close. "Please, Ma. Because I love you. I really, really love you so much." Sam playfully reached to kiss Morgan's hand.

"Back off, will you," Morgan snapped, then regarded Sam for a moment. From her own daughter's face, she glimpsed the carefree joy she felt as a child perched on the tree outside her friend Samantha's bedroom window. Morgan stared out the kitchen window at the treehouse and, in her mind's eye, saw her friend sitting rigidly on the bottom bunk bed, as she so often caught her, staring blankly at the closed bedroom door. Samantha, she called to her, there's life: your life continues in mine. But it was useless. Morgan couldn't penetrate the storm window that separated the living and the mysterious world of death.

Morgan felt her daughter tap her on the shoulder, opened her mouth, but she could only nod in agreement. Sam leapt up from the floor and hugged her, exulting in victory, "All right! I love it when you change your mind. Give me five!" She stopped her palm mid-air near Morgan's face.

Slapping Sam's still palm with her own, Morgan added a restriction that attached special significance to the sliding privilege, "Once. Once a day. Before school or in the morning."

Sam screwed her face, "What about Gramma Sofie?"

"I'll tell her," she said, compelled to add, knowing it was a waste of her breath, "just don't do it to irritate her."

"Ma, I don't do it on purpose, you know. Even if she says I do."

Morgan nodded. Distracted by Moon's call, she forced herself to focus on Sam and Gramma Sofie's daily battle of wills. Sam was strong-willed, but she was no match for a seventy-four-year-old who had spent her early childhood in a Polish *shtetl*, a Yiddish-speaking village, impoverished and regularly terrorized by the sudden violence of anti-Semitism at the hands of the government or hostile neighbors.

"Morgan," Sofie's thick inflection called from the hall bathroom. "when you can take a minute."

Morgan entered the bathroom to the vision of Sofie's corseted, pillowed bosom leaning over the sink, with her gray ringlets tossed back, her eyes facing the ceiling, her outstretched hand, a web of wrinkles, holding the prescription glaucoma drops.

Morgan took the tiny plastic bottle and moved next to Sofie's broad hips which burst open a red terry cloth robe to reveal thin, bowed legs, a reminder of a malnourished youth. Sofie indicated the urine-filled toilet. "When I went to the bathroom, I was afraid to flush, that I shouldn't wake you or Sam up."

Morgan brushed a morning kiss over the skin folds on Sofie's cheek. "It's okay, Sofie. Flush. We're heavy sleepers. We don't hear a thing."

"That I know. I could slip and fall in the hall. I could be on my back like a beached turtle, crying out, and you both would be heavy sleeping."

Sam leaned on the bathroom doorjamb, slipping the skin off a banana. She frowned at her mother, who shook her head as if not to get Gramma on the subject of deadly falls. Foot placement was critical. A bad fall could keep her confined to the house, away from her Jewish Center, the secure hub of her life.

Sam nodded repeatedly; alerted not to mention falling or sliding in the hall, she moved into the next important subject: food. "After this meeting thing, can we go to the House of Pancakes?"

Morgan palmed her daughter's forehead, "Are you sick? You'd miss *Silver Cats, Thunder Hawks* and *Defenders of the Universe* for a panel discussion?"

"*Silver Hawks* and *Thunder Cats*," corrected Sam. "Sure," she said grandly, "Nat's at a swim meet."

Morgan motioned for Sam to hand her a tissue to wipe the eye drops trickling down Sofie's cheek furrows.

Then, as if she might be blowing her whole Saturday, Sam asked quickly, "How long is it, anyway?"

"Just long enough for a half dozen of us to convince an

auditorium full of women that a career with the Los Angeles Police Department can be won-der-ful," Morgan sung, dancing Sam around, "challenging, presti-gee-ous, and, it's tacky to talk money, but *mucho dinero.*"

"Money is your God," Gramma Sofie said, blinking profusely. "You could get a nice job at the kosher butcher's. Saul says he would hire you, you should ever get hurt, you know what I am saying. And I know how to make do with chicken feet."

Morgan guided Sofie onto the toilet seat. "I know, Sofie."

"Sam. Take the bus with me to the Center. At noon is a film on Israel. Very educational. And today's lunch special is that nice sweet and sour tongue you like. A dollar fifty, but they would not charge full price for you."

Sam rattled her head no to her mother, as Sofie, bent over, pulling on thick hose over her ankles, spelled out the day's agenda. "Hershel, you like him, he and I are collecting money for Mexican laborers. You could help us, or Rebekah, she's not speaking to Hershel this week — they had a big fight you wouldn't believe — she's circulating petitions to abolish capital punishment. She could use your legs: her doctor says she has to have her knees replaced, but then she won't be able to walk until who knows when. What's the point? Sooner or later the eyes and legs go, and maybe, if you are lucky enough to have a bed, you toss and turn on it, toothless." She stood up, brushing her thoughts away with a wave of her hand, "Never mind, you want I should heat up the corn kugel for dinner?"

Morgan turned into the streetlit Academy parking lot. No Moon. She'd give him ten minutes, then she was leaving. Fencing. The word conjured up images of D'Artagnan, Cyrano de Bergerac, Errol Flynn, Douglas Fairbanks, Obi-wan Kenobi. No women. She was one of three women to belong to the L.A. Fencing Club that met on Sunday mornings for drilling and bouting. The other members ranged from novice to internationally-ranked fencers of all ages and backgrounds — scientific, professional, artistic, athletic, literary. Some fenced to increase their stamina, agility, concentration, eye-hand coordination, strength or balance. She fenced because she liked the silver lamé jacket they wore which covered vital organs, the valid part of the target that, when touched, earned points. Also, secretly, she wanted to perform as a Swordsman at the Hollywood Bowl.

Her Jeep hood faced the entrance, so she could easily see his Range Rover pull into the parking lot. She sagged back in the driver's seat, privately remarking: What a day. The EODD seminar was like everything else in her life: unpredictable. She supposed you would call it enlightening — at least Sam would remember it.

Once inside the women-packed auditorium, Morgan nodded to a retired male sergeant with a bad case of smiles, indicating for them to take a seat in the back of the packed room. Morgan was just about to sit down, when Alicia spotted her, and frenetically waved to Sgt. Smiles, who indicated for the panelist and her daughter to move forward. Alicia patted the seat next to her and nodded to Morgan.

Sgt. Smiles set up a folding chair in front for Sam. She settled, waving to her mother, who started to wave back, but stopped as Lola Day sashayed into the room with her distinct open-mouthed ruby grin. Morgan was tempted to get up and leave.

She reconsidered, less intimidated by the flak she would get from her peers — Alicia Hererra, Sara Ann Engels, Rhonda Slattery, and Alma Blocker — sitting at the dais, than the lengthy explanation she would have to give Sam for her abrupt departure.

"Ladies." Lola rapidly tapped the podium with a pencil. "Ladies. You see the ladies here today look nice with their make up on," she said, kicking off the discussion. "They have polished nails just like everyone else, so…" she smiled elaborately again, reassuring her audience, "when you get off duty, your friends will still know you're a girl." She paused for the collective chuckle, poking her head out in ostrich-like fashion, "You wouldn't want long nails anyway when you're out there having to pull your weapon on a day-to-day basis."

Morgan remembered Lola's feckless performance on the firing line in Fender's Academy training class. She wouldn't want to be anywhere near Lola when she pulled her weapon, with or without nails. Morgan looked away, focusing on the faces in the audience, trying to determine why they'd come and whether they would be impressed or repelled by the likes of Lola. "…All you have to say to your partner, when you lose a fake nail," Lola paused, inspired by an audience chuckle. "'Oh, wait a minute, can we stop?'" She smiled expectantly, telegraphing what she hoped would pass for a punch line: "'Do we have any crazy glue?'" She got a full house belly laugh.

Lola waited for the laughter to subside. Morgan stared at her in amazement.

"Our panelists here today are ladies from the 77th Division," Lola fanned her hand along the row of panelists. "All patrolling the streets," nodded Lola, widening her eyes and simultaneously raising her brows, implying incredulity, but in this one remarkable example, truth. "Everybody has to work patrol a year," she said, tilting her head to the side and nodding, as if she were trying to convince first day kindergartners that their mummies and daddies would really be back. "But you'll love patrol, just really love it."

The crowd was not sure. "Why, you'll learn things you never would have thought of. Truly. When I first came on the job, we were called to a bank where there was a robbery. And the bank teller said the robbers were two women, and I was like, *what?* Who would have thought women committed crimes like that?"

Morgan leaned over to Alicia. "Where's the head? I'm gonna throw up."

Alicia nodded to the side door, but rested her hand on Morgan's knee, whispering, "It kills me to admit this, but Iggy was right. He already told me she's a perfect puta." Alicia glanced in disapproval towards Lola at the podium, dubbing her, "La Lola Puta Perfecta."

Morgan settled, warming to Alicia's humor, folded her hands on the table and tried to drown out Lola by playing mental math: 13 plus 85 minus 22…

Lola straightened self-importantly, full of the promise of her rank. "We always think the purse snatcher is some guy in a T-shirt and Levis," she declared with an urbane sigh, "but sometimes it's a lady in heels who has a car waiting someplace."

…Times eleven is eight hundred thirty-six divided by three equals two hundred seventy-eight, remainder two… Just when Morgan thought she couldn't stomach another of Lola's elaborate laughs, Sgt. Smiles gave her a nod and a wink to get on with it, so she introduced Officer Alicia Herrera, who kicked off with some enticing anecdotes about her legal lewd conduct.

"Particularly in the northeast division," hinted Alicia, with her usual inflection that finger-pointed to a newsworthy revelation, "a big vice problem is male homosexual activity. For that assignment, in order to fit in, we have to keep in mind we're not all made for all assignments," she interjected, then continued with a chuckle. "I had to look like a male. Cut my hair real short." You had to wonder, thought Morgan, what attracted Alicia to policing, when she'd knock them dead as a heartthrob telenovela star.

Morgan shot a glance to Sam, who sat enrapt, unconsciously toying with her braid, watching Alicia sit down and Engels take her place at the podium.

Engels' time on the police force was chalked with even more juicy vice and undercover detective work. This morning, Engels was wearing an unprecedented touch of red lipstick, and, with her cropped tan hair blown back, was almost attractive. But her professional face was more sad than serious, as her mouth was naturally shaped upside-down, unless she was smiling. Morgan couldn't recall seeing her smile, except occasionally from a distance when she was talking with Slattery.

Engels skipped details about her private life as a closet lesbian, didn't mention her motivation for becoming a police officer — the youngest sister of five older brothers — or reveal her family's complete rejection of her personal and professional choices. She just jumped right in, as if she were reciting details from a memorized police report: "Approximately two weeks before I was to graduate, they pulled me out of the Academy for special assignment on the Hillside Strangler case. I went to Universal Studios and was made to look like victims who had long hair at the time. The city rented an apartment for me in the area where most victims had lived. I frequented the places the victims had gone. Twenty-four hours a day, including my days off," she smiled almost shyly, "I was tailed by our metro division, because we really had no idea how the strangler was operating."

Morgan noticed that Slattery, who was sitting at the end of the long table, was leaning over the faces to get a good look at Engels' lips moving, as if she was forming pictures from the words coming out of Engels' mouth.

"I'll be honest with you," Engels strayed from her notes and addressed the faces directly, making eye contact. "You're watched, and as a woman you're watched more. Have enough guts to do what you think is right and people will have respect for you. Just make up your mind to graduate from the Academy, and after that the world is literally open to you."

Several women, leaning forward, brightened and nudged each other reassuringly. Morgan wondered what Engels had had for breakfast. Get her away from the 77th, and she's a new woman. Must be the cheap locker room decor and trashy stench, not to mention the male aggravation.

Blocker, following Engels, took advantage of the women's enthusiasm and shot an arrow into their inflated confidence. She made an intensely personal smash by asking the group, "How many of you know of an abusing spouse or significant other and there's no action being taken?"

After a long ponderous silence, she nodded. "My husband, the father of my children, was a cop and one night he lit into my kids and me pretty good." She shook her head, shuddering, as if the memory, now only a photo in her mind, still conjured physical pain. "He inspired me to be a cop," she continued, "to wipe out guys like him."

Solemn faces nodded, wrapped up in Blocker's story. "When I first came on the department, the state did not have a comprehensive domestic violence policy, and if you want to bring up a subject guaranteed to make someone hate you, bring up police spousal abuse. Watch some male officers sneak out of the room. Why? Because it's law enforcement's last dirty little issue…I got rid of my man after that night," she grinned broadly. "But we got a mess of cop-abused wives, girlfriends, kids out there who are afraid to come forward…and they need your help."

She must have noticed the crowd's troubled squirms, so she stepped in front of the podium and gazed back steadily, making individual eye contact, "You have to approach it as serving the people: the ones who menstruate and the ones who don't," she smiled for the first time, and waited for the tittering to subside, then asked and answered, "Who wants to talk to an abused woman? I do. So will you, when you become an L.A.P.D. woman in blue. Why, you'll be out there every day to help a victim see what they can do.

"And don't let anybody tell you that our bodies aren't right for jumping, running, and exercising. They used to say that to my mother's basketball team in the '50s. Muscles, scowls, heavy breathing and competition aren't good for a girl. Well, like my ma used to tell me: 'You can look like a lady or not and still play ball.'"

Blocker excused herself, rushing out to chauffeur one of her teenage daughters to basketball practice; the remaining listeners leapt to their feet like giddy fans, and the sound of their wild applause followed Blocker past Sgt. Smiles out the back door.

Morgan noticed Sam standing on her chair, cheering and whooping it up.

Not an easy act to follow thought Morgan. But later, leaving the auditorium, heading towards the Jeep, Morgan figured she must have done all right when Sam said, "I like what you said, Mom."

"Which part?"

"All of it. Especially the part about you figuring out how your friend died."

Morgan frowned.

"You know, your friend Samantha."

"I didn't talk about her."

"Wasn't that why you joined that coronary office, whatever?"

Morgan considered a moment, then hit by the significance of her daughter's perceptive comment, rested her head on her palm. "You put that together, huh? Yeah, I'd say that's exactly why."

"But I thought she hung herself."

"That's how I found her."

"So?"

She looked into Sam's curious, blue eyes. One day she would have to tell her daughter what really bothered her about her friend's death because Sam was not satisfied for long with skimpy explanations. She had a mind magnetized to details — observing or unmasking them, filing or tossing them, identifying or decoding them. But Morgan could afford to hold off for a while longer. After all, this explanation wasn't quite as biologically simplistic as specifying the particulars of menstruation and breast swelling. This description was biologically simple perhaps, but so emotionally complex that it short-circuited Morgan's brain every time she tried to remember the night she found her friend.

A car door slammed, interrupting her train of thought, forcing her to scope the dark Academy parking lot. Ten minutes were up. It was a service vehicle, not Moon's. He wimped out, she decided, and decided as well that she didn't need to wait for him any longer. She was moving to leave when she spotted his Range Rover parked next to a half dozen black and whites, and she resisted the urge to turn around and drive away. She parked under a tree, turned off the ignition and stared at the keys for a long moment. Finally, she got out, popped the trunk and withdrew extra protective gear for Moon — pads, mask, lamé jacket.

Her mind raced: Okay, stay calm. Let's review, just review. Start with a pattern. Then trap him. The key to winning, she thought, pumping herself up, was to be different, expect anything.

She climbed the Academy steps. Her right foot ached. Had she forgotten to insert her orthodics? No big deal, she told herself. You can suck it up. Go for his torso, she refocused her attention. Go for his torso. She realized she was more nervous than on testing day at the Academy when she had to wrestle a 6'6" cadet. He threw her everywhere, but she got back up. No matter what Moon did, she vowed, she would have to get back up.

She reached the Academy gym door. It was ajar. She entered. At the far side of the shadowed gym, illuminated by light sneaking through an uncurtained window, Moon sat in a folding chair, leaning back against the wall, his hands resting on his lap. She crossed the wood floor, every soundless step shooting a muscle stab to her right calf and an adrenaline bullet to her heart. Approaching, she noticed he was staring out the window, his expression cold, rigid; even his thin lips were colorless.

"You beat me here," she tried to sound casual, confident even, but the words reverberated like shivers in the dark. She cleared her throat to make known her presence, "I said — "

"Sit down," he said, pointing to another folding chair next to him.

She sat, balancing the protective gear on her lap.

"I dreamt last night that we came here, and a bunch of Nightwatch guys showed up with their Playmate coolers, and they sat over there. The Nightwatch girls — " he corrected himself, "women were over here on this side."

She looked at him, silently analyzing that possibility. Could we just get this over with? No big build-ups.

"And we started sparring, or whatever you call it."

"Jousting."

He nodded. "Just you and me," he continued, "and the boys and girls. Right off you're slicing and dicing me — "

She glanced down at the floor, suppressing a smile. Not exactly what she had in mind, but she'd take it.

"You were really putting the hurt to me, not to mention that the boys were having a laugh at my expense, if you know what I mean. You just, I guess, pissed me off, so I threw the sword down and grabbed you by the throat, C-clamped you against the wall and said: 'Now here's what happens when I get tired of playing your fuckin' game.'"

She heard herself interrupt the silence in a hoarse whisper, "Humiliate me?"

"Teach you a lesson."

Morgan groped for a neutral tone. "This was a gentleman's challenge."

"Right," he said with a lavish hand swish, then a smug grin. "But I know that you wouldn't be challenging me to do this unless you knew I never did it, unless you thought you were going to be able to beat me into the ground. Right?"

"Not exactly. I thought maybe I could teach you something you didn't know." But her voice was thin, vibrating with self-doubt and, as if he were staring at her buck naked, she had the urge to cover up. Run and hide, but she rearranged the equipment.

"All I can tell you is once we get started my natural instincts would prevail. And when we get close enough, say within arms' length, I'm gonna take your fucking saber and shove it up your ass."

She forced herself to a more upright position as he leaned towards her and stared at her with a grin that split his face.

"And then we'd have to get down to some wrestling," he said. "Something you didn't count on. Something that might have happened 100 years ago. Something you can't do in some gentlemen's game with a referee saying, 'That's a wound. That's a kill.' That's a bunch of shit."

She watched him tensely.

"There's no referee on the street calling your moves a wound or a kill. There is no protection."

She should respond as her eyes flicked over his face, but she just ignored his hard look until he broke the ponderous silence. "What are you going to do with some dude who has a knife? Just say en guard? I know something about Kendo. Fencing's prob'bly not much different: you make a move, there's a counter move; you follow certain rules, right?"

Her head nodded yes too long.

"You can't think like that on the street. I wanted to teach you that tonight. You have to break the rules to stay alive. I think you hear what I'm saying, you agonize about it up here," he tapped his forehead, "but you don't get it."

He thought a moment. "I wanted you to understand in one easy lesson the sense of lag time we start developing from our very first fight." He shook his head more at himself than her, as if his goal were laughable.

The soreness in her throat seemed to move up to her entire face until her eyes ached. She blinked and closed her eyes for a second, tried to scour her mind: lag time. Of course, she'd heard it before. Lag time, lag time, she repeated to herself, hoping the repetition would drive home the urgency for an immediate connection.

Fender flashed in her mind. She saw him for an instant pacing in front of her Academy weapons class. Fender turning, hands on hips, an icon of authoritarianism, his chiseled scowl moving down the line of cadets, until he stopped on Morgan to deliver his lag time speech for the umpteenth time. Her attention then was riveted on Fender's lips forming every sound. "So when he moves, he will fire at the same time as you, or beat you, everytime. Every-fucking-time." His glare of steely self-control stared Morgan down.

Now, she longed for a moment alone to pull herself together, but she opened her eyes and nodded. "Lag time. Yeah, I've heard of it."

"Hitting somebody is lag time too," Moon continued whatever he'd been saying that her string of thoughts momentarily blocked out. "I know how to hit a man who figures I might hit him, but I can hit him without him knowing when I'm gonna throw that blow because I know how it feels to be in his shoes, trying to figure out if somebody's going to hit me or not: I have the experience to know what he's looking for." Moon paused, checking her expression to judge if his pearls of wisdom were falling on deaf ears.

She dropped her eyes, suddenly insulted that he would spend so much of his off time, her time, patronizing her, explaining things he believed she could never really understand. Of course, she understood. Why did he show up? Fender had probably given him his version of her poor perimeter search performance at the Academy — evidence of lag time. Well, she'd done a superb job in that mock outdoor search, chasing the "perp," a drinking buddy of Gladstone's, so it didn't come as a big surprise when Gladstone lied to Fender — said she'd fired after the "perp" and in a real situation she would have been dead. Morgan didn't need this monkey's ass to lecture her about lag time.

"This guy," Moon rattled on, "who's waiting to see if I'm gonna hit him, is going to look for a real tenseness, a real iron look to my eyes, cold stare, a dilation of my pupils, my adrenaline starting to go. He's going to watch my hands, watch my feet, every muscle in my face." He paused a moment, as if this was the direction he intended the conversation to take.

The skin on the back of her hands tightened, as though by electric shock. She willed herself to speak, "I know, you could break my face, just like that," she snapped her fingers. "I know…" *You macho crock of shit.* She gulped her thoughts, bent down and collected the protective gear. *Keep cool. Keep cool. Relax your face muscles. You blow up, he wins.* With every ounce of energy she could muster, she forced her bloodless legs to stand and soberly hold her up. Look him in the eyes…in the eyes damnit, she commanded herself. Breathe. Again. Make him wait.

She regarded him soberly for a moment. "I've gotta get home. Sam's waiting to hear how I sliced and diced you."

Then she turned and disappeared, with only the faintest limp, across the floor into discreet shadow.

11

CHOKEHOLD

The women's locker room was more humid than usual for mid-June, the third week of Morgan's assignment to the 77th. Dressing for Monday Nightwatch was like steaming oneself in a giant's pressure cooker filled with rancid mangoes and pumpkins. Old Man Worsley was still dumping his trash in the 77th alley bins. Now, his backyard was a jungle web of pumpkin vines and mango trees; his rotten produce, an inedible pulpy mass, found its way into the dumpster outside the women's locker room, and the occasional warm breeze wafted this promising compost through the only open window. Morgan felt light-headed, tried to inhale deeply and couldn't catch her breath, but assured herself the air outside would be better than in this bacteria crock pot.

The smog levels weren't good either. She sat on the corner of the bench thinking about the smog. No smog alert today, but she could feel it swelling the passage in her lungs. What if she had to chase down a suspect tonight? What if air pollution affected the Olympic Games that started in less than six weeks?

Worried about the air quality and the estimated 11,000 Olympic athletes, especially the long distance runners, soon to arrive from 140 countries, Morgan hadn't been focused on the conversation around her. Alicia was informing her Moon was taking a few days off, that he hardly ever took time off and when he did he went to the river to water ski.

"Yeah," noted Slattery, with a tinge of hostility, "with his immature friends, to water ski, drink beer and chase bikinis. What a man!"

Morgan noticed a glance pass from Engels to Slattery and realized Engels rarely talked about men. She reamed Fender at every opportunity, but he was more monster than man. About men, Engels rarely had anything good, bad or indifferent to say. Morgan was thinking maybe that was the one thing they had in common: not to use the locker room as a complaint backboard or gossip forum. Gossip, like a shared movie experience, offered a common link, a springboard for lively discussion. Morgan had been half expecting Alicia to ask for the scoop on Moon's fencing challenge Saturday night, but Alicia didn't mention it. Moon must not have said anything to Iggy.

And Morgan reasoned, as she left the locker room and went to get change for a Hershey bar, that since the midnight duel placed Moon alone with a woman officer, it was unlikely he would rejoice in her humiliation to one of his MAW sidekicks, even Iggy. He would, of course, upon his return from water skiing, gloat in the privacy of their patrol car. She banged the antique dispenser, pressing her candy bar selection, then jimmying the silver return button, until something dropped with a thud. She slipped her hand in the tiny door, withdrew a roll of mints and frowned at the machine. "Spearmints? Really?"

She walked in the squad room a few minutes before roll call, and Blocker already had Alicia's ear. "The way we deal with our cocaine problem makes it worse: we got ourselves all these centers for cocaine addiction and what not. And what I'm saying is, you know *that* money would be better spent to kick the Columbian government in the balls."

"Cojones," Alicia nodded.

Whether on the men's or women's side of the roll call aisle, crime in the 77th was so chronically drug-related that conversations invariably slid into users and abusers of rock, cocaine, PCP. Most officers scored a couple of drug arrests a day. But they could each get a dozen arrests if they wanted. What was the point? It felt like they were using straws to chip their way through a wall of ice. The tidal wave of street drugs was so mind-boggling, its current pulling under so many inner city children, that it drowned their hope to ever do anything but help keep some heads above water.

Blocker was an exception. She wasn't satisfied with throwing out a few life rafts for the homeless and the addicts. She would arrest as many narcotics violators as she could every day, all day, which meant she spent endless hours filling out paperwork; she was in court several afternoons a week, plus working Nightwatch, plus being a single mother of two children. She had no personal life.

Alicia had told Morgan she suspected it was Blocker's narcotics crusade that made her strange — too intense to befriend. But witnessing the young lives of her neighborhood children defined by addicts and pushers was a personal affront Blocker was committed to fight through her church, her community, her police work.

Blocker blazed, "I got no sympathy for anyone into drugs. It's kind of like somebody who says, 'Well, I'm gonna play with matches now and if anything catches on fire because I drop one or fall asleep, would y'all please take care of me, feel sorry for me?'"

Teddy Bear called out, "Maybe even put up some kind of burn center with a big statue of me out front."

Blocker nodded, "You got that right."

"Blocker," asked Slattery, "what's the difference between rock cocaine and cocaine?"

"Oh," Blocker said, without taking a breath, "just the way you ingest it." Slattery frowned. "Ingest it, you know. With cocaine you horn it or snort it. Makes you high, alert, kind of like an amphetamine, and you can pretty much function. But when you smoke rock, it smacks the brain within seconds." She punched a fist into her open palm.

"Guys say it's like coming for twenty minutes," Teddy Bear piped in, "so you can imagine the hook."

Bow Wow chuckled. "I've heard a lot of guys say sex isn't for shit after you use rock cocaine."

Teddy Bear shook his head. "Damn straight, they'll take rock over sex anytime. No wonder we've got such a motherfucking drug problem."

Fender strolled in, preoccupied with a crossword puzzle. He almost collided with Iggy, who was turning away from the bulletin board next to the door. Iggy was still persona non grata, so Fender ignored him. Already bent out of shape, Fender noticed Alicia sitting in his special padded seat in the center back of the room, and he poked her backside with his baton to nudge her out. She didn't move.

"Oh, you like that," Fender said, eyeing his baton. "Course mine doesn't have a vibrator like yours does."

Alicia averted her eyes, stating simply, "That's sexual harassment, Officer Fender." Alicia flicked a glance across the room at Iggy.

"Right," Fender declared with a bombastic smile, "and you should go report me. I'm sure the Captain can see you right away, and make sure while you have his undivided attention, you illustrate the proper way to eat a banana."

Lieutenant Herdahl rolled in and caught Fender in mid-pantomime. "You know, a banana," he said. Leaning over almost in Alicia's face, but not waiting for a response, he put the back of his hand on his neck and pushed his head towards his lap, then looked up at her and twitched his eyebrows.

"You're sick," Alicia said simply and turned away.

"Sit down, Fender." Herdahl barked, indicating the only remaining lopsided folding chair.

Fender bristled with a vaguely military flourish and executed a circle around the metal chair. "I'll stand," he answered, shooting her a sharp eye.

Morgan could tell Herdahl was in no mood for any chit-chat. She ran the weekly video update from Parker Center, then called out the assignments. Fender must have persuaded Slattery it was in her best interest to refuse to work with him. Whatever she'd told her supervisor worked: Herdahl partnered Morgan with Slattery; Fender with Teddy Bear. Morgan didn't think twice about carrying their equipment outside the station to the patrol car, while Slattery followed empty-handed, complaining about their car being banged up, with no air-conditioning. "No power locks even," she grimaced. "I thought all these had power locks."

"Nope," Morgan forced a smile, "but the new ones are going to be telepathic, then you don't have to do a thing."

"Excellent," Slattery said, bending her head towards her right shoulder and cracking her neck.

In the patrol car, Slattery talked endlessly. She gave a full hour recap of her childhood, focusing on what she considered to be her only achievement: tennis. And even in tennis, she didn't excel. She wasn't a winner. Although she enjoyed the game, she didn't have a competitive head. She hated being out there all alone. She preferred playing doubles, that way she could share the embarrassment of losing. She admitted to a power serve and a driving backhand. Her partner had a weaker serve, but a stronger combative mind. Believing they were going to win, her partner entered the court on the offense, a winner. Slattery stepped onto the court worrying about what she would say to her parents after they lost. How she would deal with an evening of them pretending that "winning" really didn't matter.

Slattery detailed the California teenage tennis scene, then rambled on for another solid hour about how police training had made her more aware of her environment. "It still hasn't given me more courage though. I saw a lizard's little head sticking out from my bedspread, and I just flew out of bed. I do not like things that crawl," she shuddered, adding firmly, "I never will. I don't care what I do for a living. But I made myself tiptoe back over to the bed, and do you believe it: he was seven inches."

No, it was hard to believe. Slattery was hard to believe. Morgan thinking it was hard to believe she was putting her life in the hands of a partner afraid of lizards. "So," Morgan ventured, considering everyone was afraid of something, and it was unlikely they would have to defend themselves against lizards, "no big deal, you're just not brave about lizards."

"Oh no," Slattery said with intent earnestness, "and creepy crawlers and bugs and pretty much just about anything that flies."

Morgan's heart sunk.

"Code 3," the Dispatcher's monotone charged the air, "possible peeping Tom Suspect at 1682 Florence. Car 4."

And their first call, a 314.1 Indecent Exposure, restored her confidence in Slattery.

While Morgan walked the grounds around the 1930's clapboard house, checking out the chipped paint, ripped screens, rotted wood porch, Slattery interviewed the seventy-year-old victim next to her groomed vegetable and flower garden, obtaining the necessary information to write a truly terrific sex crimes report, which she read aloud to Morgan back in the patrol car: "Victim in rear yard watering her flowers."

"Watering," Morgan repeated. "After midnight?"

Slattery nodded, reading, "'I volunteer at the hospital during the day,'" Victim states, "'so the only time I can water is late at night.'"

Morgan winced. "That's weak, but you gotta do what you gotta do."

"Oh, just wait, it gets better." Slattery continued reading, "While watering, the victim observes object sticking through a knot hole in the back yard fence. Upon closer inspection, victim notices it to be a penis." Slattery paused, dramatizing the build up, "'When I realized it was a penis and the owner was, well, rubbing it,'" Victim says, "'I just ignored it and continued watering my plants for a couple of minutes.'"

"Unbelievable," Morgan turned the corner, following a Porsche that had just pulled out of an alley with its lights off.

"Victim finally becomes upset when she sees penis pee in her flower bed," Slattery glanced over, flashing a knowing grin. "Victim runs into house, calls L.A.P.D, and returns to backyard to find suspect gone. Victim cannot ID suspect as she only saw his penis."

"Outstanding report, Slattery, outstanding."

She beamed. "Suspect was probably my ex," she half laughed. And Morgan could feel she was on the brink of a car confession. Morgan's most important conversations with Sam always happened in the car, driving, when she was distracted, yet focused just enough to listen, but unable to react — something like a mock priest at the wheel.

"He had a thing for sticking his penis in empty holes." Slattery shrugged as if there was nothing to be done about it, then confided, simply, "One morning at breakfast he told me I was not adventurous or pretty enough for him. And he had other women who were much better in bed. So what was in it for him, really." She waved her hand in front of her face, brushing away the memory, then she dipped her head, faintly admitting, "I wanted to tell him we'd never had sex when I didn't watch the digital clock." She paused a moment, remembering, then added, "And that he always came in under three minutes, twenty seconds."

She forced a taut smile. "So, I had to get a job and my hairdresser said she was becoming a cop."

Before Morgan could think of something consoling to say, the driver of the Porsche veered over and parked at the curb. She turned the corner, did a U-turn in the middle of the block, flicked off the headlights and hugged the curb, waiting. Thirty seconds later, the Porsche sped by and she pulled out behind him, giving their position into the radio mike: "Vermont and Hughes."

She hit the lights.

"Why are you flashing him?" Slattery asked.

"License plate is muddy, car is clean, no back taillight and he's trying to shake me." She had been watching the car long enough to notice it jerk a little bit between shifts, as if the driver hadn't quite mastered shifting the precision gears with an owner's smooth finesse.

The Porsche pulled into a boarded-up gas station.

Both Slattery and Morgan got out. Slattery indicated she would go, so Morgan stayed back. The earlier breeze had worked itself into a gust of warm, dry air that brushed against Morgan's face. She watched Slattery walk to the driver's side and ask, with about as much commitment as a Universal Tour guide, "Will you step out of the car with your hands above your head?" Slattery brushed an index finger across her right eye.

The driver, wearing a fashionably torn off T-shirt and red shades, didn't even bother to look up. She repeated her request. No response. So she took the polite edge off, "Step out of the car now with your hands above your head."

He stared straight ahead, "I'm not getting out of the fuckin' car. And I'm not putting my hands above my head."

Slattery's command presence turned to mush, and her voice squeaked with nervous excitement. "Do what I say. Get out right now. You've got to do what I say."

Her shrill pitch made Morgan's blood run cold. Suddenly, Morgan saw herself playing a game of doubles, with Slattery charging the net too soon. Morgan swallowed a rusty taste in her throat.

All right, she fired herself up, walking towards the Porsche. You sons-a-bitches. Then, remembering Aunt Tilly's advice on the social graces of municipal policing — if you remain calm, you keep the pressure on your opponent — she put on the hard face she reserved for work, walked up to the passenger's side and said, "I want you guys out of the car now."

The passenger, too cool in a white suit, lavender tie and gold bracelets, casually rested his arm on the door. The rider looked at her silently.

She hesitated a fraction of a second: *Let 'em go. Just let 'em go.* Then Moon's even, precise and unyielding voice ironed the wrinkles in her mind: No, do not let 'em go. Get 'em the hell out of the car. Now.

So she put her gun right up behind the passenger's head. "I'd sooner blow your fuckin' head off than read the Sunday paper," Morgan said. "Get my drift?"

The driver eased out of the car. The passenger followed, deliberately, eyeing the driver as if watching for a signal.

Morgan gave Slattery a look to move back to their car and get on the radio. When she realized her partner hadn't picked up the visual hint, she prompted her, "Back up." Slattery hurried to the patrol car to call for help.

Morgan could tell the driver had summed her up in an instant when he announced, "We ain't doing shit, sweetdick." Then he turned and headed for the driver's seat. She moved towards him, but the passenger pushed her hard, and she toppled, catching her balance before she hit the ground. As he whipped around, she leapt up onto the rear bumper and jumped down on his back, wedging her arms around his neck choking him, pulling on his tie.

"Slattery!" she yelled. No response.

Her adversary was too powerful. She could feel her entire body swing, like a tether ball on a pole, first to the left and then to the right. Enduring his merciless elbow jabs to her sides, breasts and neck, she held on as if to let go would mean instant death.

The driver sped away in the Porsche.

"Slattery!" Morgan called out, gritting her teeth and wrenching the suspect with all her might, while he turned and twisted around with her like a monkey on his back.

Finally, he started to slow down from lack of oxygen and dropped to his knees, to his back. She held the choke on until he passed out just long enough for her to handcuff him.

Just as she positioned herself to move the suspect, back-up patrol arrived with Ben Fender and Teddy Bear. "What took you so long?" she panted to Fender, as he sauntered over and watched her drag the suspect by the armpits. "Good thing I wasn't holding my breath waiting on you."

"Seems you got things under control."

"Stolen car?" asked Teddy Bear.

She nodded. "Porsche."

Fender tried to make out Slattery huddled over the dashboard of the patrol car. "Slattery putting out a broadcast for the car?"

Still lugging the suspect, Morgan attempted to look up at him, but she could barely lift her head. When she did, he was a blur.

"You better be sure," he said. "Looks like she could be having one of her frozen neck attacks. We'll dump him at the station for you."

She stood up, ice picks stabbing her own neck. "Thanks."

Fender and Teddy Bear hoisted the suspect to his feet and half dragged him at the knees across the asphalt to the patrol car. Teddy Bear opened the back door. Morgan watched Fender push the suspect into the right rear seat. She glimpsed a flash of lavender as the white suit pitched forward. Fender took his gun from his holster, placed it on the front right seat, as Teddy Bear slid behind the wheel. Fender slipped into the passenger seat behind him and slammed the door.

Morgan ran the palm of her hand over the numb base of her skull, took a shallow breath, careful not to stir the acute throb in her chest and walked stiffly towards the car. Seeing Slattery's silhouette in the driver's seat, staring out the front windshield, Morgan circled the trunk and opened the passenger door.

Once inside, she pulled the handle with effort, slamming the door. She regarded Slattery a moment, stone still, her hands poised on the steering wheel at ten and two o'clock. "Did you report the Porsche?"

Slattery nodded in the affirmative.

"Did you get the plates?"

She nodded yes again, then reached to turn on the ignition, as if progressing to the next moment would help ease the memory of the previous ones. Slattery shifted into drive. But now that the crisis was over, Morgan couldn't move forward until she knew what had gone wrong. "So, what happened out there?"

Slattery put her foot on the brake, reflecting a second, then said simply, "I didn't want to fight."

Morgan nodded, too reasonably. "*You* didn't want to fight. But you didn't mind watching me get my ass chewed up out there." Morgan gave her a moment to respond. Nothing. "What makes you think I wanted to fight?" she managed. "Sometimes you have to. I mean, what were we supposed to do, just let those animals shit all over us?"

Slattery bristled, set her foot on the accelerator and pulled away from the curb. Morgan stared at her, thinking that if Slattery had children she would understand better. Morgan sighed, looked away from Slattery's stiff portrait, and watched the passing shadowy front yards.

She remembered when Sam had been three years old and they'd been playing catch in their front yard. The ball kept bouncing into the narrow residential street. Morgan would retrieve it and they would resume catching. Aunt Tilly called Morgan to the front door, and on her way across the yard, Morgan warned Sam she could toss the ball up in the air and try to catch it, but if it went into the street, "Wait 'til Mommy gets back. Do not go into the street."

The instructions were clear, yet even as Morgan walked away, she knew Sam would test her. Morgan stepped into the foyer, listened to Aunt Tilly, but kept her eyes on Sam as she tossed the ball up and it landed on the sidewalk, bouncing, then rolling into the gutter. Sam walked toward the curb. She could easily reach the ball by stepping into the street. Morgan remembered she and Aunt Tilly had exchanged a look, knowing fully what Sam was about to do, and how Morgan would have to respond.

No sooner had Sam's tiny foot hit the curbside street than Morgan flew out the front door towards her daughter, scooped her up, gave her a few smacks on the behind, raced her past Aunt Tilly's stern face and settled Sam on her Mickey Mouse bedspread. With children, or grown-ups acting irresponsibly, sometimes you had to give them a reality check, pull the rug out from under them.

Half way to the station, Morgan was still filling out the report, grappling with how to describe Slattery's actions. Cowardly? She considered that maybe what Slattery did was quick thinking self-preservation, even smart. Maybe bravery was more stupid than smart. When she was a child, Samantha used to tell her how brave she was to stand up against Samantha's father, Mr. "Bowtie" Deaver. But Morgan always felt stupid. Alone. Weightless in a black hole trying to keep her feet on a ground that only existed in her mind. Brave would never be a word she would have used to describe herself.

Were it not for Slattery's singular observation as she parked in the division lot, they would have driven to the station in silence. "You were very brave tonight," Slattery said, then veered the patrol car into its designated parking spot, flicked off the ignition and volunteered to turn in the equipment, insisting that Morgan go home and take care of herself.

"I wasn't very brave tonight. I did what had to be done. And you gotta figure out what you didn't do and why because you jeopardized both our lives. And I'm not about to pat you on the back and tell you better luck next time. That was me and my twelve-year-old kid and my pain in the neck mother-in-law getting beat up out there. And I gotta tell you, my daughter and Gramma Sofie would've been a helluva lot more help. They'd've been right next to me pounding that guy in the kidneys with their fists or kicking him in the balls."

Morgan handed Slattery the report. "You can finish this. I got to the point where I cuffed him." Morgan brushed aside Slattery's silent interrogative. "Just put in what you did. See you tomorrow."

She eased her way out of the passenger seat, disregarding Slattery's hesitation and discomfort. Dragging her feet towards her Jeep, she considered that bravery, audacity, stupidity, call it what you will, was something she hadn't been able to teach her best friend Samantha, so she had no hope of explaining it to Slattery. Like Aunt Tilly used to say, "It's something inside you that makes you know when you have to step out into the void. You can't teach risk."

Morgan eased the back door closed behind her and limped into the dark kitchen. Baked apples, covering the usual odors of fish and chicken, warmed the air, powered up her hunger pangs, so she cracked the refrigerator door, peeking under aluminum foiled containers filled with chopped chicken liver and borscht, to find the apple strudel. The overhead kitchen light flicked on. Sam stood in her Garfield nightshirt, "God — Gosh, you're so late."

"I didn't mean to wake you up." Morgan set the apple strudel wedge, a carton of milk and a Hershey syrup can on the counter.

"You didn't. No school tomorrow, and I don't have to get up until Nat's swim meet."

"That doesn't mean you can stay up half the night." Morgan poured milk into a plastic E.T. glass, left over from Sam's pre-school years. "Is Gramma asleep?"

Sam nodded thankfully, crossed to Morgan and hugged her. "Mom, you've got to do something before I kill her." Morgan darted her a warning look. "Just kidding. But really, she said she's going to cut my hair and give me a perm, if I don't change my attitude about cooking, sewing and cleaning."

Morgan watched the last of the Hershey syrup trickle like blood droplets onto the surface of her milk. "And you told her you're not a slave, you're a kid."

"Right."

Morgan stirred her milk, grabbed her slice of strudel and shuffled into the living room, sore and exhausted. "You know, if I'm ever hurt or anything, she's all ya got. She's your father's mother, and I know she doesn't show it in obvious ways, but you are her life."

"Anybody hurts you, I'll kill 'em."

"Right." Morgan let out a weak laugh, easing herself onto the couch.

Sam knelt on the floor next to her, looking up at dried blood still caked on Morgan's chin. "What happened?"

"Made an arrest tonight."

"Looks like blood."

"Yeah, I'm okay, but I had to choke this dude out."

"Why didn't you just beat the crap out of him?"

"I did my best."

Sam checked her out more carefully, then, satisfied Morgan was all right, she raised her fist, "To the max."

Morgan tapped Sam's fist with her own, "To the max," then tackled her daughter, accidentally hitting her hard on the mouth. "You okay?"

"See any blood?" Sam asked.

She examined her. "No, you ought to have a mouth guard though, but since you don't…" Morgan playfully bugged her eyes. "Tough. Wrestle."

Later, after Morgan had read aloud a chapter from *The Magic of Oz*, she was lying in bed wide-awake with her eyes closed, listening to Sam softly snoring nearby. Turning her back to her daughter, Morgan whispered into her tape recorder about how peculiar life had become. Impossible to bring it all into focus. She felt rudderless. Fragments of arrows pointed in every direction. Where to look? For what? Her eyes opened and she saw what she'd been avoiding all night: she'd been wrenched off her tracks by the suspect she'd tried to strangle the life out of, and now what if, say, his partner would find her and snuff hers. Or worse, hurt Sam. Why would he? Irrational, she told herself, yet she couldn't rest her mind from fictionalizing a paranoid revenge-seeking scenario.

Hours later, out of a sound sleep, Sam's leg jerked suddenly and she woke up, yelling, "Stop. Stop."

"Have a bad dream?" Morgan stroked her back.

Sam nodded. "That Kiki Aru bird swooped me and was going to drop me in a muddy lake filled with poisonous snakes if I didn't tell him the magic *Oz* word."

"You don't know the magic word yet."

"I didn't tell him that."

"Good thinking."

Sam cuddled up to Morgan, saying, "I love you, Mommy." Morgan hugged her daughter close and stroked her long, straight hair, appreciating those drowsy, intimate moments that cut through her twelve-year-old's absolutely confident image. "No more nightmares," mumbled Sam. And closing her eyes, Morgan willed herself to sleep, but not until a gray dawn was breaking did she finally drop off again, dreaming, no more nightmares. Morgan knew more about nightmares than she cared to admit.

About a week before she'd requested a transfer from Devonshire, she'd considered making an appointment with Dr. Best at Parker Center again. Her nightmares were recurring, and she would wake up her daughter, who would get up to make her hot milk, bang around in the kitchen and wake up Gramma Sofie, who would get all over Sam's case for being in the kitchen without slippers.

She's such a sterling kid. It's not fair for me to complicate her life with my past. So, I'm tempted to give Dr. Best another try even though our first "interrogation" was a washout.

That had been right before last Christmas, when she'd almost cancelled her first and only appointment with Dr. Best. Lightheaded from too much coffee, too little sleep, and nauseous from severe stomach cramps, she averted eye contact the whole time Dr. Best was speaking with her. In fact, she'd stared right through him at the closed door that led to the hall. Her mind kept wondering and she imagined he had prisoners in there suffering in "silent" torment: some forced to squat for hours, others to lie on their stomachs, heads down, and still others sitting blindfolded for hours or days waiting to see him. Her dreams overwhelmed her with death and torture.

What Jacob hadn't told her about torture, she'd read — every appalling Nuremberg and Helsinki and Manzanar personal account she could get her hands on. Horrifying beyond belief. A part of her had always stayed outside the door of reality, perpetually in disbelief because she couldn't understand the cruel link that fueled the infliction of such purposeful, blinding pain. She kept looking for something to help explain it.

I'm not sure why I'm looking or what I'm looking for.

But she hadn't gone to talk with Dr. Best about Jacob or oppression and torture in a war state; she'd gone to shed light on the subject of her nightmares: the suicide of her childhood best friend.

I was there to point to the demon on my shoulder. The demon that tricks me with bright memories that turn black, like someone who hands you an ice cream cone, but it's filled with shit.

"I don't know," she'd replied, tapping her temple with her index finger, in answer to his question as they sat sipping coffee in his office. He'd asked her what she was afraid of remembering about the night Samantha died. Best was tall and thin, with a long ponytail neatly tied back and partially hidden. His gestures were minimal; his facial expression was permanently programmed on listening: direct eye contact with an occasional perceptible nod. He set down his espresso cup and offered a small nod for her to continue. "I remember every detail. It's just we were so close, I can't believe she didn't tell me."

"Tell you what? That she was going to kill herself?"

Morgan nodded. "We told each other everything."

"Maybe she didn't know."

Eyes downcast, Morgan thought hard for a moment, formulating words to express a feeling. "On some level, I don't trust my perception of the way things really are, and I'm afraid I'll mess up again — what if I don't understand something important my daughter's trying to tell me, or — "

"Morgan, you didn't mess up. Your friend took her life. Tragic, but it wasn't your fault."

Morgan shrugged, maybe not, "If only I could convince my mind of that."

"What do you mean?"

"There's just this constant chatter and images I don't seem to be able to control."

"Does it happen when you're on patrol?"

"No." She answered too quickly, and couldn't tell from his static expression if he knew she was lying.

"What kind of images?" he nodded, as though half anticipating whatever she was about to say. The buzzing intercom forced him to break away. He pushed the speaker phone button off, lifted the receiver, and listened a moment. "Let me take a look," he said. Then said aside, to Morgan, "This won't take but a minute."

A knock at the door, followed by a matronly Hispanic woman in a flower print elastic-waist dress, designed to flatter the waist she probably enjoyed several children ago. She smiled broadly at Morgan, then turned to Dr. Best and indicated the contents of the file in her hand. Best took a minute to review and sign a letter.

Morgan watched the woman lightly tap her pointed pump on the carpet as if she were keeping time to a rhythmic marimba she'd left playing on her desk radio. Her feet had to be cramped in that tiny triangle-shaped toe compartment. Morgan took a sip of espresso, resettled herself on a chair cushion and closed her eyes. She squeezed her toes, cushioned in her closed, leather sandals designed for maximum comfort and support. Her mother would be pleased, she thought. She smiled to herself as she imagined her mother stepping out from behind the floral dress, carrying a pair of trashed P.F. Flyers and wearing that threadbare apron Samantha had fashioned out of hand-woven potholders. She handed her the shoes and a pair of darned wool socks, "You've got to take care of your feet," she said, embracing her around the shoulders with both arms the way she always did when she sent her off to school. Then she walked out the door, turning to wave just before she disappeared into the hall.

Morgan heard Dr. Best's instructions to his secretary and whisked herself back to reality, or thought she had until she imagined she saw Samantha wander past the open door, searching. Naked and melancholy, the rope still attached to her neck, she stopped, her gaze sweeping past Morgan vaguely, then back, suddenly fixing on her in absolute disbelief. Samantha couldn't speak, but just as Best's secretary turned on her spike heels, revealing Best to Samantha, she eyed him and was shaking her head vehemently at Morgan when the floral skirt swirled out, closing the door behind her.

Best settled himself on a chair in front of Morgan, nodding, picking up from where they'd left off, without dropping a beat. "So what images are you seeing?"

Morgan leaned back slowly, her head downcast.

"You know, once upon a time you were a child," Best had stated, then waited, as though he expected her to confirm his suspicion before he continued. "Whether you realize it or not, that has direct bearing on your life today." He paused again.

No comment. She looked past him through the door.

Best pressed on. "As an adult, you know Morgan, we often try to forget or we simply don't want to remember traumatic portions of our childhood. And — don't get me wrong — it doesn't have to be a blatant trauma for us to block it out and discount the impact it has in our adult lives. Our job though is to observe the order to the trauma."

"You mean disorder," she looked at him.

He gave a fractional smile, "No such thing as mental disorder, just different levels of order." She eyed him perplexedly up and down. They actually pay you a salary to convince people who confront criminals every day that there is no mental disorder. "When we say something has disorder, we're only talking about our own ignorance of its true order."

Sirens moaned in the disquiet of her thoughts. "Are you saying that disorder is just an order we haven't perceived yet?"

He grinned winningly. "Exactly."

"Oh," she'd managed to keep a mocking note out of her voice. "Thanks, that really helps."

Right then and there she decided there was nothing Dr. Best could tell her to give any perspective to her tweaked world. Furthermore, anything she might tell him would be inscribed in her personnel file, so she could end up with recurring nightmares and no job.

Morgan was awakened by the phone early the next morning. She garbled, "Hello," then sat up in bed, swallowing hard, "Yes, Lieutenant. No. Right away, Lieutenant."

She hustled into the kitchen in her underwear to find Sam perched over the table reading to her grandmother from a newspaper article above the picture of a rescued giant panda munching on bamboo. "…About 60% of Wolong's pandas are on the verge of starvation." She paused, slurping a messy grapefruit.

"I have to go into work." She kissed Sam on the head and snatched a slice of Gramma Sofie's fresh honey cake. "The suspect I arrested last night died in his cell."

She hurried back down the hall, angry with herself for not checking the guy's cell the previous night.

Wondering if her chokehold could have been the cause of death, she hurried into the privacy of her bedroom to get in touch with Alicia, who confirmed bitterly, "Yeah, you fucked up. Chokehold. You killed the guy. Was he conscious when you put him to bed?"

"I didn't sign him in. I was hurting, so a couple of other officers transported him for me."

"Good God," she sighed. "Who?" Then she added quickly, "Never mind, don't tell me. They'll check on all calls you made this morning and they'll ask me if you told me and I don't wanna know."

Morgan wasn't sure who "they" were — Fender and Teddy or the lieutenant and captain, but she could already sense an inquiry.

Clicking her teeth, Alicia informed her grimly, "Look, just do your own deal and don't, I repeat do not drag any of those hungry dogs into it, or we're dead meat."

Fatigued, her body aching, Morgan had no clue what Alicia was talking about. "Dogs?"

"Those Men Against Women animals. You want that I draw you a picture?"

"Look, Alicia," Morgan said, with forced patience, "I had one bitch of a night, and now I gotta deal with this, so don't assume I know what the hell you're talking about."

"What I'm saying is I've already heard Slattery say somebody else transported this suspect, and, if it was one of the MAW guys, forget it. You don't remember who. If you say anything that suggests they had anything to do with it, they'll eat us alive out there. It'll go from slow back-up for us to no back-up."

Morgan was getting the picture. "Isn't that kind of street blackmail?"

"Call it whatever you want, just listen to what I'm saying."

Morgan thought about it. "I hear you." She wanted to tell Alicia that she wouldn't mention Fender's name, but it had nothing to do with a fear that he wouldn't back her up. After all, he hadn't exactly busted his ass to back her up in the first place. It had more to do with taking the hit for her own action, not dragging another officer into it unnecessarily.

Morgan supposed Slattery could have been re-inserting her contact lenses for the brief two minutes Fender and Teddy Bear were at the scene. If Slattery didn't know the transporting officers, Morgan reasoned it was just as well to leave it that way. Maybe it should be a harder ethical choice between accountability and truth. But it wasn't. Being responsible for her own actions was the right course. But just to be certain, she asked herself what Bruce Springsteen would do. Sure that he would have insisted on singularly taking the heat for his own brush with excessive violence, she prepared herself to confront Lieutenant Herdahl.

But Morgan was summoned into Captain Drummond's office, where he informed her he knew nothing more than she did. "It usually takes a few days for them to find out the cause of death," he said, tapping his pencil on the desk a few times before gazing up at her. "Then they turn it over to Internal Affairs for a criminal investigation."

She lifted her eyes from the floor. Internal Affairs. Damn.

"What condition was he in when you and Slattery brought him in?"

"We didn't transport him."

"Who did?"

She tried to concentrate, but her eyes were glued on the gun poster. "Two officers."

"Who?" Would he be asking this question, she wondered, if there had been an officer at the front desk, or any other witnesses to indicate who had transported the guy? Probably not.

His pencil tapping filled the silence. She shrugged. "I'm sorry to say I was beaten up so badly I couldn't see straight. Slattery called for backup; a couple of officers came and offered to transport him — "

"You mean to say — "

Lieutenant Herdahl knocked and entered, closing the door behind her. "Morgan," she greeted her, but looked to the captain, "Press? What have we told P.R?"

He shook his head, nothing, then finished his thought, keeping his eyes on Morgan. "You can count on being interviewed by Internal Affairs soon."

Morgan stiffened. "Before the coroner's inquest?"

"Probably." His eyes answered the lieutenant's frown, explaining, "She had to use a chokehold to restrain him, but by the time she had him cuffed, he was coming to. And she doesn't know who transported him."

Lieutenant Herdahl inhaled deeply. "C'mon, you're saying you have no idea who they were?"

"No."

Herdahl thrust her hands on her hips, her labored breathing punctuating the stillness, then she said, "What are we supposed to tell the press? Nothing, or that Officer Slattery was messing with her contacts and Officer Fraser doesn't know who transported her suspect?" Moon was right, thought Morgan: it did look like she was hiding a soccer ball below her belt. The chokehold whirled in her mind, wondering if Lieutenant Herdahl could've managed to fasten herself onto the suspect and spin around mid-air.

Morgan forced herself to look away, her gaze falling on Drummond's windowsill rosebuds.

The captain indicated a dark discoloration on her forearm. "I can see that you might not remember, but if the transporting officers were from this division, maybe roll call will jostle your memory."

Lieutenant Herdahl agreed, adding, "Give it some thought."

Morgan nodded. As she turned and headed towards the door, she caught a frustrated look pass between them.

She left the captain's office, silently replaying the words "criminal investigation" several times to let them sink in. But it didn't make any sense. Doubt crept back. Why didn't she just tell them it was Fender and Teddy Bear? Not telling could be interpreted as protecting them. And why would she want to protect those clowns? She remembered Alicia's warning: do your own deal. Don't bring any of those hungry dogs into it. If only she could have gotten the suspect down without using a chokehold.

Hungry dogs?

She should've never let them transport her suspect. It crossed her mind that, had Moon not taken a few days off, had he responded to the call with her, the whole chokehold scenario would have been different. She reminded herself that Internal Affairs would hold them responsible because everyone knew a woman cop couldn't choke out a man. She settled on Alicia's advice and decided not to involve any other cops. Nothing else made sense.

That afternoon she was ordered to report to Internal Affairs, downtown Parker Center, fifth floor.

Morgan and Slattery sat several seats apart in a government issue waiting room. In it were several gray folding chairs with plastic padded cushions and a massive desk, empty on top and probably inside. She wondered what was the purpose of a desk without a chair. To set things on or to establish, perhaps, an austere work tone suggested by the desk's bulk and power.

The door opened and a matronly woman in a dark suit and low pumps looked from Slattery to Morgan back to Slattery. "Officer Fraser," the woman offered a tight smile.

Morgan walked in, immediately struck by the spacious carpeted room. Sunlight poured in through the wall of windows, bouncing off the ample walnut table. A slender, well-groomed man in his thirties, wearing a tie with a print of Diego Rivera's hunched peasant "Flower Vendor" indicated a chair next to the window.

She nodded and sat.

He perched next to a well-ordered pile of folders on the imposing desk, twin to the one in the waiting room. She wasn't sure what to make of his calm, vivid blue eyes, pleasant expression, and crooked nose, possibly broken as a kid. The flower vendor tie made her think of Señor Blanco tending the Police Academy gardens. A mental picture flashed of Señor Blanco asleep in his armchair while his antiquated house went up in flames like a box of used tissues. Don't think about that, she told herself.

Then she eyed the other guy in the room: a corpulent, squat fellow leaning on the corner of the desk. He wore no tie. His dark blue caftan-like shirt was open at the neck, revealing a shock of white hair. His pock-marked face was as greasy as his Grecian formula-tinted hair. She took one look at his somber expression, sizing her up, and forced herself to smile directly at him. He was so taken aback a corner of his mouth crinkled.

The flower tie guy cleared his throat, "Officer Fraser, we'd like to hear your account of what happened on the night of June 18th."

"Where would you like me to begin?"

"Roll call's fine."

She gave her version of the night's events, then paused. Pock face's gravel voice broke the silence. "So, if you didn't do anything to the suspect at the scene except for the choking, then who transported him?"

She held his shrewd measuring eyes for a moment, then finally shook her head. "I don't know. I haven't been in the division that long. I just don't know all the guys."

The flower tie pressed in a friendly tone, "But they were guys?"

"Yes."

"Were they Nightwatch?" the flower tie asked.

"I don't know if they were Nightwatch or PM watch or late days or what they were. I don't even know if they were in the same division."

She sensed the flower tie guy was convinced, seeing him nod peripherally to his partner, but Pock Face returned no sign of agreement. He just stared blankly at her, and she could almost see the wheels in his mind spinning doubt.

While Morgan was busy telling her story at Parker Center, her daughter was circulating around her middle school lunch area, pinning "dope is dumb" buttons on her peers. Sam told Morgan she'd overheard Kyle, a sixth grade thug, comment to his friend, "Her mother's a pig." Sam started to charge after him, but noticing the principal, Mr. Buffet — a filing cabinet in a suit — approaching, she thought better of it.

Before the end of lunch, Nat stepped from the boys' bathroom, looked at Sam and lifted his glasses off his nose — a prearranged tip off. Sam entered.

She crossed to Kyle, still peeing at the urinal, grabbed him by the hair and, with Nat's help in holding him, kept punching the bully until he went down. At least, this was what Morgan could piece together later from Sam and Nat, both out of breath, tugging on her sleeve, simultaneously trying to relate details from their version of the incident.

The following day in Mr. Buffet's office, Morgan was appalled by his preoccupation with a possible lawsuit from Kyle's parents, instead of addressing what provoked the fight.

"Mr. Buffet, can you arrange a meeting with Kyle and his parents so we could discuss this?"

"No, I don't think that's necessary. Your daughter's aggressive action is out of line with school policy, so regardless of the cause, she'll be suspended for a week."

Salvaging some sense of vindication, Sam swore Nat hadn't been in the bathroom with her. And Morgan kept her mouth shut. Since it was Sam's word against Kyle's, Mr. Buffet didn't suspend Nat.

Under Mr. Buffet's close scrutiny, Sam and Nat exchanged a blank look celebrating their small, but meaningful victory. Morgan made a mental note to talk with her daughter about ethical choices — loyalty versus truth being one of life's tougher decisions.

When Morgan told Sam she would have to go with Gramma Sofie to the Jewish Center during a couple of her week "off" school days, Sam said, "But you're home during the day."

"I've got to appear in court."

"I can take my stuff to the station and hang out with you."

"I'm not exactly going to be hanging out."

She made a face. "You know what I mean."

"The station is not a kid-friendly place, neither is the courthouse."

Sam indicated Gramma Sofie watching her soaps in the living room, "And sitting in her old people classes is? I'd rather sit in the locker room for eight hours."

"Noxious gases in that locker room would make you stupid."

"So?"

"So, no."

"What if I stay with Nat's grandmother?"

Morgan looked at her, no chance. But she suspected that Sam would've preferred Nat's grandmother, a real grandmother, closer physically and spiritually to the small things in life — the tiny ant struggling across the grass carrying food, the feeling of warm mud on bare feet, the smell of brownies warm from the oven. Nat's grandmother was only responsible for love. She took him to the park, the movies, and the museum. She knew he loved skyscrapers, so she took him to the tallest buildings in Los Angeles. Born to be a grandmother, she built sheet tents for him to play in and bought him new baseball hats. She knew how to enjoy kid-fun.

Gramma Sofie didn't. Sam complained that her Gramma had a way of taking the fun out of things; Sofie, however, saw herself as a giver, not a taker. After her son was killed and her husband died, Gramma Sofie had a hard time stretching her monthly three hundred dollar pension, and even though her friends at the Jewish Center begged her to stay in the beach area, she moved in with her only living family, Morgan and Sam, and she devoted her life to her granddaughter's physical, spiritual and mental health.

Gramma Sofie thought of Sam as an extension of Jacob, an extension of herself even. When she was cold, hungry, sleepy, she assumed Sam was; she adored lily of the valley perfume and bubble baths; she liked to cook simple Jewish food, so Sam would love learning how.

How could Morgan help Sam understand that Gramma Sofie never really had a carefree childhood; her youth had consisted of learning to survive in a ghetto surrounded by fear and alienation. Unlike her cousins, siblings and parents she found the courage to leave and escaped extinction. In her early twenties, she worked fourteen hours a day, seven days a week as a seamstress in a New York sweatshop. She saved every penny to buy passage for her parents, brother and sister. Her parents came, not her siblings. And her parents missed their other children so much that, after a year, they left New York City and went back to Poland. They were all killed in Auschwitz.

After her parents returned to their home, but several years before WWII, Sofie met Thomas Fraser, an irreligious Irish-Scotsman, working as a carpenter in her factory. He told his son, Jacob, who later told Morgan, that he'd fallen in love with her the first instant he'd seen her step out of the building, lugging her sewing machine, long dark braid held firm by a loose bun, and her gorgeous chest trapped in a violet dress.

They married, struggled through the hardship of an interfaith marriage, several stillbirths and unspeakable personal loss. Then after the war, they joined one of Thomas' brothers at a beachtown in Southern California, where many Eastern Europeans were moving to duplicate the shtetl community, and where Sofie finally found a home near the Jewish Center by the sea. During the happiest period of her life, she gave pre-menopausal birth to her only child.

So how do you explain to a young woman approaching puberty, a young woman with a joy for life's freedom, that her grandmother lives every day, saying 'why me,' not because she's complaining about her situation, but questioning why things have turned out the way they have? Why she survived? How could she tell Sam, Morgan thought, that her Gramma Sofie does not see her holocaust survival as a blessing.

It took a long time for Morgan to understand, even though Jacob had explained it to her, that Sofie thought she was saved not because she had the courage to flee oppression, but because she did not love her parents and her siblings enough to return to Poland and suffer with them. And that's a heavy burden to carry for the rest of one's life. Now, in order to feel useful and needed herself, to lighten the weight of her survivor guilt, she had to help those worse off and, of course, help family members who may not figure they needed help.

While Morgan waited for the results of the coroner's report that week, Sam went to the Center with Gramma Sofie on Monday, Wednesday, and Friday, and helped her prepare hot meals for the elderly, then they sat on a bench, listened to Hershel and Rebekah argue about the Israelis and Palestinians, and watched the sidewalk parade of surfers, skaters, artists and Hare Krishnas.

Sometimes after the lunch special, Sam told Morgan she and Gramma stayed in the Center and looked at a room-length mural depicting the Center members' historical journey: a boatload of immigrants at Ellis Island, a New York streetscape, a shtetl market, a group of demonstrators carrying signs: *Better Conditions First, Power and Justice for the People.* Gramma would tell her about shtetl life as a child — sitting all day in front of a tower of potatoes and waiting for customers. After the two o'clock Jewish History talks by Rabbi Siegel, Sam helped Gramma maneuver her metal-wheeled cart on and off the bus.

On Tuesday and Thursday, Sam stayed home — washed, shopped, baked, sewed with Gramma Sofie — and waited for the end of her domestic penance. On Saturday, Nat, having received permission from Morgan and a weak acceptance from Gramma Sofie, gave Sam an early birthday present, one of Sidney's puppies. Nat must have sensed Sam had been bossed around enough — she needed a charge, someone else to boss around, and Ozma, furry, black, cuddly and confident, played loyal subject to Sam's loving discipline.

12

HEARTBREAK TANGO

He was back. Moon passed Morgan in the hall right before roll call and commented offhandedly, "Hey killer, what's happening? Beat up any innocent Negroes lately?"

What do you say to that, Morgan wondered. *It was no big deal? You neo-nazi scumbag?* She could see his little vacation hadn't offered any sort of mental awakening. "Those your new rap lyrics?" She abruptly turned into the women's bathroom. He laughed at her back. To her ears, the sound was forced, false. It faded as the door closed and, in the tile vault, died altogether.

She leaned back against the wall, her heart pounding more than she figured it should: Moon's racial slurs were nothing new. The word was already out that she'd beat the suspect to death. Three weeks at her new assignment and she knew the station was a cesspool of innuendo and lies. It was hard not to think about the suspect dying alone in his cell, wondering what he was thinking. If he were even conscious, which led her to speculate about Jacob's last thoughts. She closed her eyes and reached through the heavy web of memory to Jacob. Not now. She heard a dull sound in her ears like a refrigerator humming. A chill moved up from her stomach, numbed her breasts, neck, chin, nose.

Stop thinking about Jacob, she glared at herself in the mirror. She turned on the water faucet, fluttering an open palm in front of her face. Cool air hit the perspiration on her forehead. She hit the soap dispenser so many times that pink liquid puddled and spilled out of her palm.

Don't let that neo-nazi push your buttons, her sensible voice warned her. Don't argue with him. Don't defend yourself. She wasn't sure if she should completely ignore him during roll, maybe offer him a disinterested nod. She fantasized throwing a metal chair at his head. Why not? The women would cheer; the men would throw chairs back. No paper hand towels in the bathroom, so she walked along the hall, flicking her hands dry, wondering why she was thinking about Moon at all. In a mental fog, she wound a path through roll call and equipment pick-up, until she was sitting in the patrol car ignoring Moon's comments about the upcoming Olympics and the expected citywide traffic jams.

"I don't know," she said, "seems like everyone on my block has rented out their place and is leaving the city."

"That's what I'd love to do."

"Not me. I'm going to opening day."

"Got tickets?"

"Not yet."

"Fat chance," he smirked, "they're all sold out. The whole thing is going to be a colossal bust anyway. It doesn't take any great genius to figure out that the best way for some terrorist to humiliate the U.S. is to attack U.S. athletes. Then there's the Turks and the Israelis — "

She interrupted him, "Thank you so much for your inspiring Olympic security report." Then she finally got around to asking something that had been on her mind. "So, have you ever been investigated by Internal Affairs?"

"*Investigated* by those deadheads?"

"I guess that means *yes*."

"It means those pricks don't know how to investigate shit."

"Right." She wasn't sure if his ego were Olympic-sized, but she figured you could call it gargantuan and you wouldn't be far off. She found it curious he didn't press her for details about her chokehold technique, the transport officers, the suspect's death or the Porsche driver with the red glasses. He hadn't ignored the incident; he acted like it was just another one of many altercations not worth mentioning in the policing cosmos.

During their customary break at Tia's Tacos, Morgan supposed it wouldn't hurt to reveal her confusion about Internal Affairs tactics, how curious it was that the flower vendor tie guy, Sgt. Joe Blanco, and his cohort grease head, Sgt. Paul Francesconi, were intense about investigating her the first week, and then yesterday told her she had one final hearing to attend Friday.

"Oh, you got the spic and the whop combo. They'll dump the whole thing tomorrow."

"You think?"

"Yep."

"How do you know?"

He didn't look at her, and she knew he wasn't going to answer. Badgering him, she had learned, was no way to get him to talk, so she waited through a long silence, until he said, "This little investigation you're going through is nothing. It's just a tasty morsel for the press. That kind of stuff is nothing to Internal Affairs. If that's all they had to investigate, they'd be delighted."

Then seeming to table the topic, he chomped on a juicy tuna burrito, making her wait until she couldn't stand it. "Damnit, Moon, will you stop stuffing your face and tell me what you're talking about?"

She knew he delighted in taunting her with knowledge he might or might not reveal. He grinned. "Friend of mine works in I.A. He told me the other day when we were skiing, 'Moon, you could do just about anything. Get in a bar fight. We'd love to investigate some cop beating some suspect in a bar. But we don't have time for that. You could abuse your kid, sexually molest your mother-in-law. Beat your wife. Pass bad checks. We don't have time for that because we are concentrating on two things: crimes officers are committing and officers' involvement with cocaine. And they're all officers who have been on less than six years.'"

Morgan stared him down, checking to see if he was putting her on again. "Cocaine? Who told you that?"

"If I know it, ain't no big secret. I.A. conducts the investigation for cocaine. They got involved in that Hollywood burglary caper, remember?"

She shook her head.

"Oh, that's right," he teased her, "you were in Sleepy Hollow when it happened. Well, all these Hollywood officers were answering burglary calls, and if it was a good burglary call, before they said it was a good call, they'd go in and take all the shit they wanted."

"Cocaine?"

"Bingo. And Internal Affairs was investigating it, but they were just dumbshit sergeants like your Mutt and Jeff — "

"Something like if I passed the sergeant's test and applied to go to Internal Affairs?"

"Right." He took another giant burrito bite, mumbling, "Can you imagine you in Internal Affairs?"

"No, " she said, in mock deadpan. "I'm completely incompetent."

"There, you'd fit right in." He laughed, started to continue, then paused, swallowing. "I like your sense of humor. Mooseface, huh?" He flashed a sly smile, then went on, leaving her to sum up, evaluate and reject everything about him she had missed during his absence, and everything about him she couldn't stand.

"Well, they were investigating crimes and they didn't know the first thing about detective work," Moon explained. "So, they screwed up the entire investigation and they couldn't prosecute any of those officers. They just fired a lot of 'em, but they couldn't prosecute them in court. Now, they have eight detectives assigned to Internal Affairs who do nothing but investigate police involved in drug crime."

She sighed. "Tell that to the guy on the street paying all these big ticket salaries to investigate cops on the take. Tough to comprehend."

"What's so tough about it? The cops who are usually bought already look at themselves as a little shady. You know what I mean."

"You mean they've done it before, and it's no big deal."

"Exactly. They're not torn about some great issue, like: 'I've been in the department six years and I've never gotten away with anything, but now I want to.' Their moral precedent was set a long time ago, so they figure: 'Hell, I've come this far, why can't I continue to do this once in a while. Just once in a while.'" He aimed his drippy burrito towards his wide-open mouth.

She winced and tossed him a napkin. "It's hard for them to be good cops because they're doing what they're expected to arrest other people for."

With a full mouth of food, he garbled *bingo*.

"Damn," she mumbled to herself.

Later, deep in thought, she stared out the window until dispatch routed them a call: a decomp case in an abandoned tenement, next to a nocturnal gathering spot for hookers, alcoholics and addicts. They parked in a dimly lit alley and, crossing towards the building, approached a disheveled, broken-toothed man pushing a metal shopping cart. He veered to the other side of the alley, but Morgan got a whiff of him in passing. Or was it the chicken, ribs and hamburgers he'd scavenged for in the trash bin behind Henry's BBQ?

Inside the apartment, they joined Fender and Herrera, who had also just arrived.

They took off their jackets and covered their noses. Morgan coughed, "Must be 120 degrees in here."

Fender looked up from his notepad, "Closer to 130. How's it going, Moon?" He lit up two cigars, handing one to Moon.

"Don't ask."

The rank fumes choked Morgan like a gaseous vapor. Her eyes wept from the stench of old, oily clothes, newspapers, bags of cans, several bottle-filled carts surrounding an open barrel brimming with decomposing garbage. Morgan walked by the barrel, caught a glimpse of a half-eaten black cat, shuddered and gritted her teeth. She continued down the drab hall, strangely prepared to perform a gruesome duty when she reached the bathroom.

Next to the sweating toilet, perpetually flushing, she stared unblinking at the bloated corpse half submerged in a tub of water.

Maggots were swarming over it — the eyes already falling out of the skull.

In the other room, she could hear Moon chiding Alicia. "Lemme know if you two ladies need any help getting it outta there."

"Nope," Fender called after Alicia, "This is her favorite summer gig."

Entering the bathroom with a body bag, Alicia reached into her pants pocket and withdrew a jar of Vick's Vaporub. She opened the jar, dipped in her index finger, wiped a swatch of goo and stuffed it into each nostril, "Ah," she inhaled deeply through her mouth, and offered the jar to Morgan, "Little Vick's?" she winced, indicating the men inhaling cigars, "they've got their Havanas, we've got our Vick's."

Morgan smiled wanly, scooped up a glutinous hunk, packed it in her nostrils and nodded vigorously, bug-eyed and blinking. "It works."

"Sure," Alicia nodded. "We have to stick together."

"Hey killer," Moon yelled, "need any help?"

Morgan rolled her eyes.

"He likes you," Alicia said.

"Yeah, right. What's the color of the sky in your world?"

Fender said loud enough so they both could hear, "Actually, I hear La Chola is a muy bien bathroom cleaner."

"Pinchón!" Alicia crouched next to the corpse floating in putrid muck.

"Yo bitch," said Fender, both he and Moon laughing from the front door.

She shook her head, muttering more to herself than Morgan, "Bitch, my ass. They bitch when we don't do the work — bitch when we do. Sometimes I don't know why I put up with his bullshit."

"It's probably because the job offers everything you could want in a career," Morgan smiled.

Alicia offered a muffled guffaw, maneuvering the body bag over the feet and legs. "If you push the shoulders back," she instructed Morgan, "I can scoot this up over the knees."

Morgan nodded, looked up, but before she could respond, the partially decomposed upper body she was holding split off at the neck and left her holding the corpse's head. A wave of nausea fogged her vision, then she said, thinly, "Maybe we should try super glue."

Both women looked first at the detached head then at each other and, caught in the absurdity of the moment, burst into a flood of laughter.

Morgan yelled out, "Don't come in, Moon," laughing so hard her eyes watered, "there's been a terrible accident."

An hour later, Moon followed Morgan out of the tenement. Fender and Alicia weren't far behind. "Thanks Morgan," Alicia called after her. "Nice work on that stinker, girl."

"Thank Vick's," Morgan shot back a grin and slipped into the passenger seat.

"Yeah," Fender said to Moon, "I don't let my bitch drive either."

Morgan looked straight ahead as he turned over the ignition. She wanted to ask when she would be allowed to drive, but she lost the nerve: requesting would thrust them in a parent-child battle for the car keys.

"You smell like a medicine chest," he said. She ignored him, so he glanced over at her before he turned onto the highway. "Not so fucking bad," he admitted. "Ever think of an inside job at the coroner's office on clean-up detail?"

"Good idea. I'd start with your mouth."

The dispatcher, crackling over the radio, routed them a call: "We have a male stuck in a tree…"

Moon parked the car at the northwest corner of the park. Morgan could hear him radio their location as she crossed the sorry patch of grass and spotted the man dangling by his armpits from a thick, dry tree limb. How in the world had he managed to make it out to the end of the limb? She was about to call out a question to him when she realized he was unconscious.

She glanced back to catch Moon pause mid-gait and flash a light on some rustling bushes, but before she'd stopped to give her destination a second thought, she'd shimmied several feet up the trunk.

He called after her, "Watch the pantyhose," followed by other comments she didn't hear as she crawled out on a limb parallel to the ground.

She was a few feet from the victim before she could see his slashed wounds, bright red against his chalk-white face: a sign that probably indicated he was dead before he was hung, which meant someone had to haul the corpse up the tree. Was it some kind of a sick gang message or was the murderer trying to make the death look like suicide?

She crawled along the branch, staying focused and calm, until a thought snapped like a piece of elastic in her brain.

Climbing the tree outside Samantha's window. She's not there waiting. Why not?

As she inched closer to the victim, the ground below her started spinning. Pay attention, she told herself. Keep your mind on what you're doing. But she couldn't stop herself from remembering.

"Hey, Samantha," I whispered as I threw a leg through the open window, leaped inside and slammed the window shut. "What's hap —" I bit the end off my word, seeing her feet dangling freely against the outside of the closet door.

No…no…no…no…no. God not now, she warned, trying to wedge a mantra into the visuals swirling in her brain. Don't think about it, don't think about it, don't think about it.

But as she inched closer to the male victim and saw the rope around his neck, her mind struggled to focus in a black hole.

Samantha's blanched face, frozen in pain. I stared aghast. A rope around her neck led over the top of the closed door. I creeped toward the closet.

"No," she heard her own voice scream out loud, wobbled and re-balanced herself on the branch, her eyes riveted on the bright red slash wounds across the victim's chest, his white face —

Samantha's white face flashing repeatedly, like a neon light in my mind as I gripped the closet door handle and tried to pull it open, but it was stuck shut. So, I dragged a chair up to the closet door and stood on it to loosen the rope around her neck. I untied her, stretched out her long body on the hook rug, rushed into the hall and picked up the phone receiver…talking…talking. What am I saying?

Can't hear what I'm saying, because a second me, a double, now enlightened, turns, leaving the real me talking on the phone, and walks back into the bedroom to look again from Samantha's white face to the half of a heart-shaped locket on her white neck to the closet door handle as it turns imperceptibly, and I see now what I've never registered before, never allowed myself to consider, let alone witness.

The closet door opens and Mr. Deaver slips out. He listens to make certain I'm still talking on the phone, glances at his daughter's motionless body on the rug, listens again. He waits, then eases open the window and slithers out.

I hang up the receiver, run back into the dark room, drop to my knees next to Samantha, sobbing and stroking her forehead, "What have you done? Samantha, what have you done?"

Look up, I tell myself. Standing outside my body, I can see myself lift my heavy head, notice the closet door now open, but then pay no attention to it or its implication; instead, I reach for a spread to cover Samantha from the gust of wind coming from the open window.

The terror-filled moments passed, and Morgan didn't know if it were happening all over again. Or worse, if time had slipped backward and it was happening still.

Numb with fear, she scrambled to release the victim just as the branch cracked, releasing both of them into mid-air. She fell a dozen feet to the ground, landing on top of the victim.

When she picked herself up from the ground, Moon was right there, with a ready comment, "Nice work, Officer Fraser. Of course, you could have just talked him down."

Doubled over, her head filled with hot light shining one fluid path of inexplicable kinetic energy, she charged him, hurling her body into his stomach and knocking him on his ass. Out of sheer reflex, he jerked his fist back to haul off and belt her, but he caught himself and flipped her over, pinning her flat on her back in the missionary position.

They locked eyes, glaring.

He must have sensed she was overcome not by fear, as he expected, but utter rage. A wellspring of anger bubbled in her gut inciting a tense physical response — clenched teeth, stiffened knees, knotted stomach — and spewing thoughts that had threatened to surface, but that she'd always managed to ward off.

Good-for-nothing. The self-accusation of being good-for-nothing pounded in her head, until she yelled out: "Go ahead." She didn't know what she expected him to do, but whatever it was, she deserved it. For not being there to protect her best friend from a torturous death, no punishment was too great. And she wanted nothing more than to feel an excruciating blow to her body, followed by a dullness, a stillness deep inside her vanishing in a sheet of dark.

But aside from the head throb, she felt no such pain. And she could make out the sirens approaching in the distance, confirming she wasn't yet dead.

Moon, still hovering over her, looked up and stiffened as he must have spotted his buddies, Iggy and Bow Wow, getting out of their parked patrol car.

He pushed up to his feet, standing immense, lofty.

In the heat of abrupt intimacy, Moon stood over her, vulnerable.

Moon pulled away from the park. Aching and disheveled, Morgan stared blindly out the passenger window. The back of her head felt as though someone were driving a lead pipe into her forehead. Would this night ever be over? They drove a block in dead silence. Then he turned into a mini-mart and got out. She watched him walk away, wondering how he would feel consigned to the passenger seat. Scooting into the driver's seat, she lost herself in the world of the living and the dead. She rested her eyes on the dashboard and imagined herself wrapped in a quilt on Samantha's top bunk. She could feel Mr. "Bowtie" Deaver sit on the bottom bunk. "Samantha, you asleep, sweetie?" His voice echoed as though it were coming through a cardboard tube.

Moon returned eating tuna from an open can to find Morgan sitting at the wheel, ignoring him.

He tried to open the driver's door. Locked.

Morgan clutched the steering wheel. What could he do to possibly make her feel any worse?

He banged on the driver's window, then stormed around to the passenger side and jerked the door open. "It's my car, goddamnit. Move over." He leaned in the car, "I said, unlock the door and move the fuck over."

"Let me guess. John Wayne? No, he didn't cuss in public. What other impressions do you do? William Tell?" She smiled, offering some water.

Moon glared at her. "You're really pissing me off."

"Oh no, I don't want to piss you off."

Radio Dispatch interrupted. "3160 in supermarket parking lot. Victim hiding under a dumpsite in northeast corner."

Morgan turned on the ignition. "You smell like a bait barge," she said, "and I'd just as soon leave you here."

Without waiting for a response, she slipped the car into gear. Moon dropped in the passenger seat and slammed the door.

A few minutes later, Morgan pulled the car into the delivery area back of the supermarket and parked next to smashed crates and a thrashed dumpsite elevated on blocks.

They got out of the car. Morgan approached the dumpster; Moon walked over to the neighbors standing in a nearby cluster, whispering.

"She's deaf," said a bone-thin woman. "Lives with a foster family on the next block."

Morgan leaned over to see the girl huddled under the dumpster, then managed to get down on her hands and knees, positioning herself right in front. Her cheek to the asphalt, Morgan flashed her light on the girl's arms and legs, caked in blood, looking as though they'd been rolled in cinders. Silent and utterly still, she was curled in a tight ball. Curled next to her hand, a motionless black kitten, sleeping or dead, Morgan couldn't tell.

She was careful not to shine the light in the victim's face, but she could feel the girl staring glassy-eyed right through her. Morgan wanted to ask her if she were all right, or to tell her everything would be all right. But she was hit by the tragic scope of what had occurred to this young girl and her own dear childhood friend.

She returned the girl's vacant gaze a long moment, then something inside Morgan strangled her breath, as if jamming on her own emotional brakes to keep from driving off a cliff.

She motioned for Moon to come over and take care of it, then she pushed herself off the gravel, stepped back and watched him position himself near the girl, who was still too shocked to move.

On his hands and knees, Moon reached in under the dump. A sharp meow jerked his hand back. He whipped his head around, snapping, "Why didn't you tell me there was a cat under here?"

She looked at him dully. "Kitten," she said, pointing as it scampered away.

"Worse."

She thought he was kidding, but his initial alarm, quickly covered by a professed feline allergy, alerted her he didn't find kittens cuddly or funny.

Moon waited a few seconds, took a deep breath, then scooted the victim out from under the dumpsite. "We want to help you," he said gently, positioning himself so she could see his face. His hands signed as he spoke. "We need to know the description of the guy so we can catch him, okay?"

Motionless, she stared at a spot several inches from her nose.

"Listen," he spoke as he signed, "we don't want him to ever, ever do this to you or anyone else again. Do you understand?"

She squinted painfully at him and he nodded encouragingly, his troubled eyes searching hers. "We need his description."

She lifted a fist, trying to sign, but she shivered as if the chilling memory were tearing through her mind, ripping out all intelligible response. Closing her eyes tightly, she bowled over, whether in physical pain or embarrassed anguish, Morgan couldn't tell. Holding her in his arms like a small child, Moon picked her up and carried her to the police car.

"You're doing fine," he assured her, "you're gonna be okay. My partner here, Officer Fraser, and I are going to take you over to the hospital, get you cleaned up and into a new dress. Light green with a tie at the waist." He looked up at Morgan, shrugged modestly, then frowned at her absurd smile. "What's the matter with you?" he asked.

"Nothing," she lied, fully aware, but not knowing what to do with the realization that she liked that tender part of him she'd just witnessed. She could never tell anyone, of course. Not even Sam.

"You're not such a bad cop," she said. He caught her eyes and she smiled at him. Perhaps she was luckier than she'd thought to have him for a partner.

"Thanks," he said.

They looked at each other in silence as if their concentration had been momentarily short-circuited. They both picked up on the clumsy moment instantly. Morgan glanced away, afraid that someone who knew her well would notice the telltale smile creeping across her face.

Just after midnight, they were standing in front of a hospital elevator. "You really helped get her back on track," Morgan said. "If she could read your lips, why did you sign?"

"Not all deaf people can read lips, so it's a good idea to do both if you're not sure."

Something told her not to ask him how he got to be such an expert.

No response for a moment, then, as if he'd read her mind, he said quietly, "My son was deaf."

"I didn't know you had a son."

"He died a couple of years ago."

"I'm sorry."

The elevator door opened up, and he indicated for her to enter first. He followed, standing next to a hollow-eyed young woman with a toddler leaning against her legs. The boy was licking an ice cream cone, which was taking his mind off the bandage on his head. He looked up at Moon and, grinning, stretched out the ice cream in his grimy hand.

Moon passed a look to Morgan, offered a smile but declined the ice cream. Then, seeing the boy's expression sink, Moon leaned over and took a pretend lick.

The woman, too drained of vitality to appreciate a kind moment, shuffled the child out on the next floor. He waved to

Moon as he was stumbling on his over-sized sandals and licking up the ice cream running down his forearm.

The child's energy filled the empty elevator. Morgan sensed Moon was mentally transported light years away, recalling perhaps an image of his own child in sandals, sucking ice cream off his fingers.

By the time they'd reached the car it was almost one in the morning. The pace and tone of the night's events had quieted down considerably, so they took another break at Tia's Tacos, and Morgan reminded him about the boy with the ice cream cone in the elevator. Moon grinned, sadly, nodding, "Yeah, that kid probably has a shitty life, and a great attitude. Some kids are like that. My son always had a smile on his face. Thought the damnedest things were funny. And he was always making his mother and me laugh. We'd be in some heated argument and he'd come wobbling by in my fishing boots with a dishtowel on his head."

Morgan smiled, "Did you take him fishing?"

"Yeah. All the time. We hung out together. He always wanted to help me nail this or mow that. But," he paused, held up his hand in a gesture of surrender, then continued, "this one Saturday, he and Mister Kitty, his stuffy, were helping me cement the cracks in the front walk. Lance was always running out to meet me and tripping. So, what's he do? Hops, falls and plops butt-first in the cement. 'Ooh Dad-dy,' he says, '*assadent.*' Right.

"I had to patch up the cement, so I sent him around to his mother in the kitchen balancing half-way up a ladder, stretching to match a cluster of fall leaves on a fresh sheet of wallpaper. Just a minute, honey, she signs. Because, God knows, she has to cut these invisible paper threads that she sees hanging down from the ceiling. Meticulous. I can see her standing on the step ladder cutting threads that nobody else can see while Lance is standing below holding these wildflowers I'd sent him in to give her. I should've taken 'em in my own damn self.

"I shouldn't have given them to her at all," he paused, as if stuck in a familiar thought loop. "So," he inhaled deeply, "she finishes cutting the strings and gets tweaked at him when she sees his sandal imprint on the front of a piece of wallpaper on the floor. She said she didn't get upset with him, but she was always irritated with him when she worked on projects. She was a second grade teacher for Godsake. You'd think she'd have buckets of patience. She swears that she got down off the ladder, took the flowers and hugged him.

"But I don't believe her. She swears he signed that the flowers were from me. And she told him to go tell me that it's time for lunch. I can't, he says. Why not? Daddy says for me not to come in the front yard until he says okay. What did you do, she says, stick your little foot in the wet cement too? He tells her it was an accident. Run upstairs and put on some dry clothes, she says, and hugs him, but I don't believe her. About ten minutes later, she pokes her head out the front door. Nice work, hon, she tells me. Looks great. Grilled cheeses are ready.

"I look at the concrete job. Not half bad, at least Lance won't trip anymore. Then I push the wheelbarrow, still half-filled with wet cement, into the backyard. I'm weaving the barrow around the skirt of the pool when I get a glimpse of Mister Kitty bobbing. Mister Kitty and Lance are never far apart, and Mister Kitty's close, but not close enough to the top steps."

Moon didn't say it now, but Morgan could tell he still, all too frequently and at entirely unguarded moments like in the elevator, was stunned by a numb wave that swept over him.

Morgan thought she was holding her emotions in check, until she felt hot tears in her eyes. She'd been waiting for him to show he was human, but now that he'd revealed his pain, she didn't know what to say, but managed, "Thank you for telling me."

His face mirrored his anguish. Then, he stood abruptly, heading for a coffee refill and a tuna burrito.

She watched him charm withered Tia behind the window. Tia, trapped in that claustrophobic glass hut. She'd lost her native country and certainly loved ones about whom she'd never speak. Moon lost his son, and the missed opportunity of fatherhood. And Morgan lost her best friend and her husband. She realized they were both trapped, imprisoned by the loss of someone dear and a shared sense of self-blame.

He returned with his second sloppy burrito for the night, blowing the steam off his coffee. She couldn't help but smile to herself when he made amends in his own oblique way by relating a personal experience he once had with Internal Affairs.

"So I just made them find out and I didn't offer them any information," he was telling her. "You don't have to give those I.A. guys shit. You've got the classic Mutt and Jeff nerds."

He was teaching her the ropes of hard core police work, trade secrets that, due to lack of trust and confidentiality, experienced male officers often kept hidden from their women counterparts. "You gotta admit your I-don't-know-who-the-transporting-officers-are story is pretty dumb," Moon said, "but you better stick to it."

"Well, I don't know what happened to the suspect after they took him."

He offered her a bite of his burrito. "Tuna totally revolutionizes a burrito."

She shook her head. "I don't like tuna."

"That's your problem," he said, back on his glib track. "But you do know who the *they* are, right?" he asked. Waiting through her silence, he continued, "That's what I thought. I'm not gonna tell 'em shit, and you don't have to either. The thing is you become more of a prick than Internal Affairs. You let them dictate it. If that Joe Blanco guy is nice, civil, say: 'I don't know,' or 'I don't remember.'"

Morgan smiled at his operator-like monotone.

"I'm serious. I know you think these are good guys. Out to uncover the truth. Clean house. But you don't know these guys. They're vicious. For using the chokehold that Mutt whop, what's his name?"

"Francesconi."

"Yeah. He could bury you behind a desk forever. And they work together. Mutt and Jeff. Don't make any mistake about that. So, make it clear to them you were using the chokehold as a last resort to protect your life. You were in fear for your life. That's all they need to know."

She let him continue with the pep talk, but she was wondering about that essential part of him that she'd glimpsed but would never touch.

He glanced at her to make sure she was getting it, then continued, "But if they want to be pricks," he shrugged, "say, 'I don't know, why don't you tell me the answer.' And they'll come back with: 'Don't answer a question with a question.'" He stuffed the rest of the burrito in his mouth. "And you, right away, exclaim, 'Oh, now you're telling me how to answer.'" A coffee gulp, "Then you let 'em have it, say: 'I want a rep. I want this on tape, too. I want this terminated until tomorrow, so I can get a lawyer.'"

She shrugged, getting it. "Just fuck with 'em."

"That's the ticket." He nodded, approvingly, then launched into painting the big picture. "The first thing they're gonna do is put a briefcase on the table, but they don't open it." She assumed there was a reason they didn't open it, and, given the evening's unprecedented revelations, figured he was about to tell her.

13

Mutt and Jeff

Seated next to the streaked window overlooking downtown Los Angeles, Morgan swiveled back and forth in the maroon padded chair. She'd been staring out the window since Investigator Joe Blanco had given her a cup of hot tea, then left to look for honey in plastic packs. Today he wore a tie splashed in red chili peppers. She wondered if his wife picked out his ties. He didn't wear a wedding ring, but these days that didn't mean he wasn't married. Maybe his ties were gifts from his girlfriend. She probably wanted the world to know he wasn't a complete paper trail nerd. Could have been worse: a bowtie. The Diego Rivera peasant themes and the chilies intrigued her; bowties made her gag.

He'd been gone more than ten minutes, but it didn't matter: Morgan was engrossed in the tiny people crossing the street eighteen stories below. The human specks, no bigger than her thumbnail, moved like wind-up toys in smooth straight lines, forward, back, sideways, making it easy to think of them as more mechanical than human. Such an extreme distance had to affect the social perspective of police department employees, serious about their policies and procedures, working elevated from the real world.

Echoing in her ear was Moon's prediction of the investigator's procedure, which Mutt and Jeff followed move by move: "The first thing they're going to do is put a briefcase on the table, but they don't open it. There's this switch on the outside of the tape recorder, and they flick it on real nonchalant, and you know you're in deep shit when they advise you of your constitutional rights because now it's a criminal investigation…"

Investigator Blanco returned, shrugged to indicate no honey, set his paperwork in a neat stack in front of him, then stated, "Officer Fraser, I want to advise you of your constitutional rights — "

Having entered from a side door, Investigator Francesconi interrupted, "And everything we use administratively can be used against you in a criminal trial." Francesconi's hoarse voice diminished his authorial presence. He'd probably spent his days off at Hollywood Park yelling for his longshot, Slimebag, in the 9th.

Blanco motioned for Francesconi to back off, continuing, "Officer Fraser, your partner already told us exactly what happened. Why didn't you go for the baton?"

"I didn't get a chance to. He shoved me, and I ended up on the ground."

Blanco paused a moment, brushed his chili pepper tie with his fingertips and tried to clarify terms. "Well," he asked, his voice measured, "why did you jump on his back?"

"He knocked me down, and he was going back to the Porsche. I didn't know if he was going for his gun or not, and I jumped on his back in a chokehold because I had to try to take him down. He was stronger than I was and I couldn't handle him any other way. I was in fear for my life."

Francesconi lumbered over and stood in front of her. "We've got the coroner's report back, Officer Fraser," he said, clearing his throat. "And the suspect didn't die of a swollen esophagus like maybe we thought…from your chokehold; he died of a blunt trauma to his ruptured spleen. How do you explain that?"

Her eyes revealed her confusion. "I don't know."

Francesconi glowered. "But you do know who transported him for you."

She looked straight into his eyes, "I told you before I don't know."

Mutt leaned into her face. His liver-and-onion breath clung in her nose like a whiff of rotten eggs. "Officer Fraser, I just want you to know that your little escapade could cost you your job, and anything you hold back from us could also cost you your job. You're between a rock and a hard place, I'd say. And the only thing you can do is tell the truth, so you better start telling it right now."

She locked eyes with him another moment, forcing him to wait through his fierce exasperation for her response. He didn't wait long, "Hey, we can make this quick and painless or we can drag it out, draw lots of blood. We can keep it just the three of us or we can bring in your partner, possibly your captain." He paused, glanced at a file on the desk, adding, "Definitely Dr. Best."

She flinched, but reminded herself she'd stopped going to Best. What could he say? Francesconi sensed her restraint, picked up what was probably her psychiatric file and riffled through it. "Yeah, doctor knows Best…oh my, nightmares…poor baby has nightmares on the job.

"I don't know," he shook his head at Blanco, "Joe, I don't know about you but I only have nightmares when I'm asleep."

Moon had been right, she realized as his version of the interrogation scenario relaxed and ordered her thoughts. "Look," he'd warned. "Don't let 'em press you. Take your time. Remember," he predicted, "Mutt, the typical 1950 detective — short, fat and usually stupid — is going to try to rush you, confuse you, intimidate the hell out of you, so you'll change your story. He's going to come off really abrupt and matter-of-fact, camouflaging any technique they're using. That's why he's the bad guy.

"Now the other guy who's pretty calm is going to come between you two when things get tense. Sometimes he'll even tell his partner to step out. So, you feel comfortable that he got rid of the asshole, and he's more the kind of considerate person you want to talk with. Wrong. Whether it's acted or natural, that's how they're going to try to do it. Don't bite."

She focused on the other guy a moment. She felt like she'd met him before, maybe at some policing function. The crinkled skin around his eyes hinted that he laughed a lot, and even like now, when he didn't have anything to laugh about, his relaxed expression could break into a smile. He was calm, almost peaceful, as if he were going through the motions, asking the right questions, hoping, but certainly not expecting, that she'd reveal delicate information. And that would be okay. Que será, será.

Blanco nudged Francesconi to back off again, whispering loud enough for her to hear, "Why don't you…" he cocked his head towards the door, indicating for Francesconi to step out.

"No," he stated flatly, then, enamored with his own boldness, fired another offensive, "Look, we know you're protecting Ben Fender. What we can't figure out is why. Are you fucking him?"

She glanced at Blanco's cool eyes intently observing her. Not missing a beat.

There was a long pause as she inhaled deeply, found her feet, stood and announced in a fierce, thawed voice, "I want a rep and my *own* tape recorder, " she told Blanco, then eyed Francesconi, "so if you ever make a comment like that again, it will be your fucking job."

On the way home from Parker Center, she meandered around at the nearby City Market to quiet her racing heart. She didn't really need anything but cilantro. Cilantro and the buzz of real life. The aroma of fresh coffee beans, fresh cheese, dried herbs. And children sucking swizzle sugar sticks. When she finally did stop for fresh cilantro, she spoke with Rogelio, the grocer who lived on her block, as if nothing unusual had happened. He asked if Sam were at a baseball practice. She told him the season was over. Sam and Nat were swimming at the Y.

Morgan decided to get a dozen tomatillos for a salsa Sam liked. She set the husk-wrapped green tomatoes in a bag and, reaching for a bunch of cilantro, brushed up next to Joe Blanco.

Rogelio called out, "José, cómo está?"

Sorting through tiny chilies, Joe nodded, "Bien. Hambre."

"Y tú mama?"

"Mejor, Rogelio, muchas mejor, gracias. Y tus niños?"

He glanced up at Rogelio and noticed Morgan. He stopped and set his plastic bag, filled with enough jalapeños to make salsa for a lifetime, next to a dozen large, red tomatoes, several huge onions and bunches of cilantro. Should she whip around and hurry away, or slide around the mangoes and disappear down the aisle? Just as she'd decided on a route of discreet exit, his jalapeño bag slipped off the counter and little green bombs shot into the air, landing around her feet, forcing her to step on them or pick them up. She caught Rogelio's pained expression. Trapped behind the counter, he raised his eyes and hands to the ceiling in a gesture of helplessness.

Joe Blanco mustered an innocent face and bent over next to Morgan, kneeling face- to-face on the floor, scooping up chilies. "The bag must have slipped," he shrugged in fake disbelief, offering the hint of a smile. "Look," he cut right to the chase, "I'd probably lose my job if anyone knew I told you this, so if you tell anyone I said it, I'll deny it."

He swiveled his head in all directions, then plopped a couple of jalapenos in the bag. "Fender's a bad egg, whether you want to believe that or not. He's what we're trying to get rid of because he's already cost the department in a big way, but we can't do it without the support of cops who work with him."

He leaned in. "We know that you know Officers Fender and Bear transported your suspect. We don't know what happened on the way to the division, but I can tell you that the suspect suffered massive hemorrhaging, probably caused by dozens of severe baton jabs to his ribs."

Her eyebrows raised at the visual, "Dozens of baton jabs to his ribs? How many dozens?"

"Look, I shouldn't be telling you anything at this stage of the investigation."

"You weren't in the car. How do you know that?"

"I was a cop. It's an old boy's trick on black suspects; it leaves no marks." The jalapeños were back in plastic. They both stood.

He handed the bag to Rogelio, then turned and regarded her, seizing the moment. "If you don't help us now, you'll get reprimanded for lying to us; you'll probably get a week's suspension without pay…and in the report, it'll look like you supported Fender."

She stiffened, fingering the onion skin husk protecting a tomatillo.

He pressed on, moving into his interrogation mode. "Look, I know why you're so loyal to this guy. He was your T.O. I also know he fought with your husband Jacob — " her eyes flicked over his face, "but we have to nail him before he disgraces the entire department. His actions on the job already have us up to our eyeteeth in litigation you don't even know about. All you have to do is confirm he backed you up and we have him nailed."

His fixed seriousness touched her for an instant. She was struck by a sense of his early idealism, by the way he must have once believed people should behave to one another and now, years later, had been battered down by the cruel reality of how they actually do. But Alicia's strident warning about the MAW dogs eating the women alive slammed the door of cooperation he had managed to wedge open.

"Since you were a cop, Investigator Blanco — "

"Joe," he said, hastening to open the door to an informal confidence.

She paused, held his stare a moment, repeating his name. Joe. Joe Blanco, and thought about him in an entirely different context. Was he Señor Blanco's José? Señor Blanco who died in the fire? And Señora Blanco? Was he the José with the big desk job that got her position back at the Academy gift shop? No, it was a different Joe, and she wouldn't even ask, wouldn't tempt an emotional connection.

She continued, "You know what it would be like for me, Investigator Blanco, for any of the women in the 77th, to put out a call and not to be backed up?" She heeled a stray jalapeño next to Blanco's foot, turned, nodded to Rogelio, and walked past the mangoes.

After Blanco and Francesconi had interviewed Slattery and Morgan to no avail, the investigation didn't formally announce anything for another week. In the interim, the "scoop" was that another division had picked up the assistance call, and since they didn't announce their intentions on the radio, they had not been taped. Those "unknown" transporting officers dragged the unconscious suspect to a cell. No watch commander had been on duty to see them, so on the slate outside the cell, they only wrote FRASER as the arresting officer.

In order to protect the city, Internal Affairs publicly stated that the suspects in the Porsche had been in an altercation before they were stopped, which was why the deceased suspect fought Officer Morgan Fraser. The suspect's spleen had already been ruptured in the previous altercation. The media hype for the Olympics, only four weeks away, buried the announcement in the Metro section, and it didn't even appear in the San Fernando Valley or Orange County editions.

But Sara Ann Engels, Fender's outspoken critic, didn't buy any of Internal Affairs' rhetoric. Engels was conducting her own personal investigation to find out what happened. She hovered next to Morgan while she got dressed. "Slattery says you were outside of the car with the suspect when back-up came. Right?"

Morgan nodded, avoiding eye contact.

Alicia crowded next to them, slipped a T-shirt over lime green, string-bikini underpants, then sat on the floor and started doing sit-ups.

Engels pressed on, "You know it had to be one of the guys in MAW."

Morgan glanced at her, then looked away, but Alicia had to take the bait. "Says who?"

Engels had a self-righteous glint in her eye, "For Chrissakes, it doesn't take a detective to figure that out. Since there are no independent witnesses, and the other suspect in the car split, those MAW scumbags knew they could get away with it."

"Scumbags," Alicia echoed. "What about the suspect who beat the shit out of Morgan? Why isn't he a scumbag?"

"That's a moot point now, isn't it? Since one of your MAW buddies beat him to death. And that's not what we're supposed to be all about. Beatin' and suckin' and fuckin' — "

"Blow it out your ass," Alicia responded, more harshly than the accusation warranted, then slammed her locker and stomped out.

Morgan headed after her, pausing a second to set Engels straight. "Look, you weren't there. You don't know what happened, so why don't you just stay the hell out of it?"

"Don't tell me what to stay the hell out of," Engels fired back. "I'm sick to death of these guys doing whatever they want and getting away with it. And it's gonna stop."

Morgan hurried to catch up with Alicia in the parking lot. "Hey." She tried to put her arm around her, but Alicia shied away. "Don't let her get to you like that."

She choked back tears, mumbling that Iggy wasn't like that and they were both sick of having to apologize for being in love. "I just want to make some peace, you know," she sniffled. "Maybe help set a few people straight so they can lead a peaceful life. Do something for this piece of shit community."

"Share an espresso," Morgan interjected, causing her to smile faintly.

"Eso es. But that's really hard, when I don't even have peace in my own precinct. Not all guys are little pricks, you know." Alicia nodded back at the locker room, and they both knew she was referring to Engel's generic male label.

"I know."

"Even Lt. Herdahl doesn't get it." She shook her head, sadly, "She asked me to file a sexual harassment charge against Fender for his stupid banana joke, you believe it?" She says: 'We'll keep it entirely confidential, Alicia,' she says, 'and a righteous harassment charge along with some other charges we have on him will send a message.' To who, I ask her. 'Oh,' she tells me, 'to Fender. To all the officers who support MAW.'"

She darted a glance to Moon and Teddy Bear, exiting, then back to Morgan, in hushed tones, "So I ask her, what will those legal channels do for me at midnight alone in some alley?"

Iggy sauntered out of the back door and discreetly avoided a look in Alicia's direction as he crossed to his sports car. Then just before he slipped into the driver's seat, he glanced back at her and flashed a smile.

Morgan watched Alicia bite her lip to keep from smiling back.

Alicia sighed, "Let's make a deal. I won't let them get to me about *that* guy, if you don't let them worry you about the suspect you choked out. I'm sick of hearing about who transported him. You did the right thing," she said, nodding to herself, as she strained to watch Iggy drive away. "I always say even if you get the wrong guy, this guy for sure done something before, or he's thought about doing something."

Morgan nodded vaguely. Her tone triggered the memory of Jacob's father, Thomas, reasoning with them over Sunday dinner: "The truth is most people usually deserve what they get, so there's no reason to feel guilty for what you do."

"Dad," Jacob would stand up to his father, "C'mon, you of all people know how many people don't deserve what happens to them?"

"I'm talking about war. I'm talking about having to use your head in a time of panic," Mr. Fraser would clarify. "If you're in a rice paddy in Southeast Asia, and a guy in black pajamas is running across a rice paddy with an AK-47, are you going to shoot him or wonder if he's really a communist, if maybe he just stole those clothes from a VC soldier and he's running away? You shoot the son-of-a-bitch. You don't worry what he could have been, just what he appeared to be at that moment. How can you know past the moment?"

Alicia drove off to meet Iggy at some Latin disco in San Pedro and Morgan stayed in her car thinking and watching Teddy Bear's animated gesticulations to Moon. True, she considered, we can't know past the moment, but we can know the truth of what came before. And if her suspect didn't die as a result of her chokehold, if he died instead of a blunt trauma that ruptured his spleen, she had to find out if Fender caused the trauma.

She caught Moon's eye from across the parking lot and started to get out of her car. She wanted to ask him if Fender had beaten her suspect, if Fender had jabbed her suspect to death, but she thought about it too long and lost the nerve. Besides, how could Moon really know? What if Fender had beaten her suspect? It struck her that even if he hadn't, he might lie about it, he might say he'd beaten her suspect to protect her in some warped sense, or simply to diminish the strength of her chokehold. She let the possibilities swirl which left her confused, wondering if she would ever know what really happened that night.

14

Wash and Dry

Morgan's week suspension without pay happened overnight. A few days later when the official report came out, buried by the Olympic media blitz, it was only a slip of an article in the Metro section. But the identification of the transport officers, Fender and Bear, jarred the 77th women officers so badly that Morgan was relieved to be temporarily jobless.

During the first days of her suspension, the events of the night spun in a mind loop. What could she have done differently to stop the fight that had started in the locker room the night after the Internal Affairs report came out?

Slattery had been fiddling with her blouse buttons, watching Engels, who was sitting motionless next to her locker, still holding the report, staring at it. A frown seared her brow. Slattery withdrew a white Tupperware container and offered her homemade peanut butter cookies. Engels shook her head.

Morgan, finished dressing, was tying her tennis shoes, as Slattery passed the container to Blocker, who took a handful. Slattery chattered about the Olympic torch, giving her daily report on the location and minor problems or highlights.

Morgan watched Slattery, so pleased to share her cookies, aching for crumbs of approval. Slattery should be at the border on the 65th day when the Olympic Torch rolled runners past barley fields just north of Tukelake. She should be standing next to the Welcome to California road sign. She should be there handing out her cookies to the witnesses — townsfolk, highway workers, farmers.

The cookie container stopped in front of Morgan. She looked up, "With or without peanuts?" she asked.

"With," Slattery said, and Morgan took a couple, just as Slattery slouched past, avoiding Engels, and tilting the bowl towards Alicia, who was winding down on her power sit-ups. "Ninety," she counted, breaking into a thought. "I don't get it." She exhaled deeply, refusing the cookies, then frowning at Morgan. "Five days. For what?"

Slattery pulled the Tupperware to her waist and burped the lid.

Engels sniggered. "For lying to IA, what do you think?" Engels didn't wait for a response. She bolted to her feet, as if her insides were burning wildfire, and charged towards Morgan, pointing an incriminating finger. "For lying to IA and us."

Morgan shook her head in foolish disbelief. "I admit it wasn't very smart, but I actually thought my chokehold might have caused a swollen esophagus. Don't look at me like that. It's happened."

"Yeah, well," Blocker informed her bitterly, "now you know. Fender Bender just jammed the shit out of him."

"I know about the chokehold; I didn't see Fender beat him up."

Engels tapped the palm of her hand to her forehead with a theatrical flair. "What do you need? A videotape? Why do you defend him? You knew all along and you lied to protect that fucking fascist. Do you have any idea how this makes us look?" She waited a wretched beat. "Like them for Godsake."

"Oh," Alicia bounced off the floor, throwing her arms up to the ceiling, "she was doing it to protect us, not Fender. You act like we never tell little lies for each other. Like you never lie." She glared at Engels, who mustered a guileless face. "You make me sick," Alicia angled towards her. "You live a lie." She looked askance at Slattery, "Both of you sneak around, touch each other on the butt when you think nobody's looking, like you really think we care about your pathetic little love life."

"That's good," Blocker commented, as she slung her bag over her shoulder. "Why don't you girls get into a cat fight?" She moved toward the door, hissing as she exited, "That's just what we need. A cat fight. Rip each other to shreds."

Blocker's exaggerated hiss fell like a silent spray over the locker room. They dropped the passionate subject, until later when Alicia and Morgan were heading across the parking lot towards their cars.

"Íjole!" Alicia nudged Morgan, confidentially reprimanding her. "Five days off, no pay. Because of Fender. For that cabrón." She made a disapproving gesture, then nodded her head indicating Engels leaning up against a parked car, offering whispered reassurances to Slattery's downcast face, "But at least you got the balls to stand up for what you believe, what you did, and it was an honest mistake." Alicia veered towards the secret lovers.

"Not to mention that you're the one who told me not to reveal any MAW names," Morgan reminded her.

Alicia grinned. "Yeah, not to mention that. See what I'm saying, we try to help each other out, and tell little white lies. And even though it's hard to believe anyone would protect Fender's ass, if any one of us points the finger at him, we are going to die. For sure."

Walking next to Alicia, Morgan found herself invading Engels and Slattery's private space. "You know something," Alicia glanced over the twosome, fashioning a seeming apology, then asked, "I was wondering do those vibrator things do the job?"

Engels straightened. "Alicia, you have about as much class as a clogged toilet."

"Yeah," she shrugged. "Well, I didn't know if they work with a battery or you gotta plug them into the wall."

"What you need is to stick one in your mouth and find out," Engels said.

"What you need is to let your girl have a *real* fuck," she said, held their astounded stares an instant, then turned and walked away.

Engels lunged past Morgan, crashing into Alicia from behind, sending her sprawling onto the pavement.

Morgan caught a glimpse of several of the MAW guys — Moon, Fender, Iggy, Bow Wow — stepping out the back door as she grabbed Engels by an upper arm.

"Hey, Sarge!" Iggy called out back inside the division as Alicia scrambled to get off the ground. Engels spun around, wrenched her arm free and wheeled toward Morgan, ramming her against a car trunk.

Sergeant Ross burst out the exit and sped across the parking lot reaching the brawl just as Morgan, backed against the trunk, clasped Engels shoulders, wedged her knee between them and sent her flying backwards into Ross' outstretched arms. "She's all yours," Morgan said, brushing herself off.

Alicia spat at Engels. "Pinchón."

"All right. All right." Sgt. Ross tilted Engels upright. "Let's cool off," he leveled a look at each one individually. "Go home." He walked Engels to her car.

Slattery stood alone.

Morgan could feel Moon watching her and Alicia cross to their cars. "You need a mouth-cuff," Morgan told her.

"I say what I think. You got a problem with that, too?"

Morgan shook her head, sighing. "Yeah, like I tell my kid, just because you say 'no offense,' to somebody doesn't make what you say any less offensive."

Alicia glanced back at Engels getting into her car. "I'm not your kid, and I don't trust women who don't like men. It's that yin, yang thing, you know. Too much yin, too much yang messes up how you deal with people, you know. I hate that she pisses the hell out of me."

She waved a hand in Engels' direction, then admitted sadly, "But she's got a point. If you didn't finger Fender to protect us — *women* — that's one thing, but if you did it because you think you owe him something since he was your T.O., you owe him nada, nothing, nada."

Morgan shook her head, that wasn't it. "He tried to save my husband's life in Viet Nam. Jacob got shot and, while Fender was trying to save him, pull him out, he got hit again."

"That's history. C'mon, like I said, you owe him a big fat nada." She gave her an encouraging hug. Morgan purposely brushed her palm across Alicia's backside. "Don't mess with me, man," she warned, teasing, "you know I don't go for that shit."

They burst into grins. "What you need is a *real* one too, you know," Alicia said.

"Thanks, Doc. See you in five days," Morgan said, leaving her friend to meet Iggy and make certain she got what she'd been suggesting Engels, Slattery and Morgan needed.

Now the entire week had gone by, and Morgan didn't know quite how to explain the situation to Sam, or even if she should. Maybe she would talk to Sam today over pizza after they'd finished their Saturday commitments: helping Blocker at the food drive in the morning; laundry, in the afternoon.

Sam had actually committed she and Nat to help Blocker distribute food, but, of course, they needed a ride. Morgan had driven by this corner of the 77th at night, but, by day, she'd never seen a worse ghetto. The severe late morning sun glared off cluttered trash heaps, car scraps, disfigured washing machines and refrigerators in a vacant lot. A weathered, hunched wino stumbled across the street, spitting phlegm, apparently beyond the help of any comestibles offered at a food drive.

They drove past an immigrant father carrying a baby on his hip, guiding a couple of toddlers across the street with the palm of his hand. He probably worked sixty hours a week sweeping floors, then another twenty picking bruised edibles tossed in supermarket garbage bins and worrying about his children.

"Have you been inside any of these houses?" Sam asked, regarding her with a curious mixture of suspicion and intrigue.

"On a couple of domestic calls."

"What do they look like?" asked Nat.

"In that house over there," she pointed to a sagging clapboard, undistinguished, but for the dull red porch, "it was after midnight and I was keeping my eyes on a couple who'd been in a drunken knife fight, but I remember a half dozen or so children sleeping on heaps of clothes on the floor." She didn't tell them about the whimpering infant on the trashed couch, or the smell of urine and burnt cooking oil that was strong enough to knock you out.

"Watch it." Nat alerted Morgan to a bag lady stepping off the curb with no bag, only fleshy sags beneath her eyes. Her face was black and twisted and she stared, dazed, through their windshield. Then, as if she could read their minds, she pointed to a fenced asphalt area. Their eyes followed her crooked finger to a banner, *Food for Life*, tacked on a chain link fence that surrounded a parking lot filled with old men, women, a few children. Dogs.

In the midst of the gathering, they could see Blocker was hauling out large crates from a Mission truck and doling out food in boxes to several volunteers, who she then directed to numbered food distribution tables.

Sam looked over at Nat and nodded precisely, as if any less organization would not suit Blocker. "We're late."

"I don't think so." Morgan pulled to the curb, parallel parking into a tight fit.

They got out of the car and were immediately blasted with "When We Gather at the River" blaring over the loudspeaker. "Why can't they just give food to needy people because it's the right thing to do?" Morgan asked. "Why do we have to make it a spiritual event?"

Sam winced the way she did when she understood Morgan's sentiment, if not her words. "Now," Sam scolded, "just how many times do we do things you want to do for fun on Saturday?"

Morgan nodded. While this might not be work, she thought, neither is it entirely amusement. So many destitute people made her uneasy — helpless to do anything to better their situation. The dozens of needy humans didn't faze Sam and Nat, however, because they didn't see them as a social scar, victims of a flawed state system, perpetually without; rather, a social bruise, victims of a natural disaster, temporarily in need. They were envisioning a mega food drive in which all the 77th officers volunteered. Especially Mooseface.

Morgan laughed aloud. "If you put a gun to his head to make him give out food on his day off, he still wouldn't do it here."

"Why?" asked Sam.

She stiffened, enunciating for effect, "An officer should confine his associations and duties on his beat strictly to police work. No socializing, no getting chummy with people you might have to arrest — "

"That's stupid," Sam cut her off. "He's got some weird ideas."

The poor formed a line. Everyone in line held a number. Most women brought their own containers. Plastic bags smelled of sweat as Morgan filled them each with a block of government-issue orange cheese, six potatoes, two onions, one cup of pinto beans, two loaves of bread, two cans of soup.

Blocker had no sooner gotten Sam and Nat situated in their separate volunteer stations, then an old hag with chicken skin on her arms grabbed for Sam's entire box of rations. Wiry and quick in spite of her breakable appearance, she made extravagant swipes, lobster-like, as if she were plucking a harp, trying to reach the boxes.

Sam moved and dodged to block the woman until a teenage boy picked the hag up and put her at the back of the line, then returned to Sam. With a manner measured and calm, he shook his dreadlocks and made tiny circles with his index finger pointing first to his head then to the hag. He smiled confidentially and Sam offered a knowing nod as though it were their little secret.

Morgan watched him pass a message to Sam in sign language, grin and then with a happy spin, weave around her and skip away.

Entranced, Sam looked after him. Her eyes dropped from his dreadlocks to the glistening spurs around his ankles and stayed riveted there for a long time. Then she gazed back at Morgan with a radiant beam. Morgan didn't have the heart to tell her that as he turned and reached behind Sam's back, he'd flipped a can of beans from her box into his pack.

A couple of hours later, Nat tugged at the duffel bag in the back of Morgan's Jeep parked next to the laundromat door. He tugged again, grunting. The bag landed on the asphalt with a thud. "Cheese 'n rice," he exclaimed to Sam. "What'daya got in here, rocks?"

"Socks," said Sam, staring at the baseball field luring her across the street. "Very dirty socks. The washer's been broke three weeks." She lifted Ozma, now too big to comfortably tote around, from the backseat and hooked a red leash on her collar.

Sorting clothes into several wash bins, Morgan glanced at Sam and Nat plopping down the last of the laundry bags and hangers. "Thanks guys," she said. "You've been loads of help. I won't need you again until it's time to fold, then with your help we can be out of here before Christmas."

"What about ironing?" Deadly serious, Nat looked from Morgan to Sam. "My grandma lets me make brown shapes and buildings on old white sheets."

Sam shook her head. "Weird, you are so weird, Nat." She added simply, "Ironing is against our religion."

"My Grandma says you got no religion."

Sam bristled. "You can tell your grandma — "

Morgan threw her a hard look. "That we almost joined a group, but we had trouble getting some things ironed out."

"What?" Nat asked Sam, who eyed her mother.

"Yeah what, Mom?"

Morgan gave a slip of a smile to Sam and widened her eyes. "E-vil."

"Evil?" Nat asked, looking from Sam to Morgan back to Sam, who nodded, "Yeah, evil," then shrugged, adding, "it's gotta come from somewhere."

"You mean like vampires and stuff?"

"No," Morgan said. "More like sometimes when cruel things happen to kind people." She wanted to say that she'd always had a hard time explaining evil to Sam. She didn't know how to explain it to herself. But she didn't want to steer this into a weighty discussion drawing annoyed looks from other Saturday morning laundry patrons.

Sam dumped a laundry bag onto the counter, "Like when Gramma Sofie's family were killed in those camps. What was God doing? Taking a trip to the moon or something?"

"Oh," sighed Nat, now he got it. He could answer this question, "That's because God hasn't finished working on certain places in the world yet."

"What's he been doing?" asked Sam.

"Well," Nat shrugged, "I don't know, but when you think about it, that day a week he takes off adds up," Nat calculated. "Fifty-two times I don't know how many millions a years, but even my dad says he should've been working overtime, not taking off Sundays and holidays."

Morgan chuckled at him. She handed Sam a couple of dollars and nodded, indicating the shop next door. "Take him to the magic store and see if they have any of that stuff left that turns people into living stone."

Sam grinned and led Nat out the back door, down the alley and around to the front of the four store complex. She stopped in front of ChiliBurger Shack, counting change. "If we share a coke, we have enough for one chiliburger and two orders of fries."

Nat squinted at the price board over his head. "If we have water, then we'll have enough for two burgers."

"Water," she looked at him in disbelief. "Water. Chiliburgers and water? They don't go together."

"Says who?"

She sighed heavily and shook her head.

"Okay, forget it," he shrugged, "I know you like chiliburgers. Thought you'd want your own."

"I'll ask her to cut it in half." She stepped to the front of the line and ordered, waited for the split burger, then checked around for an empty table. Her eyes dropped to a small magnetic chessboard on a nearby counter. She inched closer, to the back of the man hunched over the game. She studied the chess pieces, mentally wrapping up the solitary contest.

"Size five." The chess player's voice startled her. "Ninety-five pounds. Ten, no, eleven years old." The chess player looked up.

"Twelve," she said. "Almost." They recognized each other and a silent moment made an impact on both of them.

Nat poked her, whispering, "It's Officer Moon."

"No," she said in mock amazement. She waved Nat off with the palm of her hand behind her back. "You can castle," she indicated Moon's king.

He nodded. "Thanks."

She stood over him in silence and watched his next few moves, chomping on her half burger, then muttered aside to Nat, "Not bad."

Sam tore a piece from the half-eaten bun and offered it to Moon. "Wanna bite?"

He shook his head.

Nat indicated a vacant table and they dashed across the courtyard, Ozma, leashed, springing behind them.

Moon took a deep breath, collected his thoughts and considered how children blew a certain kind of helium into an adult's balloon. Even if you only got out of your armchair to make dinner and do laundry, at least you were thinking of someone else's needs. He supposed his personal dirigible had busted a seam, and no gale could help him take off: without children his life was grounded in himself.

After his divorce, Moon had found himself mired in a familiar and comfortable pattern of triviality: doing the things that move time.

He had never gone in for mild emotions. And when May left him, he had been senselessly outraged. Then he channeled that entire wrath into work, and he became more devoted to the force than even he could have imagined possible.

Infuriated at her for having accused him of emotional neglect, of loving his job more than her, of denying her another child after the loss of Lance, Moon was determined to prove her wrong. He wanted to show her that he did take time out of his day to pay attention to her poignant problems with her precious second grade class.

He reminded her that he did wait for her to get home from school before he left for work. But at 3 p.m. when she returned, drained from teaching all day, brimming with anecdotes about budding prodigies, artists, doctors and lost lunch money, he was already in a private mental space getting psyched up to deal with thieves, addicts, rapists and high speed chases.

Occasionally, they had enough time to grab a bite to eat together. And he would listen to her obligingly, with feigned interest. Towards the end of their marriage they had verbally sparred often over, of all things, school busing.

Right after Lance, they couldn't even stand to be in the same room together; then, when they finished intensive counseling sessions, they never once mentioned him again. Of course, it was hard to find anything to talk about, and, when they did, their arguments were founded on contradictory premises — of the chicken or the egg variety — so they arrived at altogether opposite conclusions from entirely different belief systems.

May, desperate to have something to care for again, worried about society; she worried about defining and eradicating the social injustices she knew would one day promote anti-social behavior in some of her enthusiastic and vulnerable eight-year-olds. Moon, on the other hand, dealt with immediate reactions to specific actions, and he didn't give a damn about the cause.

The last communication he'd had with May was scribbled on a Tia's Tacos napkin: "Society. What society? I don't care about society. When was the last time society sent me a Christmas card? I'm civil to everyone and nice to nobody. That's hard for your society to understand. But I'm not a Barnum and Bailey clown walking a beat for society's personal entertainment. They think we work for them. We don't work for them. They think we care about society. We don't care. We care about what's ours. I cared about my boy, Lance. Find somebody who cares about society, May, and have a good life."

Morgan, finished with the wash cycle, tossed several loads of wet clothes in the dryers, and considered how much less frustrated she was here at the laundromat doing something about dirty clothes than she'd been at the food drive doing something about hungry people. Soiled clothes needed soap and water; famished people needed food and drink. She couldn't put her finger on why it bothered her less to wash clothes than feed indigents — probably because dirty clothes hide quietly in a basket or pillowcase.

Stop thinking about it, she told herself, and checked her watch. The kids had been gone over a half hour. She heard Ozma barking, then looked through the filmy window, and finally located Sam and Nat playing catch with a stranger across the street. Her look of concern turned to confusion when she identified the stranger: Moon.

What was he doing in the park? Seeing him in the daylight, clad in jeans and a black T-shirt with red block letters that read MACBETH, totally shattered the off-duty beer-drinking, bikini-chasing image she had carved out for him. Moon playing catch in Levis was as absurd a visual for her as Springsteen selling real estate in a suit. She admitted she'd been thinking of Moon more than she would like, but it never occurred to her she would actually be glad to see him during her suspension.

Moon caught another one of Sam's powerful throws, and when Morgan moved to the open door, away from the dryers, Moon's voice carried across the road, "She's got a pretty good arm."

Nat yelled back, "Pretty good? She's an all-star."

Morgan smiled to herself. Of all the silent wishes for Sam she boxed in her heart like antique Christmas tree ornaments, she hoped that Nat's friendship, his quiet wisdom, his unconditional affection and respect for her, would feed Sam's intuition to accept nothing less from a lover.

Moon tossed back another one of Sam's bullets. "Yeah, she's an all-star, no doubt about it. Where'd she get that arm?" His sunglasses looked towards the laundry room and Morgan ducked back inside, cursing herself. Jerk, what a jerk. She was acting like a teenager. Worse still, she was feeling outrageously sentimental.

She suspected that if she got to know Moon away from the 77th, she could be more natural with him. Honest, silly, romantic, spontaneous, sad and serious — all that she was, but was so careful not to show. She supposed her job forced her to cloak her emotions at work and at home. It bothered her she couldn't be totally honest with her daughter. She didn't want Sam to know just how dangerous the 77th was or what kind of maneuvers she did to get information off the street.

It was better that Sam believed being a police officer was an honorable profession, that she thought of police work in terms of hourly episodic television revolving around a problem discovered and resolved. That celluloid packaging of dilemmas and solutions reassured, comforted, even though it wasn't the real thing. But as long as Sam believed people could work out their problems, then the reality existed, if only in her mind.

And Morgan knew she couldn't use Gramma Sofie as a sounding board. Gramma Sofie, alarmed to see Morgan upset over work-related or personal matters, was too easily unstrung by the thought of a gun, let alone the suggestion that her daughter-in-law carried one and might have to use it. The cheerful, tireless face Morgan kept was often a mask, until she was alone, silent, completely exposed.

Morgan watched a shriveled old woman with oily hair and two yapping dirty dogs position herself in front of a washing machine.

The woman picked grass from her shaggy dog's nappy hair and Morgan told herself if she kept up her isolation she would end up alone slinking around laundromats and picking dog hairs off worn carpets. She'd made herself unavailable to everyone for so long — since Jacob died — that she was amazed to even consider getting to know Moon outside the workplace. This was all the more unsettling because it suggested she was oddly attracted to him. But how could she be attracted to a man who carried disrespect to an extreme?

He had so many negative characteristics that proclaimed no fear, no feelings, no respect towards authority figures — all expressions she saw nightly in the remorseless baby-faced street kids. Nothing about those traits endeared him to her. So, why did she even notice or allow herself to think about his positive qualities?

Her head throbbed from trying to figure it out. If she could step away from her first thoughts and allow herself the luxury of some emotional distance, she would recognize that she was still reeling, she'd been bothered all week, from her scramble with Engels in the division parking lot, and would, at this wounded juncture, naturally gravitate to anyone's, even Moon's, positive traits.

Morgan measured the softener in a lopsided paper cup, poured it into the rinse cycle. Now, leaning on a clothes folding table, she picked up the front page of the *Los Angeles Times* and got caught up in an article citing the past running times of the Olympic women marathoners racing August fifth. She planned to take Sam to Santa Monica College, where the race was scheduled to begin. She read about the popular legend of the marathon's origin: Pheidippides, a professional runner, pronounced news of the Greek victory over the Persians at the Battle of Marathon in 490 B.C., then he fainted and died. Had she been alive in 490 B.C., she would have been a professional runner; she envisioned herself running to the Battle of Marathon, pronouncing the news, hanging around to exchange backslaps, then jogging back. She would certainly not faint and die, she thought, as Moon entered the cramped laundromat.

He nodded causally to her, then opened the only available dryer, one next to her. Flights of marathon running fell from her head as she made an effort to look indifferent, moving over to the dryer to jam in another load. He inserted several quarters, shot her an "off limits" look, then crossed to the washer to retrieve his basket of wet clothes. During that brief instant, the old woman dragged over two filthy doggie beds, spewing great wafts of hair. She crammed one bed in the dryer and was about to do the same with the next one, when Moon called out to her, "Hey, that's my dryer."

"Don't see your name on it."

"I put my money in."

She shrugged, unimpressed. He got in her face. "I said I put my money in already." The dogs barked, nipping his pant cuffs.

Moon got a whiff of the germ-ridden mats and jerked them from the dryer, "People put clean clothes in here," he said. She sliced a karate chop to his forearm. He stepped back in shock, yelling at her, "Look, you have to wash these clothes first."

She yelled back, "Says who?"

He looked around for some written instruction. Finding nothing on the walls to support his claim, he wedged his body in front of the dryer and jerked the mats onto the floor. She karate chopped his shoulder blade. "I'm going to call the police."

Morgan chuckled, threw him a dubious look and indicated for him to step outside. "You can use my dryer," she assured him.

"That's not the point." He glared at the old biddy, stuffing her ratty mats back in his dryer.

"How 'bout a cup of coffee?" Morgan suggested.

They strolled to the ChiliBurger Shack and he expressed just how much he hated people who didn't follow rules meant for everyone, people who had no sense of public etiquette.

Following rules, Morgan admitted, had been on her mind a lot lately. As they drank coffee, Morgan confessed she'd been having trouble dealing with the chokehold incident. She shrugged and pushed her empty cup away. Then she told Moon that she'd also been having nightmares, envisioning Fender beating the suspect. She looked into Moon's eyes, which hadn't wavered from hers, and admitted she wasn't sure what to do.

"Nothing," Moon said. "Fender has this thespian flare thing going. But I've never known him to use excessive force."

She wanted to believe that, which would mean that Joe Blanco was lying to her about the dozens of baton blows.

The rug woman and her dogs had left the laundromat. Morgan finished folding her clothes while Moon waited nearby for his jeans to finish drying. She avoided picking out her underwear from the clump of clothes. She glanced at him, wondering if he wore underwear, imagining he did, probably white jockeys. She didn't want to think about him in underwear, but there he was right in front of her, clipping his fingernails. He looked over at her occasionally, giving a casual smile, almost as though they spent every Saturday together doing their laundry.

She knew it would be too much of a strain on her to spend time with him and not tell him, in various ways, that she liked him. That was contrary to her nature, like telling a dog not to bark when his master returned home. She was angry at herself for liking him at all, but if you stripped away his fatalistic attitude against women officers, occasionally his insights were mildly humorous, maybe even sentimental. Oh, she told herself, you're reaching, really reaching.

He handed her a coke from the dispensing machine. "Here. Somebody left some change in the return."

"Thanks," Morgan said, adding, "and thanks for catching with Sam. She could throw for hours."

"Yeah, she's pretty amazing," he said, as he watched Sam and Nat march towards them. Nat was holding a small flat dish filled with water. "If I had another kid, that's the kind I'd want."

"All right," Sam announced. "We're ready to perform our masterpiece. We need a man's human hair. Nat?"

"I'm just a kid, 'sides I know the trick."

"Right." Sam nodded and looked at Moon, who glanced skeptically at Morgan, then plucked a hair from his head and handed it to Sam.

"Thanks." Sam put it in the water, then instructed Nat. "Okay, light it when I say. But you guys," she indicated Morgan and Moon, "are going to have to get closer to see it stand on end in the water."

Sam's absorbing command made it clear she wouldn't take no for an answer, so Morgan and Moon, the spectators, leaned closer to the tiny water-filled dish in order to witness this miracle. "Okay, Nat, do it."

Nat took a deep breath and eyed Sam. "Now, Nat," Sam commanded, then reminded him, "The pizza we ordered is ready."

Nat lit the hair, and when Morgan and Moon's interest was the most intense, waiting for the hair to stand on end, Sam smacked the dish with the palm of her hand and the water splashed in their faces. Bursting with laughter, Sam scooped Ozma into her arms and bolted with Nat out the door.

Morgan and Moon exchanged a look. "On second thought," Moon said, "that's the kind of kid you generally try to sell or give away." He caught Morgan's eye and she smiled at him, pleased he had manifested a side of his nature she had hoped existed.

Sitting in a restaurant booth, Morgan served herself another slice of pepperoni pizza. She heard a car door slam and looked out the tinted window at Moon packing a clothes-filled hamper into his Range Rover. Clothes looked folded, she noted. He didn't seem the type to crumble them in all ball and iron them at home.

He turned out of the laundromat parking lot just as Sam hurried from the restaurant balancing a couple pizza slices on a napkin. His car stopped at the light and Sam sighed, but made no move to get his attention. He must have noticed her standing alone because he turned the corner and made a U-turn. Her expression brightened as he pulled up alongside her and asked, "Problem?"

"No," she said, then nodded back toward the pizza joint. Morgan observed her through the window and could imagine her daughter explaining. "It's just we got a mess of pizza and me and Nat thought maybe you wanted to come in and help us eat it. But my mom said that wasn't such a good idea." She eyed him closely, holding out the pizza. "So here."

"Thanks." He took a bite. "Just hits the spot. Thanks for having that catch with me."

She nodded, then said without moving, "See ya." Started to walk away, then paused. "Hey, how come you don't like my mother? She likes you."

Moon stopped chewing and considered a moment. "It's not that I don't like her, Sam. In fact," he conceded, "if she weren't a cop, I'd probably even ask her out on a date."

"How come you don't want to eat with her then?"

"It's not that I don't want to eat with her. We eat together when we're working." Sam waited for a better explanation. "It's like in school," he said, fumbling. "The boys have their games, and the girls have their games." She cocked her head, not even close. "Look Sam, it's just different on the street. All kinds of shit comes down on the street."

Comfortable with him, Sam nodded, took a deep breath and leaned on the car window. "Yeah, I know, my mom tells me everything." He offered her a bite of his pizza. "Thanks," she said, trying to chew with her mouth closed.

"No, Sam," he smiled at her attempt at good manners. "I'm sure she tells you a lot, but not everything. Guys get beaten up, hacked up, shot at, run over."

"And girls."

She braced an open palm on her hip, "Look here, Mooseface, women can do anything you can do. You have to know that or you wouldn't like to play chess so much." She answered his puzzled look. "The king's a total wimp, right? He can only move one square at a time, but the queen," she leaned in to him and snapped her fingers, "one move and bam, she's in your face knocking heads."

"On a chessboard, right. But on the real streets, hurt people don't always get up." He paused, then confided soberly, "I've had two partners die in my arms, and I don't want another one to be your mother."

Sam swallowed hard and looked at him directly. "My mom's a great cop. You're lucky to have her for a partner."

"But Sam," he put his hand on her shoulder, "I'm not always going to be her partner."

She shrugged. "That's tough luck for you."

15

IN THE DARK

Sitting in the patrol passenger seat after her week's suspension, Morgan was vaguely listening to Moon rag on certain useless bulletproof vests, but she was thinking about Alicia's locker room announcement that she was transferring to Narcotics. Alicia was fed up with the 77th Nightwatch, and she hoped her transfer would come through for the next cycle, so she wouldn't have to put up with any more of the petty bullshit between the men and the women. Certainly, this gender discord existed in other L.A.P.D divisions, but at least Alicia wouldn't be at the center of it. And she would make sure no one knew she dated a cop.

Moon was heading for Tia's Tacos. It was about time for their first coffee break, when they got an assist call for a PCP suspect.

On the way to the call, Moon asked her if she'd dealt with PCP. "Never," she said, and to her surprise, he gave her necessary information, immediately useful, without the obligatory runaround about her astounding mental and physical ineptitude.

"The classic PCP is a dude on dust with these wild eyes like he's looking straight through you. There's just something nonverbal, extraterrestrial about him. It's like you're talking to a walking corpse: you say, 'Put your hands above your head,' and he doesn't move. Doesn't even flinch. Nothing. So, you grab an arm, and it's like grabbing a piece of wood. And you know the fight's on as soon as you try to pull that arm back."

She painted a mental picture of a human tank, drugged into a stupor, ready to mow her over.

Moon turned down a narrow, dark street. "By the time you realize you've misjudged him," he said, "the guy's already got you by the balls."

She noticed he either forgot or decided not to offer his customary woeful glance to her crotch.

He pulled the patrol car over next to an Alameda, a cupola, surrounded by benches and a walking path that neighbors used to stroll around on Sundays. Now, it was too trashed with condoms and used IV needles to let a dog walk through.

In the moonlight, Morgan pointed to Slattery standing on the steps of the cupola with her gun drawn as of she were waiting for the right moment to leap into a twirling jump rope.

They raced over to find Engels under the dome, wrestling out from under a male whom she later described as a short, stocky, light-skinned black man in his thirties. He had short kinky hair and wore a white shirt and gray sweats.

He was plastered on top of her in the missionary position.

Engels shrieked, "He's got my gun."

Morgan reacted without thinking, "Drop the gun."

Moon brushed past her, as he drew his weapon and bounded up the steps. "Drop the gun, motherfucker." And in the next instant, when the suspect made no move to do so, Moon rested his hand on the suspect's head to keep the bone splinters from flying back in his face, and then shot the suspect in the temple.

Blood and bone chips splattered everywhere, all over Engels. Slattery gasped.

Morgan's heart beat in her eardrums, blocking all other sound, and for a brief instant she felt them all stunned still, magnetized to the suspect, sucked to the cupola's center. Then Engels shrieked, "Get him off! Get him off me!"

Moon ignored her. "Morgan," he turned to her at the top of the stairs. "Get an RA unit. Get a sergeant here. Get two more units."

"I'll do it," Slattery said, suddenly energized and directional, like an electrical appliance turned on. She spurted down the stairs towards her patrol car.

Morgan bent over a badly shaking Engels as she moved out from under the suspect. Morgan eased her down on a rotting wooden bench inside the cupola, and stood next to her. Listening to Engels softly sobbing, Morgan took a deep breath and glanced at the blood-splattered tiles.

She supposed this could be the scene of a skirmish in Beirut, El Salvador, Viet Nam. Sudden bloodshed and death made her think of Jacob. Who had been near him when he died but Fender? They were on a scouting mission together. Had he time for last words, last thoughts? Only Fender knew. She forced her mind off Jacob, but the desire to know anything about those last moments overwhelmed her.

Engels' shoulder shuddered under Morgan's palm. Whining like a trapped cat, Engels' face stiffened as though she were trying to catch her breath or keep from throwing up. Morgan couldn't be sure. She imagined Engels was still mentally ensnared under the weight of the suspect's body, so Morgan stroked her back gently. Engels' red-splotched face looked like she'd walked through a group of paint-spraying kindergartners, but the suspect's bone chips clinging to Engels' blood-matted hair reminded Morgan there'd been no kids' play here.

Ten minutes after the shooting, the Alameda was ablaze with headlights from back-up patrol cars, the shooting team investigators, neighbors and press.

Moon and Morgan were walking back to their car. He glared at Engels, drenched in blood, standing against her front fender, still in shock. "Doesn't quite have the nuts and bolts of policing under her belt, does she?" he said, adding glibly, "How many more of those splittails do we have seeping out of the sewer?"

Morgan didn't venture to think about what went wrong seconds before Engels found herself thrown on her back. Morgan could only focus on Engels' thin cry, "He's got my gun." How hard to force words from a paralyzed throat a millisecond before certain death. "I don't know how many more of those we've got," Morgan said, "but I'd be more than a little rattled if I was facing death one second, then facing a blown off head the next."

Moon shrugged indifferently.

She glanced at him askance, wondering, how many more of *you* do we have? He was unmoved by the terror a woman experiences when trapped under a man. She guessed he had never been physically restrained, so he couldn't comprehend a woman's ingrained fear. If he'd ever really loved a woman, or if he'd had a daughter, he'd at least sympathize even if he were incapable of any real empathy.

They spent the rest of the night at the station working on the report. Morgan reviewed every detail. She wanted it to be accurate, confined to the witnessed events, no personal comments or implications. Her vigilance, inspired by her devastated feelings after Fender's negative report on her as a police academy cadet for the simulated perimeter search, aggravated Moon, and he nagged her for taking too long.

She ignored him, but she wanted to tell him Fender's report had struck the very core of her frustration at having no control over so many critical issues in her personal life. Then, after that report, she felt that even in her professional life she was powerless to affect the outcome. Her actions stood the test, she shot the mock suspect before he shot her, but her voice was ignored.

How could she admit to her daughter that she was simply disregarded? Unable to convince Fender that Gladstone had lied about what he'd seen during the perimeter search, that she had reacted appropriately, and that in a real situation, she would have been alive, the suspect wounded, if not dead.

The morning after the PCP shooting, Morgan awoke after only a few hours sleep. She pulled the covers up to her neck and stared at the rotating ceiling fan, wondering how the dynamics between her and Engels would change. Surely, they would become closer in some way. A warlike experience like last night bonded dissimilar people. Maybe that was what had happened to Fender and Jacob. After all, who would have thought Jacob would connect with Fender?

It was Fender who'd put a wedge between Morgan and the women officers, with the exception of Alicia. No, she reconsidered. It was she herself who'd chilled the relationship with her peers. There would've been no hostility between her and the women if she'd initially revealed the identity of the transport officers. The women would've supported her. But Fender's high-level friends would've still influenced the IA's decision that there'd been a previous altercation.

And then what about the resulting backlash from MAW: the dreaded no back-up threat made good. Would the women have been so supportive then? It didn't matter. She buried her head, admitting in the dark, alone, the deeper reason she hadn't pointed the finger at Fender. She still didn't know what had truly happened in the patrol car that night with Fender and her suspect, but she did know that if she'd pointed the finger at Fender, her only link to Jacob, she would never crack the safe to reveal what happened the last few moments of his life.

Anyway, she consoled herself, at least Alicia had been on her side. The new rapport in the women's locker room may change Alicia's mind. Maybe she would stay. Morgan was buoyed by the anticipation.

When she walked in the locker room the following night, Alicia, slipping into her pants, greeted her. "Hey, I called you at home. Doesn't your abuela give you messages?"

Morgan shook her head, "Sorry."

"No importa. Just checking on you. I don't think abuela likes my accent."

"What accent?" Morgan smiled, then passed by Engels, "How's it going?"

Engels didn't even turn around, didn't even acknowledge she'd entered. While Morgan was getting dressed for Nightwatch, she overheard Engels, on the other side of the lockers, convincing Slattery that the previous night's PCP escapade was all in the line of duty. "You've just gotten off probation. Do you know what it means to say you did a year in the 77th? You can get any job at any one of the bureaus as an auditor, inspector, examiner."

"I don't know," said Slattery.

"I'm telling you. It'll be a whole different world for you off the street. And the department will accommodate your schedule so you can study for the state bar."

Morgan realized Engels was blaming the night's tragedy on Slattery's incompetence when it was Engels's gun the suspect had managed to get his hands on. Engels might snub Morgan, but what was she going to do about Moon? Was Engels simply going to ignore that he saved her life? Morgan could see she had no understanding of how the dynamics of these tragic, tense situations played out so, still a newcomer, she'd have to take a backseat and observe.

Blocker huffed in and slammed down her bag, "That fat ass Fender just asked me why I wasn't in the kitchen cooking up some greens."

Engels grimaced. "Just because his wife Phyllis buys that crock of stuff — "

"Shit," Alicia corrected. "You can say it, practice with me: shit."

Engels gave her a black look. "He's gonna get his someday," she said.

As Morgan headed to the door, Slattery called after her, "Hey Morgan, wait up."

Slattery followed her out the door, privately confiding, "Look, after last night I feel like I'm in the second week of Academy and wondering if this is really for me, you know."

"This isn't the Academy," Morgan said, and struck by Slattery's desperate expression that begged for direction, advice, anything, added, "It's true you can learn a lot in a year, but maybe there are some things you can't be taught, you have to just have — "

"What?"

Morgan shrugged, then locking eyes with Slattery, "Just ask yourself if somebody had a gun pointed directly at you, what would you do first?"

"I guess," Slattery shrugged, "I'd try and talk him out of it."

"Why?" Morgan held her eyes for a moment, then turned and walked out.

The candy vending machine was jammed again. With Slattery in the forefront of her mind, she hastened to the corner liquor store to pick up a chocolate Hershey's bar before roll call. Were she a closer friend like Alicia, Morgan could've told her that she knew, like most of the women, Slattery was a woman trapped in a paradox. She was indecisive about her personal life — not exactly embracing the Silver Lake gay community.

Slattery had no social friends to use as soundboards or offer advice. She didn't congregate with supportive lesbians drawn together by a shared agenda and common experiences of prejudice, exclusion and violence. She didn't even belong to any lesbian hiking groups, feminist networks, mothers' groups, witch's covens or bowling clubs.

Engels was Slattery's only source of support. Morgan knew they would sneak to a motel in Culver City of all places on Thursday nights. Engels didn't want them to be seen together. She still wouldn't be caught dead browsing through Sisterhood Bookstore in Westwood to study the cases of women her age who were condemned to insane asylums in the years before gay liberation.

Patently behind the times, Engels was still figuring out how to hide her sexual preference, yet meet other lesbians without going to gay bars. Or she had been, until she latched onto Slattery, a woman rejected by the man she thought was the love of her life, a woman so totally set back by his rejection she could renounce forever the need for a man.

How could Slattery's emotional security not be on shaky ground? Her sexual wiring criss-crossed, she waffled between being a closet lesbian and wanting a husband who didn't think she was pretty enough. A husband who detailed their flagging sex life, on the one hand, as well as offering blow-by-blow descriptions of his business trysts with story editors, production assistants and casting agents.

The women officers had been pumping up Slattery, feeding her tidbits on how to succeed in a male-dominated profession, almost as if her failure was a reflection on prospects for their future success. Morgan knew Slattery bent over backwards to try to please the men, then the women, probably thinking that once everyone got to know her, they would appreciate her flexibility. They would like her.

This job, Morgan wanted to tell her, was not about being liked.

Waiting for Lieutenant Herdahl in roll call, Morgan, early and the only woman present, was sitting in her customary metal chair next to the yellowed map of the 77th division. Sucking the almonds from a chocolate bar, she regarded the MAW guys across the room, huddled together, chuckling over a community policing joke, no doubt.

She considered Alicia and Blocker's cry for community policing; if we don't find a way to police differently, we won't make a difference. Morgan would like that. She would like finding a way to prove to women the care-taking they've done traditionally is valuable. That they didn't have to urge each other to join the men, do what they do, behave as they do, become Jane Waynes. How did women becoming men really benefit us anyway, men or women?

Morgan glanced up and realized the other women had entered, slipping so silently into their seats that the MAW guys, chattering with muffled guffaws in the back of the room, hadn't noticed — Fender decided to fill the dead air with one of his barbed commendations.

"Listen up, listen up, *pubic* announcement here," he said, bursting with enthusiasm, "I just want to say — excuse me, stop scratching your balls, Moon. I need everyone's attention here. Just want to commend Slattery last night for yet another *giant*, with a capital 'G' for girl, effort."

He took advantage of the trapped audience, continuing, "SWAT had a saying: if you can't fly with eagles, get the — " he glanced at Engels and delicately covered his mouth, "bleep, out of the sky. They can't have anybody along who might get them or anybody else killed, but..." He opened his palms in mock relief, "we don't have to worry about that here because we recognize the extra...ordinary effort above and beyond the call of duty."

Fender indicated Slattery and brought his hands together for one sharp clap. One by one all the MAW guys stood and clapped once, all but Iggy, who glanced at Alicia, then just shook his head. Morgan expected Slattery to break down or run out of the room, but she sat erect, staring straight ahead, poised as if she were in center court waiting for the wave of "boos" to subside.

Morgan stood, suppressing a rush of emotion, not in charge of the feelings that rose deep inside her. She looked at the MAW members casually grouped as though they were ready to watch a football game on the overhead monitor. "You guys are assholes."

She left the room and, walking down the hall towards the water fountain with their laughter at her back, she realized she'd just reinforced their identity.

She gulped too much ice cold water, took a deep breath and, determined not to let another emotional response escape from her mouth like a great gush of wind, she centered her thoughts, directing them first to Springsteen. It was this kind of dizzying emotion that spurred him to compose songs about rebels blocked inside with their personal fears, inhibitions, and sad memories.

Then Morgan settled on thinking about Aunt Tilly, holding the image of her wrinkled hands clasped, kneeling on the side of the bed, whispering. Morgan leaned closer, listening in her mind, refocusing her strength. It had been during Aunt Tilly's few years with her that Morgan had come to see that man could leave more than a body of weary flesh and blood marked by experiences.

Morgan had heard the outpourings of her aunt's life, outstretched palms — dedicated to social service, protecting the rights of women — and fists battling juvenile delinquency and abuse. Aunt Tilly's perception of life as something we can't determine, but can change from bad to good through truth, influenced Morgan's understanding that taking part in life's process, struggling to make her work life better through truth, would at least give her the illusion of command.

After roll call, Morgan walked down the hall toward triumphant laughter, loud and raucous, from the men's locker room. Her guess was the *Los Angeles Times* had just been delivered and Fender had cut out the PCP article from the newspaper and was reading it aloud: "…and then Officer B.Jay Moon, knowing that the suspect had a weapon, shot the suspect in the head, and the suspect expired at the scene."

"Yeah," everybody chorused, "good fuckin' shooting!"

Bow Wow passed Morgan in the hall. He paused to notice her heading towards Drummond's office and she knew he'd enter his locker room in the middle of MAW's chorus and report her visit to the captain.

Morgan waited outside the captain's office. Lieutenant Herdahl entered and indicated that Morgan follow her.

Morgan figured once behind closed doors, the captain would let Herdahl do most of the talking. She was right.

"Some members of the community and the other women are very upset," Lieutenant Herdahl said, crossing her arms in front of her chest.

"About last night?" Morgan asked. "Yeah, I can see why. It was very upsetting."

Herdahl eyed her. "So you would agree that Moon was out of line."

Morgan responded more harshly than she'd intended. "*What?*"

Herdahl glanced at the captain and sighed heavily, indicating that what she'd privately predicted to him was about to take place. "That's what some of the women are saying."

Morgan wanted to punch Lieutenant Herdahl in her smug face, much as she'd head butted Moon after she'd fallen out of the tree. But she refrained, stared at her, took several shallow breaths, then said calmly, "Moon saved another officer's life. A woman."

Captain Drummond shifted in his chair, "Yes. But it's a question of whether he should have shot the suspect at all."

"Whose question?" Morgan looked at him in amazement. They both knew he needed her corroboration with Slattery to incriminate Moon in a PCP killing. "There's simply no doubt that Officer Moon took an appropriate response."

Lieutenant Herdahl leaned in. "Not according to Slattery."

"Oh please, Lieutenant," she said, pausing to collect herself, "with all due respect…" She looked askance at Herdahl then turned back to Drummond, "I've been here not much more than a month, yet I've seen some pretty disturbing patterns in and out of the station." She wanted to remind them that during that month Slattery had struck out three times: she'd probably missed a gun on a suspect who minutes later killed an officer; she'd gotten a dust speck in her contacts and stayed in the patrol car phoning for back-up forcing Morgan to use a chokehold on a suspect; now, she'd frozen up while a suspect wrestled with her partner on the ground. But she bit her tongue: less was better. She'd put the pressure on them to lead.

Captain Drummond smiled through a tense pause. "Engels has assured us that everything was under control. That Slattery had a couple of bad nights this month, but she's got her street act together."

Morgan clenched her jaw. No wonder Engels had ignored her. In Engels' account of events, nothing out of the ordinary had happened to warrant Moon's shooting the guy in the head.

Lieutenant Herdahl nodded in the affirmative, "That's right. Slattery said Moon just raced up and shot the suspect in the head."

"He had her gun." From their blank reactions, she supposed they weren't taking this fact into account, so she clarified. "Engels yelled out that he had her gun."

"So," Herdahl processed the information, depicting the scene, "Engels yells the suspect has her gun, then with no warning, nothing, Moon shoots him in the head."

"I yelled at him to drop it, so did Moon before he shot him."

"Slattery doesn't remember any warning from you or Moon," said Herdahl.

"Well, Lieutenant," Morgan said, "then I guess it's her word against mine. But…" she hesitated, directing a request to the captain, "off the record?"

"Sure," he said with a fatherly nod, avoiding Herdahl's stare.

Morgan glanced to Herdahl, including her in the exchange. "We've taken several minutes to review this scenario, and really, as I'm sure you're aware, it happened," she snapped her fingers, "like that. And maybe because it happened so quickly, some details weren't witnessed or remembered."

The Captain nodded, thinking a moment. "You and Moon seem to remember the same details. You both get on okay, don't you?"

"Shouldn't we?"

"I mean, he hasn't beat down your self-confidence."

She paused, careful of her response, "Not yet." She was uncertain where this line of questioning was headed. Not, she hoped, an insinuation she would cover up for Moon like some people thought she had for Fender.

"Glad to see it. I wouldn't have predicted it. Would you say he's taught you a lot?"

"Depends. Some of his tactics don't work for me. I just pay attention and go home to my daughter every night."

"That's important," he said, nodding slowly. Then, as though he were doing her a favor, he added, "I'm going to put you on a report car — give Slattery a chance to work with Moon awhile. Maybe he can teach her a little self-confidence."

Report car! Her blank face covered the exclamation yelling in her head at this extreme demotion. Police officers in report cars didn't respond to calls; they showed up after the action and reported on the event.

His smile bore into her, but she stared down his bald spot, swallowing her absolute fury. "Fine." Ready to leave, but not yet dismissed, she asked flatly. "Is that all, Captain Drummond?" She eyed his drooping windowsill roses.

"Yes."

She turned, catching Herdahl's dismissive nod.

Morgan closed the captain's door, standing for a moment, wondering why she was feeling such hostility from a captain who championed women on the police force and a woman lieutenant who fought for them in sexual discrimination cases. Was it because she got along with her partner, Moon?

Still upset from the unexpected report-car slap in the face, she paused in front of the women's locker room door, wondering what emotional riptide would pull her under next. She was certain they were all waiting for her, waiting to hear her confirmation of Slattery's rendition that would finally bring Moon down. And Fender, of course, would be soon to follow.

When Morgan entered, Blocker was offering Slattery moral support. "You bumped your butt. Now get off it and move along. Do your best. That's all you can do."

"I am doing my best," Slattery said, "but I'm worried about what the guys think — "

"Stop whining," said Alicia. "Just do the job and the hell with the men."

Morgan swung in the door, crossing to her locker as their eyes burned a hole in her back. Blocker didn't wait for Morgan to open up the conversation, she came out with it directly: "What'd the man want to know, girl?"

Morgan fidgeted with the combination, working hard to

maintain a casual air. "Wanted to know if Moon and I got on okay."

A pregnant silence, then Blocker charged in. "So did you dump on the motherfucker?"

"I told the captain that we got on okay, and that he was doing his job," she said without apology, dreading and receiving their immediate cool reception.

Tentative until now, Slattery exploded. "His job! We're officers, not executioners. Everything was under control and he — "

"Who are you talking to?" Morgan cut her off. "I was there, so don't tell me everything was under control." Morgan taped her temple with her fingers. "I mean, are you blind or brain dead? Engels was pinned on the ground with this lunatic getting his rocks off on her while you were trying to find a good angle to take pictures."

Slattery gasped.

Engels asked in a thin voice, "Is that what you told the captain?"

"No." Morgan leveled a look at her, as they both saw Engels' prized sergeant position fading from view. "I told him the suspect had your fucking gun, and that was the reason Moon shot him."

"Oh great," Engels fought back tears. "That's just great."

"That's the truth, isn't it?" Morgan said.

Engels acted as though she'd completely forgotten the suspect had her gun, or worse, as if it never happened at all. Morgan gazed at her, wondering if the entire experience could have been such an ordeal she'd wiped it from her consciousness like a nightmare.

Morgan pressed her. "You were all over my ass a couple of weeks ago accusing me of covering up for Fender transporting my suspect, but I suppose it would be okay if I forgot you were screaming, 'He's got my gun?'"

Blocker and Alicia frowned. Morgan realized they hadn't heard about a gun because they were only hearing sound bytes from Engels' and Slattery's selective memories.

"I'm gonna play devil's advocate here," Morgan said, "so just stay with me."

Engels glanced away, which Morgan interpreted as resigned consent and continued, "All L.A.P.D. knows you're next on the list to be promoted to sergeant, but how do you validate getting that promotion over street cops who've been waiting ten years for it?"

"We've earned it," Blocker spoke up, her years of frustration seeping through, "that's why."

Alicia indicated the men's locker room, "They don't think we've earned a thing."

"Fuck 'em." Blocker pointed vehemently, "They're wrong. It's high time we give 'em a taste of their own poison we been choking on all these years." She smiled, with a broad, embracing gesture, "And if they can't take the heat, we'll just put 'em on report cars, let 'em write traffic tickets, handle domestic quarrels."

Alicia piped in, "Domestic quarrels? Now, don't give away the only thing they've admitted I can do."

"Parker Center doesn't know what we can do," Blocker said, "but they do know we can do domestics pretty well. So, they need to pat us on the back for something the men used to handle and they don't think we can fuck up too bad."

Morgan gave a nod of endorsement, adding, "Then when we have a situation like last night when a suspect gets a hold of an officer's gun, a *women* officer, we act like nothing happened… nothing went wrong. That's the way they act when something goes wrong. They cover it up."

Morgan caught Slattery and Engels exchange a look and she knew they'd agreed not to mention to anyone that Engels had yelled out the suspect had her gun. And she realized they'd wrongly hoped that ignoring the reality might convince Morgan not to say anything. After all, from their point of view, she'd covered up for Fender — the least she could do would be to cover up for her own gender.

"Engels," Morgan said, "I told the Captain that Moon acted appropriately. We gotta at least admit when something goes wrong, and support each other or…" Morgan threw up her hands at a loss for words, "or we don't have a leg to stand on to fight this policemen against policewomen horseshit."

Alicia brushed MAW off with a wave of her hand. "They're nothing, no different than the gangbangers in my barrio. A support group, you know, hang tough." She tried to smooth the waters, adding, "Just to keep the juices flowing. That's why they're having this kill party tonight."

Engels' nostrils flared. "A what?"

Morgan shook her head. Just when the waters start to calm, a seaquake ruptures and kicks towering waves up on shore, washing sunbathers and children out to sea.

Alicia shrugged. "A kill party. You know, fi-es-ta," she mouthed the word slowly, teasing a twitch on Engels' fixed expression. "In honor of Moon's kill."

16

KILL PARTY

Faces lit by moonlight, the MAW members — Fender, Bow Wow, Iggy, Gladstone, Teddy Bear and Moon — bunched together, aimed their guns towards the hill and, on Fender's count of "one…two…asshole!" shot at six melons along a fence. They were already liquored up. It was like the end of a football game and, just after they'd won the championship, Fender bellowed in the night sky locker room: "We don't have to justify shit anymore than the Marine Corps has to justify how they hit a beach." He punched the air with his fist, "We reached our objective, minimal causalities on our part." He slapped Moon on the back, "A fucking successful mission."

They were dominant, unbeatable, gods.

Then all of a sudden headlights turned into the shooting range parking lot.

"Who's that?" Bow Wow barked.

"That can't be Alicia?" Fender glared at Iggy, who, having endured his two-week ostracization from MAW, had just recently been welcomed back into their private parties.

Gladstone squinted. "It's her car. Alicia's car."

"What the fuck is she doing here, Iggy?" Fender was in Iggy's face as Alicia got out of the car lugging a Playmate cooler.

Moon shook his head in disgust. "Great Iggy, just fucking gr — "
Then Morgan got out of the passenger side and led the way across a
field towards the closed circle of MAW members.

Drawing closer, Alicia's mouth moved non-stop as she and
Morgan crossed the field. Within earshot, Alicia's voice carried,
"…and for his thirtieth birthday I hid these little envelopes all
over his apartment with notes inside like, 'el amor de me vida,'
'you're so sweet, look in the refrigerator,' and there'd be a box of
candy. He loved it. I know some people think I shouldn't be nice
to him — "

"Nothing wrong with being nice to somebody you care about,"
Morgan was saying. "Bet you guys move in together before the end of
the year."

"I am moving in…three doors away. I need my space."

"Three doors is space?" Morgan laughed.

"Hey," Bow Wow yelled. "What the fuck you doing here?"

Alicia belted back, "What the fuck, you think you got a monopoly
on a party? We can go anywhere we want." She unfurled a colorful
Mexican blanket.

As she spread it on the ground, Gladstone called out, "Hey
splittail, did you come over to be a sport? You gonna service us,
or what?"

"You mierde-for-brains, Gladstone," Alicia said. "I'm not
gonna serve you shit."

She opened the Playmate and set out crocks of assorted cheeses,
French bread, various chips and dips. Iggy, frozen in a spell of
indecision, stared at the food. Moon turned to the side, averting
his eyes from the scene, but there was no escaping it.

"Hey," said Teddy Bear, "can you cook me up a burger?"

Morgan tossed him a dubious look, then lifted a wine cooler
from the ice chest. Alicia tossed her a plastic glass.

She caught the glass and Moon's noncommittal glance. He
popped the lid on another beer. She took a sip of wine. He regarded
her a moment, wondering what she could have been thinking to
show up at a MAW party.

Fender snapped, "Hey, Alicia, maybe you can collect the
cans."

"And wash the beer bottles when you're done," Bow Wow added.

"Fuck you guys!" said Alicia, turning on a portable radio and popping a chip in her mouth. "We're here so you can complain about us in our presence instead of behind our backs, and we'll tell you you're full of shit."

"Hey, Iggy," Alicia called out, tossing a glass bottle of dried nuts through the air, "Catch!"

He caught it, then couldn't help smiling at her, in spite of the disapproving glances.

Bow Wow grabbed the nuts from Iggy and opened them up. "What the fuck," he said. "You might as well chip me."

So Alicia tossed a bag of potato chips into the closed MAW circle.

"Dip me," Teddy succumbed, adding quickly, "Don't throw it!" Instead, he walked over to pick it up. While he was at the blanket, he checked out what Alicia had brought, pointing to a red wax block, "What kind of cheese is that?"

"Edam," said Alicia, "very smooth. Not your type."

Moon noticed disapproving thumbs down from Fender and Gladstone. Appointed by default, he dutifully crossed to Morgan. They stood looking at each other for a moment like two people on a seesaw, equally balanced. And, in that brief instant, they recognized the intense attraction they had each only sensed. It was one of those moments in his life when Moon felt most alive, and he didn't know what to do as this energy swept through him, obscuring the risk.

Finally, Moon told her, "You just don't belong here…"

No kidding, she thought. He wasn't the final word, and she hadn't shown up because she wanted to belong to a group against women on the police force. She'd shown up because Alicia made a convincing argument for striking out against MAW mentality; mostly, she'd shown up because she was curious where these guys met and what they did. It was the kind of curiosity that drove guys and girls to crash each other's slumber parties: you knew you didn't belong and that you couldn't stay for long.

"I know," she said. "I'm not exactly interested in becoming a member."

She glanced at Alicia, now the center of a few MAW guys' attention because she was doling out food. Gladstone and Fender, removed from the collusion and comestibles, threw her an indifferent look. Then Morgan rested her gaze on Moon and half-smiled. She took a deep breath, "I just thought I'd stop by, check it out, and say hi to some guy around here they call Mooseface."

He nodded and cracked a smile.

She turned nonchalantly, strolling back across the field, alone. He saw her stop, take the last sip of wine from a plastic glass, go into a wind-up and release a pitch in midair.

Shit, he thought, I'm in hot water now. Suddenly, she'd come into his life, almost every night of his life and his life had changed. He couldn't put his finger on it. Maybe it was too much beer. Or maybe intoxication muddled his mind so that he could clearly see that she was the woman he finally wanted in his life — forget what he'd told himself about never allowing love to seize him by the balls and lead him around. But at the very moment he was feeling most exhilarated, some terror from his experience of past loves warned him that he could never have her because their needs were so out of sync. And he wasn't well-behaved about not having his needs met when he wanted them fulfilled.

The next night, in the division parking lot, Moon sat behind his steering wheel and finished writing in his log. Earley popped into his mind almost as if he'd slid into the passenger seat next to him, philosophizing that the great problem is you can't maintain yourself as a power without corrupting yourself — one of Earley's favorite conundrums. He missed Earley's open-ended questions — how can you deal with enemies without becoming enemies?

He glanced up to see Morgan head for her automobile.

Moon watched her accelerate out of the parking lot. He thought for a moment, smiled to himself, then reached under his dash for the flashing red light.

Just as Morgan was about to turn onto the freeway ramp she spotted a patrol car riding up behind.

She pulled over, bracing her arms in front of the steering wheel, and muttered, "Shit," as Moon stepped out of the driver's side.

He swaggered to her window. "Let me check out your driver's license, ma'am."

"You've got the timing of a bullet and about as much sense. You know that?"

"Put your hands on the steering wheel," he ordered her.

Looking straight ahead Morgan said, "Put your hands in your pants and play with your ying-yang." She gunned her engine, and Moon watched her turn sharply onto the freeway ramp.

He winced. "Ying-yang?"

Behind closed doors the following morning, Moon stepped in front of the captain's desk and set down a tape recorder.

"Turn that thing off," Captain Drummond said, looking up from composing a memo.

"If we're going to discuss my professionalism on the job, I have a right to have it on."

"I said turn it off."

"Whatever you say could be held against me, Captain, and I want to be certain to be straight on it from the beginning."

Aggravated but controlled, Drummond said, "I want it off. We're discussing your attitude."

"I think it's still relevant to have a tape-recording of our discussion."

Drummond glared at him, "I said turn that damn thing off."

Moon stretched the moment supremely. "I'd like to request five minutes to check with legal affairs to see if I'm within my rights on this issue to keep the tape recorder on."

"Denied. I'm not talking into that thing."

Moon nodded. "Oh, okay Captain, if you're ordering me to turn it off, then I have no choice. You are ordering me, is that correct, Captain?"

Drummond drilled a look into his eyes, "That's correct, Officer Moon."

"Well," Moon shrugged casually, "if you're denying me the right to tape this, I'd like a lieutenant present then."

Keeping his eyes on Moon, Drummond pushed the intercom button, "Lieutenant Herdahl, could you step in here a moment, please?"

Moon flicked off the tape recorder.

Herdahl entered. She and Moon exchanged a hostile look.

Drummond cleared his throat, "I hear you and your buddies had a party the other night."

"What night?"

"Tuesday."

Toying with him, Moon thought hard, "Tuesday, yeah, I think some of us got together after work."

"Who?"

"Who?"

"Yes, Moon, who did you get together with?"

Moon held up his hand, glanced to Herdahl, then in pretend shock said, "Wait a minute, Captain, are you telling me who I can socialize with after hours?"

Drummond tried another tack. "I have several witnesses confirming that Officer Fraser said she was going to a "kill party" in your honor. She refused to comment about her off-duty whereabouts. Now, I don't want to blow this thing out of proportion, but a *kill party*? C'mon man, grow up." Drummond waited through a silent moment. "Any comment?"

He looked squarely at Drummond. "Nope."

"All right. I want you to know that there aren't going to be any 'kill parties' around here. Is there anything about that you don't understand?"

"Nope."

"And no more of this ignoring fellow officers and constant criticism either."

Moon nodded slowly, thinking, then shook his head in confusion, "So, are you telling me who I can talk to and who I can't?"

"No, I'm telling you to be considerate and polite to your fellow officers. They're under enough stress as it is. Clear?"

"As mud." Moon flashed a grin at Herdahl, turned on his heels and exited.

17

WOMEN LOVE HEROES

"MONDALE PICKS A WOMAN" Morgan heard Sam scream the headline down the hall. Incredible. He'd picked Geraldine A. Ferraro, "a housewife from Queens," as the first woman to be named to a major political party ticket.

Sam probably jabbered all the way to school about getting out the teenage vote. Because if they got Mondale in the White House and anything happened to him — a big if — a woman could be President of the United States. By the time Morgan picked up her daughter from school, Sam's own possibilities had blossomed. She wanted to run for seventh grade student council president. At the very least she wanted to take the following day off from school and celebrate the making of history.

So, the following day, Friday, July 13, Morgan took Sam, Nat and Gramma Sofie downtown to the corner of 4th and Hope. They paraded across the freeway overpass with about 10,000 other Angelenos — actors, lawyers, homemakers, students, homeless, retirees — to pose for the big picture, Los Angeles' family album photo for the Olympic festivities. Gramma Sofie couldn't understand why they would go to such trouble to be unidentified specks in a billboard photo no one would see. But Morgan enjoyed Sam and Nat, swept up in the crowd's enthusiasm and unity, and that childhood whiff of eternity.

The next day Sam, Nat and Morgan finished Sam's treehouse, now surrounded with yard stakes advertising MONDALE/FERRARO. Up the ladder, under a makeshift tent of bed sheets that Sam and Morgan had draped from branches to the treehouse railing, they lounged in their nightshirts and socks. Tacked on the plywood, a poster-sized Geraldine grinned at Morgan, who had started reading aloud another chapter of *The Magic of Oz*. As Sam listened, she occasionally eyed Geraldine, stroked the new teal carpet that still gave off that dill pickle smell, then popped a piece of popcorn in her mouth. She offered Ozma, nestled by her side, a piece, then repositioned her head on her mother's lap and gazed at the stars.

Morgan glanced at Sam and longed to stop reading, freeze the moment, observe her staring and wonder what she was thinking. But stopping the flow of the moment to revel in it changes it entirely, so she kept reading, one eye on the text, and one eye on her daughter's bliss-filled face.

She nudged Sam, pointing to the place on the page. She swallowed hard, slipping into Kiki Aru's lofty pitch. "'I didn't know I was being wicked,' said Kiki."

Sam dove her hand into the popcorn bowl, "Yeah right," she commented, rolling her eyes and sucking in a mouthful of popcorn.

"'…but if I was,'" Morgan continued, "'I'm glad of it. I hate good people. I've always wanted to be wicked, but I didn't know how.'"

Sam flipped the page to the next chapter, entitled: Two Bad Ones, and spotted the queer old man she'd despised in so many Oz books before. "I knew it," Sam said, pointing to the fat body, pockets all bunched out as if stuffed full of something. "The Nome King, I knew he'd be in this one."

Morgan grinned and continued reading, "'Who are you?' asked Kiki. 'My name's Ruggedo. I used to be the Nome King, but I got kicked out of my country.'"

Sam sucked the butter off her index finger, shaking her head as if she could see it all: the Oz people had been way too nice, and since they hadn't wiped him out altogether, they'd given him the chance to strike back. Now, he was trying to convince Kiki, the not-very-bright son of a magician, to reveal the secret word for transformations so he could turn the Oz people into sticks and stones.

"C'mon," Sam sat up, reaching for the book balanced on Morgan's knee, "just tell me what happens."

Morgan waved her entreaty away.

Sam grimaced, pleading, "But you know. Tell me. I want this Nome King frozen once and for all."

Morgan smiled at her instant agitation at Ruggedo, the Nome King, knowing she herself had always been both repulsed and fascinated by his sense of cruelty, inhumanity, and intolerance. She'd grown up with the Oz books. Her own mother had taken her to one of the first Oz book conventions in a lovely cottage on a lake owned by the daughter-in-law of L. Frank Baum. A man with a mane of white hair and prominent white eyebrows played the piano. Tables were stacked with Oz books — a bonanza for book collectors; and Morgan's mother would trade her green stamp books for cheap first editions.

Older folks, who'd been collecting Oz books since the turn of the century, mingled with teenagers and youngsters. Sipping hot cider, all ages sat together — in rocking chairs or cross-legged on the carpet — around a fireplace listening to an Oz book read by an aficionado. In those moments, the quirky Oz characters united the disparate group, breaking down traditional boundaries between child and adult.

And even though Morgan and Sam knew the subject matter of the Oz books might be too young for twelve going on thirteen, the laughable characters caught in ethical and moral dilemmas transcended age. Sam would inherit their substantial collection of first edition Oz books, and it was assumed she would read them to her children. So, in an unspoken way, they were both reassured that their Oz moments together linked them with their past, present and future.

There was a knock at the bottom of the treehouse. Ozma barked.

"It's just Nat." Sam assured her puppy, then yelled out, "You're late. You didn't believe me, but I told you if they didn't wipe that Nome King dude out, he'd be back."

Sam moved to pop her head out of the tent, as Moon lifted up the sheet and peeked inside, smiling. "Late for what?"

Without dropping a beat, Sam hailed him inside. "Great, it's you." Ozma growled, and Sam stroked her reassuringly, informing Moon, "This book's better than the *Wizard of Oz*." She nodded at him, then more specifically at the book on Morgan's lap. "We just started and this boy, Kiki, steals this magic word that can change anyone into a cow or a fish or a bird and back again."

Moon nodded, undaunted. "I could use that word," he said, then glancing at Morgan's absolutely abashed expression, he indicated with an outstretched palm for her to go on reading.

Sam offered him popcorn. "You like butter?"

"Popcorn's not popcorn without it."

"That's just what she says," Sam chirped, indicating Morgan, then pointed to where they'd left off in the book.

Another knock at the bottom of the treehouse. "Pee Wee's on," Nat hollered. Ozma barked again, alerting Sam to his voice.

Sam scrambled between Morgan and Moon, lugging Ozma, "We're gonna watch *Pee Wee's Big Adventure* in Gramma Sofie's bedroom 'til she gets back. Can I make more popcorn?"

Morgan didn't even realize she hadn't answered until half way down the ladder, Sam yelled back. "Mom! Popcorn?"

"Yes," Morgan managed, her eyes riveted on the brisk friendliness on Moon's face.

"I'm sorry I didn't call first."

He didn't look very sorry, she thought. "Yeah." She nodded. "That would have been nice."

"I know, I know." Moon made an attempt at a submissive gesture. "I don't like it when people just drop in either." He averted his eyes from the hint of bare breasts under her cotton robe, and she summoned all her willpower not to touch her robe, not to apologize for his invasion of her privacy.

She tried to keep her eyes on his face, watching the vein in his neck rapidly rise and fall. "What's up?"

He nodded at Geraldine's photo. "Mondale never had a chance anyway, now he's just shot himself in the foot picking a woman running mate." His crooked grin gave him a self-pleased air. He shifted his weight. His everyday stance was more of a combat position — deceptively smooth because he'd prepared himself physically and mentally to move from a simple social moment, talking with a customer at the local 7-11, to instant combat, holding a robbery suspect at gunpoint.

Finally, staring at his cupped hands, which were awkwardly draped over his bent knee, he shrugged. "If I'd have called…it would've been harder to say it over the phone." He eyed her directly, as if he were checking out a front line, concerned how the field was shaped, feeling the rhythm of the situation, before making a quick decision.

She stiffened. "Say what?"

"Thank you."

She tossed him a suspicious look. Thank you is not that tough.

He said it again as if he were giving her the greatest compliment imaginable. And a deep terror stirred within her. The mellow sound of his voice, thank you, as though he really meant it, washed across her mind. The resonance vibrated delicious warmth that ran through her veins, as if they had been transformed into warm wine. She couldn't place why he would be thanking her, or when the last time was that anyone had taken the time to thank her for something, but she felt the sheer joy of being appreciated.

She reminded herself that when attacking, you try to chase the enemy into an awkward position. She lifted her bathrobe collar to her neck, instantly regretting the move.

He sat down next to her, saying casually, "I met with Captain Dithers today and you saved my ass. They've wanted to fry it for a long time. And our MAW meetings, especially the 'kill party,' are just the thing that could burn me."

"You didn't have to make a special trip here to thank me personally."

"I didn't. I made a special trip here to tell you that you really showed me something when you requested a report car."

"I didn't request it. Captain assigned me to a report car. I hate it. Very dull and uneventful."

"That's the point." He nodded, offering a slip of a smile. "It's safer." He stared at her hands, as if speaking by rote. "I wouldn't say we've been exactly swept away by spellbinding chemistry for one another, but who knows, shit happens." He paused a moment to give her a chance to lock into his rocky, intimate tack. "What I'm saying is I don't wear blinders when it comes to situations and people. And I don't think you do either, except when it comes to police work — the excitement, stimulation, prestige."

"Prestige!" she burst into a laugh.

"Okay." He paused, as if calculating an adjustment without entirely abandoning his position. "Maybe it's not prestige for you, but it's — "

"Look, all I'm trying to do is earn a living at a job I really like. That's not very complicated, is it?"

He smiled winningly. "And you're good." When he saw he couldn't advance, he didn't withdraw entirely. He pressed on, waiting for the right moment. "Seriously, you're better than anyone I've ever seen before."

"I do my best."

He faced her intently. "Morgan, I said you're good, but in this division that's not good enough."

Here it is. She'd heard it before and she was upset with herself for not seeing it coming again. She had opened the gates for his compliment, leaving her corners vulnerable for a direct hit. He added tonelessly, "If you don't quit, I might have to raise your daughter."

She managed to respond evenly, "Thank you, but that won't be necessary," and met his eyes.

He regarded her as though she were someone he really cared about. "I'm sorry, but that's what's scaring the hell out of me. You're really special, and I know I'm right." He waited for a response. There was none, so he topped off his black prediction with, "Sam's already lost her father, and I just can't handle another..." He winced, looking away.

So, this wasn't really about Sam's predicted loss, or Morgan knocking off an officer or an innocent bystander as a result of her piss poor police procedure. This was really more about him again, what he couldn't stand, another emotional setback.

"You think policemen are born, not created, don't you?" Morgan said.

He nodded. "Exactly. So why do you have to go against all your instincts and be something that you're not?"

"I may not have your upper body strength, but my instincts are the same."

"Not to kill."

Her voice came out in a whisper. "Oh, I've wanted to kill."

"Want. That's nothing. You gotta need to kill. And women always want to give somebody the benefit of the doubt because they can't understand a criminal mind. How many times do I have to tell you — "

"I know," she nodded, "Criminals pick on good people. Cops pick on assholes."

He heaved a big sigh, "So, who did you want to kill?"

She looked away a moment, collected her thoughts, then looked back at him, "When I was a kid, my best friend hung herself because her father was abusing her…well," she sighed heavily. "Up until the other night with you when I was climbing that tree, I always thought she hung herself, and was never able to put my finger on why that explanation didn't feel quite right." She paused. Frozen in a wild desire to escape, she focused on the treehouse ladder, and was unable to make the feeling pass.

With an enormous effort of will, she pushed on, keeping her voice as steady as possible. "And at the time, I thought I handled everything okay. I got her down off the door right away and called the ambulance and police. But I never opened the closet door, and I'm sure that's where he was hiding…her father. My own father refused to let me testify at the trial, and we moved away suddenly, all the way across the country…I was just a kid. How was I to know that when you hang yourself all the blood rushes to your head?"

Her voice cracked, continuing on its own, "But when someone else hangs you after you're already — after you're already dead, your heart stops pumping." Tears welled in her eyes and she shrugged foolishly.

"She have a white face?" he asked softly. Then after a moment in a low voice he asked, "Her father do it?"

She nodded yes. She felt crushed from the weight of revealing a truth she must have always known. Now she really had to fight the tears. With her voice quivering, Morgan explained that the night it happened Aunt Tilly had invited Samantha to go with them to the movies, but at the last minute Samantha phoned and said she couldn't.

"Well," Moon said, even more softly, "see how many years it took you to figure out that her father did it? Instinctively, I'd know it in a minute and I'd take the son-of-a-bitch and cut him eyebrows to gonads."

Her hands trembled. She could feel her chest rising and falling in stinging defeat from the realization that if Mr. Bowtie Deaver were standing right there in front of her, she wouldn't know what to do.

Moon touched her hand. "I'm sorry about your friend," he said, entwining his fingertips with hers. "You have the longest fingers," he said, then shook his head in quiet disbelief, as if realizing how he'd exposed himself unalterably.

He held her eyes, "Morgan, swear to God, if you weren't a police officer, you'd have to have a two-by-four to keep me away from you and that kid of yours. And I know you need someone…so, that's why," he balanced his proposition before tossing it into the air, "I thought if you could just stay on a report car and not go back on patrol — "

She smiled at his obvious seduction, waiting for a response.

"What, you want an answer tonight?"

"Yeah, I have to know tonight."

"Tonight? You're so direct, you're so — full of yourself. You have any idea how irritating that is?"

"What? To want to know now?"

"Yeah. You have to have an answer tonight. Yes or no, just like that. No 'maybe' or 'let me think about it.' Who do you think you are?"

He shrugged, clearly not getting it.

"You want an answer now? Fine," she said. "No." Without reservation or regret, she added simply, "There's your answer."

He shook his head. "I won't accept that for an answer."

"That's too fucking bad."

He tilted his head, staring at her intently. Leaning over, he ignored her stiff attitude and murmured, "I like you." He kissed her once on the lips.

With no movement and less expression, she said, "I'm not sure how I feel about you."

He paused, as if battling with a voice inside urging him to get up and leave. He didn't move. "Then why are you still here?"

Had he completely lost his mind? "This is my treehouse."

She pointed with pride at the flapping sheet door, and they both laughed. He took advantage of the spontaneous moment and embraced her fully.

She broke away, took a breath, laughing softly. "Moon, really, this isn't going to change my mind about the report car. Even if I did like you, I'm not ready for this."

He asked bluntly, "What's to be ready for?"

"Oh," she managed, feeling somewhat dazed. "It's been awhile." Her voice trailed off.

"Nervous?" He grinned. "You don't think I was a little nervous coming here tonight? I had to buy myself a box of chocolates to eat on the way over." He shrugged. "All right, I don't have to know if you'll stay on the report car tonight."

"I already told you I won't — "

He kissed her hard on the lips, holding her a long moment as if gathering strength to leave, then leaned into her so hard she had to wedge a flat palm on the carpet to keep from falling back altogether. Breaking away from his lips, she said, "I said I'm not interested."

He kissed her on the neck, whispering, "I know," as he peered out the treehouse to the back of the house where Sam and Nat were crouched on the other side of the sliding glass door, staring at the television.

Looked safe enough, so he leaned in closer, nudging his nose towards her neck.

"No," she inched back, blurting, "I'm not even set up for this."

He looked into her eyes and smiled. "You don't need to be set up."

She sighed, reluctantly divulging, "It's my time of the month." But she might as easily have announced that it was time to prune roses.

His fingertips brushed her neck to her shoulder. Sliding his hand down her back, he cupped her waist.

Morgan's skin shivered with goosebumps, sounding an alarm. Body parts she forgot she had sprung to attention in some wild parasympathetic race to be touched next.

She tensed as his hand moved down her thigh to her bare knee, then a wave of paralysis struck when his fingers touched the inside of her leg.

No underpants, she remembered and blurted, "No, damn it. I have — "

He frowned, pointedly, "You mean this?" he toyed with a string attached to her recently inserted tampon. Then he pressed her on her back using his free arm as a lever.

He's crazy, she thought. It felt all wrong. Too much thinking. Tense, she did a mental accounting of various body parts. Urethra, numb. Clitoris, humming. Vagina, no vacancies tonight.

Maybe this was it, uncommitted, unemotional physical satisfaction. No draining promises of adoration, devotion, monogamy.

No. Absolutely not. "It's just not a good time," she repeated firmly and made an effort to squirm away. Moon's weight, however, was already on top of her and she wasn't going anywhere unless he moved.

"C'mon," he said. "Why not?" He assumed he could fix whatever wasn't right about the time. He smiled, teasing her string another jerk, not letting go.

She stiffened. The tampon was already easing out. If she moved at all, it would slip out entirely. And how could she explain to Sam blood on the new treehouse carpet?

He unzipped his pants, and settled his flesh against her other thigh. She throbbed for an instant. He whispered. "Yes," and something about the intimate murmur of his voice close to her ear made her heart beat faster.

"Don't worry about the blood," he assured her, beaming. "I like to slip and slide in it. I love blood. I really love blood."

He twitched his eyebrows playfully and every sensation in her body turned off, every nerve ending, every thought, and every sound, except the sight of blood and brains splattering from the suspect in a white shirt and gray sweats raging on PCP. She remembered Moon's face, eyebrows quivering, set on the bloody victim like a hunter over his prey.

His words echoed in her head: I love blood. I really love blood.

"Moon," she said, forcing eye contact. "You need to hear me. I don't… want this."

He grinned. "I hear you do want this." He pulled on two strings at once. A slush, then warm liquid rushed. "Believe me, you want this."

"Dammit Moon."

"Yes, yes, you do."

Choked with anger, she wanted to scream, "Get off," but knowing that Sam and Nat were so close, she could only whisper it. She pushed flat palms against his chest.

He grabbed one arm, pinning it over her head and, with his free hand, positioned himself to penetrate.

She grit her teeth, "Get the hell off me," and pounded her fist.

"Oh, I like that." He chuckled softly, grabbed her flying wrist, and crisscrossed it under her head.

"Gotcha." He bore into her, and the winning glint in his eye dared her to do something, knowing fully that only screaming bloody murder would stop him. But she would never let Sam and Nat see her like that — powerless, submissive. Sam would be forever disappointed that she had let a man wrestle her down to the lowest position.

Morgan stared up at Moon's expression glazing over, and knew that he didn't love anymore. Tense, yet silent and submissive, her thoughts were with her, loud and clear.

In the space of a bank robbery, he'd held up her feelings for him, coursing through her veins like several shots of tequila, moving from attraction to disbelief to revulsion, settling on resignation, waiting for him to finish her off.

Waiting like so many millions of women pursued who have faltered in judgment or deed and been condemned to a lifetime of waiting for it to be over. Like her mother must have waited for her father, like all Aunt Tilly's trapped "fallen women," waited for a break, like Slattery watched the clock, like Samantha stared up over Mr. Deaver's head at the roses painted on the bunk, counting backwards from one hundred by twos. Ninety eight…ninety six…under this monster erection in a bowtie. She thought if only she'd been with Samantha that last night, stayed home from the movies with Aunt Tilly and read the *Magic of Oz*. Then gone over to Samantha's earlier…

Oh God, what wasn't working in his heart that he couldn't feel his own daughter's pain? And if he did, what was broken in him that made him not care? If only Samantha had fought back.

What if she had fought back? Morgan wasn't in fear of her life, which left time for the realization to sink in that her friend had probably fought back, had screamed even, and shocked, Mr. Deaver overreacted — smothering, choking her cries. Samantha *had* resisted her father, and here Morgan was submitting to an acquaintance rape. Echoes in her head peaked with exasperation: *Morgan, attack!* She reminded herself when the attacker is too strong, you strike the corners. Without warning, Morgan thrust her head forward and clamped her teeth over a nipple on his chest.

He cried out, "What the h — " and jerked back.

Releasing her arms, he moved to push her down, but with her hands free she pounded mercilessly on his kidneys, wrenching her hips out from under him and flipping around on her haunches.

He stood up and his pants fell down. "Son-of-a-bitch," he said, starting towards her.

"Morgan, honey," Gramma Sofie's voice floating up from the bottom of the treehouse stopped Moon in mid-step. "You all right?"

"I'm fine." She met Moon's eyes silently drilling a hole in her head. "I'll be right down."

He pulled up his pants and, reaching for his shirt, grimaced at his own blood dripping down his chest. He ducked through the sheet door with no backward glance.

Morgan stared at Geraldine Ferraro's grin. Too much of a mess to go in until Gramma Sofie went to bed, Morgan sat in a puddle of blood holding her legs to her chest, chin resting on her knees, wondering if Mondale had shot himself in the foot. Maybe it was too soon for women to be taken deadly serious. Change happened in textbooks, in the abstract, overnight; in reality, change takes time, generations.

She stared into the dark beyond the branches, unable to move or speak for the longest time. It was as if a hole in the night sky opened and released the cry of women suppressed over time, of women who had had no voice, and of women afraid to use the voice they did have. Their collective wail rushed into her head, settling on her shoulders, petrifying every limb, rendering her a human paperweight of grief.

Oh, that Sam never knows. She grafted a small hope to her heart.

But after a half hour huddled in her own puddle of blood, her heart shrunk, rejecting the weak graft, and hope turned to hate of wanting, hate of her own longing, hate of women yearning for fulfillment, belonging, love; hate of women whose personal desire compelled them to turn a blind eye to the cruel spirits of violent men, maximizing the importance of winning as an arrow to a woman's heart, to a woman's bed.

What would our countries, our cities, our streets be like, she thought, if we devoted our affection exclusively to heroes of peace, not heroes of war?

She wanted to be her daughter's hero. *Oh*, she sighed, later, under her covers, into her tape recorder, *that Sam never knows how I let her down tonight.*

18

BLOODBATH

Working a report car was a hayride assignment for physically or mentally impaired officers. Morgan's job had devolved to driving by after arguments, fights and homicides had occurred. She asked questions and helped the victims and eyewitnesses recall the particulars leading up to and following the event. It was comparable to following a tornado: the visual aftermath could only give a sense of the event, never replay live the moment-to-moment terror.

True, her assignment had bothered her at first. She'd hated the report car, then she started to appreciate the solitude and autonomy. Patrolling with a partner definitely had its disadvantages, its "temptations to corruption," as Captain Drummond put it. He'd recently given them a talk, more like a sermon, on the ethics of policing with a partner. The men and women knew his talk was inspired by the in-custody death of Morgan's arrestee; implicit in the captain's discussion was the unstated perception that Slattery had let her partner down.

Morgan allowed the same nagging questions to run amok in her head. What if Fender had beaten her suspect? What if in trying to be accountable for her own actions, she'd covered up his? His gloating over the incident sickened her so much she tried to reevaluate him, again and again, wondering if he was the guy Jacob had thought. She wanted to know if Alicia were right, if he'd ever beaten his wife Phyllis. And, especially after the episode with Moon, she made a mental note to find out.

By her fifth week at the 77th, Morgan dreaded Mondays. From the initial horrific eight hours with Moon to the chokehold and PCP shooting, Monday nights set a fire to the week. Fortunately, it'd been a slow few days since Alicia transferred out of the 77th. It was calmer than anticipated, especially since across town the pre-Olympics had kicked up an elaborate media fanfare that threatened to create record attendance and jammed highways. It seemed, however, that half of the Angelenos had left town to avoid the traffic crunch.

When Alicia transferred out, Lola Day, still a seductive snake, transferred in. And that bothered Morgan more than she wanted to admit. Worse, Lola had been promoted to P3 which meant she could actually train probationers to work on the street. The image of Doña Lola Puta Perfecta and, say, a probationer, not even someone with as much experience as their dear Slattery, reminded Morgan of a biology experiment Jacob did at home with a maze and two mice looking for cheese. The mice spent several minutes running up and down tiny corridors bumping into each other, until they finally found the cheese covered in Plexiglas. They ran circles around the transparent case until they both ended up in an exhausted heap.

After the first few minutes with her in the locker room, Morgan easily predicted Lola's attitude and presence would add more fuel to the MAW fire than Iggy and Alicia's romance ever had. Lola had told the women that first night that she decided to become an officer because she got sick and tired of telling her Barbizon models to stand up straight. Doña Lola Puta Perfecta flaunted her perfect posture and a few other truly outstanding highlights such as painted nails, layers of perfectly applied makeup, regulation short but stylishly coiffured hair, and colorful satin underwear with cupids, gum balls, stars, reptiles, Barbie dolls, hearts or unicorns, depending on the day of the week. She also sported a solid gold waist chain, which several officers said you had to see to believe. It was rumored that Doña Lola Puta Perfecta was directly indebted to these officers for her lightning rise toward her prestigious detective assignment.

Since Slattery was taking a few days off with the flu and Morgan was still on a report car, the women were speculating who Lieutenant Herdahl would assign to work with Moon.

Blocker reported that Lola had already gone to the lieutenant and requested to ride with Moon. As she reminded the women, she'd worked with all the hard-ass "vets" who hated females in the department and, as she so eloquently put it, "Moon's shit stinks just like all the rest of them."

Slattery warned her of his unrelenting reputation for harassing women, to which Lola casually replied, "Fuck his reputation. I'll just fuck his brains out."

True class. They're a matched pair, thought Morgan. And once again, she questioned Einstein's strong sense of universal connectedness: how could I be in any oneness with this woman? She looked around at Engels, Slattery, and Blocker, all staring agog at Lola and for the first time truly embraced those women, realizing they were by no means a single lens. But in spite of the weaknesses and strengths that had pitted them against each other, the men or the administration, they were collectively determined to be part of the new breed of women officers who worked hard to earn society's respect. Unlike Lola, they shared a pride in the way they'd fought to overcome incredible physical and mental obstacles in order to make their opinions known.

Captain Drummond walked down the Nightwatch roll call inspection passing Lola on her first night, commenting on her purple nail polish.

"It's not purple, sir, it's lavender." Lola smiled demurely. "If you don't like it, I'll take it off by tomorrow."

He nodded, silently indicating that would be a good idea. The MAW guys shook their heads, as if to say, "Who the hell is she?" And the women said nothing to one another, but Morgan felt a cringe spread through them and sensed a quiet fusion in their respect for each other's honorable intentions. These intentions united them for once, not against Lola, but definitely apart from her.

Morgan noticed Moon struck a stiff pose apart from the other MAW guys, and he didn't so much as glance at Lola, or anyone else for that matter. Lieutenant Herdahl assigned Teddy to Fender, Blocker to Moon, Lola to Gladstone. Lola offered Gladstone a toothy grin that he registered but ignored. Moon passed Gladstone on the way out of roll call, saying loud enough for everyone to hear, "Heads. You lose."

Now driving around in her report car, with a lot of mental time on her hands, Morgan gave some thought to how Moon was compelled to act in a certain macho way. And he probably didn't even know why. No, that's bullshit, she told herself. Stop making excuses for him. What he did was wrong. You put yourself in a vulnerable position and acted stupidly, but what he did was wrong. He can rationalize it any way he wants, but he's going to have to say something about attacking you in a treehouse.

But they hadn't said two words to each other that night in roll call.

Morgan picked up a call. She checked the address: the crackhouse across from Tia's Tacos.

She parked her report car in the midst of a dozen other patrol cars, a paramedics unit, a fire truck and dozens of spectators milling about in overcoats and bathrobes.

She ascended the front stairs, facing graffiti-sprayed porch walls and a rotted, pine banister, cracked in the middle and dangling. At the front entrance two paramedics appeared, hoisting a stretcher. The leader reached for the banister, which wobbled, broke off and crashed on the parched front yard.

They descended with caution.

Morgan plastered herself against the remaining banister to give them plenty of space to pass. They approached her bearing a corpse she recognized as Shadow, a friend of Domino, the old black man playing craps who'd helped her save face in front of Moon. Shadow's blood-drenched hand dangled from the side of the stretcher. The lead paramedic glanced at her and shook his head. "Nasty."

"Yeah," his partner said. "This guy here looks good." He called back over his shoulder. "Hope you brought a bunch of pencils and a thick pad."

Stepping into the cluttered house, jammed with 77th officers and investigators from the officer-involved-shooting section, she was blinded by the crime-scene photographer's rapid succession of flashes that froze images of the room finger-painted in blood. Blood was everywhere — on the walls, the furniture, and the floor.

She opened her report binder to note the time: 10:32 p.m., and the condition of the crime scene: blood splattered all the way to the ceiling. But she soon rested her pen, shuddering, unable to set down detail without emotion. Investigators had already yellow-encircled the position of Shadow's body in front of a unraveled web lawn chair, near Domino, bulky in a purple leather jacket, still splayed on the marred hardwood floor under a lopsided aluminum Christmas tree with several flashing red lights. His right hand loosely held a .357 Magnum, Colt King Cobra, that his fingers had probably only recently gripped.

She stared at the slow lights, working with every weak blink to inspirit Christmas, however pitiful, in July. She took a deep breath.

Her eyes followed the bloody-fingered trail of a suspect who evidently tried to crawl from the living room down the hall. She moved along the passage until she reached the kitchen where the finger tracks stopped. She looked into the kitchen and, standing transfixed, stared down at a young pregnant woman split open, like a ripe pomegranate, from close-range fire.

Fender was leaning against the shattered back door, which led to a backyard and alley, talking with a couple of detectives from narcotics division who were hauling several sports duffel bags from the trunk of a car parked next to the back stoop.

Her frown fell on Moon bounding up the back stoop and slipping past Fender into the kitchen. Moon glanced from the pregnant woman slumped on the floor to Morgan and sucked in his breath, sighing through an awkward moment, that Fender felt comfortable elucidating. "Hell of a labor," he said.

Moon offered Morgan the hint of a smile, a flash of regret, maybe. No, she told herself, no regret and she returned his non-verbal greeting with a wooden expression.

She walked towards Fender who had taken a seat at a canvas-covered restaurant booth in front of a table. Watched him cross his arms, lean back and regard Moon with skepticism. Fender must have intercepted Moon's eye contact with Morgan.

A narcotics detective tossed a sports bag on the table in front of Fender, unzipping it to reveal a wad of crumpled clothes.

Fender looked up at Morgan. "You doing the report?" She nodded. "Sweet," Fender said, half-smirking at Moon. "Sweet."

Fender's twisted smile yanked Morgan into the moment. She jotted down details of the blood-splattered kitchen — blotches on the back wall, the kitchen cabinets, the table legs. Peripherally, she saw paramedics set up a stretcher next to the woman's body.

She swallowed hard, then watched the detective open another sports bag to reveal a crumpled bleach-blotched navy sweatshirt on top of a full load of crack.

Fender cried out, "Yes!" He bounded from his seat. "Been trying to get a hit on these sons-a-bitches for months."

Charging from the kitchen, he hurdled the pregnant corpse and hurried down the hall to broadcast the big score. Morgan glanced down and noticed that the splotched canvas seat where Fender had been sitting was soaking wet and tinged pink.

Moon crossed to Morgan, distracting her. "You can hardly blame him," he said. "The asshole who hit my partner Earley worked out of here."

Morgan got a glimpse of the pregnant woman's guts spilling out as the paramedics hoisted her up. What appeared to be a tiny hand poked out of the stomach just as Engels stepped into the kitchen entryway. Engels gasped and fell back, cupping her palm over her mouth. Dumbfounded, she watched them maneuver the stretcher past her into the hall.

Morgan barked at the paramedics. "Cover her up for godsake."

Sara Ann Engels stared down the hall, statuelike, for a long moment. Morgan caught the suffocation in her eyes. "Sara Ann," she called softly. Engels' head turned slowly, her mournful eyes connected with Morgan in speechless horror. Morgan maintained a steady voice and lifted a beckoning hand. "Can you help me out here?"

Later, in the stifling locker room, Morgan felt the whoosh of air on her face as Blocker unfurled her pantyhose in front of her locker. Morgan was breathing with difficulty as though she'd recently finished a 10K run. Probably the smog. Los Angeles was suffering the longest smog siege in a decade. South Coast Air Quality was downplaying the smog picture, but the air pollution would affect the Olympic athletes. Especially the marathon runners.

Blocker grunted at the din of wild cheers, yelling and banging that came from the men's locker room. It had been intruding into the women's space for a good twenty minutes. "Shuddup," she yelled. "Fucking animals."

She huffed at Morgan, slipping on a T-shirt, and indicated Engels, sitting alone, as if in a trance, right next to the wall that separated them from the men.

Morgan and Blocker exchanged a look just as Engels lurched up and pounded on the wall with her fist. Laughing and catcalls shrieked through the barrier. With no warning, Engels snapped, rushing out of the locker room in her underwear, without looking back.

Morgan jerked up her pants and raced after her, leaving Blocker struggling into her panty hose.

Buck-naked, Fender was atop Bow Wow's shoulders. Iggy was dousing their leader with soda. Teddy Bear was leaning towards Moon in the shower, talking confidentially, when Engels burst through the locker room door.

Shocked silence.

Engels stared up at Fender for an instant, as if everything she came to say fell out of her head.

"Lit-tle girl," Fender reprimanded her, grinning supremely. "Get the fuck outta here, unless you want — "

Out of control, Engels screamed and flung herself towards Fender, knocking Bow Wow against the lockers, scratching and clawing to get Fender down. Iggy reached over to pry her off, but he was at a bad angle.

Morgan rushed in, shouting, "Engels!" She leaped to assist Iggy, but Engels knocked her to the floor.

Moon and Teddy Bear broke out of the showers as Sergeant Ross, followed by Blocker, stormed in, thundering, "Shut up. Every damn one of you!"

Morgan watched Moon and Teddy Bear pull Engels off Fender and, feeling a chill, looked down. She glanced at the crumpled uniform she'd fallen on, touched it and felt that it was completely wet. She glanced up at Fender, still naked, tottering in high spirits on Bow Wow. Then she casually scooped up the uniform and walked out, unnoticed, except for Sergeant Ross who she was sure noted her dark bundle, but without comment.

Morgan didn't go home that night. She left a message for Gramma Sofie: tell Sam I'll be home to take her to school. I have a lot of paperwork. Then she went back to the crack house and proceeded methodically from room to room. From the living room down the hall into the kitchen, she searched for details, jotting them down on a pad. She noted the front lock was broken, evidenced by the heel marks at the bottom of the door, by a swift boot.

Domino shot near the fake tree, Shadow coming down the hall from the kitchen. He'd have been coming out of the kitchen towards the living room, and must have entered just after the door was blasted in and Domino drew his gun, according to Fender, and was shot.

But what about Reggie, the other suspect in the kitchen, and the pregnant woman, RaVonda? According to Fender's report, Shadow surrendered, hands in the air, then the bathroom door popped opened, RaVonda stepped out, and Shadow drew; Fender shot him, and he dropped in front of the lawn chair. RaVonda tried to escape down the hall. Fender warned her: stop or I'll shoot. She didn't stop, and he nailed her midway down the hall.

How did she make it all the way down the hall to the kitchen, and why? Morgan followed what must have been RaVonda's last mad dash to the kitchen.

Why did she have to get to the man at the sink? Why did RaVonda have to get to Reggie? She checked the officer-involved-shooting report to confirm again that both Teddy and Fender said they had entered from the front door.

Something caught Morgan's eye. She took a step backwards and studied the yellowed linoleum floor. In the corner just above the baseboard, between the sink and the back door, she noticed a dried brown splotch. It looked like honey oozing out from a crack in the wall onto the floor. She leaned in, examined it a moment, then stepped away. Probably chocolate ice cream.

Still gooey, it reminded her of something she couldn't quite place until a still shot of Teddy flashed in her mind: Teddy Bear lobbing brown saliva at the firing range that first day she'd found out about her transfer to the 77th.

But Teddy had never even been in the kitchen. She referred to the officer-involved-shooting report again. Never made it out of the living room until after Fender ran into the kitchen and tagged Reggie. She got down on her hands and knees, swiped the still sticky chocolate blotch with a sample cloth and slipped it securely in a specimen bag.

She sighed, exhausted, and sat on the back stoop to review her notes.

An hour later as the sun came up, Morgan was still hunched on the back stoop, dozing off. A siren wailing down Century Boulevard startled her awake. She checked her watch. Barely enough time to make it home to braid Sam's hair. Reaching down to pick up her notepad resting next to the hose nozzle, she noticed a wide ring of moist dirt. Result of a puddle? She checked the nearby hose nozzle. No visible leaks. A quick survey of the dry yard offered no sign of plant life needing water. Yet to make a mud puddle that large in diameter, the water had to be running hard for more than just a few minutes.

So what? No time for musing about puddles. She shot up and, heading into the kitchen, swayed, light-headed, bumping into the off-white slip-covered booth where Fender had been sitting hours before. She looked down, brushing her fingertips over the pink-tinged water mark, still damp, that encircled the area previously occupied by Fender's rear end.

She stood for a moment staring at the watermark, as if some unknown force kept her feet planted until her head figured it out. Then cursing herself for not having suspected it sooner, she hurried back outside and scooped several tablespoons of dirt into another plastic specimen bag.

19

BEWARE OF ROSES

Morgan dropped Fender's uniform off, along with the samples of moist dirt and brown ooze, to BSS Williams, her friend who'd been training cadets at the Police Academy, now back in serology specializing in identification of body fluids in major crimes, usually homicide and sexual assault. He warned her he was already up to his eyeballs in his nickname BSS — blood, saliva and semen — but to check with him later in the day. He'd see what he could do.

She phoned home as she was leaving the lab to tell Sam she'd be back in time to braid her hair for school. But the early morning city traffic was deadlocked, and she arrived home too late. She whipped her Jeep into the narrow driveway and beeped her horn at Sam, long hair flowing unbraided, racing out the front door as the school bus turned onto their street. Morgan parked and bolted from the car.

Sam brushed a kiss by her cheek and slipped an envelope into her hand. "Can you give this to Moon? It's an invitation to my birthday party Saturday."

Right. July 21. Your birthday party. Morgan nodded, vaguely remembering some weeks before talking about a water party with squirt guns, hoses and water balloons. Morgan didn't have time to go into the potential embarrassment of giving Moon anything, let alone discuss the improbability that he would show up at a thirteen-year-old's squirt gun party. She marveled at her daughter's confidence, energy and grace as she glided down the drive to meet Nat who was toeing the dirt next to the bus stop.

Sam waved to her before she stepped on the bus, then plopped herself on a seat near a rear open window. With her long hair caught in the wind and billowing magically, Morgan thought she looked remarkably like the princess of Oz who occasionally admitted deserving mortals, like Dorothy, into the Emerald City.

Morgan dragged herself up the stoop to face Gramma Sofie's scowl at the threshold. Nothing was said. Gramma Sofie turned in a snit, scuffing down the wood floor in her pink satin slippers. She disappeared behind her closed bedroom door. Her box-springs squeaked as she sat on the side of her bed, removing her slippers and tucking them neatly under her rocking chair.

Morgan turned into the room next to Gramma Sofie's and closed the door. She passed the goldfish without feeding him and flopped on the bed, staring at the cottage cheese ceiling. After a minute, she leaned up on her elbow and rummaged in her nightstand drawer, sifting through several of Jacob's letters until she'd found one of his last missives.

She read through the part about the gray, soapy food and clammy, fetid air until she came to the paragraph about camaraderie. "Imagine being in a jungle ocean dog-paddling with a couple of dozen wounded guys. No rescue in sight. Surrounded by sharks, we watch out for each other day and night…I've been on watch duty with Ben Fender, that all-city linebacker I was telling you about from Tampa. He's a helluva funny guy, an instinctual soldier, not much on sentimentality. He comes off as a hard-line, tough guy, but he got a letter from his wife the other day. Sent him a rosebud, found out she's pregnant, and he just broke down, sobbing…"

The rosebud image swirled in her head until it started toward her like a projectile, scratching her in passing, reminding her of the prickly details she'd yet to figure out in her attempt to reconstruct exactly what happened at the crackhouse. She assured herself she would figure it out. She'd already gathered some physical, trace and impression evidence that could answer a few puzzling questions.

Morgan made a mental list enumerating the crime items she had left to review. She had to check with the medical examiner for the victims' times of death, if death occurred at the location where the bodies were discovered; she needed to take a look at the crime lab photographs of the scene, the sketches made of the body positions. She had to get a crime lab investigator out there to dust for prints, something they automatically did on homicides whether they were criminal or innocent. But she hadn't seen anyone dusting the previous night. Why not?

She realized she wasn't treating this like any other officer-involved shooting, accepting all the information given by the officers, Fender and Teddy Bear; rather she doubted the accuracy of the information in the officer-involved-shooting report, and she was conducting her own private investigation for a criminal homicide, the unlawful taking of a human life, perhaps with premeditation, and since Fender was the shooter, possibly with malice aforethought.

She called the crime lab, got an investigator to dust the crime scene, and verified the time and location of the victims' death, then returned to the serology lab later that afternoon. After she'd turned in the specimens to Williams that morning, she'd called Teddy Bear and reconfirmed the officer-involved shooting report. He swore he'd never been in the kitchen before RaVonda and Reggie were shot. What about after? No, not after.

She dismissed her suspicion that he was lying until Williams held up the plastic bag with the chocolate-colored shavings from the kitchen wall and announced it was dried saliva and chewing tobacco, probably Red Man. Her interest was piqued. She didn't need chemical match of his saliva with the spit and tobacco juice to know Teddy had lied. He'd been in the kitchen. But was it during the shooting?

The wheels in her head were turning so fast Williams had to wave an unmarked manila envelope in front of her face to get her attention. "I didn't mark confidential on this one because then everybody would read it."

"Good thinking." She reached for the envelope.

He backed up. "Not so quick," he teased and, with a gently amused expression, dangled it over a trashcan. "I could just drop it and nobody's the wiser."

She stared at him with concern, but no real comprehension, then brightened, "The uniform? Wow, that was quick?"

"Yeah, I was up all morning. Look, I know that you want these results, but you see once I turn this info over to you, the *report officer*, the ball's in your court and…ignorance is bliss."

"Says who?" She made a swat at the envelope.

He backed up further. "Think about it."

"C'mon." She lunged and grabbed the envelope. "You just want me to hang around so I have to take you to dinner."

"No." He shook his head, eyeing first the envelope then Morgan. "Now I want you to do the right thing."

Morgan escaped to the nearest bathroom, locked herself in a stall and opened the envelope. She read the analysis that revealed the woman victim's blood type was in the moist dirt sample and "saturated in uniform."

Saturated in uniform.

Morgan reread the phrase several times, clarifying for her own edification, saturated in *Fender's* uniform. His uniform was permeated with the blood of the woman he shot in the stomach. Not Domino's blood. Not Domino's friend's blood. Not Reggie's blood. How could his uniform be saturated with only the woman's blood?

Maybe he had picked her up and moved her after he'd shot her. That would account for a concentration of her blood in localized patches on his uniform shirt. But traces of her blood were in his uniform pants. His cuffs. Saturation implied that her blood touched every fiber of his uniform, as if he'd dunked himself in a vat of her blood dye.

Naturally, the officer-involved-shooting report offered no explanation. Her investigation now was completely off the record. Off the map, she thought. Almost immediately, the patronizing smirks she'd allowed herself to suffer, in the name of Fender, gave her a headache; she hated herself for her wretched, inferior overtures to get along with Fender, The Grand Dragon, and his MAW clan…to get along for what? For the sake of the department, for the protection of the women, for the memory of Jacob?

And come on, she clawed at her brain, spit it out, for her own conceited, obstinate, ignorant self.

"What have you done?" She pounded the metal wall again and again. "What have you done?" she hollered, pounding the shivering borders with both fists. The envelope dropped, its loose pages strewn with bloody details, floated to the sticky tile floor. One page tilted precariously on the seat of the exposed toilet. But the papers could have vaporized and taken her with them for all she cared.

She flopped back and forth against the tinny prison, in a frenzy of rage, screaming, "This is insane. Don't we have enough problems? We have enough goddamn problems!"

She caught her breath and in the split second of silence heard a faint sound bounce back, "…enough problems? We have enough goddamn problems!"

The echo rang through several seconds of inert shock, rearranging her wits, until she shuddered, as if jarred suddenly awake by a rough hand, clearing her head from a groggy sleep. She took a deep breath, then bent over, hair brushing the lip of the toilet, as she scooped up the analysis form tottering on the seat and those that had landed between the bottom of the bowl and the filled Kotex dispenser.

That evening's Nightwatch went as smooth as glass. No bickering in the locker room. Blocker, Slattery and Engels dressed in silence, punctuated by Doña Lola Puta Perfecta's humming of her favorite Carpenters hit, "Close to You."

Roll call was other-worldly, lifeless; everyone sat stone silent. Morgan noticed Fender, unmoved in the corner, wearing a uniform. She wondered when he had discovered his other uniform was missing. Had he reported it? Herdahl announced the assignments, entertained questions and, when there were none, dismissed them, watching the officers, detached and distant, file out the door.

Fender brushed by Morgan on the way to his car in the parking lot. He nudged her with the butt of his shotgun. "Aren't you 'bout done with that report?"

Her eyes flicked over the shotgun, then rested on Fender's face. She could say something. No. Let him squirm.

"Bet you're doing a dynamite job — turning over every stone." He pressed for a comment, so she sprayed lighter fluid on what she could sense from his gaze was a burning concern, "Got a couple more stones to dig up yet."

During her entire shift, Morgan had only two calls, both minor domestic disputes, but when she returned home at 2:30 a.m., she picked up a call on her answering machine: a child screaming *Mommy, Mommy.* An icy shiver traveled from her head to her bare toes.

She roared into Sam's room and found her wrapped burrito-like in her blanket, sound asleep. Gramma Sofie's bedroom door was closed, but Morgan could hear her soft snoring. Morgan replayed the message several times. She didn't recognize the child's voice and there were no other discerning sounds. A second message from Alicia: "Call me pronto, chica. I have some information for you." Too late to return calls. She ejected the tape, slipped it into her bag and went into her room.

She kept her underclothes on and pulled the quilt over her head, cocooning herself on her pillow, striving to believe the call was more a prank than a threat. But even tucked in her shelter, she couldn't convince herself the screams weren't intended to intimidate her.

But who? Fender had no reason to suspect she'd swiped his uniform unless someone in serology had blabbed. She remembered what Joe Blanco told her about Fender's friends. They were everywhere and they were tight.

What about BSS Williams? She flipped the covers off her head and reached for the phone. He wasn't Fender's friend or he wouldn't have given her the blood work report on the uniform. She dialed his extension at the lab, then hung up before anyone answered. Better to talk with him in person.

She mentally reviewed what she had to do when she got up. Check with the crack house neighbors and the paramedics who responded to the call — ask about specific details; review her notes at the crack house, what she may have missed; meet with Joe Blanco — eat crow; talk with Teddy Bear — what would he say about chewing tobacco in the kitchen? She sighed, what a torture that was going to be.

Oh, and remember to call Alicia. What did she want? Since Alicia worked mornings in narcotics, Morgan hadn't spoken with her all week. Alicia would definitely have heard about the crackhouse bust. That's probably why she called. With her thoughts whirling beyond any possibility of sleep, Morgan got up, slipped on her bathrobe and slippers and padded down the nightlit hall towards the kitchen. The morning paper thumped on the front walk.

Instinctively, she moved to retrieve it, but as her hand paused on the front door knob, she remembered the child's scream: *mommy, mommy*. And here she was heading outside in a bathrobe and slippers at 5 a.m. with no gun. She unlocked her gun from the secured desktop drawer, slipped it in her bathrobe pocket and walked down the steps to retrieve the *Los Angeles Times*. The morning edition's bold headlines read: *Jackson Delivers Apology*. Once back inside the house, feeling pretty silly, she secured her weapon in the drawer and walked to the kitchen.

She was in the midst of an article detailing Jesse Jackson's dramatic speech, announcing he would support Mondale, when the phone rang, startling her. She reached for the receiver, hesitated, then picked it up. "Hello."

A familiar voice whispered, "Morgan…it's me."

"'licia?"

"Iggy's still sleeping."

"I'm glad somebody is. What's up?"

"Iggy says you haven't filed your report on that bust the other night."

"So?"

"Fender's pissed."

"That's news? Besides, since when did you give a rat's ass about Fender's attitude?"

"He's pissed at you. Iggy says he thinks you're up to something, gonna try to frame him."

"Frame him? That's rich. Don't worry. I'm just writing up a report. Doing my job."

"Fender's calling you a cunt and other stuff you don't want to hear."

"I can imagine."

"No, you can't. Iggy says it's different. He's never talked about you like that, and he's acting up."

"What do you mean?"

"He can't do anything to stop you, so Iggy told me tonight that Fender was bragging about beating up on Phyllis with a chair, chanting: More-gun…More-gun…More-gun…"

"Jesus H. Christ."

Morgan held the receiver to her ear, listening to Alicia breathing. "I told you. The cabrón, he's a psycho son-of-a-bitch."

Morgan nodded. "Right."

"Morgan," Alicia paused, "remember what I told you about the hungry dogs?"

"Yeah."

"Well, this cabrón is not hungry, he's rabid, and I don't know if he's just talking big or what, but, think about it: if you turn in a report that the I.A. comes down on him for, suspends him or something, living with him — forget it, if he's already beating her with a chair."

"I hear you. Thanks for the news flash. Get some sleep."

Morgan hung up, poured herself a glass of cold milk, added a long stream of Hershey syrup and mentally penciled in "visit Phyllis" on her to-do list. Now, on top of the damn crackhouse report, she had to worry about Phyllis and her kids.

How was she even going to see Phyllis without Fender knowing? She considered calling Moon, asking him to do her a favor, amuse Fender, while she paid a call on Phyllis.

Would Moon tell Fender? Maybe not. She considered Fender's stick-together pledge, his MAW deal, then she reminded herself what MAW stood for: Men Against Women. What are you, brain dead? She admonished herself. Moon practically raped you. No, he did rape you. No practical about it. What makes you think he's going to take wife beating seriously?

Morgan had to see Phyllis before meeting with Joe Blanco at three o'clock. She would have to take a shot in the dark. Drive by the house around noon. She remembered from Academy days that Fender enjoyed a workout ritual before lunch. If he were gone, Morgan would have a brief window to talk with Phyllis alone; if not, she would question Fender about the crackhouse. He would give her the same line of bullshit he'd been dishing out, and he wouldn't suspect anything.

Just after twelve o'clock, Morgan turned onto Fender's wide residential street. A wood-paneled stationwagon, probably the one Morgan had seen Phyllis drive to the Academy, was parked in the carport. Morgan pulled into the driveway in front of his suburban ranch house, and parked behind the stationwagon. She thought about parking at the curb, but decided the driveway made more of an assertive, yet casual statement. That way, if Fender came home, it wouldn't look as though she was trying to hide anything. Don't fantasize, she told herself, walking up the front steps, if Fender comes home and sees me with Phyllis, he'll go ballistic.

Morgan rang the doorbell and waited, adjusting the black leather shoulder bag which contained a Polaroid in case she needed to take photographs to document evidence.

She'd started taking photographs a couple of years ago when a victim had called the Devonshire police in a hysterical state from the gated community she lived in with her fiancé, a valley judge. She claimed he had beaten her up. When Morgan arrived, she found the victim, bloodied and cut, sobbing in a neighbor's kitchen. The woman was six months pregnant and had been badly kicked in the stomach as evidenced by the red footprint still imprinted over her navel. The victim said she lived in constant fear of her fiancé's volatile temper.

Morgan completed a detailed report, then a couple of days later was dumbfounded when the woman sent a letter renouncing all her accusations, requesting that the case be dismissed. The City Attorney lost in court, and Morgan realized that if she had taken photos of the cuts, bruises and footprint, they could have prosecuted the abuser without a cooperative victim.

When Phyllis, under a straw hat, opened the front door smiling, Morgan's worst fears were dashed, until she noticed a seeping gash peeking out from the broad brim. Morgan introduced herself. Phyllis nodded as though she'd been expecting her, "Ben's not here. He's at the gym. I'll tell him you stopped by."

"That's okay. Would it be all right if I talked with you a minute?"

"Sure." Phyllis backed away from the door. "I was just pouring myself a glass of iced sun tea. Want some?"

It was easier than Morgan anticipated. They settled at the white Formica kitchen table animated by a ceramic rooster centerpiece. Phyllis didn't cry or accuse. She listened. Morgan explained about the crackhouse and her investigation into Fender's actions, "There are too many loose ends overlooked in the officer-involved-shooting report, and really there's no reason Fender — Ben's going to bring it up if he's not asked."

Phyllis, emotionally flat, offered no personal comment until Morgan described RaVonda, the pregnant woman shot in the stomach. Phyllis softly stated, "Ben shot her," then sagged into the padded chair, dipping her shoulders and drawing her knees to her chest. Hiding under the sunbonnet, she shivered.

Against a beige wall in the living room, she allowed Morgan to take photos of fresh cuts, old scars, fading bruises — all hidden by baggy clothing. Phyllis led her outside to a trash container and stood silently while Morgan documented a tangled mass of smashed lamps, a broken chair, and empty beer bottles.

Had he ever abused the children? No, Phyllis bit her lip, but the oldest one, her ten-year-old girl, swore just that morning that she'd kill Daddy next time he beat up on her mother. Morgan dipped her head, nodding, and soaked up the child's threat, connected to her own vivid memory of protecting her mother against her father's attacks.

Morgan informed Phyllis that with the photos as evidence she could assume the responsibility of convicting Fender, and remove the burden to testify from Phyllis and the children. But Phyllis warned that he would sweet-talk her, then try to threaten her not to testify. Which was, all the more reason Morgan told her, why she would have to leave him.

The reality finally exposed and documented in instant photos brought tears to Phyllis' eyes. Viewing her own raw gash, bruises and painful scars spread out in a dozen photos on a coffee table next to school photos of her children clarified her path. The photos, undeniably grim, convinced her she'd passed through a life-altering door and there was no turning back.

Morgan cautioned her to act normal, to give no notice or explanation to her family or friends, and to be strong and silent until the moment came when she would have to escape with her children. Morgan wondered how Moon would have handled it. Would a male officer have devised an escape plan? Probably not. She tried to remember where she'd heard it was all right to hit someone as long as it was with a stick no thicker than a thumb. Somewhere. Was it still such a pervasive part of the culture that a man had a right to control his wife and children? She wondered how many officers, judges and DA's were men, and how many still thought that way? This would only change when more women became officers, prosecutors and judges.

But what would Springsteen do? He would help Phyllis escape.

Morgan was more sure than ever, that, as a woman officer, she was finally on the right rail car heading in a positive direction of social change. At that particularly hopeful moment, she wasn't considering how hard some people worked to sabotage certain trains.

When Morgan backed out of Phyllis's driveway an hour later, she waved to a neighbor eyeing her, an elderly man in an L.A.P.D hat, mowing his lawn. She'd left Phyllis in this police hamlet making beef stroganoff for Fender's early dinner. Morgan had given her a hearty hug, the kind Aunt Tilly would have given a "fallen" Portland woman.

Phyllis, however, was lifting herself back up, standing on her own two feet, even though neither woman had any idea whether, when the moment came, the abused cop's wife would have the strength to guide her five young children swiftly out the door.

Driving to Parker Center, Morgan enjoyed a stirring revelation. Like her Aunt Tilly, who shone a light on the social condition of economically exploited women, Morgan was flashing a high beam on cops who beat up on their loved ones.

At Parker Center by three o'clock, Morgan's head throbbed so intensely she could track the pain to the source from the back of her neck down her spine to her left thigh, calf and finally to her right numb instep. Settled in Detective Joe Blanco's brown Naugahyde chair, she glanced at him as he adjusted his eyeglasses and continued reading her report. She stared across his above-standard walnut desk through the massive filmy 11th story window that looked down on Los Angeles Street.

So far, Blanco had been simply civil. Nothing more, nothing less. "Coffee?"

"Yes."

"You take it black?"

"No, with honey."

"Right. Sorry, no honey. Sugar?"

"No."

"And I bet Nutrasweet's never touched your lips."

"What makes you say that?"

"Just a guess."

"What about a coffee, hot cocoa combo?"

"Sounds good."

He nodded, pleased he'd been able to work out a deal. That was his job. Working out deals.

Morgan wasn't about to make it easy for him.

After she'd burned him and lied to him during the IA investigation, she was surprised he offered her anything beyond a urine sample. After all, he had no idea what to expect from her and was probably wondering why she'd gone to the trouble of making an appointment to see him in the first place. Why she'd told his partner, Francesconi, she wanted to see Blanco alone and would not divulge the reason.

The reason, of course, was Francesconi — his snorts and disapproving gestures rendered him just a notch above a swine with a couple of lobotomized human skull parts.

Her eyes followed the people below, blurry moving specks. All those people were going someplace, on the way to something. And a hundred years from now, all new people would be going someplace.

And if she did absolutely nothing about this crackhouse report, about Fender, no one would be the wiser. Joe Blanco here with the Diego Rivera tie was the only one really driven to expose the truth. In a century, who would even care, let alone remember?

Blanco set down her report, removed his glasses. He stared at her, waiting through a long, heavy silence. She wondered if this was when she should tell him about the threatening phone call, about what Iggy said about Fender, about Phyllis' open wounds. No, not now, she decided. Don't drag it out.

It was late. She was desperate to get out of there. No sleep in two nights. Sucking alertness aid pills like breath mints, her nerves were misshapen scraps ready to be sewn into one of Gramma Sofie's patchwork quilts.

Staring somberly at him, she considered that this administrative representative of the office of Internal Affairs was the man Moon scoffed at and Fender satirized. Did Blanco ever stop to realize that he wasted his shabby reality trying to gather evidence to incriminate the leader of MAW, a non-existent group? The Los Angeles Police Department never publicly revealed the existence of the sexist clan. She wanted to invite Blanco to investigate Jimmy Hoffa without mentioning the Mafia. But his steady gaze cautioned her not to get too lofty, rather to proceed with the report under his folded hands.

"I've never filed a report that implicates an officer in a homicide," she said, "so before I turn it in, I wanted to know if I've left out anything."

He offered a nod of complete understanding. "Very thorough…down to Fender's entire uniform. You really stretched on this one." He stared at her with a hint of intrigue.

She squirmed. "Like I said, if I'm going to file this report, I want to make certain I've got what I need."

He gave her another long, hard stare, as if waiting for her to read his mind. "Officer Bear," he said.

Morgan pointed, indicating the report. Teddy Bear was in the report. "He's there."

Blanco nodded. "You need Officer Bear. As Fender's partner. But you've got to question him."

"I did." Had he even read the report? She was profoundly annoyed until a sly smile animated his bland expression.

"Yes, you questioned him about what happened, and he told you his version. Now you have to go back to him and inform him of your version…jog his memory." This stiff, almost awkward bureaucrat behind a solid mahogany desk, who loved jalapeños and probably was a king of salsa in some Latin bar in Pacoima, gave Morgan her first lesson in how prosecutors get officers, criminals to roll. "Make it clear to him that we will accuse him, he'll get time, unless he comes forward and confirms your finding."

She shook her head. She knew these guys like her daughter's hair. "He'll never roll on his partner."

Blanco leaned forward and, with a peremptory wave of the hand, revealed he knew them much, much better, "Don't put money on it," he assured her.

He handed her a microcassette tape recorder. "Cover yourself in case Teddy Bear recants later."

She nodded, pausing to give herself a pep talk. Tell him everything. Go for it. Something she couldn't put her finger on and didn't have the time to analyze told her to trust this guy with the Diego Rivera tie. This uptight investigator stared at her, listened and every once in a while smiled that same crooked grin Señor Blanco used to manage when she complimented his vibrant Police Academy garden.

Morgan wasn't offering any appreciation for Investigator Joe Blanco's job well done; she was admitting to withholding Fender's name in the chokehold incident. "I just wanted to clear the record," she added, deliberately making eye contact.

"Thank you," he said, simply.

She took a sip of his coffee, hot chocolate combo, wondering what he was thinking.

"I'd like to share that with your captain." Off her nod, he added, "He was a little skeptical about allowing you to finish investigating such a sensitive shooting that implicates Fender, but I told him you were just the person for the job: thorough, honest, no red flags — Fender would get suspicious if we brought in a special crime unit to comb through the house, but you — "

"No threat, I know," she said. Then she asked him, without pausing, without stopping to think about it, "Does your mother work at the Academy gift shop?"

"Yes." She felt his eyes on her, waiting for an explanation, waiting for her to lead him through the personal door she'd opened.

But she returned abruptly to the business at hand. Now that the Fender admission was over, she could feel her caffeine saturated alertness pill wearing off. She pressed on to move her meeting agenda along. "If I pull this report on Fender off, I need a favor." She withdrew the dozen Polaroid snapshots from her notebook. He flipped through the photos soberly, then asked her, with more apparent concern than curiosity, if Fender had touched the children. No, she assured him, but she'd need a guarantee of a safehouse for Phyllis and the children and a restraining order on Fender.

He nodded, "Consider it done," then glanced at the Olympic headlines and asked, "What about a few tickets to the opening ceremonies? I've already paid for them."

"Phyllis is going to have her hands full. Besides, she has five kids."

"I was thinking more along the lines of you."

She said she'd think about it, and left Blanco's office, vaguely realizing she'd just accepted a date with Señor Blanco's son.

Morgan asked Sgt. Ross, whom she liked all right simply because he was the first person she'd talked to at the 77th, to slip Teddy Bear her report before roll call. Blanco assured her she could trust Ross implicitly. Better not involve Drummond yet. She told Ross to mention discreetly that she needed to talk with Teddy before she filed the report.

Ross could decide to turn it over to Fender before Teddy Bear, but it was a risk worth taking. She was sure Ross had seen her steal away Fender's uniform and, so far, she didn't think he'd said anything to Fender. Ross had probably told Drummond. And Drummond told Joe Blanco. What a rumor mill: it was impossible to keep secret any aspect of an investigation.

After work though, Morgan found a note on her front car seat. "Meet me at the Beach Cafe on Pacific Coast Highway at 6:00 a.m.,T."

She arrived home and immediately let Ozma, spinning in joyful circles, outside in the backyard, then she checked Gramma Sofie and Sam, both sound asleep. Flicking on the message machine, she heard a vaguely familiar man's voice, energetic, like a morning disc jockey: "Tell her what she's won…A trip. She's won a trip. Good. Now, what's the bad news? Tell her where…oh, now that's pretty far away… who'll take care of Jacob's little girl?" Click.

She played the message a dozen times, listening for any hint to identify the caller. Nothing. She knew she'd heard the voice, or perhaps the message enough times that she was acquainted with the inflection. The voice didn't belong to any of the MAW guys. Naturally, Fender would've gotten someone she didn't know to make the call.

Veering off the road on her way home, now she was wide-awake.

She set the alarm for 4:30 a.m., took half a sleeping pill and dozed off in Gramma Sofie's recliner next to the phone, with Ozma cuddled at her side. She dreamed Fender was behind the wheel of a van speeding down an icy mountain highway with Morgan, Nat, Sam, Gramma Sofie and Ozma swerving in the seats. He lost control and the van spun over an embankment. Morgan checked to make certain everyone was all right, then jimmied the crushed van door open. She spied Fender tromping through the snow, hurrying to reach the door before she was able to help the passengers escape. He shrunk with each threatening step towards her. When he reached her he was was the size of a hot dog. The puppy snarled. Morgan yelled, "Sofie, hold Ozma." But Ozma, crazed by the smell, made a beeline for the open van doors, tumbled into the snow next to Fender and gulped him without so much as a sample lick.

The alarm went off and Morgan was already in the kitchen making coffee, contemplating the meaning of Ozma eating Fender. She wrote a note to let Sam know she might not be home in time to braid her hair for school. But Morgan hinted she was working on a birthday surprise. She wanted to tell her daughter about the Opening Ceremony Olympic tickets, but it wasn't a sure thing. She hadn't yet made up her mind, and Blanco could change his. After all, he did work for Internal Affairs.

But Morgan had a feeling that an outing, a threesome activity, couldn't hurt, and if it worked, maybe a real date would be next. She had to admit she liked this Joe Blanco, and it wasn't simply an attraction to his artistic ties. Her open mind was motivated, in part, by the screaming tabloid headline she'd glimpsed at a supermarket: Bruce Betrays Fans — marries Julianne Phillips. A platinum blonde model. Morgan didn't have time to read the article, but she imagined his supporters were mourning that he hadn't married a Jersey girl, a factory worker. His marriage was a wake-up call for Morgan: if Bruce, the rock-and-roll greaser preaching for the common man, could marry a blonde model, Morgan could at least date an Internal Affairs detective who wore Diego Rivera ties.

Her Jeep in reverse, she let out her clutch and pressed the accelerator, but the car didn't move. She sighed. Just after 5:00 a.m., and already things were going too smoothly. Walking around her car in the dark, she was absolutely unfazed to find every tire slashed. She put the gears in neutral and pushed the car a few feet down the drive to give her enough clearance to back Gramma Sofie's Cadillac out of the garage.

Teddy Bear had picked an ocean café far from their precinct and a time when most cops who'd been working all night had the good sense to be sleeping. Even stopping to fill the Cadillac with gas, Morgan arrived before him and was on her second cup of coffee when he moseyed in and sat across from her facing the immense stretch of sand and sea.

He set the envelope containing her report on the table between them. The waitress, young, beautiful and dark-tanned almost the shade of Teddy's naturally nut-brown skin, had performed only cursory service before. Now she rushed to the table and offered a robust good morning, pouring Teddy coffee and passing a long look over Morgan's head. "Blue plate?" she asked him, in an all too familiar way that implied more than just an appreciation of his plate color preference.

Teddy nodded. "Thanks, Tammy."

She smiled adoringly and bounced away.

"Tammy?" asked Morgan.

"I slide over a few mornings a week," he said, taking a deep breath and staring through the tinted window. "The water helps me keep things in perspective."

Tammy set a basket of muffins in front of him, a large O.J. and ice water. "Thanks." He nodded and waited for her to finish fussing with the napkins on the table next to them before he glanced at the manila envelope and muttered, trying to downplay the contents, "You're making a mistake if you file that, you know." He gazed at Morgan, unflinching.

She dipped her head, entertaining the possibility. "Yeah, it won't be the first time."

He stabbed a chunk of butter and spread it on cinnamon bun. "But it'll be the last." He took a bite, taking a second to enjoy the sweet cinnamon. "Want some?" he offered.

"No thanks."

She didn't know where he was hoping to lure her with his "last" comment, so she ignored his bait. "When this report becomes public, IA has assured me they'll reel you in with Fender."

"No doubt." He crunched an apple hunk.

"Teddy, c'mon. I know from that damn tobacco spit that you were in the kitchen, but you and Fender both agree you weren't the shooter, so why are you holding out? Maybe you were involved in the shooting. The whole scenario is fuzzy. The officer-involved-shooting report doesn't hold up. But this blood work on Fender will hold up with or without your testimony. And you know they're just chomping at the bit to bring Fender down. He's not worth five or six years of your life for Chrissakes."

"How do you know what he's worth?"

"I know how you guys work. No partner's worth doing time for. That's the first thing Moon told me."

"Moon's got a big fuckin' mouth."

She sat through a long silence while he jammed a piece of pumpkin bread into his jowls. It was clear he'd brought her out in the middle of her night to talk her out of filing the report, not to talk about what had happened that night at the crackhouse. Fine. She could get home just in time to braid Sam's hair.

Tammy poised the coffee pot over her cup. "More?" she asked.

"Thank you, no." Morgan reached for the envelope. "I've got to go."

"Oh, that's too bad. You don't have time for breakfast?" the waitress said, adding brightly, "It's the body's most important meal."

"I'll grab a bite at home," Morgan responded, smiling, glancing at Teddy. "I have to get back in time to braid our little girl's hair."

Tammy covered her many exposed perfect teeth, darted a pained look at Teddy, then made a beeline towards the kitchen, where her disappointment was not lost on the sympathizing cook.

Teddy's dumbfounded expression wavered. Amused or pissed? Morgan couldn't tell until he raised his eyebrows and said, "Now why'd you go and do that?"

"I thought you were more sensitive than that, Teddy." He eyed her suspiciously. "You like coming here to look at the water? Don't fuck with your server. Better to keep her intrigued and aloof, dreaming up ways to slip aphrodisiacs into your juice, than tick her off so she's conjuring up ways to lace strychnine in your muffins."

Morgan stood up, caught a glimpse of Tammy peeking at them from the kitchen area and felt her profound disappointment. "Don't worry," she said, "I'll tell her on my way out I was just kidding about the *our kid* thing."

He nodded thanks. "She takes good care of me. Always remembers to put ice in my water."

"Sweet." Morgan smiled. She felt Joe Blanco tapping inside her head, reminding her not to let this guy go. Morgan added, casually, "Seems like the type who'd probably wait for you four or five years. See you later."

She crossed the room, careful not to look back, but she could see his reflection in the window. And he wasn't looking out at the ocean, but rather into the kitchen. She could see by the way he was rubbing his thumb unconsciously back and forth on his knife hand, that he was trying to understand his life…asking: where did I go wrong? How did I come to this?

By the time she'd unlocked her car door, he'd crossed the parking lot and was standing next to her. "Can we sit down by the beach?"

They strolled towards the ocean and sat on a sand dune, out of earshot but within sight of the cafe. Morgan leaned the microcassette recorder on some nearby seaweed. It recorded the breaking waves as they watched them in silence. Then something unexpected came over Teddy. As she listened, Morgan knew that much of what he expressed, his even tone, his profound grief, his teary eyes she could never put in her report. But she let him tell it his own way.

"I've always thought Fender's a good cop with an attitude. I like that. I got an attitude. I was raised not to trust whites just like he was raised to hate blacks. But we got beyond that, teased each other to hell and back. And he might've called himself a racist but, on a one-on-one kinda deal, he's not. He really liked Earley. You didn't know Earley, but ever since he got blown away because Slattery didn't do her job, Fender's just been too hot to handle, every which way…

"When we transported your suspect that night, he was in the backseat with Fender and he started mouthing off about a cunt cop. Now, Fender's given a few punches and jabs here and there before, nothing serious, but he lit into this dude. 'I don't care,' Fender says, 'if she is a female. Fuck with any cop and you fuck with me. Do you understand, nigger?'

"Dude didn't answer, so Fender got in his face, called him nigger until the dude spit in his face, 'Fuck you, white trash,' he says. And that's one thing you don't call Fender: *white trash*. Probably makes him feel, you know, disposable. So, Fender just lights into him with his flashlight. Couldn't see much 'cause I was driving, but I could hear the gut shots and the dude thrashing around, slamming his feet against the seat. Messy." Teddy shook his head, looking off in the distance a long time. "But I figured it was a one-time deal, Fender'd get the picture. You can't work out your grief about Earley on a suspect.

"But it turns out everything flips him out now. Way out. Slattery and Engels, Alicia and Iggy, you and Moon, just puts him over the edge. There's not one thing he likes about his job, not one person he likes to work with. I'm thinking that maybe he needs a vacation, but if I make noises about it, forget it. So, I go to his wife, Phyllis.

Phyllis Louise and their five kids. This woman's a saint, I'm serious, and she has, you're not gonna believe this, no clue about Fender and his job."

Morgan could believe it, but she didn't say anything that would interrupt his flow of thoughts. "Fender never talks about his work," continued Teddy Bear, glancing at her uncertainly. "Never brings it home…he's Officer Ben on their street, mows the blind neighbor's grass, supervises street car washes in his driveway, runs a boy scout club, coaches a Little League team. 'Why do you think Ben needs a vacation?' Phyllis asks me. She doesn't even mention Earley's death. And I'm asking myself if his own wife doesn't know about the one thing that has sent him over the top…" Teddy Bear's voice trailed off.

Then he turned slowly towards Morgan. "That's when it hits me that this guy is carrying some heavy shit. He's gotta be wound tighter than a top. I keep my eye on him. As soon as Lt. Herdahl told us to keep our eye on that crackhouse I wished she'd just suck the words back into her face. We were already driving by the place a dozen times a night, now Fender wants to park there. Which is what we did for about five hours that night. I'm around the back of the house and am just about ready to call it quits, when a car pulls up near the stoop and parks.

"I radio to Fender, who's across the street in that abandoned restaurant. He radios back that a threesome — two men, one woman — are approaching the front. They enter as the car headlights go out. 'They're in,' Fender says. 'Wait a minute and I'll take the front; you fuck 'em in the back.'

"The kitchen window's half open, so I can hear this guy Reggie, the driver of the car, at the sink washing cups, calling out to somebody in the living room. 'Hey, Domino,' Reggie says, 'you know me, man, I wasn't with no other woman.' Moving down the hall, Domino yells back, 'You don't gotta convince me, Reggie. You best get out here and talk to RaVonda when she gets out the bathroom.'

"I burst through the screened back door: Freeze! Reggie does, still got the cup in his hand, and we can hear the front door blast open and Fender yelling: 'Freeze! Police!'

"Fender told me later that the suspect near the Christmas tree, Domino in your report, moved like he could be reaching for a gun, which you know since they found a gun in his hand. So that hangs. Fender shot him.

"Then I hear the other guy shout, 'Don't shoot. Don't shoot.'

"A bathroom door opens and a woman screams, 'He's got no gun!' Fender shoots once, twice. Then the woman shrieks, 'Reggie!' And we're talking shrieks so loud Reggie gives me this God awful panicked look.

"I tell him, don't move, everything'll be all right. We hear the woman screaming, running down the hall, until Fender nails her in the shoulder and she skids down the wall, to where she pulls herself into the kitchen doorway to see Reggie, who I'm still holding at gunpoint…

"She reaches out to him, and I swear to God time stops and plays this moment over and over and over in my mind. They lock eyes like in some movie, and she stretches her arm out to him, just a few feet away, and she's reaching, gritting her teeth, then she heaves her body towards Fender, and he plugs her a couple of times in the stomach. She flops on him. Reggie dives for her and Fender shoots him. But the instant before he shoots him, Fender darts me a look.

"My knees are numb, swear to God, numb, and I'm looking from Reggie to that woman to Fender, who's standing there with a stupid ass grin on his bloody face.

"He has her blood all over his uniform, his neck, his arms, his shoes. He goes out back by the stoop to wash his uniform off with water. He calls me out there, starts laughing, roaring, and squirts me in the crotch. Piss off, I tell him, I didn't get blood all over me!

"He gives me another stupid ass grin, 'No, looks like you got so scared you took a leak.' He slaps me on the back and I jerk away from him. Man. I'm so fucking pissed at him, I can't fucking speak. 'What? What?' he gets in my face, 'what're you gonna do?'"

And Teddy Bear's words flowed like a great wave of emotion, both cresting above and pulling in undertow. "I stay in his face for a minute, thinking, for Godsake, I gotta do something — something, I'm gonna do something, I'm thinking, because you are a motherfucker cop. The kind of cop I never want to be. I'm walking down the hall, into the living room, and I realize this motherfucker just gunned down four of my people. If I don't do something about it…I am…"

Teddy Bear paused, swirling in the moment, then slowed down. "I don't know when it happened that he changed so much, maybe over time, maybe it wasn't just Earley's death that flipped him out, maybe it was something that happened to him in Viet Nam or when he was a kid and it's been buried in him forever. Couldn't be just one thing, had to be a bunch of things.

"Didn't make any difference. I was so mad at him I couldn't talk. So, I grabbed the hose from him and wet down my whole uniform. He laughed, headed back inside the house, messing up the place, fixing the scene for his story, and a chill went through me when I realized: I'm gonna do nothing. It's his word against mine. And my word means nothing."

Morgan left Teddy staring out to sea, and then stopped to have a word with Tammy.

Driving from the café parking lot, she noticed Tammy exiting the rear door, carrying a tray of food. Morgan watched her in the car's rearview mirror, easing her bare feet across the sand, careful not to spill the ice water.

20

BIRDS WITHOUT A NEST

Moon's Range Rover was in the Saturday morning car wash line. He was bent over the front seat picking toothpicks, peppermint wrappers and paper clips off the front carpet when he spotted a small white envelope that had slipped down between the passenger seat and door. He opened the invitation to Sam's water-play birthday party and was perceptibly touched. He even tossed it on his dash after the Rover was washed and ready for a day of errands.

The invitation slipped back and forth on the dash all morning as a subtle reminder. Finally, he decided to just stop by a minute at Sam's party. What could it hurt? The kid was crazy about him. How could he disappoint her? He wouldn't have admitted it, but he hoped that stopping by, paying attention to Sam, might help his relationship with Morgan. They hadn't talked since the night in the treehouse, and he hadn't given it nearly the thought he figured she had. Women thought about relationships too much. They reviewed every detail, attributed a network of meaning to every action or oversight. Moon's buddies talked about chicks constantly but it was more dick specific to whether or not they could talk some lame chick with bad make up into giving them a decent blow job.

Simple facts, black and white. They liked a chick or not. She was hot or not. They sunk it or not. So, the treehouse episode was easy for Moon to interpret. It reaffirmed his self-fulfilling prophecy that he couldn't maintain a successful relationship with a woman.

Late in the afternoon, he pulled up and parked in front of Morgan's house just as a pre-teen appeared from the backyard, launched a skateboard over the hedge, hopped on and power skated down the sidewalk.

Passing a long buffet table decorated with crepe paper streamers, he was puzzled by signs of a celebration that never took place — an uncut birthday cake, perfect chicken salad sandwich triangles, water pistols, water balloons, party hats in a neat line. Moon grabbed a handful of unshelled walnuts. Looking up, he saw a figure hunched in the treehouse.

He approached the treehouse ladder and met Nat, standing guard. "Party's been canceled. She doesn't want to see anybody," Nat warned.

"Thanks," Moon said, as he patted Nat on the shoulder and climbed up, greeted by Ozma's protective bark.

Sam, holding Ozma in her lap, was staring into the tree boughs. Moon sat down cross-legged next to her, but she ignored him. He inhaled deeply. Taking a moment to observe the treehouse embellishments, his gaze trailed along the collage of Marine newsprint, yellowed articles, and war medals she had varnished along the wooden hand railing in memory of her father. Moon noticed the only framed picture was of a full-dressed Marine laughing with an ecstatic two-year old clinging to his back. Her hair-braid, like a long stem rose, was clenched between his teeth.

Moon glanced down at a long braid lying across Sam's lap, and then, checking the nape of her neck, spotted a few short curls hanging from under her snug baseball cap.

He lifted the brim gently and exposed a tousled head of ringlets. Moon frowned, "Your mom do this?" Sam ignored him. "Where is your mom?"

Nat climbed up the ladder and took his shoes off at the edge of the carpet. "She had to work on some report all day," Nat told him. "We were gonna just postpone it until this evening, then…"

He passed a look first from Moon then to Sam's shock of hair then back to Moon. "Big mistake. Gramma Sofie's friend was over and said she'd cut Sam's dead hairs or something. Just a little bit, you know." Nat shrugged. "Guess she had a mess of dead hair. Now she swears she's not coming down until it grows out."

Moon nodded. "Yeah?" He was impressed by her pledge. "How fast does your hair grow?" Sam shrugged. "You could be up here a long time."

She darted a look at him, as though realizing she'd charged herself with a pretty heavy expectation.

"Don't worry, if I know your mother, she'll clear it up so Gramma Sofie'll leave your dead ends alone."

Moon withdrew two safety pins from his shirt pocket, locked one inside the other, and said, "In the meantime, I need your advice. Somebody gave me these as a joke, you know, and I can't figure it out."

Nat moved in closer.

Sam regarded the pins curiously, so Moon positioned himself nearer, continuing his feigned confusion, "See, you're supposed to be able to separate them without opening the pins."

Nat looked dubious. "I don't think so."

Moon handed them to Sam, her hostility waning a moment as her attention focused on twisting the pins. She gave them back to Moon, placing one in each hand separately.

Nat's mouth dropped open, silently marveling at her.

"Thanks." Moon nodded, pleased. "How'd you figure that out?"

She turned her head away slowly without a word.

"She's not speaking to nobody either. 'Cept me. Morgan did that after her mom died. Didn't speak to nobody 'cept her best friend."

"That so?" Moon nudged her. "Hey," he said, refusing defeat. "I know how to get water from a quarter."

"She can already do that," Nat muttered, as though he were really trying to help Moon out.

"Okay." Moon stalled, thinking, regarding her, struck by a glimpse of female mystery in her youthful dignity and arrogance. "Okay, okay," he relented. "I wasn't going to show you this until I knew you better, but I can show you something you've never seen before." Nat checked out Sam's glazed eyes and shook his head dubiously at him, but Moon persevered. "And after you've seen it, no living being will ever see it again."

Sam regarded him with speculative interest. He pressed on, withdrawing a walnut from his pocket. He cracked it, revealing the kernel in the palm of his hand, "Ever seen this before? Nope. Say bye." He popped the nut meat into his mouth. "And you'll never see it again."

"All right!" Nat exclaimed, totally in awe.

Sam averted her eyes and locked her jaw.

Tenderly, Moon slipped his arm around her shoulders and said with feeling, "C'mere, Mooseface." He lifted one of her curls with his index finger. "Curls look really good on you. Really. I'd tell you if they looked stupid. Now…" he paused, motioning for Nat to lean over and indicated his, dark, wiry hair, "on Nat?"

Sam lifted her eyes to Nat's winning grin and the very thought made her crack a smile.

When Moon showed up for work that Saturday night, Fender was not there. Word was out he was in some "hot agua." And Morgan, the one person who could tell him what was going on, was mysteriously off for the night. To make matters worse, Lt. Herdahl finally partnered him with Lola Day, who'd given every indication she was anticipating riding with him.

Out on patrol, he gave Lola more than his usual cold-shoulder treatment; he was utterly silent. Lola talked. He drove.

On a domestic dispute, she calmed an irate husband by cajoling him into a community self-help alcohol program. Moon stood by writing the report, stone faced.

When he returned to his patrol car, Lola was already there, applying lipstick. He snorted.

Her eyes shifted towards him. "We're cleared for supper. Why don't we stop at my place and I can fix us something to eat."

Silence, then Moon asked without looking at her, "How far do you live?"

"Not far," she replied. She told him the address and he pulled out of the tenement parking lot. On the way Lola chattered to him, stressing her one asset: public relations. "I can get along with just about anybody…I love kids…But I think sometimes I'm just too empathetic, you know. Thin-skinned, but when I get my feelings hurt, I lose my temper and I'm like the Incredible Hulk…Oh, you can just park around back in my spot."

Moon parallel parked in front of the apartment complex, turned off the ignition and sat staring out the windshield.

"Don't you want to come up?" she asked in a low intimate voice.

He turned, staring at her blankly. "All right."

Lola fidgeted with the door key, then, once inside, floated past him, waving towards the kitchen for him to make himself at home. She disappeared down the hall.

Moon gazed out the grimy window, then ambled towards the kitchen. He opened the refrigerator door. A jar of kosher pickles with one lone pickle floating in brine. A small pizza box. Several white cartons to go. A quart of skim milk. He shook his head, closed the refrigerator door, then on second thought, opened it, unscrewed the top off the jar and popped the scrawny pickle in his mouth. He left the lid on, but not screwed to the jar.

He was hastening to the front door when Lola called out from the other room, "Moon, could you come here a minute?"

He paused, shook his head in almost amused bewilderment, then sauntered down the hall until he stood at the bedroom doorjamb and beheld Lola, poised naked but for a white gauze shirt. She stood in front of the light streaming in from the open bathroom door. Holding a glass bowl of fruit, she smiled brilliantly.

Moon regarded her up and down, glanced at his watch, then crossed towards her. He looked at the too perfect bananas spread on top a shiny red apple. "Is it edible?" he asked nonchalantly.

"Guess," she said, setting the bowl on the bed with a saucy laugh. She rested her palms on his chest. He put his arms around her waist, pressed up against her. She flinched intimately, cocking her head back with an elusive, breathy laugh. He fingered her top button, slipping it through the hole, loosening the transparent fabric, exposing a nipple.

She inched towards the bed, but he didn't budge. "Why don't you just suck my cock right here?"

She fastened on his intent eyes. "Is that all you want?" she taunted, her smile tinged with self-satisfaction.

"No," he said in a hard, flat voice, regarding her. She was everything he'd assumed she was and more, he thought, as he ripped the remaining buttons off her top, revealing her chest.

She froze.

He stared at her for an intense moment, waiting. When his silence moved into an awkward moment and showed no signs of abating, she dropped her eyes and reached towards his pants' zipper. He pushed her hand away and looked at her for another instant before he spelled it out in no uncertain terms. "What I really want is for you to get the fuck out of my car and off my police force today."

Word spread through the men's locker room after Nightwatch that Fender had called for a meeting at the park, and Moon was so hacked with Lola Day that he was primed to let off some steam and cook her in one of their sizzling MAW roasts.

So, a couple of hours before dawn the Grand Dragon's troop — Moon, Gladstone, Bow Wow, Iggy, Teddy Bear — were all there hanging around the bleachers chugging beer, talking in hushed tones, waiting for their leader to approach.

"I called this tribunal," Fender said, standing in front of them, one clenched fist at his hip, with the same nasty glint in his eye Moon had seen that night when he'd ripped the G-string off the stripper, "because we can't take another night of their splittail bullshit."

Moon nodded, wondering what Fender would've done if Lola pulled that naked, fake fruit shit with him. He would have followed his macho motto: if she has a hole, I gotta pole and probably fucked her, then announced the graphic details in roll call. And would that have bothered her? Moon doubted it. Fender would be another trophy. In fact, Moon considered, Lola Day mirrored the testosterone venom women complained about in men. And similar to most of the guys he'd known, she bragged about her sexual exploits.

He was loath to admit that it bothered him she didn't crumple at his rejection. On the contrary. She'd said, with a smirk, "Your police force? You want me off your police force. Fat chance." She'd slipped into her uniform, grabbed the only real apple in the bowl of plastic fruit. "Lunch," she smiled casually, indicating the remaining bananas. "Help yourself." Then she'd returned to the patrol car as if nothing had happened.

Now Fender was shouting that he'd saved the city a whole shitload of money by offing those scumbags in that crackhouse — and what thanks did he get?

Moon knew the MAW guys would listen to his ranting as usual. They were like soldiers who listened to their leader before he revealed his combat strategy because they were used to the way he pumped them up to feel the rhythm of the enemy so they'd know just the right moment to strike.

Fender continued, parading back and forth in front of his troops. "I get Engels, one psycho splittail, coming at me in my locker room. My own goddamn locker room, where another splittail lifts my uniform and is supposedly writing a report that some jackass over in IA tells me could slam me with criminal charges. Criminal charges! The animals have finally taken over the fucking zoo."

Moon looked around at the men and noticed they'd stopped drinking beer, listening without comment to Fender rail as usual about how women had changed the whole department. "And what've we got to say about it?" Fender clamped each one of his disciples with his hardboiled glare.

Teddy Bear stared at the dirt, and Moon noted this was probably the first time in the history of MAW meetings that not one of them looked as if he were having any fun. The air was electric — jaws clenched, faces taut, eyes hard — with disappointment, anger, disgust. Only Fender was letting off steam, at them. Half inebriated, preoccupied with other thoughts, they were less animated, less involved, less swept away in a united active voice. "Who are you? Men or women? What've you got to say for yourselves for god-fucking sake?"

They were stiff and silent — to the untrained eye, a hard bunch to read. But Moon could see Fender didn't realize he'd gone too far; he'd already gone out on such a high, weak branch, no one could follow and expect not to fall and fracture limbs. Fender probably thought they were so silent and serious, paying such close attention to him, because they were comprehending that he had to move them to a higher level of combat now, where there'd be more personal risk, more emphasis than ever on lying and trickery.

Bow Wow finally broke the silence. "Jack shit, that's what we got to say about it, Jack shit."

"Thank you." Fender gave a small bow, then turned and threw up his hands to the rest of his sorry troop. "Are you gonna let these splittails keep fucking us?"

Bow Wow shrugged, disgusted, as if jack shit was pretty much all they were ever going to have to say about it. Fender scanned the other noncommittal expressions and fell silent for a moment.

That was when Moon could tell it hit him, but he ignored it at first, giving a quick headshake and markedly looking off across the baseball diamond. Then he looked back, and like any good commander, aimed for unity in the face of division. "What is this?" he said, half chuckling in amazement. "What? Are we wimping out here? Hey!" He made eye contact with each one again, then tried to sweeten the moment with some sport-like physical contact, an affectionate fist to the forearm for Teddy Bear, a couple of shoulder touches for Bow Wow and Gladstone, a butt slap for Moon, ending with a hug for Iggy. "We're all we have. We're it. We're the L.A.P.D.!"

He hopped up on the first bleacher seat and punched his fist in the air, shouting, "L.A.P.D.! The last of the greatest fucking police departments in the world. We've got to stand together on this one — "

"Fender," Moon held up his palm for him to stop. Moon knew he had to keep it short and to the point. The MAW men had come to the park at Fender's request out of loyalty to each other. He felt all their eyes on him. Now, they wanted to go home. "Fender," Moon continued, somberly, "you made a mess, and you didn't clean it up."

Fender stepped down from the bleacher. "What are you saying?"

Moon shifted his weight, irritable and tired. "C'mon. You know exactly what I'm saying. Like in Newton." He jarred Fender's memory to a particularly shaky escapade in the "Shootin' Newton" division. "We made a mess and we cleaned it up. Now, what are we looking at here? You got a weapon found on Domino, the driver of the car, you nailed. Then his buddy, Shadow, you said looked like he was going for a piece, you nailed him. Okay. So far. But then you hit the woman in the stomach — "

"She lunged at me, I thought she was coming at me with a knife."

Moon talked over him. "Pregnant woman. Okay, so she lunged, but she was un-fucking-armed. Maybe you should've put a butcher knife in her hand."

"She lunged; I was in fear of my life." He grinned, glancing around the group as if he expected a laugh. Not even a smile. Shooting an unarmed pregnant woman in the gut offended even these men, who'd all seen their share of questionable shootings. But this was overkill, unmanly, nothing they could boast about, and they enjoyed bragging about their collective and individual vagaries.

"The dude you hit in the kitchen," Moon was careful not to glance at Teddy Bear, "never made a move for a piece. You know better than that shit. You fucked up big time, man."

Moon sent a shock wave into the group, leaving Fender speechless, hit in the corner with his defenses down. Moon had stepped on Fender's weapon before he had a chance to scoop it up, so Fender had to take a moment to step back, make some adjustments. He glanced around briefly at the severe expressions, struggling for eye contact, team spirit, a rally in the face of certain defeat.

He sighed, appeared to relax, like an impassive boxer in his corner between rounds of sparring. Then, when everyone least expected it, he turned, yelled, "Die, you fucking whistle blower," and planted a crashing right jab in Teddy Bear's head.

The punch hit Fender's partner squarely in the jaw and knocked him so suddenly to the ground that Fender had a few seconds to jump on him and pound on his head with total force before Moon wrestled him off Teddy.

Moon took a few half-jab pokes in his midsection before he wrested a right arm behind Fender's back. "You fuck," Fender gasped, swinging his other arm in a weak hook, "you're fucking her." On his knees, arms wretched behind his back, he screwed his head around to glare at Moon. "Am I right or wrong?"

Moon took a deep breath and shook his head sadly. "Your priorities are so screwed up, man. I'm hearing it with my own ears and I don't believe it. Your picture's going to be all over the front page of the *LA Times* once she turns in that report, and you've got your nose in my sex life."

"Tell me you're not sticking her," he persisted, catching his breath.

Moon assured him that he wasn't sticking her, but Fender waved a hand, as if brushing them all away. "Fuck. Fuck all you dickheads."

21

GRAND DRAGON'S TRUTH

Sunday morning, Fender walked out of his front door with Phyllis and his five kids, dressed for church. He noticed Morgan leaning against her Jeep across the street.

Morgan reached for the report on her back seat, then headed for his front walk, reminding herself she didn't even have to be there. She was only showing him the report before she turned it in because she thought it was the right thing to do. He'd been her training officer. He'd fought with Jacob. Admittedly, the report was her moment to confront him, to show him that written facts and details could wield more power than oral lies and harassment.

She had to face him with her findings. She had to face him so he could look into her eyes and know she wasn't beaten down by his intimidation — anonymous phone calls, tire slashing, death threats. It, too, was her moment to call him on all the duplicity and mafioso policing that had led to his crackhouse guerrilla warfare.

Morgan watched Fender say a few quick words to Phyllis, who Morgan could tell was nervous by the way she shuffled the kids into their station-wagon. Fender walked to meet her at the curb.

That Phyllis completely avoided even glancing in Morgan's direction was a good sign that she hadn't slipped back into victim's remorse. She was still going to go through with the plan. Morgan imagined her slipping out as usual during part of the preacher's sermon to nurse their baby in the nursery. Only she wouldn't do any breastfeeding in God's house today.

She would quietly whisk the other four children out of Sunday school on a pretense, any pretense. She'd been living with pretense so long that wouldn't be a problem. Then she would calmly lead her young children across the car-packed asphalt parking lot. It would be the longest walk of her life. But once she had them safely seat-belted in the station-wagon, she would drive two blocks to the Texaco station on the corner where a contact from the witness protection program would escort her across the border to a Rosarita Beach safe-house.

Morgan forced herself to maintain eye contact with Fender as he approached her, but the heavy air forced her eyes to drop before he even spoke. When he did speak, she felt, for the first time, a pang of regret for what she'd written about his actions at the crackhouse. Maybe she'd been too harsh.

"I don't know what you trumped up for that report, Morgan," Fender said. "But if you want me to apologize for shooting first, forget it. Maybe I shot too quick, but I'm alive."

She must be crazy. What was going to happen to his kids without a dad? Maybe when he found out everyone knew about his wife abuse, he would stop. Turn over a new leaf. It could happen. The kids' carefree yelps were escalating in the station-wagon. Her heart pounded wildly. What had she done? She said simply, "Well, you were wrong. You did what you thought, but you were wrong."

He fixed his gaze on the station-wagon, unable to speak. When he did, his voice cracked. "This will destroy my life. You know that."

The vise on her heart was so tight, blood thrashed every which way except to her knees, which were numb. How did he know what was in the report would destroy his life?

"You turn in that report, I'm a dead man." His eyes shifted towards her, beseeching, trying to promote an understanding between them with a crooked grin. "What can I do to get you on my side, to help you understand that this report will be the death knell not to just me, my family, but the L.A.P.D.?"

"You mean because you shot RaVonda, a pregnant woman, in the stomach?" Morgan said, her voice now working on its own volition, disconnected from the sloppy confusion in her brain and heart. "And shot another suspect, Reggie, in cold blood." His eyes glanced over at the bound manila report in her hand.

"Not to mention the driver of the car, who didn't have a piece, and Domino, who did have a piece, but," she couldn't help interjecting, "this really impressed me, that even in your haste to rinse all the blood off yourself, you still remembered to take the gun that Domino never reached. Where was it? Probably the small of his back, and you placed it in his right hand."

Fender eyed her. "If you put that in there," he said, glancing at the report, "you're gonna look as stupid as the shit you are."

"Maybe, maybe not. The suspect was left-handed."

"So you say."

She wouldn't give Fender the satisfaction of knowing she remembered the night Moon had insisted she pick Domino and his buddies up for playing craps in the alley. She'd visualized Domino tossing the dice with his left hand. She always noticed people using their left hand because she was left-handed, and her suspicion Domino was left-handed had motivated her to check with the coroner, who confirmed it. But she would let Fender think she was bluffing, and he would have to call her.

Fender focused on his station-wagon filled with all the rest of his life. He was careful not to look at her now. "Do you have any idea," he murmured tightly, "what effect this report could have on the city of Los Angeles?"

"Why? Because the victims you shot were all black?" She palmed her forehead in mock amnesia. "What a dumbshit. No, I never thought of that." She handed him the report.

Without looking at it, without looking at her, he said, "I'm asking you to destroy this report. I'm asking you as a friend. A partner." He looked off down the street impassively. He was making an effort at humble communication and he hadn't had much practice. She could sense from the thin tone in his voice that he would have destroyed the report for her. She thought of Jacob. If she destroyed the report for any reason, it would be because Fender tried to save Jacob's life. She replayed their ambush scenario in her mind, then rattled by the disquiet of her thoughts, she finally asked herself: What would Springsteen do?

After a ponderous silence, she informed Fender, "I wanted you to have a chance to take a look at this before I turned it in."

"What's the point?" He turned slowly back towards her, making a last gesture towards his vehicle. "This is my life you're fucking up." His children wrestling in the car diverted his attention again. He watched them a moment, gave a weak smile to Phyllis who was trying to contain them, then shook his head ruefully, and looked at Morgan. He looked at her as though he were seeing something for the first time. His small stiff nod confirmed the light that she saw go on in his head through the flicker in his eyes.

"What?" She fastened her eyes on the veins popping in his neck.

"You might as well know…about Jacob…he was one of my best supporters. I don't know how to depict him in war. He was just a decent, nice man with no business fighting. You'd be a better soldier than he was. I know you've always wanted to know what happened that last day when we walked into that ambush. He took a couple of hits in the leg, not bad. He was okay and I was dragging him out, then this gook came flying out of nowhere, shooting at me. I held Jacob in front of me, used him as a shield is all, Morgan, a fucking shield. Those bullets he took were meant for me."

He handed her back the report, turned and crossed towards his station-wagon, lifting a small boy from the open back window, hoisting him on his hip and walking around to the driver's door. "Okay, Jacob little buddy, it's your turn to drive."

Morgan felt sick, paralyzed by Fender's final piece to the puzzle of Jacob's death. She'd been waiting so many years to hear about Jacob's last few moments with Fender, to understand what really happened, how he died and Fender didn't, that when the information was sent like a rock from a slingshot, it was all she could do to keep her balance and not topple like a hit tin can onto the pavement. The station-wagon backed out the driveway, surged down the street. Morgan stood for a long time holding the report, trying to swallow her grief and anger and confusion.

It wasn't until she returned home and she and Sam picked up on an unfinished *Magic of Oz* chapter that she had time to reflect.

Sam plopped her newly tousled head of hair on a pillow and cuddled next to Morgan in bed. "We have to finish this in time for the Oz Convention in two weeks because I want to make a laminated board game for the Oz display table."

Every part of Morgan's body ached to sleep, but something in Sam's anxious eyes told her this was an important moment to stay awake. She supposed it had something to do with turning thirteen, something neither of them could mention but they both knew: this would be the last book they would read aloud together, and its special magic, the warmth of a mother and daughter cuddling and laughing, was important to value even as it happened because the sense memory would keep them close, if not always together, during those mysterious, confusing teenage years.

Sam held the book in front of Morgan's face. "Okay. Okay, I'm reading." Morgan could hardly keep her eyes open, but she managed to read words that painted clear pictures of human nature, motivation, and then, Fender's manipulative genius struck her.

"How do you think the Nome King's going to trick Kiki into giving him the magic secret?"

"That's for L. Frank Baum to know and us to find out." Morgan nudged her, and found where they'd left off. "'Ruggedo, on his part,' Morgan continued, 'decided that he could, by careful watching and listening, surprise the boy's secret, and when he had learned the magic word he would transform Kiki Aru into a bundle of faggots and burn him up and so be rid him.'"

"What'd I tell you about this guy?" Sam exclaimed. "He lies like a rug."

Morgan smiled at her word play, then continued, "'This is always the way with wicked people. They cannot be trusted even by one another. Ruggedo thought he was fooling Kiki, and Kiki thought he was fooling Ruggedo; so both were pleased.'"

After a few minutes, Sam had dozed off, so Morgan stopped reading and turned out the light. She supposed that was true: wicked people cannot be trusted even by one another.

It was then, staring at the leaf shadows dancing on the wall, that she comprehended Fender's combat strategy par excellence: she realized the degree of his relentless deception, of his twisted thinking, plotting up until the last instant.

For a brief moment, he'd essentially become Morgan, as the hero must become the enemy to understand the enemy's weakness and plan the best strategy to win. He'd gone into her head and attached himself, his wife and children onto the lifeline of Jacob's memory.

And it didn't matter to him that the last visual he offered Morgan of Jacob was as a human shield. It didn't matter because she would still connect them, Fender and Jacob together protecting each other until the end. Somehow she would forgive him for using her husband to save his own pitiful life.

After all, it had been some time now. And she was a woman with a child to come home to every night. Morgan would probably even respect him in some oblique, unintelligible way for having the courage to finally tell her what happened, admitting like an ornery schoolboy how he'd really messed up.

She could feel herself drifting off as she saw herself placing the report on Captain Drummond's desk, moving the reality of the crackhouse bloodbath into someone else's lap. She could see herself, unmoved, closing the captain's door, walking right past personnel, knowing without a doubt that she didn't have to stop and check Fender's file to find out he had four girls, Lindsey, Meg, Grace, Brittany and a boy, not named Jacob, but Doug.

22

BLUES IN THE NIGHT

O n the morning of the opening ceremonies for the Olympic
Games, Morgan couldn't find a hat. She didn't want to
wear her L.A.P.D. cap, and she politely declined Gramma
Sofie's plantation belle sunbonnet which gave Gramma Sofie the
chance to soliloquize more detailed excerpts from articles about
skin cancer than anyone cared to hear. Nat saved the moment,
offering his Pirates baseball cap. It fit. And he was so happy to
have been invited he didn't need a hat anyway, but Sam insisted
he wear her Mets cap from last year. They hadn't won the
championship, but she'd pitched a no-hitter. He consented. It
was snug, but it was Sam's.

Waiting for the troops to settle on hats, Joe Blanco sat in the
kitchen eating a piece of Gramma Sofie's cheesecake. She filled his
ear with the details about how her Jewish Center collected money
for Mexican laborers, and he amused her with stories about his
mother's duplicate bridge club. She'd taught him bridge his tenth
summer. Chest your cards, she used to tell him. Chest your cards,
Joey, don't let Mama see what you've got.

Morgan never suspected that Joe Blanco was a man deeply
affected by relationships, touched by the simple pain of ordinary lives,

until the day after she had turned in the report on Fender; Joe invited her to lunch at a popular tamale stand in East Los Angeles.

They sat across from each other at one of the picnic tables in a covered alcove. Salsa music pulsated from an overhead speaker. Joe wanted to tell her what wasn't going to happen to Fender. He waited until she'd swallowed a couple of bites of her chicken tamale before he told her no criminal charges would be filed.

It took a few seconds for the information to sink in. "No criminal charges? No murder charges?"

"The DA has to file the charges," he said.

She raised her palm, indicating time out. "Drummond, you, your greaseball partner Francesconi were all over me about the choke hold."

He offered a disheartened shrug, agreeing that it didn't make any sense. "It's more about saving face."

"My face? Your face? Not Fender's face."

"The DA is just happy to force Fender off the streets because it sends a message to guys like Fender."

"You guys are really into sending messages. What's this one? Kill a few unarmed suspects and land a desk job? And what kind of message does that send to the suspects' family members? The whole damn community?"

He sighed heavily, then took a moment to glance around at several chalky bricklayers sitting at the other end of their picnic table next to a couple of gardeners laughing and chugging blended fruit drinks. "You're not going to like this, but most people don't care about the suspects' family members, much less the whole damn community."

He dipped a chip in salsa and seemed to be thinking about Fender and the whole mess, but he cocked his head to the overhead speaker, as though suddenly transported by the familiar church bells, a few repeated organ chords, wind chimes, then a lone horn and a mandolin to accompany a man's resonant voice singing in Spanish about how he has committed his whole life to dance one time with this woman he loves. Joe stopped chewing and listened, mesmerized by the familiar hymnlike tone or the soulful tale, Morgan couldn't tell. But she felt herself slipping out of English, out of Fender, out of the 77th, as she fell into the singer's longing.

He lives with the hope, he sings, as he waits by his true love's front door for her to come home from work, and that when he asks her to go dancing, she won't say no, that, even though he's unknown to her, she will perceive all that he wants to say but can't; he lives with the hope that when she steps off the bus and sees him standing at her front door, she will accept him as her soulmate, however imperfect; but when she steps off the bus, absently reading a book, she saunters up the walk of the house across the street. She unlocks the door and enters without seeing him. He checks the address numbers written in pen on his palm.

He stands for a long time, but he can't make himself cross the street and ask her today. So, he'll come back tomorrow; if she accepts the dance invitation, he will have everything. And he walks home, happy that he has one more night to hold on to the hope of her love forever because in that hope lies his existence.

When the song stopped, Morgan was crying.

"*Está bien.*" Joe Blanco nodded, placing his hand on top of hers. "Pretty melodramatic, but it gets to me too every time I hear it." He smiled, offering a modest shrug that suggested he had stood waiting at the wrong address before.

Now, Gramma Sofie stood at the front door and hugged her three hats good-bye: Pirates, Mets, L.A.P.D. Joe Blanco donned his straw Panama hat, gave her a hug and reminded her confidentially to chest her cards. Without so much as glancing in her daughter-in-law's direction, she invited him to Sunday dinner, and Morgan noted he was smart enough to graciously decline.

Conversation and laughter electrified the ride to the Los Angeles Coliseum. Sam and Nat read over every competition and bickered about the next day's individual bicycle road race in Mission Viejo, 190 kilometers for men, 70 for women.

Morgan was prepared for Joe to discuss what the Los Angeles Olympic Organizing Committee called "the law enforcement challenge of the century" — protecting the Games of the XXIII Olympiad and the resulting highly publicized 'Star Wars' security operation, but he never mentioned any aspect of policing. Never brought up her report on Fender at the crackhouse, or her recent reassignment back on the street, off a report car, riding with Moon.

Instead, he laughed about the first rehearsal with the 300 placard-bearers and how the water sprinklers kept turning off and on, showering them. David Wolper himself, the producer for the games who would open and close productions, had to race around looking for an attendant in a green uniform.

Joe expressed his optimism for the games, how he believed, like Peter Ueberroth, the Olympic president, that this was a chance for L.A. to put its best foot forward, to use the enthusiasm of the games as an opportunity to build community support. So, he completely avoided mentioning the smog, the death threats mailed to some African and Asian Olympic committees in the name of the Ku Klux Klan, and the threats to the Turkish Olympic team from the Armenian Secret Army for the Liberation of Armenia.

He focused on the humorous problems, and made them laugh over his visual rendition of the volleyball stanchions that were mistaken for weights and transported to the weight-lifting arena in Westchester instead of the volleyball arena in Long Beach.

Morgan couldn't remember when she'd felt so relaxed. For so long, nothing had seemed funny. Or was it simply that she was losing her sense of humor? Spending too much time around pessimistic people, maybe she was beginning to view situations through their cynical eyes.

Before they'd even found parking near the Coliseum, Nat and Sam had already coerced her into accepting Joe's invitation to attend the closing ceremonies, too. By the time they'd found their seats in the packed stadium, she'd agreed to a real date the following Saturday night in honor of the women marathoners. She would go with him to a Latin dance club, La Piñoteca, and salsa.

Finally, settled in her seat with a Coca-Cola and a hot dog, she took too big of a bite and mustard slipped down her chin. Joe smiled kindly and handed her a napkin, and she nodded appreciatively. It didn't make any sense that she was sitting next to this man, a detective, the Internal Affairs cop who, just weeks before, had had her suspended a week without pay for lying to him.

It didn't make any sense that after the hugely inspiring placard show, he took her hand and squeezed it. She returned the pressure, and, for the remainder of the day, they clasped hands like teenagers. It didn't make any sense, but she knew it was right.

And that night, lying alone in bed, she tried to remember where she'd put her black Capezio flats. They probably would be comfortable dancing shoes. She couldn't remember when she'd worn them last, or if they would be wide enough for her new rigid insoles. What if her feet had grown? A smile crept across her lips when it struck her she could buy a new pair.

Gramma Sofie stared into her plate for the entire dinner, nibbling on the sweet and sour pot roast and stabbing bits of baked potato. Before dinner, she'd caught Morgan drinking baking soda in water; now, strangely intense, she was finally unable to restrain herself about Morgan being taken off the report car and reassigned to active patrol. "I don't like to criticize, and you know I don't condemn nobody what is a working person, but I knew as soon as you got back on the street again — "

"Sofie," Morgan intercepted the oncoming lecture.

"You could look for another job, less dangerous," Gramma Sofie persisted. "That's all I'm saying. At my age, I can say some things. And my Jacob, were he here, he would say no. And why? That you shouldn't get hurt."

Morgan eyed her crossly.

"He wouldn't let you, and you know this. So, I want to please talk for Jacob — "

"Sofie, what good — "

"You are interrupting. You could wait your turn to talk. I should speak for my son. He's sitting inside." She tapped her heart with her open palm several times, then continued. "And before it is growing too late, I'm wanting to remind you he gave his life, and I don't think he wanted to do that. All his life he was a student, always with his nose in a book, and he loved to help people worse off. He would be a doctor."

Gramma Sofie glanced at Sam's downcast eyes. "Your mother knows in her heart, this is not a job for a woman with a child. That I shouldn't have to say."

"I'm doing okay." Morgan nodded. "And so is Sam."

"What about me?" Gramma Sofie, quickly heating to outburst, knocked her veiny hand so hard on the table she bounced her fork on the floor. "I'm frightened to death. Jacob even is wanting you to know that every minute you go out, I am sick to death until I hear your footsteps on the front walk." She choked up. "And every night I pray that the Lord should protect you."

"Look," Morgan said more sharply than she intended. "You know what it's about. This is my job." She looked away, sighing, "I love this work, Sofie. Have you ever done anything you've loved?"

Gramma Sofie thought a moment, then shook her head no, dipping her eyes into her open palm and breaking into a sob. Morgan touched her. "I'm sorry. That was a mean thing for me to say. You never had the support I do."

Morgan darted Sam a glance to go console Gramma Sofie. Sam made a face, and Morgan jabbed her under the table with her foot.

Sam set down her fork, scooted her chair away from the table and made an elaborate circle around the chairs to reach Gramma Sofie and give her a hug. "You're doing a good job. Pretty much. I love you," she said, uneasily aware of the extraordinary power she held over her thin-lipped grandmother.

Gramma Sofie bit her lip through a grateful nod. Morgan watched her closely, waiting a moment to make sure she wasn't going to start crying again. They exchanged faint smiles and Morgan took another helping of pot roast, with a look-I'm-having-seconds gesture. Morgan knew she was a continual reminder that it should have been Jacob having second helpings, it should have been Jacob sharing his mother's whirl of memories, wishes, sentiments.

Morgan took a deep breath and directed Sofie's attention to a real consideration. She asked Sofie's advice — should she put those little plastic things on her new black flats? Every dress item was a major decision for Sofie because everything had to last. Heel protectors, Sofie said and nodded definitely: they save the heel from wearing away.

Now Sam was asking Morgan if she'd go over and take a look at Nat's Apple computer thing. He says he's getting a box so he can send messages to people with other computers. He could send me a message without calling on the phone, she pointed out, but I don't have one. Sam glanced first from her mother to Gramma Sofie and then back to her mother.

"You have a phone," said Morgan.

"Mom," she sighed, "a computer. I don't have a computer. An Apple computer is the best, Nat says."

"Right." Morgan nodded. "They're only about a million dollars. How did Nat get one?"

"His uncle works for Apple, and gave him his used one."

Gramma Sofie offered Morgan a piece of cheesecake, asking Sam, "What's the good of a computer, when you have a typewriter?"

"A typewriter?" Sam looked at Gramma Sofie, took a big breath and and started to explain. "Okay, Gramma, a computer has a brain. Did you read about the new high tech private eyes who use computers to track down counterfeit stuff?"

"That's nice," Gramma Sofie said, adding to Morgan, "I used a whole package of zwieback for the crust."

"Thanks," Morgan said. "I'll have it after work," she assured her, offering a big grin to Sam, "with hot milk, you and *The Magic of Oz* in bed."

Gramma Sofie gave Morgan a suspicious look. "It's your heartburn, isn't it? Acting up again."

"Nope, I'm fine," Morgan said, standing and motioning to Sam. "Okay, why don't you walk me out, honey?"

Morgan gave Gramma Sofie a peck on her rouged checks, lightly kissed her own fingertips and tapped them gently over Sofie's heart. "I'm listening to you and I will be very careful."

She chased her daughter out the door, looked back at the house and shook her head. "That was close."

"Yep," Sam nodded.

"Don't ignore her tonight."

Sam nodded dutifully and Morgan embraced her as they walked towards the Jeep. "You really showed me something in there, honey."

"Gramma Sofie's okay. She's just, you know — "

"I know," said Morgan, "but if you only had one baseball, and you knew for the whole rest of your life you could never have another baseball of your own, how would you take care of it?"

"I'd give it to Nat to look after."

Morgan laughed and reached into her purse, withdrawing some magic snaps in a small box. She slipped a spitwad-sized snap from the box and threw it on the driveway. A tiny firecracker pop brought a big grin to Sam's face. "Here," Morgan handed the box to Sam. "Share them with Nat."

Sam shoved the box in her pocket. "No way."

Morgan opened the driver's door, but sensed something was wrong, "You okay?"

Sam shrugged. "Sure. I just don't like it when you and Gramma Sofie argue about your work."

Morgan sat in the driver's seat and pulled Sam towards her. "Without you, I couldn't do this." Sam pressed close leaning on her knees. "This is really a family job, honey. I need your support. You get me going every day, so whenever it gets hard on you, we have to make time to talk about it, and if it gets too hard on us, we'll find another line of work, okay?"

Sam stopped chewing on the inside of her right cheek. "Mom, I'm really proud of you for going back on the street." She forced a smile. "But you already know that."

"Yeah, but it feels different when you tell me."

Sam hugged her tightly around the neck, pressing against the chain with the mitzvah Morgan always wore. Morgan smiled at her a long moment, studying her to identify some confusion she sensed Sam was struggling to keep from showing on her face. Fear? Hurt? Anger? It was gone before Morgan could be certain.

She gave her daughter a bear hug, popped in her Springsteen tape and backed out of the driveway, glancing in the rearview mirror at Sam. She wondered if Sam felt separation anxiety. How did Sam feel every night while she stood in the driveway with her thumbs up and watched her mother's car disappear around the corner. What did Sam do afterwards?

Morgan imagined Sam meandering around back, crossing the yard to her treehouse. She would climb the ladder, hearing Gramma Sofie call from the kitchen window, "Sam. Samantha."

Sam would flirt with pretending not to hear, but they'd played out that scene before and it wasn't pretty. The end, to Sam's chagrin, was always the same: Gramma Sofie would holler several times from the window, then step out on the back porch and ring a strident cow bell. Finally, when all else failed, Gramma Sofie would march across the yard to the bottom of the treehouse and threaten her granddaughter within an inch of her life.

Sam must want to take Gramma Sofie by the shoulders and shake her: stop trying to protect me. Leave me alone. But she never did.

Tonight, Morgan sensed their dynamics would be different. Sam would wait for Gramma Sofie to appear at the back door. When moments passed and there was no cowbell, Sam would consider how tired she must be. And Sam would realize how hard it must be for Gramma Sofie to watch Morgan go to a job Gramma Sofie hated. And suddenly a revelation would swoop her outside of herself, when it dawned on her that what she and Gramma Sofie had in common — loss of Jacob, her father, and anxiety over Morgan, her mother — should bring them closer together, not keep them apart.

Back again on the street working with Moon, Morgan wasn't interested in winning Moon's acceptance anymore, in taking his hazing and dishing it back. Waiting for him to bring up her report on the crackhouse, or maybe express some regret for his terrible behavior in the treehouse, she didn't offer much in the way of conversation until they stopped for their first break.

"C'mon," he finally said. "I know you've missed me and you're just tongue-tied."

"No, that's you. Officer Tongue-tied." She was amazed at his astounding capacity to pretend that nothing much had happened between them in the last few weeks.

He looked up. "I'm gonna go order, you want a tuna burrito?"

"You know I hate tuna." She slammed down her pen. "You read my report? You think that's right?"

He shrugged. "Look, I wouldn't do it, you wouldn't do it, Fender did. You gotta understand: it's us against them."

"No, no it's not. That's what you guys want people to believe so you can pump more training into SWAT and boy cops on bikes."

He ignored her deadpan look, strolled to the serving window, and ordered a tuna burrito bandito with extra salsa.

She hated herself for thinking she could have shared anything intimate with this man. When he returned, they exchanged a brief glance, as if they were snapping a picture of uncensored thoughts going on behind each other's eyes. "The entire community knows Fender just gunned that guy down. And nothing is said."

Her right calf twitched, alerting her to a soon-to-be throbbing foot. She'd forgotten to switch her orthodic inserts from her running shoes to her work shoes. Damn, she cursed herself.

Moon started to say something, but a radio dispatch cut him off, "Burglary, narcotics, suspect still on premises, code 30 ringer at the self-storage warehouse 6514 Century."

Moon jotted down the address. "Nickerson Gardens," he informed her. Morgan whisked her paper trash into a nearby can and headed towards the patrol car.

A Tia's Tacos employee yelled from behind the serving window, "Burrito Bandito." He slapped a bag on the counter and grinned at Moon. "Grande, señor." Moon grabbed the bag and caught up to Morgan.

He focused on his take-out wrappings, but Morgan was still thinking about Fender. "It's an outrage that criminal charges are not filed against him, and the worst thing that'll happen to him is a cushy desk job. Makes me want to throw up."

"I can see that."

She glanced askance at him as he hovered over a bite of his tuna-dripping, humongous burrito. He stopped, mouth wide open, and offered it to her. "You know, it's hard to believe, but I actually missed working with you."

She looked away, sighing, not at his rank manners, but that flash that flared up in her when she was around him, that electric discharge that an adversary who kept you on your toes sparked. "You're sure as hell not any great shakes, but you are…"

She searched for the right word as they reached the car. He instinctively made a move for the driver's door, but she was way ahead of him.

He veered to the passenger side, grinning. "…an officer and a gentleman," he said. A glob of refried beans and tuna dripped on his shirt.

She glanced over at him and said flatly. "Yep, that's you: Mister Cool Beans."

She pulled out of the parking lot to answer the burglary call, as he set the flashing light on the dash and observed her rigid expression. "If it's any consolation," he said, "his wife and kids have left him, and a desk job'll kill a guy like Fender."

"Yeah, that makes me feel a lot better."

"He went off the deep end."

"It was murder, Moon. We both know it. Then he just covered the hell out of his ass."

He nodded, "Yeah, I read your report."

"You didn't. You actually read someone else's report?"

He picked his teeth with the corner of his burrito wrapper. "Skimmed it."

She glanced over at him, indicating his queen chess piece. "The braid's a nice touch."

He nodded, thanks, and they stared straight ahead, enjoying the moment.

But in typical Moon fashion, he could not let a tender moment float sweetly away. He had to shoot it down. "Bet you scored some bonus points with those skirts in I.A.," he said, wiping his tongue over his front teeth and sucking in air. She was tempted to inform him she'd gone with Joe Blanco to the Olympic opening ceremonies, and she'd accepted his invitation to see *Cats* the following weekend at the Shubert Theater in Century City, but she decided it would be just as well to exclude Moon from the dynamics of her personal life. Keep him on a need-to-know basis.

Minutes later, Morgan rolled by the Secure U-Store-Warehouse. Burglary suspect possibly still on premises. No sign of activity, but they'd decided to use 'diagonal deployment,' one of them visually guarding the front; the other, the back, until assistance arrived, so they could move into a perimeter search and inspect the inside private storage cubicles. They parked next to a pile of metal, and crunched across gravel to the front door.

Moon indicated he'd move to the rear.

"No, you stay here," Morgan said. "I need the exercise." Her right foot was asleep. Walking would stimulate circulation.

"Well," Moon grinned. "I didn't want to say anything, bubba, but…"

"Bubba my ass, I'm Morgan to you," she whispered over her shoulder.

"Fine," he held up his palms. Why upset her more?

She headed toward the rear, her back almost kissing the decayed stucco wall as she moved alongside the building towards what looked like a hole in a rotten wood fence beyond the deformed mass of car parts — hoods, doors, trunks — hunched together. She checked her watch and heard a garbage can toppling over in the alley.

Slipping through the hole in the fence with her gun drawn, Morgan spotted the suspect with a backpack running toward a chain link fence. "Police! Freeze!" she commanded.

The suspect glanced at her, then scrambled madly up the fence. Pursuing him, she stopped, got in the ready position, aimed her gun, and yelled out again: "Police! Freeze!"

He stopped at the top of the fence, in profile, his left hand gripping the chain link; his right, clenching an automatic weapon poised.

"Drop it!" she ordered, shouting at him to herself: C'mon, you son-of-a-bitch, just drop the fuckin' piece.

His head swiveled in her direction as if he'd heard her mind and she was dead serious.

She hesitated for an instant, then added with not the slightest quiver in her voice, "Drop it! Or I'll blow you the fuck away!"

He sized her up, gaped at her, then nodded, no problem, no hurry. "Okay, baby, okay, just give me time to get down," and shifted his back to her.

Baby my ass, she thought and yelled. "Drop the gun! Now!"

He made a move to get down from the fence. Hearing a loud clink on the fence links, Morgan lowered her eyes for a split second to notice his tennis shoes with spurs, and a flash of still photos cut through her mind in a millisecond: Sam's crooked smile passing out food, a wrinkled hag with chicken skin grabbing…Sam's crooked smile…boy with spurs on his tennis shoes picking up the old hag and —

"Drop the gun!" She screamed out loud, then inside, You shit, you shit…don't make me —

She imagined him whirling around, shooting in one fluid motion, the force thrusting her back, bouncing her against the alley wall. Sam, she had the snapshot of her daughter standing in the driveway waving goodbye. Sam! She cried inside, knowing she couldn't shoot first, but if she waited until he turned and shot, it would be too late. What about Sam?

Numb, she could feel her right leg start to buckle, as he whirled around in one fluid motion, "No!" and shot. Once.

According to the police report, Moon heard Morgan shout. "Police! Freeze!" And he sprinted towards the hole in the fence.

The suspect's first shot missed, then she and the suspect both fired. Her shot hit him in the neck; his, in her chest.

The force propelled her backwards.

Her mind wrenched around to see a vision of childhood, as she lightheartedly climbed up Samantha's tree, leapt in the open window to find her friend weaving potholders and humming one of Aunt Tilly's alluring ballads, possibly, 'Tonight My Sleep Will Be Restless,' Big Mac's favorite.

Moon cuffed the suspect to the chain link fence, then hurried to Morgan, slumped on the ground, shaking his head miserably, "Oh, fuck, fuck." His eyes fixed intently on her expressionless face, as if the power of his living energy could will her alive.

He bent down, with absolutely no shred of hope, and checked her pulse, and feeling the beat of hers recharged his own.

She regained consciousness and cursed him non-stop, while he opened the top of her uniform to check the wound. She could feel a tug at her neck, knew, in his haste, he'd broken her neck chain and could feel her mitzvah slipping. She tried to tell him, ask him to look for it, but he was picking her up and moving her back across the alley away from the suspect she'd shot, now howling in grotesque pain. Or had she been howling before she passed out again?

He ran to the front of the warehouse to move the patrol car closer to the fence.

By the time he pulled the car around, Engels and Bow Wow had responded to the back-up call and were hurrying towards the back of the warehouse.

Moon braced Morgan and looked to Engels who, running up, was aghast at the wound, but didn't glance away, freeze or throw up. She forced herself to keep eye contact with Morgan in case she came to for an instant.

"Get her feet," Moon told her.

"You're not waiting for RA?"

"Not this time."

Engels lifted Morgan's boots, stopping for an instant as if to notice how Morgan was positioned up against the alley wall a distance from the suspect, slumped, unconscious against the chain link fence — a detail that somehow missed the police report, but was later revealed.

Engels asked, "Have you moved her since — "

But Moon cut her off, "Let's go." Balancing Morgan's feet, she followed his lead towards the patrol car parked just on the other side of the fence. Several feet away, Engels' eye caught something tiny glistening in gravel, reflecting the streetlight.

By the time they had her on the front seat and Moon in the driver's seat, resting her head on his lap, Morgan's eyes fluttered open, enough to recognize Engels. Just as Engels closed the passenger door, Morgan, too choked to speak, lifted her hand, gesturing for her to come along. Too late. Engels reached for the back door handle, but Moon, waiting for no one, lurched the car into forward, flipped on the siren and screeched from the alley onto Century Blvd.

He fidgeted with a jacket tossed over her chest, readjusting it up to her neck. "Better?"

She nodded, "No lag time. Fender was wrong."

"Fuck Fender. Even Fender would have been proud of you."

"I'm not Fender."

"No, no you're not."

He reached by her side and clasped her hand, squeezing it, "Keep talking. C'mon, did I ever tell you, you have really beautiful breasts."

She cringed. "Shut up," she whispered, squinting hard at him to focus.

Sirens screaming and lights flashing, he careened around a corner, bumped up over a sidewalk, through a hedge and shot diagonally across a vacant parking lot. He looked down at her and winced. "Seriously. Now, I've never told that to a partner before. Fender definitely did not have beautiful breasts. Massive hunks of flab. I didn't have the heart to tell him."

She couldn't bear the pain, garbling, "Stop."

"Am I getting kind of blurry?"

She nodded wanly, fading. He leaned closer and whispered, "Keep your eyes open. C'mon, stay with me." Her eyes closed. "Talk to me, goddamnit."

Her eyes fluttered open, as she fought to focus, "You piece of shit."

He nodded, "I know," and squeezed her hand.

The car burst from the other side of a parking lot. Intent, he looked at the distant green light at the end of the street. "Almost home."

She moaned, "No matter where you go, I'll find you."

He shook her, "I'm not going anywhere. C'mon. Stay with me."

The spotlight turned red. "Sam." She managed a weak smile and slipped away, murmuring, "I'll find you."

The car seemed to speed forever up the hill towards the red stoplight.

The realization that she would die struck him suddenly and concisely, but he rejected it, screaming in his head, *Oh Lord, no, please don't let it be this woman.*

This time he didn't try to stop the tears that rolled down his face. Her death, so close, ripped open the memory of his son's death too long hidden behind the curtain of his mind. He accepted, without knowing why, that he was deeply afraid when he lost control. When something happened so suddenly, it took the heart out of him.

As the police car stopped in front of the hospital emergency entrance and paramedics scrambled towards the car, Moon held her, unwilling to let her go. And like a paralysis victim with movement frozen but who can still hear and feel, she sensed him lean over her motionless face, his eyes filled with tears, and brush the hair from her brow.

For a moment the knowledge of all his years of experience was wiped away. He cursed himself, "Forgive me, partner," he whispered.

She took a shallow breath, retched Sam's name, making sure someone brought Sam to the hospital pronto, shivered in pain, then called him a "fucking piece of shit" one last time.

23

Blood on the Moon

Moon disappeared for weeks after Morgan was shot. He took a leave during the "continuing investigation," fading into the Simi Valley orange groves on his brother's orchard.

When he returned he drove straight to Morgan's house. Crossing the backyard, he blocked his eyes from the sun long enough to spot where he suspected he would find Sam, sitting alone in her treehouse.

Aware but unmoved, she turned her back to the footsteps scaling the ladder. Tired, face set, mind occupied elsewhere, she wanted him to go away. His eyes moved from the dark marks on the carpet to the yellow-edged picture recently tacked on a railing: Morgan, sitting on a carousel horse, has her arms wrapped around the waist of a man who is holding a baby, Sam, on his lap.

Moon squatted next to Sam, staring at her short-cropped hair.

Finally, without looking around at him, she stated in a neutral tone, "You got a staring problem, or what?"

"Yeah," he half-smiled, withdrawing a wadded handkerchief. "I thought you might like to have this back." He unwrapped Morgan's gold mitzvah and placed it in her hand.

She glanced at it, "It's not mine."

He shrugged, "Well, it's got your name on the back."

She eyed him skeptically, until he turned it over and showed her the inscription on the back: "Samantha loves…"

A thoughtful frown creased her brow. *Morgan* was inscribed on the other half of the mitzvah her mother always wore.

"Samantha loves Morgan." The image of her mother sneaking out of her bedroom and climbing the tree to her best friend's window hit Sam like a brick in the throat, smashing the air from her lungs, compressing her into a small corner next to the railing as the treetop whirled over her head, sucking up all the oxygen until she had to gasp to catch her breath.

She burst into tears.

Moon slipped his arm around her, scooting her shaking body onto his lap, where she dropped her head and sank into his shoulder. He told her how tough her mother was all the way to the hospital that night. And Sam's mind, all her being was stuck there with her mother halfway up the hill screaming at Moon to drive fast. *For Godsake, get my mother to the hospital quicker so I can see her. Faster. Faster. She's running out of air. Just get her to emergency. I'll be there in a minute.* Racing with Nat and Gramma Sofie down the slippery hall, past faces in slow motion, to a room with a wall of white coats moving in slow motion around her mother's shoe soles.

Nat would nudge Sam to a closer corner where she could see her mother's still face, her body shielded by a man in a white coat reaching over her passing knives, pinchers, plungers, to another white coat, a surgeon bent, intent over her chest.

Sam remembered holding her breath. Holding time. Holding hope. Hearing her through the blur of forms and clink of instruments "…if you only had one baseball, and you knew for the whole rest of your life you could never have another baseball of your own, how would you take care of it?"

Sam wondered if she hadn't told her mother she was so proud of her, maybe she wouldn't've gone back on the streets?

Nat guided Sam across the foggy room, past the white coats who'd broken the shield to let her through. Her head was too stiff to tilt down, so she stared straight ahead, and noticed for the first time Moon standing in the shadows.

Her eyes trailed inexorably to her mother's moist brow. Sam touched her hand, and her mother's eyes opened, misty, then closed, but in that brief moment Sam looked into her soul — certain her mother knew she was there with her.

The retelling of the hospital night emergency screwed up Moon's face like Sam had only seen on the expression of movie victims in extreme pain over the loss of a loved one. But she had no words to relieve his suffering. She knew she would relive, at the oddest times, that endless moment in limbo on the brink of her mother's death.

"I wanted to apologize to you." Moon said, "A lot of people will say things about me, and I'm not going to say much, but I wanted you to know that I know I really blew it."

She looked away, bit her lip. She might have said something, but Gramma Sofie shouted, "Lunch," from the kitchen window. "We can't wait any longer." Nat opened the back door, and Gramma Sofie, walking in reverse, pulled a cart of sandwiches and six tall ice-filled glasses.

Pushing the other end of the cart, Morgan, chest bandaged, appeared in the threshold, holding napkins.

She noticed Moon and paused, as if considering several remarks before deciding on, "Do you ever call first?" They exchanged a curious look.

"Sam," she said, "you want peanut butter and jelly or jelly and peanut butter?"

Privately, Sam managed to utter into Moon's collarbone. "I want to be a police officer. A captain."

He patted the back of her head, "I know, Mooseface. I know." He put his arm around her waist to lift her up, and motioned for her to go down the ladder. "First things first though: let's grow your hair."

At the bottom of the ladder, Sam hurried towards Nat, pouring lemonade. Moon approached Morgan's steadfast gaze.

"You look good," he said, managing not to drop his eyes to her bound chest. "How do you feel?"

"Better." Revealing nothing, she set the tone for their exchange.

"I didn't come to the hospital to see you — "

She dismissed his explanation with the wave of her hand. "That's fine," she said with finality in her voice that suggested she didn't want to talk about anything that had to do with the shooting. "Sandwich?" She indicated the tray of crustless white bread triangles.

"I hate peanut butter. Feel like I'm gumming a mouthful of crap."

"That's lovely. Thank you for that report." She took a bite from a bread point, then stared at him, waiting. He'd come to see her, so what did he want to say?

He took a deep breath, "I wanted you to hear it from me…I'm retiring."

"When?" She responded simply, as if he'd told her he was going to the gym.

"Before the end of the year. Gonna roll my pension into an IRA, something like that, and manage my brother's citrus farm."

"That's quite a career leap: leader of MAW to CEO of O.J.?" she said, ignoring his grimace. "Why don't you take your money and do something fun?"

He smirked at the word, as if it conjured up possibilities beyond him.

"Fun. You know, like water skiing. Go to Lake Havasu and ski 'til you drop."

He nodded, glancing at Sam, who'd recuperated from her doldrums and was comparing her nibbled bread sculpture with Nat's.

"No," Morgan said, softly, realizing he had no friends to take water skiing, no one to share fun, "you may not take my daughter water skiing."

He looked back at Morgan, seeming to search her calm eyes. What had she told Sam?

What had she told the captain? Drummond didn't seem to know the suspect had lifted Moon's gun. In fact, no one mentioned that Morgan had moved her body to protect Moon. That she'd been shot in the line of duty guarding her partner. No one had said, helluva job Morgan. She'd received no commendation. No mention in the newspapers other than "…officer-involved shooting. Officer in critical condition. Suspect, wounded, suffered complications in surgery, resulting in an embolism-induced coma." Morgan didn't have to say anything: eventually, the suspect would come out of his coma and probably remember the woman officer purposely moved to intercept a bullet intended for her partner. Morgan didn't even care if the suspect forgot; she knew. More importantly, Moon knew.

Morgan offered no answers to his silent questions. Her thoughts and opinions, wishes and dreams, were as closed to him as the photos in the scrapbook of an amnesia victim. And staring into his wordless expression, she knew he would linger on, living worse than a mind in oblivion: he'd missed or messed up opportunities; unlike Fender who blamed everyone else for his miserable life, Moon blamed himself. Too late.

Morgan heard footsteps on the driveway and a sonorous male voice rushed a chill up her legs. Joe Blanco, in a Hawaiian midnight blue shirt with slivers of silver moons, stars and spirals, holding roses in one hand and, in the other hand, his mother, Señora Blanco, turned the corner of the house. Seeing Moon, he stopped, nodded politely, and then stood discreetly aside.

"Officer Fraser," Señora Blanco called out, "díos mio." Her drowning eyes spoke volumes. Morgan crossed to her, delicately embracing her with one arm and kissing her on the forehead. Señora Blanco's frail frame quivered. The threesome remained close a moment, heads bowed, while Señora Blanco crept her fingertips onto Joe and Morgan's handclasp, then closed her eyes and sighed softly.

Morgan sensed Moon watching, then heard him brush by, whispering, "Bye, bubba." She listened to his fading footsteps crushing the gravel drive and squeezed Joe's hand feeling, at that moment, nothing but lucky. She had a suspicion she would never see Moon again, and she was right.

Tonight Her Sleep
will be Restless

1998

In her mother's kitchen, Sam was shredding sharp cheddar cheese with Gramma Sofie's battered grater. She wore white shorts and a tank top. Her pony-tail was lopsided and strands of hair, as if loose from a strong wind, swept her temples. She smiled because she had remembered something Gramma Sofie said about a senior she'd dated her sophomore year at UCLA. Men come in some version of three odors: floor wax, stale smoke, imported cheese.

She smiled, not as you'd smile at a witty remark, but a treasured gift.

Nat, rolling pie crust dough on the counter, asked why she was smiling. She told him.

Floor wax tells you that a man spends too much time doing things for himself; stale smoke, for his friends; imported cheese, for his family. Always choose cheese, Gramma Sofie had told her.

Nat said, "You can tell she was raised in a land-locked country." He flicked a floury index finger over the tip of his nose, "No scent for sea salt."

She thought about Nat's love of the water. He slept with a half-filled glass on his nightstand, and dozed off to a tape he'd made of ocean waves gently breaking. Whenever possible, he was in some form of water, swimming or diving.

They had just gotten back from snorkeling in Avalon Bay. It was the first time they'd spent a day together since he'd come home from a six-month cross-continental road trip with DuWayne Jester, the owner of a floundering scaffolding business. Nat and DuWayne had been surveying Jester's scaffolding contracts that he wasn't going to meet unless he made Nat a partner and took advantage of his structural engineering skills and business sense.

And Nat, a frustrated artist and draftsman in high school, had always wanted to pursue an artistic career. Unlike his father, an accomplished plasterer, who didn't aggressively collect money for finished work and ended up doing janitorial work for Burbank airport, Nat had matured into an entrepreneur, headstrong and direct, yet still sincere — and dead serious about not wanting to work for anyone else.

Initially, Sam had worried about what it would be like seeing Nat after being apart for so long. When she'd come back home after her first year away at college, he'd lifted her off her feet and hugged her so hard and for so long, she could hardly breathe. "Nat," she'd gulped, "put me down, 'chrissakes." He set her down and grinned, his eyes glassy. "I missed you."

"I missed you, too. But I don't crush you to prove it."

When he picked her up at the airport this time, he hugged her, but not as hard or as long. In fact, Sam noticed he touched her much less, but they still chattered and joked.

What had happened in their lives amazed them, and they teased each other on the boat back from Avalon. Sam's spontaneous childhood antics that prodded Nat into swordplay, building, and climbing pointed toward an adult life filled with impulse and escapades. Instead, she spent most of her day holed up in a library reviewing case law, or in a windowless office writing briefs, or a stuffy room interviewing victims.

Nat, always the more careful and judicious, preferring to observe rather than scale the thrashed Academy wall, had chosen to stay indoors and build tents. He taught her to use step-by-step methodology to solve polynomial problems. Now, he was traveling around the world engineering huge outdoor play structures to help build skyscrapers.

They had taught each other more than how to build treehouses and solve complex algebra problems. They taught each other to have faith in their own abilities.

She watched Nat mixing cinnamon sugar and pretended to be eyeing him as if she'd just met him. But unlike all of her other friends, she didn't remember meeting Nat. Her first memory of him was maybe at four, building a sheet and blanket fort between two separated rocking chairs. She couldn't remember who decided on a rocking chair frame, but the purpose was to simulate an earthquake. She saw herself in a photo on the refrigerator, wildly rocking and giggling. She imagined Nat inside, yelling, "Earthcake. Earthcake."

She scanned her yellowed and blotched childhood photos under magnetized tape strips on the refrigerator door. Would she move that energy-guzzling hulk all the way across country? If she left it here for the new house owners, she'd have to take the pictures off. A lump swelled at the thought and her nose tingled: remove the picture collage that she'd watched her mother carefully arrange? She darted a glance at Nat, teared up, then looked away.

They had carefully avoided talking about her upcoming move. He hadn't even congratulated her about landing a job in Washington, D.C. as the lead attorney identifying and working with family violence cases for the Bureau of Justice Assistance system. He knew about the employment prospect because they'd been instant messaging while he was on the road, and she let him know about the job when she applied for it, rattling off her responsibilities: "I'd be working with officers every day, reviewing their on-scene police reports and supervising plea bargaining offers which would be so great because I've been developing written prosecution policies."

"Sounds good," he e-mailed back. "What about that tome you've been writing about your mother?" He always directed her focus back to the tough stuff.

"Don't remind me. I'm sorry I started this damn book. It's driving me nuts. Too many holes. What really happened the night of the shootout with Earley and Boots? What happened with the suspect who died inexplicably in his cell? What happened at the MAW meetings in the park? What in the hell was going on in

Moon's mind when he shot that PCP guy in the head? What really happened at the crackhouse with Teddy Bear and Fender?"

She'd worked it all out from her mother's point of view, from looking over Morgan's notes, listening to her tapes, researching public information, guessing the rest, but there was so much more.

"Ask Moon," Nat e-mailed.

So, a couple of months before, she met Moon for lunch at Barney's Beanery in Hollywood, and reminded him about the book she'd been writing about an important historical time, 1984, and she needed him to confirm critical details. No bullshitting either. He nodded his gray crewcut several times. Then he said, careful not to commit himself, "Let me look over what you've got."

Moon read the chapters about the men, admitted to Sam that he'd once thought blacks were incompetent, but he'd changed his mind — not across the board, of course.

Down deep he still believed women's suffrage destroyed the "natural" harmony between men and women. Once he got beyond why women, blacks, gays and short people should never have been allowed on the force, he was a goldmine of information that public records didn't reveal and people didn't know or wouldn't tell Sam — details about the night Earley died, the first time Moon saw her mother's silhouette at the crime scene talking with Fender, the way Teddy Bear told him Fender had mercilessly jammed Morgan's choke hold suspect with a baton in the back of the patrol car, how Fender, the Grand Dragon, stonewalled women and humiliated Iggy. Moon assured her he hadn't had to think about blasting the PCP victim — he just did it; he told her he didn't have to be an eyewitness to know what had really happened at the crackhouse bloodbath either.

"He had something to say about everything," Sam e-mailed Nat, "but he wouldn't talk about the night my mother was shot."

"He will," Nat fired back through cyberspace. "Then you won't see him again."

"What makes you say that?"

"Just call it male's intuition."

She could almost feel Nat's enchanting smile and his eyes that looked at her as if they were breathing in every detail. Nat listened to her, paid attention to her, seeming to enjoy the process of thinking aloud together. No conclusions, just moment-to-moment expressions of opinions and feelings. They communicated with each other like jazz musicians play together or improvisation actors perform. But he'd never told her how he felt towards Moon. She knew.

Nat had a way of writing people off he didn't trust. People who disappointed him in the extreme, he stopped seeing them socially, stopped working with them. He once explained he didn't like himself, didn't like what he felt obligated to say and do, when he hung around with people he didn't trust. "So, it's more about me," he said, "about being fake. I don't like fake."

"But what if someone disappoints you because they don't want to be fake?" she'd asked, both of them knowing she was referring to Moon's refusal to come to Morgan and Joe Blanco's wedding in '86; to their twins' baby shower in '88; to Gramma Sofie's memorial in '92; and, finally, the last straw, Sam's graduation from Duke's law school in '95. For Nat, Moon's avoidance was hurtful because he thought it disappointed Sam; for Sam, it was simply Moon's survival. He hated loving her mother. He hated himself, so he pretended to forget her, refused to be in her presence, much like Nat, now, refused to be in his.

Sam rewrote the manuscript, and had handed it to Moon a few days before. He finished reading it, called her and asked to listen to her mother's tapes. Morgan had given them to her, said she didn't care what Sam did with them. Nat was the only other person who'd listened to them, but she handed them over to Moon. What did she have to lose?

Now, she and Nat were slumped in the kitchen nook, gobbling down steaming apple crisp and figuring out how Nat could accept the partnership with DuWayne, turn the company around, and maybe start his own scaffolding business. But where would he start his own business?

She'd e-mailed when she found out about the job in D.C. but she hadn't e-mailed about selling the house. You can e-mail at midnight, but words alone don't capture inflection, gestures, expression, and silence.

And Nat had avoided asking questions about the obvious: she would have to move to D.C. She would be closer to her mother, Joe, and the twins, who'd moved with her to the southeast when she started at Duke. She wouldn't be coming back to Los Angeles as often, and Morgan wasn't ever moving back. She had a new life as a wife and mother of twins, and she was a detective in Raleigh. She'd put the house in Sam's name. It was vacant now, but Sam had been renting it since Gramma Sofie passed away. Nat and Sam slapped on a few coats of paint. But since the '94 earthquake jolt, it had been in need of minor structural and plumbing repair her insurance wouldn't cover. What was she going to do with the house? She had flirted with giving it to Nat. He could move in, use it as a safe haven between his international scaffolding design trips, and she would come visit often. And Nat would've kept the pictures on the refrigerator, she was thinking, until —

A visual locked her thought and jaw, sticking the mushy apples to the roof of her mouth. She looked at the refrigerator door and imagined again a hand, another woman's hand, not her mother's, removing the photos, one by one, and dropping them in a manila envelope. She looked from Nat to the refrigerator then back to Nat. Her face flushed.

"What'ssamatter?"

She shook her head nothing.

But, typically Nat, he wouldn't let the moment go. "Eat a worm?"

No, she smiled, sniffing. They never talked about Nat's girlfriends. She knew he'd dated, but she didn't ask questions, and he never brought it up. It felt wrong not to ask something on her mind, so she swallowed and set down her fork. "You know," she tried to sound casual, "I've been meaning to ask you if you're seeing anyone."

He scrunched his brow and pointed to his mouth full of hot pie.

"Very funny," she said, noting the twinkle in his eyes.

When she heard Moon's Range Rover rattle into the driveway, Sam considered that maybe asking Moon over to talk her first night back with Nat wasn't such a good idea.

More distant than usual, Moon didn't even come to the back door to say hello, which was fortunate since Nat was choking down the rest of his pie.

She touched Nat's arm, "You don't have to go." She needed Nat's support actually, and thought, maybe this one time, he would stay.

But he scooped his scaffolding designs off the kitchen table into a manila folder, shaking his head. "Oh no, this is your baby. What are you afraid of, that he's going to say no?"

"Yes."

He shrugged, smiling amusedly at her. "I'll stop by later. It's fiction…" he winked, "well, mostly." He reached down patting a goodbye to Louis, then Ozma, her fourteen-year-old puppy.

She stood and looked into Nat's face, the face of her dearest friend, the face she didn't remember her life without. "It's got some holes," he admitted, "but you don't need him. Just use your imagination. What else can he help you with?"

"The truth."

He brushed wisps of hair from her forehead, which might have been an excuse to touch her, then rested his long fingertips on the nape of neck. "Which one?" He smiled enticingly. And they exchanged a glance, asking now what? She moved to wipe the flour off his nose, then stopped herself. Something had been settled between them, but she wasn't sure what. Did he mean which truth? That would be something Nat would ask. Or did he mean which one of them had to remind the other that they must soon go separate ways?

Sam watched his every body part move out of the kitchen — his sweeping left hand tucked the manila envelope under his armpit, his sturdy cocoa thighs, outlined by the pressed hem of his beige khaki shorts, and his broad shoulders tilted slightly through the narrow kitchen doorjamb. She listened for his car to start at the front curb, and when she heard him pull away, she knew he was going on a date, which was why she'd hesitated to brush the flour off his nose.

Standing like a statue in front of the kitchen window, she watched Moon slipping the reel-to-reel tapes under one arm and balancing a shot glass on a half bottle of tequila; he lugged the tape machine up the rickety treehouse ladder and sat cross-legged until long after the golden sunset rays shot through the branches.

And Sam, drugged by her sensual day at sea with Nat and the imminent reality she had to face with Moon, kept her post at the kitchen window watching him stare into space. Finally, she couldn't take the suspense any longer, so she climbed the ladder and sat next to him.

"That whole sex scene was a little too much," he said flatly.

"Hi to you, too."

He took the last slug out of the bottle, and said nothing.

"Too what? Graphic?"

"Yeah, it made me dislike Moon in a way I hadn't before."

She was amused by his detached critique, more like an editor guessing the reader's reaction to unconsensual sex than an actual participant.

"I mean, you write Moon and Morgan very sexually. I like the guy, then after he does that — I mean, it really kind of pissed me off: I want them to be together, then everything gets out of control and they don't hook up." He paused a moment, sighed heavily.

"So you think I should tone that part down?"

"Well, yeah."

"How?"

"Well, for one she didn't wrestle me."

Sam had transcribed the tapes verbatim. "I can't change her words."

"No," he nodded, "I guess not. I just thought you were after the truth."

"I am. That's what she said."

He half winced to himself. "Don't you suppose I would remember if she wrestled me, bit the hell out of my nipple?"

Speechless, Sam stared at the near faded photo of the toddler on the carousel.

He opened the front of his shirt. "Be a helluva scar, don't you think, if she ripped off a hunk of skin."

"You mean, she just let you rape her?"

"Rape? You young people today don't understand rape."

"What's not to understand?"

He glanced at her askance, then shook his head, annoyed that he had to spell it out, "Most women don't like to mess around when they're, you know…"

"Having their period."

He nodded, continuing, "But guys don't mind that."

"No?" She asked evenly, careful not to betray her biting thought that guys aren't the ones cramped and bleeding, so of course they don't mind.

He thought a moment, then summed up his take on women's sexuality. "My experience is women want it, even when they're on the rag, okay, but sometimes have a hard time expressing it — or they think guys will think less of them, I don't know — so they say no. And you just have to figure out what they really want."

Working hard on maintaining a blank expression, Sam stared at him. "Read their mind?" He nodded, as if thankful she'd caught on. "Well, we've spent some time together over the past dozen or so years, Moon, and I never once got the sense you were telepathic."

He looked away, sighing deeply, as though he clearly wanted to table this topic.

Something told her not to let him off so easy, not to let the memory fade gently into dusk. "Why do you think she would do that?"

"Ask her." He shrugged. "Maybe she liked me." He bugged his eyes out at her, like that's so impossible?

Sam tapped Morgan's tapes with her fingertips. "She says she liked you. She probably could have loved you, if you were more lovable. But she also says she asked you to stop, that it wasn't a good time, that she didn't want it like that. So, maybe she *really* didn't want it like that which is another way of saying no."

He nodded as though a vague sense of her emotional state washed in front of his eyes. "I figured maybe she was a little nervous."

They glanced at each other long enough for both of them to recognize neither of them believed that.

"So you basically ignored her, just fucked her." Sam indicated the general vicinity on the faded teal carpet where it'd occurred. "And left her."

He hated it when Sam used four-letter words. So, he stared at her with his blank expression practiced to hide his thoughts, an expression demanding concentration that could have been better spent communicating them.

Sam didn't buy that he simply "figured she was a little nervous." Moon had the heart of a man who felt the emotions of others but trained himself not to be stirred by sentiment.

Understanding that Moon had more empathy than he communicated had always made it easier for Sam to get along with him. He was like a dry plant, withering next to a faucet rusted shut. Nat said that was a false analogy: a plant, by definition, does not have the power to turn on a faucet, Moon does.

Over the years, both Nat and Sam noticed the inexplicable power she held over Moon. She tried not to abuse it, but she felt sorry for herself occasionally and took advantage of his peculiar generosity. At her high school graduation, he said he wanted to give her and Nat a little extra money for the All Night Party. He started to hand Nat a hundred bucks, then he stopped in mid-gesture, turned and handed it to Sam. A Kodak moment: trusting the girl with money.

He'd always made a point of asking her about her plans, wanting to at least know the twists and turns of her personal and professional life. But he had never asked, even once, about this manuscript over the several years she'd been working on it. Occasionally, she would mention in passing, "Oh, I had a telephone interview with Slattery today," or "I'm having lunch with Captain Engels tomorrow," or "Nat and I are going to the movies with Alicia and Iggy." He would nod, keeping his eyes on the newspaper, "I hope that helps you out." He never queried about how the book was coming along, so Sam didn't imagine he would want to read it.

And now that he'd listened to her mother's tapes, Sam knew the whole reason she'd written this book was to come to the one truth they'd never discussed, the truth only he knew.

So she prepared to ask him by assuring him she wouldn't change anything in the book. She would also keep the part about Morgan wrestling him and biting the hell out of his nipple because if her mother didn't do it, she wished she had and that was the advantage of writing: you could change reality, go back and react in ways you would have wanted. And, Sam promised, "No matter what you tell me I will not change the ending, but I need to know and you need to tell me what really happened in the warehouse the night my mother was shot."

Sam didn't know if she'd caught him at a bad time or just the right time. His eyes moved from the stained rug to the picture of Morgan on the carousel. He was probably thinking about her, really thinking about all that she didn't say to him and why, clearing up his own questions about why she'd been unusually distant that night.

He smiled to himself. "She was in my face most of the time, you know, asking questions about gear and procedure, commenting about everything from the weather to my haircut. But that last night she was not at home." He made little circles in the air with his hand. "I had to do most of the talking.

"I figured she was pissed about Fender, pissed at me for not saying what I knew really happened to her. If she hadn't stuck her neck out, you know, Fender would've basically gotten away with murder."

He looked at Sam. "She got a rash of shit from men and women that she probably didn't talk to you about. Been better for her to have just kept quiet because she'd defended him all along, covered up for him before." He shook his head. "She took a lot of heat.

"From yours truly, too. Even that night…well," he paused, "I wasn't a total shit. Least I confirmed what Teddy Bear had already told her about the real scoop with Fender beating up her suspect in the car. Wild man Fender," he sighed, holding his forefinger in front of his nose. "And I was this close to telling her what happened that night at the crackhouse with Fender was nothing — just the tip of the iceberg, nothing to what happened a couple of years before in Shootin' Newton, first night back after my son drowned."

"I had a rough time handling it," he confided. He bowed his head. "Had some allegations of brutality that night in Newton, too, Fender and I, under cover of authority. Nothing really. They just charge you for beating the hell out of someone when you're in uniform."

Sam was careful to keep her facial expression even, but her mind raced: assault and battery under cover of authority.

Almost as if reading her thoughts, he winced. "Torture. A couple of cops in the division were ambushed and shot. Both were down when Fender and I arrived. Fender was first at the scene. The four suspects ran into a second-story apartment. We kicked the door down, grabbed one of their girlfriends by the hair and stuck a gun to her head. We wedged her in front of us and walked up, saying, 'We're gonna blow her fucking brains out if you have a gun.'"

He paused for a long moment, until she finally couldn't stand the suspense. "What did you do?"

"They didn't have a gun," he inhaled deeply. "So, we basically just tortured the hell out of 'em. Two policemen, four guys. We broke 'em. Their faces were mush," he recalled matter-of-factly. "It was a fair fight, but if we could have found a gun on 'em, we would have killed every one of 'em. They don't know how lucky they were.

"One guy had something like 70 stitches in his head. Knees cracked. We had 'em on the ground begging those cops' forgiveness, swearing they'd never be gang members again. So there were a few…dozen or so allegations.

"We had a demonstration outside the division chanting my name and Fender's. Internal Affairs investigation lasted eighteen months. We were both on a photo line-up, but I was picked out by twelve people. I was the last one interviewed," he noted, with a tinge of pride. "Prime suspect is always the last interviewed.

"Not one policeman rolled. They didn't get any of our unit. Thirty-eight guys. I didn't get one day."

Sam remembered Fender's cover-up with the hose at the crackhouse. "Did you have blood on you?"

"Everywhere," he smiled, like a boy recounting an awesome slide at some water park. "Immediately after we beat those guys, we went downstairs with the garden hose. We had blood all over our legs, everywhere. With a navy uniform in the dark, you can't see, but you get in the light, looks like somebody splashed you with red paint. Had to clean our badges off, our faces. Fender and I checked each other, then we went out and were directing traffic. Captain came down and said, 'Where are the suspects?' 'Oh,' we said, 'we think some of those officers over here got 'em, and they took 'em to the station.'"

Remembering her mother's report of the crackhouse bloodbath and Fender's beating of Morgan's suspect during transport, Sam knew Fender and Moon had trumped up an oversight. "Oops, somehow they got to the station," she said, "and nobody knew who arrested them. Amazing."

He shook his head. "Internal Affairs knew who did it. Your step-dad knew."

"Joe? You think?"

Moon, never on a first name basis, always referred to him by his surname or as Sam's adopted parent. He nodded, "Yeah, Blanco knew. But there was nothing he could do about it. Most of the guys worked 77th, Hollenbeck, Shootin' Newton together. We were tight. Fender kept us tight. I mean, we murdered the bad people back then. We all knew what to say. Didn't have to call each other at home, check stories and shit. Blanco knew he wasn't a big enough asshole to really ever crack our group without a little help from on the inside: your mother." He shook his head, holding up his hand in a sign of resignation. Thinking about Morgan and Joe Blanco, together, was unpleasant for Moon; mentioning them in the same sentence, unprecedented.

Wind rustled in the tree. A chill passed through Sam, leaving her nauseous, dizzy with the realization that his revelation of that assault and battery night was his way of initiating her into the folklore of the men's club to which her mother never really belonged, yet fought to understand. Ultimately, Morgan drove in the first stake that broke it up.

"What about the night my mother was shot?"

"What about it?"

He went for another slug of tequila from his empty bottle, then grinned broadly, "I could tell you, but then I'd have to kill you."

"Okay." She stared at him, hard enough to make him glance away.

Then he confirmed the scenario at the warehouse until just before Morgan was shot. He said he'd left out a few details in the police report because he didn't think Morgan would live, and if she did, it would be her word against his. And who would care what the suspect had to say? As it turned out, the suspect came out of the coma and had a hard time remembering his own name, let alone what really happened the night he was shot.

Moon told Sam, "I hear Morgan yell, 'Police, freeze,' and I sprint along the side of the warehouse to the alley. By the time I step through the fence Morgan has the suspect turned around, hands behind his back, ready to cuff. I can't believe she hasn't fucked it up. When I step between the fence and Morgan, I must've come up too close to the suspect's right side, just as something, screeching in flight, hurls towards us from a pile of trashed car parts. I looked away for a split second to I.D this airborne object as a cat…take my eyes off the suspect long enough for him to whip around, flip his right hand backwards, knock my wrist with his forearm and grab my fucking gun.

"He's about to shoot me from a few feet away when Morgan steps between us. I mean she steps right between us. She and the suspect both fire. Her shot hits him in the neck; he nails her in the chest. Holy crap. It all happened so fucking fast.

"The suspect drops my gun and Morgan's still holding him at gunpoint, so she kicks it back to me, then hits the ground hard, lands on her right kneecap first. 'Fuck,' she yells at me. 'You goddamn fuck!'"

Moon shook his head at the powerful memory. "She was pissed."

Sam stared at Moon as the story spilled into the night. Waiting for so long to understand what was never clear to her, invisible, Sam penetrated as deeply as possible into the real story, and the truth, a hurricane pounding her head, brought her crashing to the ground, trapped in mangled power lines, his words driving into her skin like needles.

All the way on the freeway to the hospital, Morgan called Moon every foul name imaginable and then some she just made up. He was in-fucking-competent, and, she swore, if she died, she would be his worst fucking nightmare for the rest of his life. But no one that ornery could die.

She was meaner than any man he'd ever known. And he was absolutely sure if she lived she'd make certain that the world would know, Officer B.Jay Moon, frightened by a tabby cat, lost his gun and got his partner shot. Even the department couldn't allow him to fade like old wallpaper into a desk job in some remote division. No, what happened to Fender would look like a commendation compared to what Morgan would make sure happened to him.

Then he admitted to Sam a reality that grieved him to face: he'd been a model cowboy cop, pretty damn competent at kicking in doors and kicking ass, but he'd never actually been in a position to know if he'd take a shot to save his partner's life. His son, Lance, certainly, but Moon didn't know, and now would never be certain, if at that crucial millisecond, he would use his own body, without thinking, to protect a partner.

Sam felt him shift himself away from her, as if this admission disgraced his last pretense to honor, and severed his emotional connection with her.

Sam huddled over, chest to knees, covering her ears, closing her eyes, senseless by all he'd revealed.

Trapped in a tunnel resounding with "Tonight My Sleep Will Be Restless," bagpipes that cried from loss and separation, and a lonesome guitar solo that evoked both the hardship of a solitary journey and the resilience of the human spirit, she didn't hear Nat come to the treehouse. She only knew she awoke to crickets and found herself lying under a blanket in the crook of his arm listening to his heartbeat.

Moon was gone.

She told Nat what Moon had said: he'd finally admitted that her mother's body block to save his life was the single most courageous act he'd seen.

Nat kissed her forehead. She studied his earnest face, closed her eyes and slipped into a dream roaring down Pacific Coast Highway in the passenger seat of her mother's Jeep, Springsteen blaring.

When she was far away from her mother, Sam often dreamed Morgan had died that night fourteen years ago. Having almost lost her, Sam was more aware of her own ultimate, utter isolation. She lived on the edge of loss, always shoring up for the worst: she never hung up the phone without thinking *what if that's the last time we talk;* she never hugged her mother goodbye without holding her for an extra second; she never walked away without turning back and waving. And in Sam's dreams, no matter how hard she tried to convince herself Morgan was still alive, she never believed it; it was as though she'd lost her mother in battle, then when Sam woke up, her throat dry, skin clammy, nose tingling, she felt silly. She should have known her mother would prevail one last time.

Only Nat knew about Sam's anxiety attacks. And he said he understood why she would feel more connected if she moved closer to Morgan: when Sam wasn't around him, he told her that a part of him always felt switched off.

In this dream on the Pacific Coast Highway, Sam had something to tell her mother, so she reached to turn down Springsteen.

Silence. Morgan glanced at her, waiting. And Sam didn't know which to tell her first. That she was beginning to appreciate the wonder of Nat, or that she finally comprehended something of the mystery of Moon. That the opponent her mother'd almost loved, the partner who'd almost got her killed, had privately confessed to his captain how Morgan was shot. Then he'd resigned. The police department kept the details under seal for their own protection. Sam understood now why her mother would never answer questions about that night. What was the point? She was lucky to be alive. Sam also understood why Moon had sat on his porch every night, picking scabs and pouring tequila into open wounds.

Sam expected her mother to philosophize, like she did so often now, about the old ideas of protecting the people — trying to help her daughter understand how law enforcement has been affected by the notion of one man against the world who's got to solve immediate problems alone. But Morgan didn't say a word.

She just held Sam's hand, slowed the Jeep to a stop on the road next to the beach and pointed to a man in a dark blue uniform at the water's edge. A horse came into sight. And the final image of Moon that Sam sensed more than saw was him getting on his paper doll horse, riding off into the sunset, across the water and falling off the horizon.

Morgan turned and smiled at her daughter, and Sam could feel her mother's energy burning inside, generously warming her heart. Then Morgan revved the engine, spun back onto the Pacific Coast Highway, and flicked on the volume. Springsteen's wail cracked from the speakers. "…You can't start a fire sitting 'round crying over a broken heart…" and Sam watched her mother's hair flying in her face, "…this gun's for hire…" as they headed into a tunnel "…even if we're just…" and understood at once how desperately she loved her mother, "…dancing in the dark…" The near loss of her mother's magic had blinded her to anyone else's and had driven her instead to find order in the chaotic bits and pieces that shaped her mother's life, making it possible to reveal that Morgan Fraser actually beat the lag time, that millisecond, Fender predicted would kill her.

Morgan was silent, but Sam told her she'd quite unexpectedly discovered another connection; she'd found a curious similarity between the men and women policing the 77th and the Yiddish men and women at Gramma Sofie's Jewish Center. The emotional urgency that drove arguments, conflicts and resentments seemed to be connected by their closeness to death, to their extreme dependence and their ambivalence about living or working with people brought into close contact more by chance than choice. Engels and Fender bickered bitterly at the 77th, she pointed out to her mother, just like Hershel and Rebekah did at the Jewish Center — intense, hostile interactions perhaps assuring themselves and others they were active, committed and still alive.

Morgan nodded, betrayed a small knowing smile, then turned Springsteen up louder as if his amplification connected her to life.

Sam woke up before they reached the end of the tunnel, before she had the chance to tell her mother how much she loved her. Before she could thank Morgan for her childhood, for reading their Oz books, for wrestling with her, for braiding her hair, for catching her wild pitches, for building their treehouse. But for the first time, she understood that her mother's tragic childhood memories were not hers because Morgan illuminated other memories, and her guiding ray, brilliant and totally original, was her daughter's personal lighthouse.

On the other side of the tunnel, Sam's heart was blown open to Nat, still staring at her, kissing her tenderly, deeply on the lips, then holding her. She watched him gazing at the stars for a long time, and realized she'd been falling in love with him her whole life. It was only now that she felt secure enough, whole enough herself that she knew how to nurture the love of a man who let her know she was the one he breathed for.

Sometime later, before they moved to their first townhouse in Washington D.C., schlepping the balance of their childhood —

Ozma, Louis, and Jax, Louis's three-legged father — Nat and Sam would sit by a beach campsite and burn the planks from their imperfect treehouse, scorching Sam's mind with flames of more than she cared to remember, more than she could forget. Nat would hug her close and tell her his grandma assured him Sam's restless journey to reveal the truth would vindicate her mother and allow Morgan's loved ones, her childhood friend Samantha and Sam's father, to finally rest in peace.

Sam would hear her mother's voice calling to her, as she must have when she was a toddler, half-wrapped in a bath towel, balancing against the toilet: "Walk, Sam. C'mon, honey, walk to Mommy." And Sam would find her balance, take one step, then another. And toward her mother's smile, she would wobble, naked.

Acknowledgments

I am grateful to the late Beverly Lewis, Bantam Vice President, for her interest in this controversial topic, for her willingness to take a chance on me, and for her personal attention to Morgan's relationship with Sam, in whom Ms. Lewis recognized the strength of her own daughter.

Thanks to Pamela Painter for giving initial manuscript notes. To my Queens University writing workshop peers, my dedicated and talented faculty, especially Fred Leebron, Peter Ho Davies, Jane Alison, and Pinckney Benedict.

Gratitude to the Los Angeles police officers I interviewed, whose insights guided me deeper into the truth. To the National Center for Women and Policing. To Los Angeles Parker Center for opening doors that enabled me to shadow women cadets at the Los Angeles Police Academy and go on ride-a-longs with LAPD officers. To the women in "El grupo" for their hard questions.

Thanks for support from the University of North Carolina, School of Filmmaking, former Dean Jordan Kerner, as well as screenwriting colleagues, Dona Cooper, Bill Mai, Ron Stacker Thompson.

Gratitude to John McKinny for his early enthusiasm and wisdom. To Gabrielle Thompson and Christine Norris for their copy-editing. To Cathy Watson for her e-publishing guidance. To Claire McKinney for her imprint promotion direction. To my siblings, family and friends for a lifetime of emotional support.

And profound thanks to my late husband, Daniel, and sons, Ryan, John and Daniel B for *everything*.

LAURA HART MCKINNY is a producer, writer, and professor who has taught screenwriting for over twenty years as a founding faculty member at the University of North Carolina School of the Arts, School of Filmmaking.

Born in Miami, Florida, Laura zigzagged from the South to the East to the West back to the East coast. She has a Bachelor of Arts from UCLA and an M.F.A. from Queens University. A chapter from her upcoming novel, *Rosebud, S.D.,* is published in *Boomtown,* an anthology. Laura most recently produced the feature film *Susie's Hope,* and has written and co-produced the feature documentaries *In Broad Daylight* and *Remembering Frederic: Life of a Genius,* as well as the filmed stage adaptation of *The Land Breakers,* a novel by John Ehle. She has three sons and three grandchildren, and lives in Winston-Salem, North Carolina.

Cover artist Hayden Tedder lives in Winston-Salem, North Carolina. She is a member of Delurk Gallery and her art can be found in galleries, restaurants, coffee shops, and private collections.

www.ingramcontent.com/pod-product-compliance
Lightning Source LLC
Chambersburg PA
CBHW031133120726
47905CB00006B/1680